BELOW
THE SURFACE

BELOW THE SURFACE

A MARIA KALLIO MYSTERY

LEENA LEHTOLAINEN

Translated by Owen F. Witesman

amazon crossing

Text copyright @ 2003 by Leena Lehtolainen
Translation copyright © 2017 by Owen F. Witesman
All rights reserved.

Previously published as *Veren vimma* by Tammi in Finland in 2003. Translated from Finnish by Owen F. Witesman. First published in English by AmazonCrossing in 2017.

Published by AmazonCrossing, Seattle

www.apub.com

Amazon, the Amazon logo, and AmazonCrossing are trademarks of Amazon.com, Inc., or its affiliates.

ISBN-13: 9781542048743
ISBN-10: 1542048745

Cover design by Cyanotype Book Architects

Printed in the United States of America

CAST OF CHARACTERS

THE LAW

THE SMEDS FAMILY

Alma Smeds: .... Rauha's mother

Andreas Smeds: .... Sasha's older brother

Rauha Smeds: .... Sasha's mother

Sasha Smeds: .... Champion rally driver

Viktor Smeds: .... Sasha's father

SUPPORTING CAST

Einstein: .... Maria and Antti's cat (deceased)

Jaakko .... Halonen: Hunter

Annukka Hackman: .... Journalist, Atro Jääskeläinen's wife

Jouni Jalonen: .... Graphic designer

Kirsti Jensen: .... Antti's academic colleague

Atro Jääskeläinen: .... Publisher, Annukka Hackman's husband

Sini Jääskeläinen: .... Atro's daughter

Antti Sarkela: .... Maria's husband

Iida Sarkela: .... Maria's daughter

Taneli Sarkela: .... Maria's son

Jouko Suuronen: .... Sasha Smeds's manager

Terttu Taskinen: .... Jyrki Taskinen's wife

Jani Väinölä: .... Skinhead drug dealer

1

I'd never killed a person before, but now I had to. As I walked toward the shore, I heard Annukka splash into the water. She'd piled her things next to a stump just back from the lake. I knew there was a pistol in her purse, and I intended to use it.

Stealing toward the stump, I opened the purse. My hands were gloved, I was wearing a disposable raincoat, and I had plastic bags over my shoes. A hat covered my hair. I would leave no trace.

The pistol felt heavy as I took it out. I checked to make sure there were rounds in the magazine. It was full, but I hoped one shot would be enough.

Annukka swam quickly. Soon it would be dark, but I could still see her head bobbing on top of the water. Releasing the gun's safety, I took aim. I heard only a muffled pop when the weapon fired. Annukka's head jerked. Her body came to a stop and started rocking gently, kept afloat by the wet suit she was wearing. I waited a few minutes, then went for the keys and phone in her purse. I turned off the phone. After taking a roundabout way to her car, I began searching it. I didn't find what I was looking for and had to leave empty-handed before the darkness grew too thick. My own car was half a mile away from Annukka's. I didn't run into anyone as I walked along the edge of the forest. When I reached the car, I drove through downtown Kirkkonummi to Eestinkylä. I didn't see a single car along the way. I threw the pistol, the keys, and the phone off the Vårnäs Bridge into the river and took off the protective clothing I'd been wearing—I could get rid of that later.

When I arrived home, I finally began to shake.

2

That morning I would have preferred not to look in the mirror. There were bags under my eyes, and my hair was nothing but tangles. At the breakfast table, Iida didn't want to eat her porridge and Taneli complained that his was too hot. He was right, of course. I'd woken up late, and their breakfast hadn't had time to cool.

Outside it was sleeting again, so I packed the children's rain gear in their backpacks. Iida wanted her winter boots instead of her rubber ones. In the end I gave in because otherwise I'd be late for my morning meeting. Antti wasn't going to be home for another two days. The children screamed in the hallway, demonstrating the futility of my attempts to teach them how to behave in an apartment building. In the elevator, I mentally cursed whoever had just smoked in there. When we finally got to the car, the back window was still covered in ice, even though the heater had been running for two hours. Probably time for a new heater.

First I took Iida to her preschool group, then Taneli to the three-year-olds' class in the basement of the day care. Taneli's inside slippers were missing, even though I clearly remembered putting them in his cubby the previous afternoon. Finally we found them next to Roope's slippers.

In the car again, I put on the Rehtorit, who sang "Cops Are Heroes," but I didn't feel the slightest bit like one. How could two weeks alone with my own children leave me so exhausted? Things had even been easy at work, mostly simple, routine cases. When Iida had come down with the flu the previous week, I'd been able to stay home with her without any problems.

But all the sleepless nights left my hands shaky. Whenever Antti was away I had a hard time falling asleep. I watched tearjerker movies, listened to music with my headphones on, and drank too much whiskey. Whenever I was alone my thoughts raced, and I had to flee into imaginary worlds and ragged harmonies.

Inside the station garage I pulled into my reserved spot. Next to me was my boss, Jyrki Taskinen's, Saab, clean and shining in spite of all the sleet. I just had time to drop off my jacket in my office and grab a cup of coffee before the meeting. My subordinates were already waiting.

Ursula was giggling with Puupponen, and Puustjärvi was dozing. The others were awake but quiet. There was no sign of Koivu. I sipped some coffee before starting.

"Good morning. Where's Koivu?"

"He's with a client. He'll come when he can," Autio said.

All of our cases were being handled, and none of them was difficult. They were just straightforward pretrial investigations that we'd be able to send to the prosecutor in no time. Rapes, assaults, one knifing, some domestic violence. That was our world.

Flags were flying all over the city since it was Finnish-Swedish Heritage Day. Puupponen, always a paragon of political correctness, suggested the flags should be flown at half-mast. The office Christmas party season had started over the weekend, which meant a rise in fights in taxi lines and attempted rapes. The number of incidents per day would only increase until it peaked on the holiday itself.

Our unit's party was scheduled for a week from Friday with the rest of the Criminal Division. I was looking forward to dancing with Taskinen.

With the meeting well underway, Koivu appeared at the door, cleaning his glasses. He didn't look very chipper either. His three-month-old was still keeping him up with colic, and there was no end in sight. A couple of times I'd found him sleeping in the break room in the middle of the day.

"What kept you?" I asked. "Was it something important?"

"This guy Atro Jääskeläinen's wife, Annukka Hackman, has been missing since Tuesday afternoon. He's frantic."

"He should be grateful," muttered Lähde, who, based on his stories, was married to the worst nag and tyrant in the world.

"Well, he isn't. He can't reach her cell phone, and none of their friends or relatives know anything. He wants us to try to ping her phone to see if it shows where she is."

The name Annukka Hackman sounded vaguely familiar, but I couldn't place it.

"Is the wife the faithful type?" Ursula asked.

"I tried to ask, but the husband just got more agitated."

Lähde snorted. "His old lady'll come back when her lover runs out of ammo," he said, then we moved on to the next case.

Later that morning, when I got tired of filling out overtime reports and started thinking about lunch, a message flashed on my computer screen notifying me of a new case. All I had time to do was glance at it and see the word "body" before Puustjärvi walked in, looking red in the face.

"Some hunters shot a lady in Lake Humaljärvi thinking she was a moose!"

"Holy . . . Were they drunk? And where is Lake Humaljärvi? Somewhere in Kirkkonummi?"

"Yep."

"OK, you go since you know the area and take Koivu with you."

"Got it," Puustjärvi said obediently, and I almost thought he was going to salute. "I'll have to drop everything else."

5

Nodding, I started reprioritizing cases in my mind. The minor assaults would have to wait. Puustjärvi left the door open behind him. I turned and looked out the window. The sleet had stopped, but the sky was dark gray and a north wind was keeping the flags flapping horizontally.

I imagined how the frigid wind would feel on my cheeks, and the thought was suddenly enticing. Standing up from my desk, I grabbed my coat from the closet and switched shoes. In the hallway, Puustjärvi was telling Koivu about the discovery of the body, and Ursula and Puupponen came out to listen too. Apparently the woman had been swimming when the bullet hit her in the head.

"Do we have an ID on the victim?" I asked.

"No. She's blond, but there isn't much left of the bottom half of her face. And supposedly the hunters were all sober."

"Let's get going then," I said to Koivu and Puustjärvi.

"You're coming too?" Koivu asked. Ever since returning from maternity leave, I'd stayed strictly behind my desk. "You feeling the need to read some careless hunters the riot act?"

"No, I just want a break from my desk," I said. I hadn't been out jogging for ten days, and I was in serious need of fresh air.

"And slogging through a wet forest seems like the best way to get that?" Koivu asked.

"Koivu, you can kiss my . . ." I said happily, suddenly glad I would get some time in the field with him. Ursula gave us a strange look. After she'd been working with us for a couple of weeks, she'd asked Puupponen whether Koivu and I were a thing. Puupponen had laughed so hard he nearly fell off his stool in the break room. He knew Koivu was like a cross between a close friend and a little brother to me.

"How did they manage to think a woman was a moose?" Puustjärvi asked as we were turning off the Ring II Beltway onto the West Highway. We were letting him drive because we weren't in a hurry. Puustjärvi was always conscientious about following the speed limit.

"They drove a moose into the lake and were trying to shoot it. Someone hit the woman instead," Koivu said, a yawn nearly stifling his speech.

"So the woman and the moose were in the same lake? Hard to believe. Was the woman downwind?"

"Am I a cop or a weatherman?" Koivu asked.

"And what kind of a crazy person goes swimming in November? Lake Humaljärvi doesn't even have a good beach, just bushes everywhere," Puustjärvi said. "Maybe it was suicide. Maybe she got in the line of fire on purpose."

I thought of the hunter who'd unintentionally killed this woman. I'd met people in similar situations before: a truck driver who had a drunk walk in front of him, train engineers who'd noticed a person on the tracks too late, a father who'd left his one-year-old alone in the bathtub just for a second. For a moment I regretted not staying behind my desk.

The sky was clearing, but the sleet melted slowly. The weather changed on a daily basis, and apparently the freezing temperatures were taking today off. We had to leave the car a good distance from the path that led to the lake because the narrow road was already backed up with the vehicles belonging to the hunters, Forensics, and the Kirkkonummi Police. I pulled on a pair of rubber boots for the hike.

Near the shore the trail became difficult where heavy forestry machinery had torn deep ruts in the ground. I started to get out of breath. I hadn't quite managed to regain my previous fitness level since Taneli's birth. By the time we reached the shoreline, sweat was running down my back. A pantsuit and a leather jacket were poor outdoor clothing.

The body was covered with plastic. The hunters had pulled it out of the water and desperately searched for a pulse, to no avail. I nodded to Hirvonen from Forensics and introduced myself to the officer from Kirkkonummi who was in charge of the situation. Then I forced myself to look under the plastic. The woman had curly blond hair and was wearing a black wet suit. She lay on her stomach, and the bullet had pierced the back of her head. I didn't have any interest in seeing what it had done to the bottom half of her face on its way out.

"She wasn't shot today," Hirvonen said. "Look. She's stiff, and see these blotches on the side of her forehead? There's probably more of that under the wet suit. The water washed away most of the blood and brain matter. She's been in the water for hours, maybe all night."

"And that isn't a wound from a moose rifle," Koivu and I said at the same time. "That weapon was something smaller caliber," I added.

"Was someone trying to shoot a moose with a pistol?" Puustjärvi asked in confusion.

"My guess is we're looking at a twenty-two, either pistol or rifle. The bullet came out through the jaw. Probably no point dragging the lake for it, since bullets that small usually disintegrate," Hirvonen said with a sigh.

"We'll see what other leads we can find," I said and turned away for a moment. I felt impossibly tired and full of adrenaline all at the same time. This accidental shooting was turning into a homicide. I hadn't solved a case like this in more than three years.

"Has any identification turned up?" I asked.

"No, or any clothes either, although I doubt she came out here in the forest in nothing but a wet suit."

"We're looking right now," one of the Kirkkonummi cops said.

"Koivu, what was the description of that missing person you were talking about? Mrs. Hackman."

"Blond, average height, thin."

That fit the victim in front of us, but it didn't prove anything yet. We all stood where we were, mindful not to trample any tracks. Of course it would have been better if the hunters had left the woman in the water. Now it was hard to say which side of the lake she'd been shot from. The wet suit was buoyant, so the body could have drifted on the water for who knows how long. We'd have to find out what the wind direction had been during the night. I took out the notebook I always carried, even though I rarely interviewed anyone anymore. I started making notes about everything that needed to be done. My sweat had dried, and a chill ran through me. I asked Koivu to organize interviewing the hunters. They'd be able to show us where the body had been floating. Puustjärvi could take care of getting the forensic investigation started. In all likelihood, the hunters and police had already unwittingly fouled the tracks. We would still find something, though; we always did.

I didn't have to wait long before Koivu came back accompanied by a shortish man with wet hair who was shivering so hard with cold that I had a hard time understanding him. At least I made out the name Jaakko Halonen. I wondered whether interviewing him made any sense, because despite his claim that he was fine, I could see the symptoms of shock.

"We trapped a bull moose thinking it wouldn't go in the lake, but it did. I think a couple of us took shots, but none of us hit it. We heard it climbing up the bank on the other side. I was looking for it with my binoculars when I saw her . . ." Halonen swallowed. "She was floating near this side. An old hunter like me knows a body when he sees one. Penttilä suggested getting a boat, but I went into the water myself. I had to go see if we could still help her. I'm sure your investigators will be able to tell which one of us . . ."

"How close to the shore was the body floating?" I asked.

"Less than ten meters, and she was light . . ." Halonen began shaking harder.

"Thank you. That'll be enough for now. Don't worry about who's to blame. She wasn't shot with a hunting rifle. Thank you for pulling the body out of the water." There was little chance he'd intended to interfere with the evidence. Still we'd have to check for any possible connections between Halonen and the body.

"It wasn't me?" Halonen asked and began to shake even more violently.

"If you were shooting at that moose with a hunting rifle, then no, it wasn't any of you. Could someone in your party take you home or maybe to see a doctor? Hatakka, could you handle that?" I asked, addressing one of the Kirkkonummi officers.

Once Halonen had been escorted away, my phone rang. It was Puustjärvi.

"I'm a couple hundred meters east of the body. We found a pile of clothes and a purse. Will you come have a look?"

I went immediately. Voices came from the forest, and I assumed the forensic team was coming for the body. The path along the lake was difficult, winding along bare rock and occasionally stopping at large boulders. Why on earth did this woman want to swim here? Based on the wet suit, swimming in cold water was something she did regularly, but why come swim in the middle of nowhere when there were more accessible shorelines?

The clothing and handbag were at a relatively flat spot near a gently sloping, exposed bedrock shore where getting in the water would have been easy. The clothes were neatly folded inside a plastic bag. The lingerie was on top, a bra and matching dark-blue satin panties. This wasn't cheap underwear, and the rain gear, thermals, and high-top hiking boots were expensive too. Whoever this woman was, she'd known how to choose the right footwear for this terrain. The underwear was strangely out of keeping with the pragmatic sportiness of the rest of the clothing, though. The plush, dark-blue towel didn't have a monogram, so no clues there.

I waited for Forensics to take their pictures before picking up the handbag. It looked new, and the leather was stiff. The wallet was intact. Carefully I opened it. Inside were credit cards, two twenty-euro bills, and a new-style driver's license. The picture showed a stylish blond woman. Maija Annukka Hackman, born April 8, 1970.

"I think we found Annukka Hackman," I told Koivu, who had caught up to me.

"So she wasn't off cheating," Puustjärvi said.

"Nope. Not unless she had a date with a naiad," Koivu said, trying to lighten the mood. Probably he felt it was his duty since Puupponen wasn't around.

When I looked at Annukka Hackman's driver's license more closely, I remembered why her name was familiar. Hackman was the reporter who'd interviewed me a few years earlier for the weekend supplement of one of the tabloids. It was just a little before my second maternity leave. I'd hesitated to agree to the interview because I didn't like the theme of the article, which focused on "women in unique occupations." In my mind female police offers were already commonplace, although there wasn't exactly an oversupply of female detective lieutenants yet. Hackman had also interviewed a professor of theoretical physics, an army officer, and a fire chief. Two things had fascinated her most: that I was visibly pregnant and that the murder investigation I'd led the previous spring had connections to Espoo city politics. Hackman had tried to paint a picture of me as a fearless champion of justice who couldn't be held back even by pregnancy. The article was so embarrassing I'd tried to put it out of my mind.

Still, Hackman had given a very effective and professional first impression. She'd done her homework on policing and the gradual increase of women in the force. But the whole time I had felt like I had to watch what I said. Hackman had tried to create some sort of woman-to-woman connection that would make me tell her things I wouldn't tell a male reporter. Seeing through the ruse had been depressingly easy. I didn't know what paper Hackman had been writing for these days.

Her husband had filed a missing person report, but that could be a cover. We always looked for the perpetrator in the victim's inner circle first. I looked at my watch. One thirty. The day care closed at five.

"Puustjärvi, if you'll stay here and continue with the field team, Koivu and I can go deliver the bad news," I said. Turning to Koivu, I asked, "Do you have the husband's info with you?" Being the bearer of this kind of news was hard, but it was part of the job. Koivu and I had done this together more times than I could remember.

Annukka Hackman and her husband, Atro Jääskeläinen, owned a small company called Racing Stripe Publishing, which produced a motorsports magazine of the same name, as well as a website. The company was located in a neighborhood in southwest Espoo called Nöykkiö, and the street address, 26 B, indicated that it was next to their home at 26 A.

"Did Jääskeläinen's concern for his wife seem genuine?" I asked as Koivu was turning out of downtown Kirkkonummi back toward Espoo.

"Hard to say. I wasn't at my sharpest this morning. You know what it's like being up all night."

"Unfortunately. How's Anu holding up?"

"You know her. She never complains. She just keeps getting paler every day. We've tried everything for the colic. Fennel tea and all that. I guess it has to end someday, though."

Koivu's wife, Anu, also worked in our unit but intended to apply for a transfer as soon as her maternity leave ended. I missed Anu's methodical attention to detail and sharp wit, as well as having another woman around to laugh at our male colleagues' strange logic. At first I'd thought Ursula might be a sort of replacement for Anu, but I couldn't have been more wrong.

"We'll have to ask Jääskeläinen to identify the body. And the bottom half of the face isn't a pretty sight. Do they have any children?"

"Not together, but Jääskeläinen has a daughter from a previous marriage who lives with them. Her name is Sini, and she's sixteen. According to her father, she didn't know anything about where her stepmother was, and he avoided saying anything else about her."

"So stepmother and daughter didn't have a good relationship?"

"Apparently. But usually it's the teenager who runs away, not the thirty-something stepmother."

Neither of us was about to rule out the possibility that the girl had shot her stepmother. A few years ago I might have, but recent events had shown me that teenagers were capable of anything. In addition to Atro Jääskeläinen, Sini would be a prime suspect.

For a few seconds I leaned my head back and tried to figure out how I would tell Atro Jääskeläinen the news. Maybe we should have asked the police chaplain to join us, but I didn't know whether the family belonged to the church. I did have contact information for the parish crisis group and the mental health office in my bag, though. When I started as a cop, groups like that didn't exist, and there were frequently times when I hesitated to leave grieving people alone. I still felt helpless around them, but I'd learned to hide it better than when I was younger. I knew I still worried too much about other people's problems and tried to help too much when there was nothing I could do. Even though people claimed knowing was better, I had no desire to tell Atro Jääskeläinen that he'd just become a widower.

3

When we pulled off the highway, Koivu asked me to read the map. And for good reason: this part of east Espoo had gone from fields and forest to sprawling housing developments so quickly in recent years that even the police had a hard time navigating all the new streets. The lots had been chopped up as small as possible, and you could pay a hundred thousand euros for less than a quarter of an acre. Out of necessity I'd become an expert on Espoo housing policy over the past few years.

The Hackman-Jääskeläinen residence was a duplex with Racing Stripe Publishing in the northern half of the building. A recently planted hedge was still too short to block the view of the construction site to the west of the house. There were two cars in the driveway, a red Audi and a beat-up yellow VW Beetle with light-blue stripes running over the hood and top. We walked to the office first but didn't manage to ring the bell before the door opened.

The man in the doorway was average in height, maybe a couple of years past forty, and plump like someone who doesn't get much exercise beyond walking to his car and back. Round eyeglasses gave his face a childlike look.

"Are you from the police?" he asked, out of breath.

"Yes. I'm Detective Lieutenant Maria Kallio, and this is Sergeant Pekka Koivu. Are you Atro Jääskeläinen?"

"Is it . . . is it about Annukka?"

"May we come inside?"

Jääskeläinen didn't move from the doorway. I knew that expression. It was the look of a person who understood that the worst was coming but wanted to hold out hope for just another moment.

"Where is she? Is she alive?"

Taking Jääskeläinen by the arm, I led him inside like I would have led Taneli to the dinner table if he didn't want to go. In the entryway was a low bench, and I sat Jääskeläinen down on it. Then I told him the bad news, that his wife had been murdered, without revealing the exact cause of death or where the body had been found.

"Are you sure it's Annukka?"

"Your wife's purse and wallet were found near the body, and the description matches. We'd like you to come in and identify her as soon as you're up to it."

For a moment Jääskeläinen said nothing. His eyes welled with tears and his hands clutched his thighs.

"Annukka," he said, as if repeating the name might somehow bring his wife back. "Annukka was writing an unofficial biography of Sasha Smeds for our company. It was supposed to go to press next week. There are things in the book that no one knows, and it's going to sell big. If Sasha wins the British rally in a couple of weeks, he'll be the new world champion."

Suddenly Jääskeläinen loudly burst into tears. Rarely had I seen a man weep that way, howling like a little child.

"It was supposed to be our breakthrough . . . in Finnish and English . . . Annukka was so good. Now it's all ruined. Annukka's gone. Who killed her? Why wasn't she more careful? Why didn't she defend herself? She always had a gun with her."

"A gun?" Koivu and I both exclaimed.

"Your wife carried a weapon?" I asked. Few Finns carried guns. Even as police detectives we were rarely armed. In my whole career I'd only been forced to discharge my service weapon once. "Why did your wife carry a gun? What kind was it?"

Jääskeläinen didn't answer. It is always frightening to watch someone completely lose control of themselves, and that's what was happening to Atro Jääskeläinen. He was crying so violently now he couldn't speak.

"What's going on here?" A slender man with a ponytail stepped out of a red door at the end of the hallway.

"Detectives Kallio and Koivu from the Espoo Police Department," I answered. "And you are?"

"Jouni Jalonen. I'm the graphic designer here. Are you here about . . . ?" Jalonen didn't finish his question as he stared at Jääskeläinen sobbing uncontrollably.

"Unfortunately Mrs. Hackman has been murdered," I said.

"How?" Jalonen's voice shook.

"We aren't at liberty to say."

"Oh God . . . Atro, I'm so sorry," Jalonen said, but he didn't reach out to touch Jääskeläinen. Koivu and I exchanged glances.

"Do you know if Mr. Jääskeläinen has any family who could come stay with him?"

Jalonen shook his head. "Sini will know. Atro and I don't work together directly that much. I'm just on contract to do the layout for the magazine."

Jalonen had the prematurely lined, gray skin of a smoker, and the nicotine stains on the first two fingers of his right hand told the same story, as did the smell of him.

"How well did you know Annukka Hackman?" I asked.

"Annukka? She wasn't an easy person to get to know. She was a damn good reporter, but she kept her distance."

Jalonen promised to keep Jääskeläinen company until the crisis group arrived and Sini came home from school. Together we took Jääskeläinen next door to his house and found some sedatives in the medicine cabinet. But he refused to take anything and just continued crying. We left him sobbing on the black leather couch in the living room. Identifying the body could wait until tomorrow.

Jalonen did know enough to tell us that the pistol Hackman carried was a Hämmerli-brand .22 caliber. Hackman was a recreational shooter, and her carry permit was in order. The gun had a silencer, because she used to practice in the family's garage.

"The impression I got was that Annukka feared for her safety mostly when she was on long drives alone working on stories. And I guess she had an old boyfriend who bothered her, but I don't know much about that." Jalonen put a cigarette between his lips and looked at us inquisitively. "Is there anything else, or can I go back to the office?"

I'd need to write up a search warrant before I could have our team go through Annukka Hackman's things, and Koivu could interview Jalonen later, so we took off.

"A twenty-two like that can also fire long rifle rounds," Koivu said once we were sitting in the car.

"And because we didn't find it in her bag, she might have been shot with her own gun. Let's have Forensics get going on dragging the lake after all. Maybe the murderer threw the pistol in the water. The perp must have been someone who knew Hackman carried a gun. At least that narrows down the pool a little bit."

We turned off the beltway toward the police station. Even though my family and I had moved away from this area two years ago, seeing the old familiar landscape of rolling fields still stung. Our former rental house didn't even exist anymore. In its place stood three new houses worth three hundred and fifty thousand euros a piece. We hadn't even considered buying one of them, since we wanted to preserve the illusion that there was more to life than paying a mortgage.

"Find out everything you can about Hackman," I told Koivu. "Employers, former lovers, vices. That book about Sasha Smeds sounds interesting and might have something to do with the case."

I didn't know much about rally cars, but avoiding the name Sasha Smeds would have been impossible over the past few years. The previous season he'd narrowly lost the world championship, forced to drop out of the final rally during the third special stage because of engine trouble, after which the team pulled him from the competition, allowing their other driver to take the overall championship by a single point. After that, the conversation in the Finnish media about the unfairness of motorsports was intense. Apparently this year Sasha was doing even better than the previous season.

"Smeds is even with Carlos Sainz, and there's only one rally left. Don't you read the newspaper?" Koivu asked me as we ate a late lunch in the station cafeteria.

"Not the sports section. I've never been interested in men wearing racing suits in metal boxes. I prefer to look at them with less clothing on."

"Antti probably knows everything about rally racing," Koivu said, teasing me. A couple of years earlier my husband had attended an environmental protest against the Jyväskylä Grand Prix. The protesters staged their own "race" with toy cars. After Taneli's birth he'd gone through another of his intense do-gooder phases, but lately he'd maintained a steady level of disgust with everything. Hopefully the work trip he was on would perk him up a bit.

"A tell-all book a publishing company thought was going to make them piles of money might be a motive for murder," I said, bringing the conversation back to the case. "Put together a team to search Hackman's belongings tomorrow. I'm glad to come too if I survive my leadership meeting. I could probably be there around noon," I added as I got up from the table. "But for now I have to hit the day care before I head back to the White Cube."

The "White Cube" was the name Antti had given our new apartment. It had two bedrooms, a balcony, and a sauna, all totaling about a thousand square feet. Our bedroom and the kids' room had views of a small pine forest. That had been a deciding factor for us, because at least we could see birds, squirrels, and rabbits in the forest. The living room and kitchen looked out on the more urban landscape of the parking lot and the next building. A lot of people would have felt at home there, but we didn't.

"When is Daddy coming home?" Iida asked for the thousandth time as I drove home.

"Two more nights, dear." Antti was at an EU climate conference in Edinburgh, which was the culmination of a project he'd been working on for the past year. His contract with the Meteorological Institute ran out at the end of the year, and there was no word about an extension. Nowadays even a doctorate didn't ensure a permanent job in the academic world.

At home, I fed the kids, did the laundry, and read two bedtime stories. I wasn't really present, though. Annukka Hackman was on my mind. Was the interview she did with me still somewhere in the stacks of newspapers we kept? Taneli fell asleep easily, but as I started rummaging through the random files in our room sometime after nine, I could still hear Iida tossing and turning. I finally found the crumpled newspaper article mixed in with some book and music reviews Antti had kept. Annukka Hackman and the photographer had demanded that I wear a police uniform for the photos. Because I was so pregnant, the only thing I could fit into was a pair of men's tactical coveralls, with sleeves and pant legs several inches too long for me. I looked ridiculous.

The headline of the article was "The Mother Who Investigates Murders." I'd asked Annukka Hackman if she would have used a parallel headline for a male detective. Puustjärvi, Koivu, and Lähde were all fathers who investigated murders, and their families affected their work too. In fact, statistics showed that the fathers of small children worked the longest hours. Koivu, in particular, fit that description.

Detective Lieutenant Maria Kallio, age 35, has a master's degree in criminal justice and heads the Espoo Police Violent Crime Unit. There aren't many female detectives in Finland, and the typical image of a Finnish homicide detective is still a tall, broad-shouldered man with a beer gut.

Kallio comes from a Northern Karelian family of schoolteachers. Her choice of profession was easy, though, and she made it into the police academy on her first try. That isn't common. Kallio was at the head of her class in technical subjects and, after graduation, she worked for a couple of years in the Helsinki vice squad. Ambitious as always, she soon applied to law school at Helsinki University—once again she was accepted on the first try.

The article listed each stage of my career and commented briefly on my half-year digression into legal practice.

Apparently Detective Kallio isn't interested in money— as a lawyer she earned several times more than she does as a police officer. Her selection as the head of the Espoo Police Violent Crime Unit in 1996 was a veritable miracle since she was already scheduled for maternity leave. Employment policies like that only work in the public sector. It would seem that the selection was influenced by Detective Kallio's success in solving the murder of the figure skater Noora Nieminen. After returning from maternity leave, Detective Kallio led the investigation into the Rödskär serial killings and made waves in Espoo politics when she solved the murder of Councilman Petri Ilveskivi. According to rumors, Kallio's superiors were under fierce pressure to quash the investigation, but Detective Kallio stood up to them.

"Maria, the pace of your work seems intense. How do you mesh murder investigations and motherhood? Are you a superwoman like we see on TV?"

"Not at all!" Kallio exclaims, obviously agitated. "My daughter has a father too, and we found a lovely day care that's been a good fit for her. Finnish women work, and it doesn't matter whether they're police officers, teachers, or textile factory workers."

However, there aren't many mothers whose lives are in danger when they go to work and who have to deal with murderers. One of Detective Kallio's colleagues was killed in a dramatic standoff in January 1996, and it was pure luck that Kallio didn't end up a victim of the same prison escapee. Later a bomb was placed in the Kallio family mailbox during the Espoo politics investigation. Kallio won't comment on whether she always carries a gun.

"I don't feel like more guns and walls are the solution to the increasing violence in society. We need to find the causes of violence and focus on prevention," she says, showing an idealism uncommon among the police.

"Doesn't constantly dealing with the dark side of life get to you?"

"Family is the best antidote to that," is all Kallio will say.

Detective Kallio married in 1995. Her husband is a mathematician, and they have a four-year-old daughter. For security reasons she won't mention their names in the media. A second child is coming in the spring. Kallio is an avid athlete and plays the bass guitar. The family's pet is a fifteen-year-old cat named Einstein.

That mention made my eyes tear up. Einstein had died two weeks after we moved into the urban confines of the White Cube. He'd had a free-roaming life at our old place, but that wasn't possible in our new home. We'd thought about giving him to Antti's parents in Inkoo, but Antti's father was seriously ill and my mother-in-law wasn't interested in looking after a cat too. Sometimes I got the feeling Antti missed Einstein even more than I did—he'd been Antti's cat originally.

Explaining to Hackman why I didn't want Antti's and Iida's names mentioned in the article took forever. And I felt uncomfortable having to correct my colleague's titles and the year of my marriage, when I didn't think they had anything to do with the subject of the article. Hackman would have liked me to talk more about my private life and the feelings I had about my work, and she was disappointed when I wouldn't. For a second when I was really irritated I'd thought about saying that dead bodies turned me on, but fortunately I had the sense to keep my mouth shut. With my luck, that would have ended up as the headline.

Just then my phone started playing Pelle Miljoona's "Violence and a Drug Problem," which meant the call was coming from work.

"Hi, it's Kemppinen from the front desk. I have reporters asking about the shooting at Lake Humaljärvi. Should I transfer them to you?"

"What, right now? Didn't Puustjärvi write up a press release?"

"Both tabloids and the news wire want to know the identity of the victim. They got a tip that it was some other reporter."

Maybe reporters were like cops: when one of their own gets killed, they put even more energy than usual into finding answers. It was 10 p.m., and of course they wanted this homicide for their morning headlines.

I tried to remain objective about the press, so I decided to take the calls. Maybe working was better than staying up drinking whiskey and watching dumb movies. I selected the first number Kemppinen had given me. I decided not to reveal Annukka Hackman's identity. I could always say that the family hadn't all been notified yet.

In the end it was eleven o'clock before I made it through all the media inquiries. At seven the next morning when I turned my phone on again, four more callback requests were waiting in my voice mail. We'd have to hold a press conference at some point in the afternoon.

That morning the whole unit was present for our daily meeting. Koivu looked more alert than the previous day. Ursula was painting her nails dark brown, and Puustjärvi sat next to her, grinning. I left the Hackman case for last, because it would involve the most discussion and delegation.

According to Puustjärvi, nothing definitive had been found at the lake other than Hackman's car, a red Peugeot 406, which had been sent to the lab. The car keys were missing, as was Hackman's cell phone. In the glovebox the team had found a receipt from a gas station in Kirkkonummi, which showed that Hackman had filled up there the day before yesterday at 3:40 p.m. After visiting the gas station she'd apparently zeroed out the trip meter; it indicated a distance equivalent to that between the station and the lake.

"We aren't getting a location when we ping Hackman's phone, so it might be at the bottom of the lake too. The dragging starts today," Puustjärvi said.

"OK, you continue liaising with the Kirkkonummi folks and handle any possible witnesses in the area around the crime scene," I said. "Koivu, how's your profile of Hackman coming?"

"Sini Jääskeläinen called me yesterday. She claims she knows who killed her stepmother. Before Hackman married Jääskeläinen, she dated a guy named Hannu, and apparently he stalked and threatened her. He claimed she broke a promise to marry him."

"Hannu? Did the girl know his last name?"

"She says she doesn't. I'll find out from her dad."

"So one line of investigation is this Hannu character. Fine. What else?"

"Maija Annukka Hackman, maiden name Väänänen. Born in Espoo, graduated magna cum laude from North Tapio High School in 1989. Her marriage to Jääskeläinen is her second, and it started a year ago in the spring. Before that she was married to Janne Hackman, and that marriage lasted from December 1993 until the following summer. She studied marketing communications, and landed her first job as a summer reporter for a local radio station, then *Society* magazine for a few years, then moved into newspapers at *Iltalehti*. She's been a freelancer for the past two years, and she founded her own communications agency, which merged with Racing Stripe Publishing earlier this year. She specializes in motorsports and personal profiles. She's done articles on everyone from government ministers and race-car drivers to single moms and lady cops." Koivu grinned at me.

"OK. You focus on Atro and Sine Jääskeläinen. Ursula, could you start going through Hackman's coworkers and contacts? This Sasha Smeds book is particularly interesting."

"So I get to interview Sasha Smeds?" Ursula asked, faking the innocence in her smile.

"If necessary. Puupponen, are you the one with the autopsy report?"

"Nope. There isn't one." A wry expression appeared on Puupponen's face. "Kervinen is on duty, but he won't open her up. Hackman was an old girlfriend of his."

"Girlfriend?" I'd always had a hard time imagining Kervinen being interested in living people. "Why didn't you say so up front?"

"One thing at a time, you always say. Hackman and Kervinen dated a couple of years ago. Apparently Hackman was dating Kervinen and Atro Jääskeläinen at the same time and then chose Jääskeläinen."

"But that means . . ."

"Yeah. The threatening ex-boyfriend is our very own Hannu 'Carcass' Kervinen. He was pretty tense on the phone," Puupponen said with a forced laugh. Even though Kervinen wasn't technically part of our unit or department, he was still part of our investigative team. And interviewing a colleague can be tough. Many of us had more than enough experience to know that.

I sighed. "Maybe it's best if I handle this one. Koivu, you can come with me. We'll talk to him together. Let's look at our schedules after the meeting and then you can set up a time with Kervinen—"

"What do you mean, you two will talk to him?" Ursula half stood from her chair. "I've never had anything to do with Kervinen, so I can stay neutral. You've known him for years. And Koivu was supposed to interview Jääskeläinen. Maria, let me handle Kervinen!"

Ursula Honkanen had landed her place in our unit thanks to her indisputable competence. She was twenty-eight years old. After initially studying economics at the University of Tampere, she grew bored of how theoretical everything was and joined the army, after which she applied to the police academy. She'd spent a year in Lahti working white-collar crime but then transferred to us as resources were shifted nationally from financial to violent crime. Ursula was an attractive woman, five foot ten and thin, with short blond hair. I'd heard Puupponen and Autio debating whether she was packing any silicone, since certain parts of her seemed out of proportion with the rest of her slender frame.

"Ursula, the Smeds angle might be important and requires some delicacy. You said you'd be happy to interview him. Does anyone know where he lives?"

"Inkoo. That's where half the rally drivers in Finland live," Puustjärvi replied. "But I doubt he's home now. The Australian rally just ended."

I divided the rest of the tasks, then started polishing another news release with the department press officer. Publicity was frequently useful, since regular people liked helping the police. But sometimes it was also difficult to decide which facts would help an investigation and which would hurt it if made public. The moose hunters knew that Hackman had been shot and someone had leaked that to the press. Now it was time to release the victim's identity. Koivu confirmed that all next-of-kin had already been notified.

"Kervinen's on his way over," Koivu announced after I wrapped up my meeting with the press officer. "He took the rest of the day off. If there's a bright side to this, it's that we won't have to bother Jääskeläinen to identify the body. Kervinen confirmed that it's her."

I'd never particularly liked Hannu "Carcass" Kervinen. He didn't engage in the dark humor most pathologists seemed to indulge in, something I'd always figured was a natural, human defense against the macabre nature of their work. In fact, Kervinen didn't joke at all. To him, bodies were strictly research subjects that only aroused an intellectual interest. Maybe that was a defensive measure too.

"Bring him to my office and ask for some coffee and sandwiches. We won't have time for lunch since we have the Jääskeläinen job in the afternoon."

"Are you coming along on that too?"

"You help me here, and I'll help you there. Did you sleep last night?"

"Five hours straight. I think that's a record."

I laughed, remembering all too well those nights when Taneli was an infant. I'd often sleep on the living room couch with ear plugs in while Antti attempted to calm Taneli's cries in our bedroom. I never would have survived those first months alone, especially with Iida demanding her own attention as well.

"Do you know if Kervinen's married?" I asked Koivu, who immediately started a search on his laptop. I couldn't remember seeing a ring on the medical examiner's hand. We'd never talked about children during either of my pregnancies. Still, Kervinen was a couple of years younger than me, and unattached men that age were rare. More than once I'd gotten the feeling that Kervinen didn't even know what sex was. Apparently I'd been wrong. It was hard to imagine him threatening anyone, though.

For far too long, the most dangerous thing a woman could do was to leave a certain kind of man. Often there had been previous violence in the relationship, but not always. Sometimes it took being left to set off the late-night phone calls, the skulking in bushes, and the hate mail. The recent legislation creating a system for restraining orders had been long overdue. But the Hackman-Jääskeläinens hadn't filed a complaint against Kervinen. Maybe Sini had exaggerated the harassment. She hadn't even remembered Kervinen's last name after all.

Koivu stood up to go get Kervinen as Puupponen came by and announced that the autopsy would be performed in the afternoon. He offered to go observe. If Kervinen was the murderer, he probably took steps not to leave any evidence. Shooting was a clean method for a killer since it didn't require close proximity to the victim. Kervinen would have known to protect himself from gunpowder residue as well.

When Koivu walked back into my office a few minutes later, carrying a tray of coffee and food, I almost didn't recognize the man he brought with him. Usually I saw Kervinen in a lab coat, carefully coiffed and groomed. Now his caramel-colored hair stuck up wildly, the collar of his shirt protruded from his winter coat, and his shoes were wet. Kervinen's frequent changes of aftershave had been a topic of general derision in the department, but today he only smelled of sweat. He sat down in an armchair but didn't want coffee or tea, and seeing the sandwiches made him look like he was going to be sick. His usually precise hands trembled. I didn't recognize the expression in his eyes, but it scared me.

"So you identified Annukka Hackman?" The conversation had to start somewhere, and the only thing I could think of was to get straight to the point.

"I thought it was just some routine case. I didn't even look at the name. I just opened the bag. Those eyes . . . and that upper lip . . . But no lower lip, and no jaw. Oh dear God! And then Puupponen calls and asks if it's an interesting case. Was he fucking with me?"

Koivu and I glanced at each other. Kervinen didn't seem like he was in any shape to be questioned.

"Hannu," I said, trying to sound comforting. "None of us had a clue that you'd dated Annukka Hackman."

"Dated! I was engaged to her. I even bought a bigger apartment so we could move in together. Then she went off with that Jääskeläinen bastard. She was such a goddamn opportunist! Doesn't her marriage to Janne Hackman tell it all? She just married him for his Swedish last name. That's the only reason. 'Väänänen' wasn't fancy enough."

"How did you two meet?"

"She was doing a story on the pathology department. That was right when those dismemberments and a few other sensational murders happened, and she was interested in what I knew about that. I guess she thought forensic pathology was like on TV, that I was solving crimes with the police or something . . . Then when she learned the truth, she wasn't interested anymore." Kervinen rocked restlessly in his chair. I'd never seen him like this before. I'd only ever known Dr. Kervinen, the professional; the person sitting before me was the private-life version of that man. He was a stranger.

"You said Annukka was an opportunist. What else can you tell me about her? How else would you describe her?"

Kervinen slapped his hands on his knees. "The same as you. She had this obsession with finding out the truth and telling the world. She thought people had a right to know what politicians and celebrities did in their free time. She could have been a good detective. She was ready to do anything to get a juicy story, and that was probably why she went to bed with me. And I don't believe she cared about Jääskeläinen either. She wanted to do a book about Sasha Smeds, but no respectable publisher wanted to get involved with a project that didn't have Smeds's consent. She needed Racing Stripe to publish her exposé."

I prodded Kervinen to tell us more about their relationship. He responded in a violent tirade, entirely opposite the slow, reserved way he spoke as a pathologist. Occasionally he fingered a bundle of keys clipped to his belt loop, which also held a couple of small scalpels in plastic cases. Kervinen had bought a diamond ring for Hackman. He'd also sold his beloved studio apartment in the historic center of Helsinki so he could purchase a two-bedroom flat in Tapiola. But as their moving day approached, Annukka announced that she'd decided to marry Atro Jääskeläinen instead.

"I understand that wasn't where you left things."

"I didn't do anything bad to her. I just wanted her to take responsibility for her actions, for breaking our engagement and ruining my life."

Stalkers often had ways of justifying their actions, especially if the motive for the harassment was unrequited love. Presumably Kervinen had believed that if he tried hard enough, if he rang Hackman's doorbell at six in the morning and sent endless text messages, she'd come back to him.

"Have you ever really been in love?" he asked. "So in love that you feel like you'll die if you can't get what you want? That your body won't listen to your brain?"

Koivu didn't answer, and neither did I. Finally I asked the question I had to ask.

"What were you doing the night before last?"

"I was sitting at home listening to music and missing Annukka. I've missed her every damn day since she announced she wanted Jääskeläinen instead of me. Every goddamn day. Maybe it'll get easier now that she's dead."

Perhaps Kervinen thought we'd suspect him in any case so why not serve up a motive on a silver platter? I leaned toward him, even though the stench of his perspiration made me cringe.

"Can anyone testify that you were home?"

"No."

"Then you're headed for powder residue testing."

Kervinen stood, and for a second I thought he intended to strike me.

"God, Kallio, don't you have more respect for me than that? I'm a professional. If I'd shot Annukka, I never would have left a trace."

"So being tested won't bother you. I imagine we already have your fingerprints. We'll come back to this later."

Kervinen sat down again, but then stood when he realized the conversation was over. I asked Officer Rasila from Patrol to take him to the forensic lab.

"That was something," Koivu said after Kervinen left. He tended to be embarrassed by large displays of emotion.

"It was that. Isn't it strange how everyone in love automatically thinks that no one could ever feel anything so powerful and genuine?

Let's check Kervinen's phone records from Tuesday night. His landline might save him or a ping from his cell phone might betray him."

Koivu took a sandwich and poured himself a cup of coffee.

"Sini Jääskeläinen gets home from school at three. We can meet up with her if we leave soon."

"Good. And I want to have a look at that book about Sasha Smeds. I'm curious about this previously unpublished information. I want to know what it is."

4

I've always found it interesting to visit complete strangers' houses. They make up the facades in the drama we present to each other. I've never been much for decorating, and I've always avoided knickknacks and frilly curtains. When Antti and I were looking for a new home, we toured several houses and apartments. Antti didn't want a row house— he thought they were the very lowest form of residential living. Many of the houses we visited were being sold because of a divorce, and they exuded a certain sadness. Maybe we were superstitious, but we didn't want to move into any place like that.

At first glance, everything appeared normal in the Hackman-Jääskeläinen home. But tiny details revealed that someone had lived there who didn't exist anymore. In the master bedroom, there was an empty cell phone charger and on the living room table sat a dry bouquet of roses. There were blond hairs on the curlers in the bathroom. On the kitchen counter was a coffee cup that said "Annukka" and had pink lipstick on the rim. I'd seen grieving parents preserve a lost child's room like a museum, and once I had to comfort a man who was hysterically throwing away all of his dead lover's clothes on the day he died because seeing them hurt too much. Maybe Atro Jääskeläinen wanted to preserve the touch of Annukka's lips on her coffee cup; maybe he would never wash it.

The Hackman-Jääskeläinens had only lived in the house for six months. They'd bought it almost complete after a previous buyer backed out of the construction contract at the last moment, Jääskeläinen explained. He was calmer than he'd been the previous day, but he smelled of beer and his speech was slow.

"Was Annukka a cold-water swimmer?" I asked.

"Not anymore. Apparently, a few years ago, she was into it, but the wet suit she has now is from when she did triathlons. Annukka got bored easily and switched sports a lot. Recently, she's been really interested in rally racing, and she's even ridden in a few cars to see what it's like."

"In Sasha Smeds's car?"

"At the beginning of the book project, yeah, but lately it's been with less well-known drivers." Jääskeläinen listed some names I'd never heard before.

"Did Annukka tell you she was going to Lake Humaljärvi to swim?"

"She didn't say where she was going. She just said she was going out to check on something important. She said she'd be gone a couple of hours. Annukka doesn't like anyone keeping tabs on her, but of course I was immediately concerned when she didn't come home on time, especially given that Kervinen guy . . ."

"Why didn't you file a police report about his harassment?"

"Annukka said she could handle it. She was sure Kervinen would chill out after a while. Do you think he killed Annukka?"

"We're looking into that. Do you have any idea what your wife went to the lake to check on?"

"No! I don't know what she was doing there. As far as I know, she'd never been there before." Suddenly Jääskeläinen stood up. "I'm grabbing a beer. Do you two want one?"

I would have, but since I was on duty I declined. The beer was dark and German, and Jääskeläinen poured it into a glass with a certain reverence before waiting for the head to collapse.

"How did the Sasha Smeds book project start?"

"Annukka interviewed him for our magazine last year. Smeds has an interesting family. They all live in the same house: Sasha's parents, his brother, and Sasha's wife, Heli. The brother and wife are organic farmers. Andreas was also a promising driver, but then he screwed up his career and had to quit. Of course, Sasha had the world championship stolen from him last year. That was some serious drama. And this year's championship is going to be really tight; it's going to come down to the final rally in a couple of weeks."

"Did Sasha participate in the book project?"

"In the beginning." Jääskeläinen sipped his beer, and I could practically taste it on my own lips. I wondered if I should stop by the liquor store on the way home and drink a bottle or two after the kids fell asleep. "Sasha didn't like the angle Annukka chose, so he backed out. But that doesn't hurt the marketing. Unauthorized biographies are perfectly common out in the world. In Finland we're just too considerate to celebrities."

But celebrities weren't considerate to themselves or their loved ones. They exposed everything about themselves there was to expose, I thought, and remembered a story Ursula had been reading aloud in the break room about the unique sexual proclivities of a former beauty queen's boyfriends. In my job I was always learning too much about strangers' intimate business, and I had no interest in reading more in the tabloids.

"Where did Annukka keep the manuscript for the book?"

"In the office. The source material and backup copies are in the safe. Don't think I'm going to let you take them."

"They're evidence for the investigation, and if I have to, I'll go to a judge to get them," I said firmly.

"And then you'll sell the information to the highest bidder?"

"That's not how I operate." I could only speak for myself, though, because I knew that more than one of my colleagues made a little extra on the side by letting the papers know whenever a celebrity got pulled over for speeding or drunk driving.

The door opened, something was thrown on the floor, then there was a clatter of coat hangers.

"Dad, who's this?" Sini Jääskeläinen appeared in the living room. She was a standard-looking sixteen-year-old with her hair cut short in one of the current styles. She wore jeans with exaggerated bell bottoms and a sweater that left her navel bare. Koivu introduced us to her, and she looked like she wanted to leave.

"Were you two home the night before last?" Koivu directed this to Sini.

"The night before last? I had aerobics and then I went with Laura to McDonald's in Tapiola. I came home at about nine thirty to watch *The Sopranos*."

"Could we get Laura's phone number?"

Sini glared, but then she looked up the number on her phone. I didn't want to ask about her stepmother while her father was listening. It took Atro a few seconds to realize we were checking his daughter's alibi.

"Come on, you don't think Sini shot Annukka, do you? She's just a kid."

"Whatever, Dad, I am not! At least not to all the guys I run into who are your age but want to get in my pants. But I didn't kill Annukka. Why would I? She was OK."

"How about we go have a look at Annukka's papers?" I suggested to Jääskeläinen. I thought Koivu could get more out of Sini than I could.

Jääskeläinen stood up and brought his beer with him. To get to the office, we had to go outside along a covered walkway. The wind rustled the hedge, and a drill whined in the yard next door. Inside, the graphic designer, Jalonen, was on his computer.

The safe was high quality and could have stood up to almost anything. Even an experienced safe cracker would have had a hard time with it. Jääskeläinen had to use the crib sheet he kept in his wallet to get it open. There was a large box of Smeds materials: newspaper articles, video recordings, notes, and rally results. And disks, backup copies of the backup copies. I would need a garbage sack for all of it.

"What computer did your wife use?"

"She used a laptop and the desktop in her office."

We would have to search both, which was something Ursula could add to her task list. She was extremely good with computers. Someone could come back for those, but I was going to take the papers now. I wrote out receipts for all of it for Jääskeläinen.

"I don't have a clue about her passwords," he said bitterly.

In the car Koivu said Sini hadn't given him much.

"I get the feeling Sini and Annukka didn't pay much attention to what the other was doing. I doubt her father keeps track of her either. She seems to live her own life. She eats dinner at restaurants with friends and just comes home to sleep. Her friend backed up her alibi from six on. They were in aerobics class together, then went to McDonald's, just like she said."

"So in theory she could have been with her stepmom at the lake, but she would have had to find a way back by hitchhiking or using public transportation."

"Or a taxi. Some of these teenagers have a crazy amount of money," Koivu said.

"If she hitchhiked from anywhere near the scene of the crime, someone might call it in as a tip. Let's check the buses and taxis in the area. We'll see if canvassing the houses nearby turned up anything. The latest reports are probably waiting in our in-boxes."

After I dropped Koivu off at the station, I went to pick up my kids. On the way I plugged in my hands-free earpiece to call Ursula and ask if she'd made contact with the Smeds family. Apparently none of the five family members had answered the phone.

"They have cows that have to be milked twice a day. Someone has to be home," Ursula said.

"Take a trip out there then. Maybe take Autio with you."

"Now? It's almost four. I can't. I've got other plans."

"This morning you were dying to meet Sasha Smeds."

"He probably isn't even coming home between the Australian and British rallies. He's probably training near Versailles at the Citroën rally facility."

"Ursula, just do it!" I hissed, then hung up even though I knew I should have given Ursula a real talking-to. For some reason it was easier giving orders to men. Somehow it seemed strange that my recalcitrant subordinate was the other woman.

Being so surrounded by men, I was used to the few of us women in the department sticking together. Last week our women's soccer club had played its final matches of the season. Ursula hadn't participated.

"Soccer? Just with women? No thanks. I prefer other sports," she'd replied when I told her about our club. I suspected that if the club had been for men and women, she would have come to stand on the sidelines and hand out water bottles.

I was at the day care at five to four. Iida was in the middle of a game with Roosa and had no interest in going home. Roosa joined in the tantrum. By the time I got them calmed down by promising that they could continue their game tomorrow, I was exhausted. Luckily I didn't have to bother making dinner; we had frozen macaroni casserole at home. During my second maternity leave, I'd systematically learned to cook something other than simple foods, and to my surprise I'd even learned to like cooking. Ingredients usually behaved the way they were expected to: egg whites whipped to stiff peaks, flour soaked up water, and butter melted in the microwave. The outer leaves of a head of lettuce might be a little wilted, but underneath the rest would be fresh. You could throw away a rotten tomato without a second thought. People were different. The ones I had to deal with in my job tried to hide and to hustle, and I never knew when I started a case what final result I'd end up with. Criminal investigation was like setting bread dough to rise but with someone else choosing the rising time and baking temperature.

I had the power to interrogate and arrest, but I had no influence over the consequences of a crime. Domestic violence charges were dropped; rapists got off with suspended sentences and came back a few months later to be interrogated about their next attempt. A pedophile stepfather claimed his wife and daughter were crazy, and the prosecutor couldn't find enough evidence to get a conviction. Sometimes I thought about going into prosecution since I had a law degree after all. My own vengefulness scared me sometimes.

After dinner it was time for the kids' shows. I'd have at least the running time of *Tiny Two* to read the Smeds papers. I left the bedroom door open a crack and started going through the contents of the box. Our unit secretary had made copies of everything, which Koivu had. He understood more about rally racing than I did and would be able to spot anything out of place that I didn't have an eye for.

Hundreds of articles had been written about Sasha Smeds in the domestic and foreign press. Annukka Hackman had been a systematic person; the articles were in chronological order. The first newspaper article was from 1983 when eleven-year-old Sasha had won some sort of go-cart race. His sparring partner had been his brother, Andreas, who was two years older. Their parents, Rauha and Viktor, were farmers in Degerö. That was in Inkoo very close to Antti's parents' summer house, so I knew the area.

Reading all the articles would take days, and I was more interested in Annukka Hackman's manuscript. I tried in vain to find a paper version. There were two disks, one labeled "Sasha Manuscript" and the other labeled as the backup copy (clearly, Hackman wasn't about to risk losing her work to a corrupted disk). Our only computer was with Antti in Edinburgh, so that reading would have to wait for tomorrow. I found the previous year's articles in which Smeds explained how team orders were just a normal part of motorsports.

"Of course it's disappointing that I was so close to the championship, but the team would have done the same thing for me if they could have ensured me the win," the article quoted Smeds as saying. He was trying to smile in the picture, and the caption said the small brunette next to him was his wife, Heli.

A scream from the children's room interrupted my reading. I hadn't even noticed that they were done watching TV. The scream was followed by another, then I heard Taneli burst into tears. I rushed to their room. Taneli lay wailing, surrounded by Duplo blocks. Blood dripped from his forehead. In her hand Iida had a red hammer used to pound blocks through holes.

"What the hell's going on in here?"

"Taneli broke my Lego dollhouse!"

Lifting my son off the floor, I wiped off most of the blood with Iida's doll blanket. Head wounds often bled a frightening amount even when the injury wasn't serious.

"No matter what he broke, you still don't hit him!" I yelled at Iida. I knew I shouldn't shout. It made Iida cry, and I wasn't far from tears either.

"Let's go put a bandage on that," I said as I tried to calm Taneli. Band-Aids made children think the pain would go away, just so long as no blood was showing. In the bathroom I washed the blood out of Taneli's hair. It looked like the wound was only superficial. Still I decided to let him sleep with me. Hopefully Iida wouldn't feel rejected.

Iida and Taneli had three and a half years between them, and sometimes I thought that was at least one year too long. Iida wanted to play quiet games of house and princesses with her dolls. Taneli spent his time with cars and toys that made as much noise as possible. At least they both liked stuffed animals, but it terrified me the way their games diverged along traditional gender lines, even though Antti and I tried to break those roles. Taneli was putt-putting around with toy cars before he could talk.

I got the kids calmed down by reading them a Moomin book, but I still felt bad about shouting. Maybe I was expecting too much of Iida to think she could ignore all of Taneli's provocations. She probably needed more company her own age outside of school. Antti was more patient than I was and could always seem to calm troubled waters and find something sensible for each child to do.

After the Moomin story, I turned on the TV. One of the endless news programs was on.

"Today the Finnish Road Safety Council launched a new campaign to cut down on young drivers speeding," the announcer said. "The public face of the campaign is rally star Sasha Smeds, who had just enough time to visit his home in Finland before the final race in the World Rally Championship in two weeks in Great Britain."

The Road Safety Council ad began. It started with Sasha Smeds spraying champagne on an awards platform. Then it shifted to a close-up of Sasha's face, and his jubilant expression turned serious.

"I only drive fast on the racetrack. On the road I always follow the speed limit. I never get behind the wheel when I've had alcohol, and I don't let my friends either. You should do the same!"

Then the picture shifted to a tricked-out Citroën hatchback with Smeds behind the wheel. There was also a woman who looked like a model, two school-age children, and a golden retriever. The woman wasn't the same one who had posed with Smeds in the newspaper picture. A lot of rally and Formula 1 wives had created their own careers in advertising, but apparently Sasha Smeds didn't want to get his family mixed up in his sponsorship business.

"Sasha, isn't it a contradiction for you to be acting as a role model for safe driving?" the reporter asked. Smeds was being interviewed at the Helsinki-Vantaa airport. Maybe Ursula was right that he would be impossible to contact before the decisive race.

"I don't think so. One purpose of car racing is to develop new safety technology. You're free to check if I have any speeding tickets," Smeds replied. He was obviously prepared for these sorts of questions.

"The campaign also talks about drunk driving. Your brother, Andreas's, rally career ended because of a drunk-driving conviction. What do you have to say about that?"

"My brother made a mistake, but he's suffered the consequences and made up for his bad choice."

Sasha Smeds was a handsome man, a typical Finnish blond of average height. High cheek bones and a slightly hooked nose gave his features personality. I hoped the Road Safety Council campaign would be a success. With our Traffic Division we'd just wrapped up an accident case in which a boy who had recently received his license ran a car his classmate was driving off the road on the West Highway. The result had been three dead. I had a running joke that the most dangerous part of my job was my commute to work in Espoo traffic.

If Taneli intended to rebel against his father when he was a teenager, fixating on rally drivers and starting to drive himself would be one of the best possible ways. Then Iida would become a chick who only cared about her looks and attention from boys, and whose mission in life was to find a rich man to support her, I thought darkly. I felt like the worst mother in the world whenever my thoughts began to stray from the children nestling into my lap to Annukka Hackman's murder.

The home phone rang just after eight as I was finishing brushing the children's teeth. Taneli whined sleepily, and I asked him to crawl into Mommy and Daddy's bed. Iida looked sulky since she had to sleep alone in her room.

"Hi, it's Jyrki."

"Hi," I replied, confused, since my boss always called my work phone.

"I was just wondering . . . Could you go out for a beer?"

This surprised me even more, since Jyrki Taskinen wasn't one for sitting in bars.

"I'd be happy to, but I can't. Antti won't be back from Edinburgh until tomorrow."

"Oh, yeah, I remember you mentioning that. What about . . . what if I came over to your place for a minute? I'll grab a couple of beers at a convenience store on the way. Who knows, they may have something dark."

"Sure. The kids will be asleep in a few minutes. I've spent every night alone for almost two weeks."

Taneli was already snoring gently in our bed on Antti's side with his stuffed cat Elvis under his arm. I read Iida a story and gave her a good-night hug. I tried to think how I could have screwed up the Annukka Hackman murder investigation already. Why did Jyrki want to see me tonight of all nights? Our families were friends, and I knew his wife, Terttu, and his daughter, Silja, pretty well, although Silja was a professional figure skater in Canada these days. At work Jyrki and I tried to have lunch together once a week, but trying was often all we succeeded at. There had been a cool period in our relationship before Taneli's birth since Jyrki had tried to get me to drop the Petri Ilveskivi investigation under pressure from his higher-ups. After that we had more than one strained conversation about solidarity and trust, and nowadays our friendship was stronger than ever.

Iida fell asleep quickly too. I remembered that I still had a few drops in a bottle of Laphroaig—I'd asked Antti to bring more from Scotland. I poured myself one finger and glanced out the window. A taxi drove up and Jyrki climbed out with a plastic bag. I was starting to get nervous. The downstairs bell rang, and I buzzed him in. Then I heard Jyrki's steps on the stairs. Antti didn't use the elevator for environmental reasons, but Jyrki avoided it for the exercise.

"Are the little monsters down?" Jyrki asked when he arrived.

"Yep. There's a cold one in the fridge. Do you want it while the ones you brought cool down?"

Jyrki handed me the beer, and I found pretzels in the bag as well. Jyrki didn't usually eat junk food.

He sat down at the kitchen table. I didn't bother saying that the living room would have been more comfortable. I lit a candle and poured him some beer. We chatted about work just long enough for me to realize he hadn't come about Annukka Hackman's murder. He clearly needed to work up to whatever was on his mind.

"Terttu said she didn't want us talking about this yet, but I can't keep it to myself anymore. Terttu is at Meilahti Hospital right now for tests. At first we thought it was normal menopause complications, bleeding and stuff . . . I guess you know since you're a woman. But they found cancer in her uterus. We're finding out now how bad it is."

Jyrki rotated his wide wedding band. His blue shirt was pressed, and his hair was combed neatly as always.

"Terttu's really scared. I wanted to stay with her at the hospital, but she wouldn't let me. They're taking the biopsy tomorrow, and it'll be a couple of weeks before they can analyze it."

"Oh, Jyrki. I'm so glad you didn't stay home alone." I placed my hand on his shoulder, and he grabbed it and squeezed. Years ago one of my coworkers accused me of sleeping my way up the career ladder, even though Jyrki and I had never shared anything more than a friendly kiss on the cheek.

"Terttu's afraid of dying, but she keeps pushing me away and won't talk. She won't even let me touch her." Jyrki had emptied his beer glass, so I got him a refill and asked if he wanted a sandwich. He didn't and just munched pretzels as if he didn't realize what he was eating.

"This spring it'll be twenty-seven years since we got married. But suddenly my wife is treating me like a total stranger. As if her health is none of my business. She can handle it alone, although obviously she can't. Maria, don't let Terttu know you know. I'm not even supposed to tell her siblings yet."

"Have you told Silja?"

"No. Terttu said she doesn't want to tell Silja until we're sure the situation is really serious."

Jyrki wasn't much different from a lot of Finnish men: he didn't have a best male friend to talk to when things got difficult. He and I had made a career of picking up the pieces for these same sorts of men: a wife would leave, taking the children, and the man didn't have anyone to talk to so he turned to a knife, a gun, or lighter fluid. Although to be honest, I doubted that talking would have always helped—there were feelings you just had to live through despite the pain.

Hannu Kervinen had expressed his disappointment to Annukka Hackman, and his calls and letters hadn't helped anyone. I tried to comfort Jyrki, even though I knew words wouldn't make the fear go away.

"All of a sudden there's this feeling that we can't plan for anything. For a long time we've intended to go to Canada to see Silja, but my work has always gotten in the way. You always think you've got forever."

"What if you booked the trip now and went for Christmas?"

"We have to see what the doctors say first. Terttu might need to start treatment immediately." Jyrki sighed and stared at his ring. "But let's talk about something more cheerful. How's Koivu adjusting to being a father?"

I related all the news from my unit and about my own kids, and a couple of times I even got Jyrki to laugh. After his third beer he called a taxi.

"Thanks, Maria," he said after pulling on his coat, then he hugged me long and hard. Just before he let go I felt a kiss on my hair. It felt like an electric shock.

When I went to my room, I found Iida there too and didn't bother carrying her back to her own bed.

Both children were sound asleep, and Taneli's head wound hadn't bled anymore. Still I couldn't go to bed yet, so I sat up emptying the bottle of Laphroaig and praying for Terttu Taskinen, even though I didn't have a clue to what or to whom I was praying.

5

When I turned my phone on after I woke up the next morning, seven call notifications were waiting for me, all from the same number. I had turned the phone off when the kids were going to sleep, and what Jyrki had told me shocked me so badly that I forgot to check my calls after he left. To my disappointment none of them was from Antti. The male voice that I heard speaking in the voice mails was completely new to me. Actually, it was more shouting than speaking, and in each successive message he seemed more agitated.

> *Hi, this is Jouko Suuronen. I'm the manager of Finnsport Representation. I need you to call me as soon as possible about your subordinates' rudeness to my client, Sasha Smeds.*

That was the first message. In the final message, which came after midnight, Suuronen started resorting to threats.

> *If you don't contact me immediately, we're going to have our lawyers start looking into your activities.*

What the hell had my guys been doing? Or, more precisely: What had Ursula done?

I can't function in the morning before a couple of cups of coffee and some carbs. After fueling up, I got the kids dressed and took them to day care. Taneli claimed his head didn't hurt anymore. I made the day care ladies promise to call me immediately if he started acting strangely, even though I knew I was being overprotective. I called Suuronen from the car in the day care parking lot.

"Hello," said a bleary voice. Cell phones had made people stop introducing themselves on the phone. They were such personal objects that the identity of the respondent was considered obvious.

"This is Detective Maria Kallio, Espoo Police. I'm trying to reach Jouko Suuronen."

"Kallio. Well, it's about damn time!" Suuronen seemed to wake up instantly. "What the hell are your people doing harassing Sasha Smeds? What game are you playing at saying he has to come in to the Espoo police station at nine o'clock today or he can't leave the country? Sasha's headed to France tomorrow to prep for the Rally GB. The world championship is at stake. Do you understand that? Do I have to fucking spell it out for you?"

"Everyone has an obligation to assist in murder investigations." I found that my arms and legs were shaking. I was angry at Ursula, who obviously hadn't done what I'd asked and gone out to the farm to interview Sasha in person, but I was even more furious at this cursing bully. "I'm glad Mr. Smeds will be coming to the police station bright and early. That way we can get his interview over quickly. I think that will be in everyone's best interest."

"Sasha isn't coming to the police station, at least not without a lawyer!"

"Do you make all his decisions for him? How well did you know Annukka Hackman?"

"You listen here . . . Oh shit—" Suuronen hung up the phone. I burst out laughing although I just as easily could have cried.

Suuronen and Smeds could make the media dance to whatever tune they wanted, and of course I'd be the one who'd end up having to take responsibility for the mess. But I had applied for this unit commander position myself, so I couldn't complain, although sometimes I thought that life would be easier if I could go back to being a sergeant in the field instead of sitting behind a desk.

There was good news too during the morning meeting: Annukka Hackman's autopsy had demonstrated that the shot easily could have been fired from her own gun. The time of death was estimated to be Tuesday the fifth of November between three o'clock and eight o'clock. There still wasn't any sign of the gun, and dragging the lake hadn't turned up anything. Eyewitness sightings of Annukka Hackman's car and other people near the lake on the night of the murder were plentiful, and the forensic investigation was making progress. But we were burning through money. Because three days had already passed and we were still in the dark about so much, we had to use all available resources.

"Jalonen, the graphic designer, had some interesting things to say about Jääskeläinen and Hackman's relationship," Koivu said. "I asked if they seemed like they were in love, and according to Jalonen, Jääskeläinen was definitely in love, but Hackman seemed more interested in her book project and her newspaper articles than in her new husband. Once he overheard them having an argument about how Annukka worked too much and never had time to go out." Koivu glanced at me and grinned. How many times had I vented my frustration about Antti's complaints that I didn't have enough time for the family?

"But what was even more interesting is that I received a text message from Sini Jääskeläinen last night. She claims she knows her dad was home around six on Tuesday evening because she called him on the family's landline," Koivu said.

"Ah. And why did Sini feel the need to tell you that?"

"Good question, boss. According to the phone records, there was no call from Sini's cell phone or any other phone to the Jääskeläinen landline anytime that night."

"So Sini suspects her father. Since you seem to have a good rapport with her, Koivu, you keep working that angle. Ursula, what's going on with the Smeds family?"

"I finally got in touch with them. Smeds's wife claimed they hadn't even heard about Annukka Hackman's death. Which is hard to believe since it's been all over the news! Then she wanted to know what Hackman's murder had to do with them. So I said it would be best for Sasha to come down here this morning at nine o'clock if he didn't want to get arrested."

Based on her appearance, Ursula was really throwing herself into this meeting with Sasha Smeds. Her makeup was fit for a nightclub, and her short skirt showed off her perfect thighs and calves, which were accentuated by her high-heeled pumps. Black lace flashed under her fitted blazer. Puustjärvi couldn't keep his eyes off her neckline.

"Did Smeds say he'd come?"

Ursula blushed a little. "I didn't speak with him, only with his wife. Sasha was resting, but his wife said she'd pass the message along. Do you want me and Autio to question him?"

"I doubt he's going to show up just like that. His manager contacted me and claimed that Smeds didn't have anything to do with Hackman. What time was it exactly when you spoke with Heli Smeds?"

"Heli Haapala. She kept her maiden name. I called there again right after we spoke and got her on the line."

"Great. Let's keep an eye on the situation, and call me if he does show up at nine. It might be a good idea to hear from other members of the family too. Ursula, you'll be getting Annukka Hackman's computer today. Will you check what's on it? Jääskeläinen claimed he didn't know the passwords. Try to figure that out and call in the experts if you need to. OK, everyone back to work."

As everyone else filed out, Koivu handed me the daily papers. "Have you seen these?" he asked. Annukka Hackman's murder was on the front pages of both tabloids. "Star Reporter's Tell-All Biography Murder Motive?" asked one. The other was even more brazen: "Sasha Smeds Connected to Murder?" Atro Jääskeläinen had decided to market Annukka's book regardless of her death. One of the papers even had a picture of me taken years before during some press conference.

"Was there anything else interesting in the phone records?" I asked Koivu.

"I'm still going through them, but first I'm going to talk to Sini Jääskeläinen. She must not have known how easy it is for us to see what calls someone's made. She seems worried about her father, and that's interesting."

I was back in my office by 8:45. During the meeting a dozen new calls had come in. There were also just as many e-mails, all about the same thing: What was the status of the Annukka Hackman murder investigation? I sighed, then looked at who had both called and e-mailed and started typing replies.

Because the investigation is ongoing, the police department can provide no further information at this time.

I didn't want to make the media's job any more difficult on purpose, but discretion was best now. The phone rang again. This time, the call was coming from an unknown number.

"Espoo Police Violent Crime Unit, Lieutenant Kallio speaking."

"Hi, it's Sasha Smeds. Am I speaking with the head of the Violent Crime Unit?"

"Yes. We're looking forward to seeing you today."

Smeds sighed. "I know. Did my manager, Jouko Suuronen, speak with you this morning?"

"Yes, I did have the pleasure of speaking with him."

Smeds laughed. "Jouko isn't at his best early in the morning. I'm sorry if he behaved inappropriately. And my wife wasn't able to explain to your officer that my whole day is booked with interviews. A film crew from Sweden is going to be here soon, and in the afternoon there's a Belgian car magazine coming. And then tomorrow I'm headed back to France and then England. Annukka's death is a terrible tragedy, and I'm happy to help the police, but I really can't make it over to Espoo today."

"How well did you know Annukka Hackman?"

"She was practically a family friend until . . . Look, I could probably make an hour between twelve and one. Couldn't you come out here? I'm sure you can understand that I want to concentrate on getting ready for this next race. The world championship is riding on it."

I knew this was a game. Smeds wanted to smooth over Suuronen's and Ursula's slipups, as well as keep the media off his back. He only wanted to talk to the people in charge. My curiosity began to win out. I might never have another chance to meet one of the best rally drivers in the world.

"Twelve o'clock sounds fine. We know where you live. I'll bring a couple of other officers with me. See you then."

I was annoyed enough with Ursula that I didn't notify her immediately and instead clicked through my e-mail, then looked up the report on Andreas Smeds's drunk-driving case. In September 1996 Andreas was caught driving seventy miles an hour in a fifty zone with a blood-alcohol content of .19. He got off with a fine. The next year he had two more drunk-driving arrests, but now the incidents were worse. I didn't find any other criminal records for Andreas Smeds or anyone else in the family. On a lark I also looked up Jouko Suuronen's name. He had some speeding tickets and one assault conviction from two years ago, a fight in the line to get into the "it" nightclub at the time. Fines and compensation to the tune of thirteen thousand marks.

I called Ursula, even though it was stupid because her office was only ten yards away.

"Smeds didn't come," she said irritably.

"I know. He called me."

"You?"

"We're meeting at his house in Degerö at noon. You're coming. It'll take a little under an hour to get there, so let's meet at my car in the garage at ten past eleven."

"What's going on here?" Ursula sounded like I'd tried to take away her boyfriend.

"Let's talk about it in the car. Do you have Hackman's computer yet?"

"Yes. I haven't had time to look at it because I was waiting for Sasha."

I didn't want to humiliate Ursula by leaving her out of our interview with Sasha Smeds. We hadn't really done any field work together, because I didn't do that much anymore. But Ursula participated actively in our morning meetings, and according to her colleagues she was quite aggressive in interrogations.

I put one of the Annukka Hackman manuscript disks in my computer. A file list appeared on the screen. Introduction. Childhood. First Race. I opened the file labeled "Childhood."

Alexander Johan Smeds drew his first breath on the rainy spring day of April 11, 1971. His parents, Rauha (b. 8/13/1938) and Viktor (b. 11/20/1938) were farmers. They had one previous son, Andreas (b. 7/2/1969). Rauha Smeds was born in Degerby on her family's farm, which is today called Smedsbo. She lived there until the age of six. Then world events intervened: in September 1944, Rauha's family, like many other Finns, was forced to leave their home when the Porkkala Peninsula, which includes the village of Degerby, was leased to the Soviet Union as a naval base for a term of fifty years.

The family didn't move far, though. Rauha's father, Albert, was a man of culture, a theosophist and pacifist. That may have been where his daughter's name, meaning "peace," came from. Alma, her mother, was an exception in predominantly Swedish-speaking Degerby because her first language was Finnish. They stayed as close to their former home as possible, in Innanbäck, and despite strict security, they slipped onto Soviet territory now and then to gaze at their old place. In 1955 Rauha moved, first to Kokkola and then to Stockholm. Following the early withdrawal of Soviet troops in 1956, the Smeds family were among the first former residents to return to their homes. In 1960 Rauha married her second cousin Viktor, who was from Kokkola, and the couple also took up residence at Smedsbo. However, their first child was nine years in coming.

Sasha had an idyllic country childhood surrounded by cows, horses, cats, and dogs. In the summer he rode his bicycle to school and in the winter he sometimes skied. Both brothers were interested in engines from an early age. For his third birthday, Sasha received a soapbox car his father had made.

Hackman had interviewed Sasha Smeds's childhood friends and schoolmates. She'd done her background work carefully, and there was none of the sensationalism in this section that I had expected. It simply told of a normal, albeit bilingual, childhood in the southern Finnish countryside. She did argue that Sasha had a bit of an inferiority complex about his older brother, but that wouldn't have surprised anyone.

Then at age nine, everything changed for Sasha when he got behind the wheel of his first go-cart.

Both Sasha and Andreas remember the immensity of the experience. Their mother wasn't at all excited about motorsports because it clashed with her environmental sensibilities, but Viktor understood the boys' innate need to drive fast and took them to the go-cart track. Once there, the Smeds boys' phenomenal talent became obvious.

My phone started playing Eppu Normaali's "Bar Fly," which meant Antti was calling.

"Hi! Where are you?"

"At Heathrow. This place is awful. Is everything all right?"

"Yeah," I lied, not mentioning Taneli's head wound or Terttu Taskinen's cancer. "Is your flight on schedule?"

"More or less. Should I pick up the kids? I've missed them."

"Let's get them together. I'll see you just before five at the day care. And hey—bring me some Laphroaig!"

"Already bought it. See you soon."

The call left me feeling warm inside. Only a few more hours.

Before we left for Degerö, I went down to the cafeteria and had a salad for lunch. Puustjärvi and Ursula were sitting behind a large potted plant and didn't seem to notice me. I didn't want to eavesdrop on their conversation, but unfortunately I didn't have anything to read to distract me. Ursula was trying hard to get Puustjärvi to go out with her that night.

"You can go out for a beer. You aren't going to be able to go anywhere after the babies are born. Say you have to work overtime. Come on. It'll be nice to get to chat in peace for once."

Puustjärvi's wife was in the final stages of her pregnancy, and—surprise surprise—they were expecting twins. Puustjärvi had bemoaned the fact that he had to buy a new car since there was no way four kids were going to fit in the family's old Subaru. Ursula seemed to be arranging more headaches for the poor man. I'd thought she was focusing her wiles on Puupponen, who was single. Apparently she liked the challenge of men who were taken.

As she and I were driving to Degerö, I didn't comment on what I'd overheard, and Ursula wasn't in the habit of talking about her personal life with me. Instead she told me everything she knew about Sasha Smeds. He was in his second season as Citroën's number-two driver, and before that he'd been a relief driver for Toyota. His co-driver lived in Monaco, but to the delight of the Finnish taxman, Smeds had chosen to maintain his domicile in his home country. The family land had changed ownership from Viktor and Rauha to the boys about five years earlier, and now Heli and Andreas managed the farm and dairy operation.

"Sasha and Heli don't have any children, but Sasha still spends as much time as possible at home. Andreas doesn't have any family. Heli came to the farm about six years ago as a temporary worker and ended up staying. She doesn't look like much, so she's probably jealous of all the models who constantly hang around the star drivers."

"Have there been rumors of any extramarital relationships?" Of course nothing interested readers more than sex and money.

Ursula shook her head. The day was overcast, and when we crossed the bridge over the bay into the forest, everything looked colorless. There were just a few leaves left on the trees, but somehow the lack of color was calming.

"This is really far out here," Ursula said as the Degerby church tower came into view.

I laughed. "During rush hour, it's faster to drive from the station to here than to the other side of Helsinki." During the summer I'd spent long stretches at Antti's parents' cabin in Inkoo, which was only a little farther, while my father-in-law was having surgery and my mother-in-law was living with her daughter's family near the hospital. Leaving the seaside to return to the White Cube had been painful. In November, though, it wasn't so idyllic anymore: streetlights were unknown here, so after dark even going out for a walk was difficult.

I turned onto the road that led to Degerö. The landscape of rolling fields around us looked like something from the British Isles. The houses all looked comfortable, and the yards were well manicured. A lane lined with spruces led to Smedsbo. I wondered if the trees had managed to grow this tall in less than fifty years or if the Soviets had spared them.

The buildings on the property were arranged neatly around the barnyard. The main building was a red two-story house with white trim around the windows and doors. Surrounding the house were a barn, a hay shed, and a collection of smaller feed-storage buildings. Looking at the structures you could imagine you were in the nineteenth century, but the illusion was broken by a couple of cars and a tractor visible through the open door of the garage. Unlike many of the buildings in the area, these hadn't been destroyed by the Soviets. Upon closer inspection, I noted that the garage was newer than the other buildings. As we drove up, a young man in coveralls stuck his head out. Pretending not to notice us, he went back to working on one of the cars, a fast-looking red Citroën convertible. I doubted they mass-produced models like that.

When we climbed the front steps, we found the key in the door lock: we were really in the country now. A German shepherd rushed to the door to meet us. It didn't bark, though, and generally looked gentle. Behind the dog came a small woman with pigtails whom I recognized as Heli Haapala. She was wearing an apron and had smudges of flour on her cheeks.

"Sasha will be here soon. He's just answering an e-mail. Come on in the living room. Would you like coffee or tea?"

"I'm always up for coffee," I said as we entered the house.

The house was built in the traditional farmhouse style, with the living room and dining space combined. In one corner stood a loom, and there was a baking oven in another. Close to twenty people could have fit around the table. Sitting down at one end of it, I looked out the window into a field with a few cows grazing. Seeing cows outdoors this late in the year was rare, but maybe it had something to do with Smedsbo being an organic farm.

Heli Haapala set out coffee and *pulla* sweet rolls and made a couple of trivial comments about the weather. Her movements were smooth and efficient, and her body had the wiry muscle of someone used to physical labor.

"How well did you know Annukka Hackman?" I asked her while we waited for Sasha.

"I didn't. We just talked a couple of times there in the beginning before we realized what kind of book she was writing."

"What kind of book was that?"

"The kind we didn't want. Sasha happens to be a star driver right now, but the rest of us have normal lives and don't need anyone talking about us."

The living room door banged open, and I turned toward the sound of footsteps. Sasha Smeds was slenderer in person than in pictures or on TV. His smile looked unaffected and was reflected in his eyes.

"I'm sorry you had to wait. I just had to reply to a question from my racing team management. So are you Detective Kallio?" Smeds walked over to shake my hand, then he introduced himself to Ursula.

"I'm Sasha. It's a pleasure to meet you both." Apparently he wanted us to use his first name. "I'm glad this worked out this way. Take some pulla. Heli baked them today."

I told Sasha that I intended to tape our conversation.

"So is this an official interrogation?"

"Yes. How did you meet Annukka Hackman? Whose idea was the biography?"

"Annukka did her first interview with me for *Society* magazine when I started driving for Toyota. Female reporters usually don't know much about racing, but Annukka knew a lot about the technical side of things and clearly paid attention to the sport. Then she moved over to *Iltalehti* and they started sending her abroad to report on the rally circuit. Those press conferences are usually all men, so Annukka really stood out from the crowd. She asked tough questions too. It would have been hard not to get to know each other since we crossed paths so much every year. I wondered a little when she went freelance, though, since she was such a good racing reporter. Well, then she found Atro Jääskeläinen and *Racing Stripe*."

I'd understood that the racing world was even more closed to women than other sports. The drivers were 98 percent men, and the woman's role was to sit in the spectator seats being terrified or show off her legs next to the prize platform. I could imagine how Annukka Hackman might have felt at press conferences, since I was frequently the only woman at the meetings I attended too.

Sasha grabbed a pulla from the bowl and started to fiddle with it like a stress ball.

"The idea for the book started last fall when it looked like we were going to win the world championship. Annukka had just married Jääskeläinen, and we were at the wedding. When I danced with Annukka, she suggested writing a biography to be published in Finnish and English. I talked with my manager, and he approved the project. At first the idea was to have it ready for last Christmas, but when the championship didn't go the way it was supposed to, they decided to put it off. Annukka said she didn't just want to throw something together based on articles other people had written. She wanted to write a real book. So we decided it would come out this year in November for Father's Day, just before the final rally of the season."

Smeds spoke calmly, barely taking his eyes off me. He was used to answering questions and conversing with strangers.

"What was it like working with her?"

"Until this summer, it was great. No thanks," Sasha said to his wife, who'd gone to get us more coffee. "But could you bring some apple juice?" Turning back to me, he smiled warmly. "Too much coffee isn't good for your body." His expression was boyish and charming.

"So what happened this summer?" Ursula asked. "Why did your working relationship change?"

Heli returned with Sasha's juice, then quickly disappeared back into the kitchen.

"Of course I understood that Annukka wanted personal details for her book," Sasha said. "Like childhood memories and my love story with Heli. But I didn't think my brother's problems with the law belonged in the book, or my manager Jouko's divorces, let alone my father's heart condition or my grandparents' political views. And who would be interested in that anyway? When our disagreements got too big, I quit the project. Jouko has already been in talks with Finnish and foreign publishers about a different kind of book, but of course what Annukka was working on made that complicated. Did she manage to finish her book before she died?"

This question was directed at me.

"You'll have to ask Atro Jääskeläinen about that. When did you last see Annukka?"

Smeds thought for a moment, then yelled into the kitchen:

"Heli, do you remember when Annukka last visited here? Was it the week before May Day? It seems like it was a little before the Safari Rally."

Heli stuck her head through the door, and her cheeks reddened a little.

"No, it was later, in early July. We were leaving the next day for the French trials. Remember? It was the day before Andreas's birthday and I was just baking his cake and . . ." Heli swallowed and turned back into the kitchen. Smeds stared after her.

"Heli always remembers everything. She's right; now I remember too. Annukka was lucky she didn't get that cake in her face."

"So the meeting wasn't particularly friendly?"

"In the end Heli threatened to call the police if Annukka didn't leave. Jouko had told us to do that if she showed up. I didn't want any trouble like that, but they were all talking about filing for a restraining order. I thought that was overkill."

"Where were you on Tuesday afternoon and evening?"

Smeds snorted.

"I guess you have to ask that. I was home asleep. I got back from Australia early Tuesday morning. The jet lag was intense. I can sleep anywhere, but I get the best rest here at home next to my wife."

Outside it had started to gently rain. A cow sauntered toward the barn, looking unconcerned. It was so quiet here that the whirring of the tape recorder sounded loud. Smeds worked surrounded by noise, so maybe he needed this sort of atmosphere at home. I found myself envying him for living in such a peaceful place.

On the table was a slip of paper full of incomprehensible letter combinations. *LK 30, RK 20, OC,* and so forth.

"Notes," Sasha said when he saw me glance at it. "On the other side of the field I have a practice track about three kilometers long.

The Swedes are here to film a practice run. I don't need any pace notes for that track, but they wanted to see them. Annukka rode with me a couple of times, and once she even tried to read the notes for me. She did well for a first timer." Sasha drained his apple juice.

"Of course we couldn't stop Annukka from writing her book," he continued. "So Jouko hired some lawyers. We made it clear to her that if she wrote a single word that wasn't true, we'd sue. Jouko was handling it, but Annukka still tried to appeal to me to back down that last time she was here."

"Did Annukka Hackman ever hit on you?" Ursula asked.

Smeds laughed but couldn't hide a slight blush.

"I wouldn't say she hit on me, but she was flirty. I think she caught on pretty quickly that I'm a one-woman kind of guy, though."

A bang came from the kitchen as if Heli had dropped something. I made a mental note. Heli seemed to be protecting her husband; I imagined that everyone around Sasha Smeds did that. Rally racing might not have been quite on par with Formula 1, but there was still an awful lot of money involved. And it was a sport that ultimately depended not only on teamwork but on Sasha's ability to stay focused.

"Did you know Annukka Hackman carried a gun?" I asked.

"Everyone knew. Annukka thought I should too, at least abroad, like during the Safari Rally. She saw the world as being full of enemies." Smeds smiled sadly. "And I guess she wasn't wrong. Hopefully you catch whoever did it."

Sasha Smeds was no stranger to the spotlight, so I knew we were dealing with a carefully constructed persona here: the affable boy next door, every mother's ideal son-in-law, who just happened to be a top athlete. But you couldn't build that profile without having the right material to start with. Sasha Smeds was impossible not to like.

The living room door opened. First a shadow appeared on the rag rug. Then a man stepped in. He was a little over sixty, with a hooked nose and high cheekbones that were even more pronounced than Sasha's, as well as a leaner face. His walk was slow, like that of a much older person.

"My father, Viktor Smeds," Sasha announced. "Dad, this is Detective Kallio and Officer Honkanen from the Espoo Police."

At that the color drained from Viktor Smeds's face. He staggered and collapsed to the floor.

6

"Dad!" Sasha made it to Viktor's side before I did, but didn't know what to do to help him. I turned Viktor into recovery position, loosened his collar, and checked his breathing. His respiration was fine, and only a moment passed before he opened his eyes.

"Rauha . . . Vad har hänt med Rauha . . ." Viktor said to his son in Swedish.

"Nothing happened to Mom. The police are here because of Annukka Hackman," Sasha said. Then he turned to his wife, who had rushed in. "Heli, why didn't you tell me Dad is still in such bad shape?"

Sasha and I helped Viktor into a bedroom to rest. Viktor felt brittle, even though he couldn't be much older than my own father, who still radiated vigor and health.

"Dad had bypass surgery a month ago, and his recovery hasn't gone the way they hoped," Sasha said. "Mom went to the store in the village, and Dad always worries about her when the weather's bad. Even a professional like me has to be careful on some of the roads around here. Heli, will you call Sandberg just in case? He's our family doctor," Sasha explained to me. "Those Swedes will be here any second. Did you have anything else for me?"

"I'd like to talk with the other members of the family too if they aren't needed for the taping. Not your father, though. We'll interview him later if the need arises. Does he speak Finnish?"

"Not as well as the rest of us, but he gets by. Dad's from up north in Ostrobothnia in the Swedish area and lived in Sweden for a long time when he was younger."

Through the window I saw a van drive up with the SVT1 logo on the side. The young man in coveralls we'd seen working in the garage came out to greet the new arrivals. Apparently he was more favorably disposed to television reporters than police.

"Heli, the Swedes are here! And the police want to talk to you too," Smeds yelled in the direction of the kitchen. Instead of waiting for Heli, I went into the kitchen myself where I found her kneading a dark bread dough. Bread pans waited on the table, but instead of the traditional baking oven, she was preheating a fancy convection model. The kitchen was generally pretty modern—apparently Sasha had been willing to invest in proper equipment for his wife. Did Heli Haapala handle all the cooking for her in-laws too? In the modern world a mother-in-law and daughter-in-law easily working alongside each other in the same kitchen seemed rare, but maybe the Smedses were a more harmonious lot. I could barely stand even Antti being in the kitchen when I was making food.

"So this summer you threatened to call the police if Annukka Hackman didn't leave," I began. Heli stood with her back to me, forcefully kneading the dough. Her apron reached almost to her ankles, and her hair was pulled back in a ponytail.

"Annukka was trespassing. Sasha was really busy, and Annukka was just harassing us with her questions. Andreas almost attacked her . . . It was a horrible mess."

"Andreas attacked Annukka?" Ursula had come into the kitchen.

"I said almost." Heli slapped the dough into a bowl, then used a knife to scrape the rest off her right hand before washing up at the sink.

"None of us had anything against Annukka. As a person, I mean. We just couldn't accept her wanting to cash in on our lives."

"Wasn't Sasha promised a cut of the sales?" Ursula asked.

"I guess. Jouko handled that. But when we decided to quit the project, we told Jääskeläinen at Racing Stripe Publishing that we didn't want a cent of his money."

"I understand that in the book, Annukka writes about how you and Sasha met. Did she interview you as well?"

"Yes. Stupid me, I agreed, even though I've never wanted to appear in the press simply as Sasha's wife. I have my own job. I'm a farmer," Heli said as she tilted her head and her ponytail swung past her shoulders.

"So you're not just a housewife?" Ursula quickly asked.

"What do you mean 'just'? How is running a house not important? I own a third of this farm, and Sasha and Andreas own the other two-thirds. I'm a farmer just like the men. Now, I'm sorry, but I have to serve coffee to the television crew."

Heli disappeared into the living room, then brought back our coffee cups and the plate of pulla, which she refilled. Entertaining interviewers seemed to be routine. I walked after her, even though it felt silly.

"Where were you last Tuesday afternoon and evening?"

"In Espoo at the fabric store. And no one was with me to testify about it." Heli smiled quickly as if to show she knew we were looking for an alibi.

"How many cars are there here?" I continued.

"Six. One SUV we all use for bad weather and driving in the forest. Sasha's Citroëns, a station wagon and a convertible, and my Picasso. The Hyundai belongs to Andreas; he won't take a sponsorship car from Citroën. Rauha won't either. The green Škoda that just drove into the yard is hers. Viktor isn't driving right now. Sasha's race car will be here until tonight, but it isn't registered and doesn't get driven anywhere but on the practice track."

"Were you using your own car on Tuesday?" If so, we'd need to check whether there had been any sightings of a silver Citroën Xsara Picasso near Lake Humaljärvi.

"Yes, I was. But I don't even know how to shoot. I don't approve of violence of any kind, and neither does anyone else in this house. You're going to have to look for your murderer somewhere else! Now I'm sorry, but I have to go feed the cows."

We heard the Swedish TV crew tromping in. Sasha laughed with them. His voice sounded a little lower in Swedish than in Finnish. I'd noticed before how personalities could change from language to language, with characteristics appearing or disappearing. Antti had defended his dissertation in English, and I remembered how surprised I was by his self-confidence. Whenever I had to speak Swedish, I always started talking too fast, as if I found it irritating and wanted to get out of the situation as quickly as possible.

"Let's talk to Andreas and Rauha Smeds too," I said to Ursula. As we headed toward the entryway, the front door opened and a woman came in with her arms full of shopping bags.

She was even shorter than I was. Gray hair hung loose around her face and her eyes were filled with alarm. Maybe Sasha had told his mother about his father's episode.

"Hello, Mrs. Smeds, I'm Detective Kallio from the Espoo Police. I'd like . . ."

"Like whatever you want, but I'm going to see my husband now!" Rauha Smeds set down the shopping bags. The contents of one of the cloth bags spilled out on the floor: organic wheat bran, ground beef, and vegetable bouillon cubes. Rauha Smeds ignored her purchases and disappeared through the door we'd taken Viktor through. I put everything back in the bag, then walked out into the yard to find Andreas.

Andreas Smeds had stopped working on the convertible and was now working underneath the older-looking white Hyundai. Only his shins and dirty black hiking boots were visible. The cheap Škoda and the Hyundai seemed to belong to a different world than the flashy Citroën and the large Land Rover.

"Andreas?" Since Sasha had wanted us to call him by his first name, I did the same with Andreas. Perhaps Swedish Finns did that with everyone, like the Swedes did.

Andreas's legs twitched, then bent as he began to shimmy out from under the car.

"Oh, it's the cops," he said before his face appeared. "My hands are too dirty for shaking." Andreas stood up. He was a little taller than his brother and blond like all the men in the family. He had deep-set blue eyes that avoided my gaze. I introduced myself and Ursula, who looked at the red streamlined convertible in awe.

"I don't have anything to tell. I didn't know Annukka Hackman. She was only interested in my DUIs, and I didn't want to talk about that. I thought Sasha was stupid to ever start working with someone like her. But Sasha wouldn't kill over his reputation. Headquarters handles all the unpleasant business."

Andreas Smeds's face was expressionless, and his voice was calm, but his fingers revealed his agitation. He rubbed them on his pants, leaving grubby streaks.

"What do you mean by 'headquarters'?"

"Jouko, Sasha's manager, and of course the Citroën people. And the Finnish people, who love their rally heroes, as long as they win. And a few scandals don't hurt either. The people have to have something to read after all."

"Were you concerned that there might be sensational revelations in Annukka's book?"

Andreas laughed, but there was no joy in it. "There's nothing sensational about my brother that doesn't happen on the track. He's a good man. He doesn't drink, and he doesn't sleep around. He really is as lily-white as they say in the papers. And he's a hell of a driver. And he was at home asleep on Tuesday when Annukka Hackman was killed. I can testify that Sasha's cars were here the whole time."

"So you were home then too?"

"How else do you think I can testify for my brother, Detective? Dad was at a follow-up appointment, and Mom was with him. Look somewhere else for your murderer."

"Where was this follow-up appointment?"

"At the Mehiläinen private hospital in Helsinki. Sasha Smeds's father doesn't have to wait in line for public health care."

Antti's father hadn't either. His bypass was scheduled for just before Christmas. In the public system he would have had to wait nearly a year, and he probably would have died in the meantime. Luckily Tauno Sarkela had been able to earn and save enough to cover the surgery. We didn't have the resources to help, and Antti's sister didn't either after buying out her ex-husband's half of their house in Espoo.

Outside I started hearing people speaking Swedish and the rumble of a tailpipe. I hadn't seen Sasha's race car—apparently it had its own garage.

"The show is starting," Andreas said with a snort. "Do you have anything else for me? I need to go see if Sasha needs me."

We followed Andreas into the yard, where a bright-red Citroën covered in sponsor decals had appeared. Sasha had pulled on a racing suit, and a helmet hung from his hand. A member of the film crew was attaching a small video camera behind the driver's seat of the car. I walked over because I'd never seen a rally car up close. First I marveled at the tires. The studs were less than half an inch long and they were much denser than those on a normal winter tire. These tires had no business on an asphalt road.

"Vem ska komma med?" Sasha asked his visitors, who all hemmed and hawed. I peeked in the car. There were no rear seats, but there were roll cage bars across the door openings. Multipoint seat belts went from the belly over the shoulders.

"Am I not going to have anyone be my map reader?" Sasha asked in Finnish. "What about our esteemed police officers?" he asked, turning to us. "Care for a ride? One lap around the track only takes a couple of minutes."

I was sure Ursula would jump at the chance, but she avoided Sasha's gaze. Maybe she was afraid the helmet would mess up her hair.

"I can't turn down an offer like that," I said. Annukka Hackman had been addicted to rally racing. Maybe I'd understand her better if I shared her experience.

"Excellent. Andreas, will you bring Detective Kallio a helmet?" Sasha opened the co-driver's door for me. As soon as I sat down, Andreas was there, fastening my seat belts and putting on my helmet. It was massive but surprisingly light. For a moment everything around me sounded muffled, but then Andreas attached the headset cord, and I heard Sasha's voice.

"They're going to be filming me and the view out the windshield, but they won't see you. I haven't told the film crew that you're a cop. You ready?"

"Let's hit it," I said and tried not to show how nervous I was. Of course I'd driven fast before for work, but this was different.

The car instantly accelerated to what must have been sixty miles an hour as Sasha raced down the lane through the field into the forest. I nearly shrieked as the car headed straight toward a snowbank, but Sasha turned at the last second. After the next curve I started to relax. Sasha knew every meter of the practice track and exactly how his car would react. Sometimes we skidded sideways, sometimes we were perpendicular to the narrow road, and we nearly flew over one hill. But Sasha drove confidently, obviously enjoying himself, and I couldn't help but get caught up in the speed. When the lap was over, I felt like asking for more.

Still, I found that my legs shook when I climbed out of the car. Although my mind enjoyed the experience, my body disagreed.

"Were you scared?" Andreas asked as he opened the door for me. "Did you get her to scream?" he asked his brother, who was taking off his helmet.

"No, even though I got it up to a hundred and sixty-five kilometers per hour. Damn." Sasha laughed and I joined in. Although the ride had only lasted a few minutes, I felt the same way I did after an hour of running.

We said good-bye to the Smeds family and walked past the outbuildings to our own car.

"Did you get anything new out of Sasha?" Ursula asked once we were out of earshot.

"Asking questions didn't even cross my mind, and I don't think this line of investigation is really going anywhere anyway."

"No? I thought all of them seemed to have plenty to hide. The father passed out when he saw us, and Andreas hates his brother. Maybe he shot Hackman and hopes Sasha will be blamed for it. If he wants to he can undermine his brother's alibi, and he could also stash Hackman's pistol in Sasha's things. What about issuing a search warrant for the house?"

"I can't justify it. We don't have enough evidence," I said and opened the car door. "Do you want to take a turn driving? I have to write out some notes." What I didn't say was that my hands were still shaking from the adrenaline, and I wasn't ready to get behind the wheel yet.

I'd never ridden with Ursula before. As she set out from the farm, she drove confidently and quickly. A dog watched us go, and the rain made the landscape look like a watercolor painting that hadn't dried properly.

"I don't think Andreas hates his brother, but why has he stayed on the farm?"

"He quit school after the ninth grade, just like Sasha. Maybe no diploma and three drunk-driving convictions make it hard to find a job."

"Do you know if the drunk driving caused any injuries?"

"When Andreas got caught the last time, he'd broken his leg driving into a tree. Maybe that calmed him down." Ursula turned on the radio and tuned it to Radio Nova. They were playing Phil Collins yet again. I wrote down a few thoughts that had occurred to me and things we needed to do. We had to get Suuronen in for an interview, along with Sini Jääskeläinen. We had to investigate all the usual gun dealers and fences, in case one of them had ended up with Annukka Hackman's gun. Autio could handle that. I started humming along with Collins. His new single actually sounded OK. Was this a sign I was reaching middle age?

Suddenly Ursula slammed on the brakes and steered onto the shoulder.

"Oh my God!" she exclaimed.

Two cars came at us side by side, one in the opposite lane and the other in ours. We were near the village of Degerby, and both directions were no passing lanes. The speed limit was fifty miles an hour, but the passing car was doing at least seventy.

"Did you get the license plate?" Ursula asked, panting. "If I hadn't swerved in time . . . If someone had been on the shoulder . . ."

"I'll call Traffic. It was a blue Audi. This isn't the first time someone has almost gotten killed like that on this road," I said, trying to calm Ursula down even though my own heart was pounding. "Maybe the Audi driver thought he was Sasha," I added, forcing a laugh.

Ursula continued driving, but I could see her shaking, and she didn't dare go over forty-five. A line of cars started to form behind us. At the next intersection I told her to pull over.

"Let's switch drivers. You had a real scare."

"I'm fine!" Ursula snapped, but she stopped anyway. "I didn't do anything wrong!"

"No, you didn't. You did exactly the right thing and prevented an accident. It's no wonder you're in a little bit of shock."

I took the driver's seat, and Ursula moved to the back seat and leaned her head on the headrest. In the rearview mirror I could see the color gradually returning to her face.

"Of course you're going to tell everyone at work about this," she said after calming down.

"Why would I? I would have been just as scared as you were if I'd been driving. Will you promise not to tell my husband I took a ride with Sasha Smeds?"

I couldn't interpret the expression that flashed across Ursula's face. Then she opened her handbag and started touching up her lipstick.

I dropped Ursula off back at the station and was at the day care by around four thirty. There was still no sign of Antti. According to the teachers, Taneli had been calm and in a good mood all day, and Iida had been singing constantly about Daddy coming home. We waited in the yard—the children played and I forced myself to chat about the weather with a couple of the other moms. Then through the drizzle I saw a thin figure with a familiar loping stride.

"Taneli, look! Daddy!"

Taneli scampered off toward his father, and Iida sprinted hard to get to the gate first. I think I took a few running steps too.

"Big hug!" Taneli yelled, copying the Teletubbies. Neither Antti nor I paid any attention to the mud the children smeared on us as we all held each other.

That evening we ate pizza and played Star of Africa, with me and Taneli on one team. The previous spring Iida had learned to read, so she sounded out the foreign city names on the playing board, her mouth full of Scottish toffee.

The kids were over the moon about their dad coming home, and getting them to sleep was tricky. Antti had to read to Iida twice as long as normal, while I put his dirty traveling clothes in the laundry. Antti didn't use aftershave, so his clothes only had the mild scent of his skin and shampoo, familiar yet provocative. I hoped Iida would go to sleep quickly. I poured myself a dash of whiskey from the bottle Antti had brought, but just a dash. I wanted to keep my senses keen. I thought of Atro Jääskeläinen and Hannu Kervinen, who had fallen in love with the same woman, and felt sad for both of them.

"I think she'll fall asleep now." Antti came out of the children's room. "I feel kind of sticky. I'll have to take a shower. Or should I wait for the sauna to heat?"

The sauna we had now was hardly better than none at all: it was barely the size of a large closet. Our family could just fit in it but wouldn't for long. The steam from the electric heater was stifling and had a hard edge for someone used to the mellow heat of a wood stove. In the summer the sauna made the whole apartment sweaty.

"Go ahead and shower. I'll join you," I said hopefully. I'd always liked making love in places other than the bed: in the sauna, on the beach, on the entryway floor. Our shower was so cramped that getting frisky there required some acrobatics, but my longing generally made me forget the hardness of the wall tiles.

"It's nice having you home again," I murmured into Antti's hair later as we lounged on the living room couch, wrapped in towels and sipping Laphroaig.

"That was probably my last work trip for a while. The project isn't going to get its funding renewed. I'll have to ask around for more work. Maybe the university has adjunct positions available. I met a guy from Cambridge in Edinburgh, and they're starting a graduate program in category theory. They might have work for me next fall."

"In England?"

"Don't worry yet. I might be able to do it in blocks, like one week every month. I'm just going to see what happens. You're working on a murder, right? And one of the suspects is that rally star, Sasha Smeds? I read it in the papers on the plane. Seeing your picture always makes me happy."

"No one but you would even recognize that as me. I visited the Smedses' home today. They live just a few kilometers from your parents' cabin. Nice area."

"Do you remember a couple of years ago when I went to that protest at the Jyväskylä Grand Prix? Sasha Smeds had to drop out of the rally because of engine trouble. I have to admit we felt some malicious glee. Someone came up with the idea of inviting him to our protest, and he actually came."

"Really?"

"Yeah. He even tried to convince all us tree huggers that rally driving doesn't actually pollute that much. Supposedly the cars have the best possible catalytic converters, ones they're testing for normal cars. And the Safari Rally and all that creates jobs for poor Africans." Antti laughed sarcastically and stroked my back.

"Sasha does seem like an easy guy to like. And besides, he's an organic farmer."

Antti took his hand off my back, drawing away from my side and sitting up straighter.

"And you're not usually that naive! The organic farming is just a PR stunt: he produces a few liters of organic milk to compensate for all the pollution and the bad example rally racing sets. I wonder how many times that dude has even milked the cows!"

I was surprised to see Antti so agitated. He was usually quite calm— if one of us got uptight, it was usually me. I stared at my husband in shock.

"So you're saying that someone being a rally driver automatically makes them a bastard?"

"Doesn't it?" Antti stood up. "I'm tired from the flight. I think I'm going to go to bed."

My irritation felt like tiny needles on my scalp and in my throat. I was annoyed that Antti had ruined his homecoming with a fight. I knew this wasn't just about rally racing or his uncertain employment situation. Antti had been tense ever since we moved into the White Cube.

Before the move, we'd debated where we would go and how big of a mortgage we could manage. Antti hated banks and didn't want anything to do with them, but we didn't have a choice. Rents in Espoo were insane—purchasing an apartment was the best option. We had about fifty thousand euros in savings when we started, but now all we had was debt. Sometimes I suspected that it bothered Antti that I earned more than him, but I always pushed that thought out of my mind. Antti wasn't that kind of man.

I poured myself more whiskey and retreated into my work files. Let Antti sulk in peace. I had brought home the disk with Annukka's manuscript and a few video cassettes. After finding some headphones for the VCR, I put a tape in and started to watch. Based on the backdrop, it was from the Safari Rally. Sasha's red Citroen wound through the desert, and people dressed in traditional East African clothing swarmed out of the way. In places the crowd was dangerously close to the track. I wondered whether it worried Sasha that someone might jump in front of his car at such a high speed. Behind him were cars with vaguely familiar names on their sides: Didier Auriol, Tommi Mäkinen, Marcus Grönholm.

I fast-forwarded the cassette through more racing and segments of reporting about the competition. I found it all pretty boring. I'd never watched a rally race before. I'd only watched Formula 1 once at home with my dad just so I'd know what it was all about. In contrast, my son, Taneli, loved it all. More than once, I'd found him watching a race on TV and enthusiastically mimicking the sounds of the cars and the shouting of the announcers.

I tried another cassette. This one was from Finland, from the national championships, with a Mitsubishi in the lead. It was Andreas driving this time, and according to the caption it was archival tape.

"According to information obtained by the *Checkered Flag Report*, this year's Finnish national rally champion, Andreas Smeds, has been arrested for drunk driving. Smeds and the Mitsubishi team will be holding a press conference tomorrow."

The recording went blank. I was just about to rewind it when the picture came back. On the screen I saw an empty table with a bunch of microphones and two bottles of mineral water on it. There was a buzz in the room that went silent when two men dressed in dark suits appeared from behind a curtain. One turned out to be the Mitsubishi spokesman, and the other was a young and anxious-looking Andreas Smeds, who stared at the tabletop instead of looking at the flashing cameras.

The Mitsubishi man first stated that Andreas had been arrested for drunk driving and announced that as far as the team was concerned, he didn't need to retire. These things happened, especially when you were in a high-profile career with so much pressure. Then he turned the microphones over to Andreas, who tried to lift his gaze from the tabletop but couldn't.

"Um, yeah. As Mr. Ahlfors said, I was caught driving drunk last night, at a police checkpoint on Hanko Road. No one was injured, but I still think it's best that I end my racing career now. I'm extremely sorry for doing such a stupid thing, and I want to apologize to the entire motorsports community and the Finnish people."

After Andreas stopped speaking, the room was quiet. Then, after a few moments, the spokesman opened the floor to questions. Instead of waiting to be called on, the reporters just started shouting over one another.

"Andreas, weren't you supposed to move up to the World Rally Championship series? Isn't it crazy to stop now on the edge of an international career?" asked a man whom I recognized as the *Checkered Flag* reporter at the time.

"Maybe it's crazy, but it's my only option in this situation."

"Is it true that the team would have let you continue? Aren't you really being pressured to quit?" asked a female voice, and the camera shifted for a moment to Annukka Hackman. I paused the tape and looked at her. She was wearing a stylish black pantsuit and only a little makeup, and her hair was shorter than it had been when she died. Annukka hadn't wanted to look too feminine in the majority male audience.

"I made my decision yesterday morning before I talked with the team representatives," Andreas replied, and Ahlfors looked irritated. People had a tendency to make dramatic decisions in moments like these. Perhaps Andreas should have slept on it for another night.

"How could you be so stupid to get behind the wheel when you were drunk?" Hackman continued, and the crowd of reporters guffawed at the directness of her question. Andreas blushed.

"I don't have any explanations or excuses."

"Where were you coming from?" a male voice shouted.

"That doesn't matter. I shouldn't have driven drunk, and I'm going to accept the punishment the court imposes on me," Andreas said quietly.

Would a similar public shaming work on other reckless drivers? I was willing to bet that most of them would have come prepared with better explanations for their stupidity. There would be stories about tight schedules and miscalculations and the need to get home to see a sick child.

"What are you watching?" Antti had appeared behind me.

"Andreas Smeds, Sasha's brother. He ended his rally career six years ago after getting caught driving drunk."

"Well, at the very least we know he could never be a politician," Antti said with a laugh then sat down next to me. "Come to bed. I've been sleeping alone for two weeks." He wrapped his arms around me. "It's nice to be with you again, even though this place . . ."

"I know. We'll figure out something soon." I turned off the VCR and followed Antti to the bedroom. But I didn't fall asleep because all I could see on the backs of my eyelids were alternating flashes of Carcass Kervinen and Viktor Smeds's pale face.

7

I didn't turn on my phone on Saturday until after noon when I got back from my run. Again I had ten voice mails and a text message, all of them callback requests from Jouko Suuronen. This time they were about his own interview, which Ursula was trying to set for Monday.

I'm going to meet Sasha in France on Monday. Tell your officers to meet me there, Suuronen said in his final text.

I ate a sandwich and drank a large café au lait before I called Suuronen. I didn't have to call him. If I wanted to be cruel, I could have just stopped him at the airport. Ursula had the weekend off, and I did too, theoretically. But I was the boss, and bosses didn't usually have the option of invoking the laws that governed working hours.

"So Sasha didn't turn out to be your murderer?" Suuronen snapped. "And now you're attacking me? Goddamn it! Of course I knew Hackman. I tried to talk some sense into her when she started going rogue with her book. I said that if one single thing wasn't true, we'd see her in court. And we don't plan to back down on that, even though the bitch is dead now."

"When did you last see Annukka Hackman?"

"At the Jyväskylä Grand Prix. She tried to worm her way in to talk to Sasha, but I had security run her off. Goddamn bitch! Luckily she didn't manage to bother Sasha, and he won handily."

"You said you're traveling to France on Monday. What are you doing tomorrow morning?" If Ursula wasn't willing to pull overtime, I could go see Suuronen myself.

"Tomorrow's Sunday, and I'll be hungover."

I laughed. "So we'll talk when you're hungover."

"You aren't going to give up, are you? Fine, let's meet tomorrow at one here at my place in Westend. I imagine you can look up my address."

One o'clock was near our family Sunday lunchtime. Antti wouldn't like it. I tried to get in touch with Ursula, but couldn't reach her. I wondered if she'd convinced Puustjärvi to go out for that drink after all. But that was really and truly none of my business.

I left a message on Ursula's cell and started cooking Antti's favorite food, potato wedges and baked pike. I put a bottle of white wine in the fridge to chill.

After I'd wined and dined Antti enough, I worked up the courage to tell him I was going in on Sunday.

He sighed. "You promised when you went back to work that you weren't going to do overtime anymore."

"I guess I did," I admitted and wondered why I'd made a promise like that when I knew I'd end up breaking it.

Ursula didn't text me until Sunday morning. *Sorry, my battery was dead and the charger is missing. I'm at Levi in Lapland catching the first snow, and I'm not coming back until the last flight.*

Ursula hadn't mentioned any skiing plans on Friday, but of course she didn't have to tell me about her leisure activities. And whether or not she was telling the truth in her text message, she did have the weekend off. I called the station, and Liisa Rasilainen happened to be on call; she promised to go to Westend with me.

Jouko Suuronen managed a wide range of athletes: ski jumpers, track-and-field stars, and a couple of swimmers. I wondered what the division of labor was between him and the Citroën people. I'd always thought the team would handle the racers' sponsorships. Having so many people hovering around you, taking care of everything, probably felt strange. What word had Andreas used? Headquarters.

Sasha and Heli probably never had the chance to get tired of each other, with him spending half the year traveling around the world for races. At least they didn't have children. I never could have been a professional athlete's wife. No hockey stars for me. You'd never know where in the world your husband might be sent next, and building a life of your own would be nearly impossible. I remembered what Antti had said about Cambridge and shivered.

Liisa Rasilainen picked me up at home. I wanted to arrive in Suuronen's driveway in a police cruiser—his attitude irritated me that much. Liisa was also in uniform, and it suited her. I'd tried to recruit her to the Criminal Division and our unit, because I liked working with her, but she'd stayed in Patrol for salary reasons.

"Do you really suspect Suuronen?" Liisa asked as we parked in front of a large house in the wealthy neighborhood of Westend. Apparently managing athletes was lucrative; the place must have been worth a million euros. The lots around us were large, with space for landscaping, two-car garages, and swimming pools. Many of the yards were behind high walls and gates with electronic locks. However, Suuronen's house only had a low, recently trimmed hedge around it. There was a new-looking Citroën parked in the driveway. I didn't notice a security camera until we were at the door.

Based on his voice and manner of speech over the phone, I'd expected Suuronen to have an unpolished appearance, especially since he'd promised to be hungover. But the forty-something man who answered the door was clean and well kempt. He was wearing a dark-blue suit and tie, and his aftershave had an understated scent. There was no hint of a hangover about him. His eyes were bright and his dark hair was neatly combed.

"So I get two lady cops, do I? Does the department have men at all anymore?" he said in greeting. He was just as rude as he had been on the phone. "Come on in. Do I have to make you coffee?"

"No," I said with a laugh and followed Suuronen into a living room with a high ceiling and an enormous television. The room smelled of tobacco smoke, and Suuronen lit a cigarette before sitting down on the brown leather sofa. I took the armchair across from him, and Liisa sat in its twin. It appeared that Suuronen had no small children: no Legos on the floor, no juice stains on the couch. He'd been married a couple of times in the early nineties, but each union had ended quickly.

"Couldn't we have handled this over the phone? I only knew Annukka Hackman professionally and didn't have any interest in her beyond that. Sasha said you were asking his family for alibis for last Tuesday. I came back from Stockholm on the five o'clock flight. My car was at the airport, and I was in traffic on Ring I until seven. The gridlock here is worse than Athens these days!"

"Whose decision was it for Sasha to withdraw from the biography project?"

"His."

"Why?"

"I thought Annukka Hackman was a good reporter. She had a nose for news and, for a woman, she had a surprisingly good understanding of the motorsports world. At first everyone was excited about the biography, including the team, the sponsors, and me. It was a good derivative product for Sasha's brand. But then Annukka said she didn't want to paint a glossy portrait; she wanted to tell about the Sasha behind the stardom. And not just about Sasha's life as a driver but about his background and his family."

Suddenly Suuronen stood up and walked to the bookshelf. He opened a cupboard door, and I caught a glimpse of a respectable collection of bottles. He opened a carbonated mineral water, which overflowed onto his pants, and I noticed that his hands were shaking. He drank straight from the bottle and continued speaking where he stood.

"Sasha wanted to keep his private life to himself. And Heli doesn't want to be trotted around as Sasha's wife, no matter how hard the women's magazines beg. And to tell the truth, she isn't media sexy in the way a lot of other drivers' wives are. I think Heli was probably behind Sasha's decision, or maybe Andreas. I say that because Annukka also wanted to write about the end of Andreas's career, and he can't stand to have anyone even talk about it. He always goes back to drinking, then his family suffers."

"So Andreas has an alcohol problem?"

"He's sort of a situational drunk. He hits it hard for a few days and then goes sober for months."

Could Annukka Hackman have been shot by someone under the influence? He might have driven out to the lake drunk. As a professional driver, he probably thought he could drive fine, regardless of his state of intoxication. After all, he hadn't been caught because of the state of his driving before; he'd simply been stopped at a routine police checkpoint. But could he have shot a gun precisely if he was drunk? We still didn't know how many shots the murderer had fired before hitting Hackman. Dragging of the lake hadn't yielded any results: the gun was still missing.

"Do you know whether Jääskeläinen still intends to publish the book?" Suuronen asked.

"You'll have to ask him yourself."

"If the police suspect someone was murdered over the book, it'll be good for sales. It'll be too bad for Jääskeläinen if you catch the murderer too soon." Suuronen gave a malicious smirk. "Annukka Hackman stepped on a lot of toes." Suuronen proceeded to give us a list of motorsports influencers and some business leaders whose sponsorship activities were impacted by Hackman's reporting over the years.

"That should give you girls plenty to investigate. Leave the Smeds family alone. And me too. Now I have to leave for my next meeting."

Suddenly Suuronen stepped in front of me and started to shake my hand.

"Keep your fingers crossed for Sasha this weekend," he said. "Annukka's death has really rattled him. Hopefully this won't affect his driving in the championship rally. There's a hell of a lot riding on this."

Suuronen wiped his brow, which was suddenly bathed in sweat.

Then he turned and disappeared into the next room.

"So that's what a high-flying sports manager is like," Liisa said with a laugh once we were back in the car. "You want me to drop you back at home?"

"Yeah, thanks. You have time next week to hit the gym with me?"

We arranged to go on Wednesday. At home it smelled like lasagna. To my great relief, Antti wasn't sulking, and Iida was proud of the table she'd set and the napkins she'd folded into bunny ears. The joy infected me too, and I put out of my mind the fact that interviewing Suuronen had been pointless.

On Monday morning there was a message waiting on my desk saying that the forensic team had found ten bullets in the lake. Some of them were obviously old, but all of them had been sent to the lab.

Puupponen and Ursula were giggling like two teenagers again in the morning meeting. Puustjärvi sat as far from them as possible, looking miserable. Koivu said he'd interviewed Sini Jääskeläinen.

"At first she claimed she called her father on their landline. When I told her there was no such call in the house phone records, she tried to claim she has a special cell number that doesn't show up. That isn't true either. I asked her to come in today at ten to give her a little time to think. She's obviously lying. Either to protect her father or—"

"Herself," Ursula said. "Don't write her off just because she's sixteen. Have you checked if she or one of her friends has a moped? A lot of girls do now, at least if their parents have money."

"Good observation, Ursula," I said. "So far we've only been focusing on cars. Will you check that and also what flight Jouko Suuronen arrived on the day of the murder? Puustjärvi, what's new with the cars?"

"We're cross-checking all the suspects' vehicles. We haven't had any hits, but we're still working on it. There was one moped spotted near the lake, but it was just an old guy who fishes there," Puustjärvi said. "I was thinking about interviewing a few more people this afternoon. Can you go with me, Ursula?"

"Ville and I are going to talk to Hackman's old coworkers from when she was in TV," Ursula replied and flashed Puustjärvi a smile that made him blush.

"The only connection between the moose hunters and Hackman is that one of them went to elementary school with Hackman's first husband. And that first husband lives in Singapore. So that's a dead end too," Puustjärvi said bitterly. Even though we knew Hackman hadn't been shot with a moose rifle, I had wanted Puustjärvi to look into any ties to make sure. I wasn't surprised there was nothing.

Kervinen's gunpowder test results hadn't come back yet, and his phone records showed no calls on Tuesday night. But on Monday he had called Hackman's cell phone. One of the last calls Hackman received on Tuesday had come from a pay phone at the Kirkkonummi train station. For all we knew, that had been Kervinen too.

After the meeting I went to Koivu's office to review a pretrial report for another case that was headed to the prosecutor. Koivu had done good work. A little before ten, the duty officer downstairs called and asked Koivu to come escort Sini Jääskeläinen up.

"I'll look through the rest of this quickly while you go get the girl," I said to Koivu. The parties in the case were a mother and her fifteen-year-old daughter, whom she'd been beating for years. At the girl's own request she'd finally been placed with a foster family, and now she wanted her mother charged with aggravated abuse. I stared at the report wondering at the mother's ingenuity in always finding new ways to torture her child. The girl should have been taken away years earlier.

The sobbing was audible before the door even opened. Sini Jääskeläinen walked in to Koivu's office and collapsed in his chair.

"Completely hysterical," Koivu whispered to me. "Stay if you can. Apparently she was crying when she got here. Should we call her dad?"

"Sini," I said cautiously and touched her arm. "Sini, there's nothing to worry about."

Sini lifted her face from her hands and looked at me, then broke into even louder wails. I could only barely make out the halting words among the tears.

"Will I go to jail? I'm already sixteen."

"For what?" I asked, finding myself fearing the answer. A few seconds passed before Sini could talk again.

"For lying to the police. Is that, like, perjury? Madde's dad is a judge and Madde said you can go to prison for perjury."

Koivu gave me a feeble smile. I'm sure he was thankful that he didn't have to try to comfort Sini alone. "So what did you lie about?" he asked with such exaggerated sweetness that it was my turn to grin.

"About talking with Dad . . . On the landline. I never call him on that phone. I tried to reach him on his cell to get him to pick me up from aerobics, but he didn't answer and neither did Annukka. So I went with Laura to McDonald's to hang out. I thought it was weird Dad didn't answer. He always answers when I call, and his battery is never dead."

"Did your father's voice mail pick up?"

"No. The phone just rang and rang and rang. And when I tried Annukka it just said 'the number you dialed cannot be reached.' Where will I go if it is Dad . . . ?"

Sini's mother, Marjut Jääskeläinen, had died in a traffic accident when Sini was five years old. A drunk driver had driven through a yield sign right into the side of her car. Atro and Sini had lived alone for ten years. It would be no wonder if the arrival of a stepmother had triggered jealousy in Sini.

I found a little piece of grubby paper towel in my jacket pocket and handed it to the girl.

"Tell us the truth now and you won't be charged with anything. Why do you want to protect your father?"

Sini blew her nose repeatedly, and finally I went to my office to grab a packet of tissues. I wondered if some *salmiakki* would calm Sini down. I always had a bag in my desk for various emergency situations. Usually I was the emergency situation, though. I grabbed the bag of licorice, but Sini didn't want any candy. Koivu, on the contrary, grabbed three at once.

After stammering for a while, Sini finally managed to tell us what was bothering her.

"I heard Annukka talking with Hannu on Monday. They were arranging a date for Wednesday. If Dad heard about it . . ."

I asked Sini to start from the beginning. She'd come home earlier than usual on Monday and was sitting in the living room half in the dark when Annukka came in with her phone to her ear.

"She was obviously nervous, apologizing for not responding to some messages, and said they needed to meet one more time to talk through things. She suggested dinner on Wednesday at the Tapiontori Restaurant for old time's sake. Once Hannu yelled at us from outside our living room window that he always had to pay for their meals at Tapiontori, and I remember Annukka shouting back that he should send her a bill. I don't know what she was planning. Probably to cheat on Dad. Back in the beginning she was sleeping with both of them."

"Did you tell your dad about the phone call?"

"No. I didn't want him to be sad. But when Annukka hung up, I stood to show her I'd heard it all. At first she tried to downplay it, saying that she just didn't want Hannu pining over her for the rest of his life and that he has to find someone else. That was what she was going to tell him. As if she hadn't already said that a million times. Maybe Annukka told Dad herself, because she was afraid that I'd turn her in."

Koivu and I exchanged glances over Sini's head. The phone records matched her story.

"Do you happen to own a moped or a motorcycle?" Koivu asked. Sini stared at him as if he was an idiot.

"Dad has a scooter, and I drive it sometimes. Was it someone on a scooter?" Sini started crying again.

Koivu tried to change the subject, asking her about school and aerobics, and managed to slip in a few questions about Sini and Annukka's relationship. Sini claimed that Annukka had been OK and that her father had been in a much better mood ever since he'd met her.

Outside the sun shone for the first time in weeks. The light made Sini's face look even redder. Koivu promised to arrange for someone to take her home even though she probably should have been in school.

"So we need to come back to Jääskeläinen and Kervinen," I said to Koivu when he returned from escorting Sini downstairs. "Will you get Hannu in here by tomorrow and interrogate Jääskeläinen yourself? When did they say the gunpowder results would be ready?"

"At the end of the week. Oh, I forgot to tell you, Anu says hi. She wants to know how you convinced Antti to take paternity leave after Iida was born."

I burst out laughing and said that it had been the contentious atmosphere in the university math department, not me, that did it. Apparently Anu wanted to get back to work. Koivu and I agreed that they'd come to our place for a visit as soon as our work calmed down a bit.

I tried to get Taskinen to join me for lunch, but it didn't work for him so I headed downstairs to the cafeteria alone. There was space at Puustjärvi's table, so I sat down there with my vegetable soup.

"Have you already been up to the lake?" I asked.

"I'm just leaving after lunch. I'll go straight home from there. I have to take the rugs out to beat. Kirsi isn't up to housework."

"Let's go in my car," I suggested. Puustjärvi had started riding the train so his wife could have the car after she went on sick leave in the twenty-second week of her pregnancy.

"You're coming too?"

"I want to see the crime scene again. Last time there was too much going on and too many people. Maybe the place will tell me something now."

I'd always believed that murder scenes had messages for me. I tried to walk through them, placing myself in the role of the victim and the murderer. It was always fraught, but it usually helped. No one knew why Annukka Hackman had been swimming in Lake Humaljärvi on a November evening. The wet suit indicated that the swimming excursion wasn't any sudden whimsy. For a moment I thought about borrowing one from the department's equipment room, but I rejected the idea. Walking the shoreline would have to do.

In the car Puustjärvi said he'd talked to the residents of the nearby houses. One was absolutely sure that around four he'd seen an SUV parked on the edge of the forest. Puustjärvi had pictures with him of various SUVs, one of which matched the Smedses' Land Rover. There were only a few dozen of that model registered in Finland. We arranged that Puustjärvi would call when he was done. I parked at the turnout where Annukka Hackman had left her car six days earlier. Despite the sunny skies, the wind was cold and whipped my hair in my face and made my eyes water. Branches swayed and grasses rustled in the wind. If the wind had been blowing this hard on Tuesday night, Annukka might not have heard someone following her. How familiar was she with these woods? A lot of city dwellers would be afraid in a dark forest, even though there were far fewer dangers here than in the middle of a brightly lit city.

There were waves on the lake, and it seemed crazy to even consider swimming in the frigid water in this lonely place. The nearest cabins, on the other side of the lake, were empty in November, and the farmhouses past the fields on the opposite side were too far away for anyone to possibly see a swimmer.

Because we didn't know where on the lake Annukka had been swimming when she was hit, we couldn't determine the shooter's location. A hundred-yard range allowed too many possibilities. I started walking east from where Annukka's clothing was found. Gradually the shore turned craggy and extremely difficult to traverse. I slipped on a moss-covered rock and fell on my back onto some lower rocks. For a moment it hurt so much I couldn't move. Then my phone rang.

"It's Petri. Where are you?"

"Here on these goddamn rocks!" I said and groaned. "I'll start heading for the car. I'll see you there." I started back, occasionally having to clamber on all fours and feeling like a complete idiot.

Puustjärvi met me en route, and he looked chilled. "They thought the SUV they saw was a Toyota, but the witness, a sixty-year-old woman, wasn't sure."

"So it wasn't a Land Rover?"

"No. Did you know the northern border of the Porkkala Naval Base went through this lake?" Puustjärvi asked.

"No. My father-in-law told me some of the local history, but it was more about down around Inkoo."

"My mom is from Kirkkonummi, and her parents worked on the Pickala Estate and lived on the grounds. The order to leave back in '44 was a huge blow, especially since, at first, the area was leased to the Soviets for fifty years. Mom's parents were the same age then as I am now and thought they'd lost their house forever."

The evacuation of the Porkkala Peninsula had also been mentioned in Annukka Hackman's manuscript. Could her swimming the lake have something to do with that? I didn't have time to contemplate the question further, though, as Puustjärvi's phone rang. He glanced at the number with a strange expression on his face.

"Hi, Mirja. What? Oh no. When? To Jorvi? Are you OK with the kids?"

As he talked, Puustjärvi started striding toward the car, and all I could do was follow. My back still hurt. I heard Puustjärvi promise to make a call. Then he turned to me.

"Kirsi was taken in an ambulance to the hospital. She's having some sort of hemorrhage. Our little Ninni almost fainted. The kids are at a neighbor's house now."

"I'll take you to Jorvi." I did a quick calculation and figured I could still make it to the day care before five. When we reached the car, Puustjärvi tried to get in on the driver's side, even though his hands were shaking so hard he could barely open the door.

"I'm driving," I said. "You call the hospital. We'll put the light on top to get around the traffic. What week is Kirsi in?"

"Thirtieth." Puustjärvi was almost crying. "I said having a bonus baby was a risk, but Kirsi still wanted one more. A woman over forty with twins. This has to be punishment . . ."

I backed the car into the road and took off much faster than was safe. Puustjärvi called Jorvi Hospital, where they said that, based on the information from the paramedics, they were preparing for an emergency C-section. They were worried about a placental abruption.

I turned onto Gesterby Road, which was paved but narrow and winding, and I had to dodge a van coming at us in the middle of the road by going a little off the pavement toward a ditch. Puustjärvi tried to call Kirsi's cell, but all he got was voice mail.

"Dear, it's Petri. I'm coming to the hospital. Everything will be fine," he said into the phone, practically whimpering. When I finally reached the highway, I could see that he was now crying. Then I had to concentrate on driving. A steady line of cars flowed toward us, and a truck veered onto the wide shoulder to get past me.

"If Kirsi dies, it's my fault . . ."

"Hardly anyone dies in childbirth in Finland, and even preemies under one kilo can be saved. And how would it be your fault when you just said it was Kirsi who wanted another child?"

"On Friday . . . Me and Ursula . . . Kirsi hasn't wanted to in months. She says it hurts too much and she's big and clumsy. But I still shouldn't have. I've never cheated on Kirsi before. But Ursula is just so nice."

I braked at some traffic lights, then floored it after they changed, trying to think what I could say to Puustjärvi.

"After work I went for a beer with Ursula in Tapiola. Then she said she was hungry and had some paella at home that just needed to be warmed up and asked if I wanted to join her. Stupid me, I went with her. We never even got to the paella. Oh God. I've been out of my mind all weekend."

"Think about that later. Kirsi needs you now, and your children need you. All of them." I turned onto Ring III and got stuck behind a Russian semitruck. I remembered Puustjärvi's bleak expression during the morning meeting and Ursula giggling with Puupponen. Of course my subordinates' private lives were none of my business—unless their misadventures threatened to ruin the working culture of the unit.

I slipped through a small opening past the Russian truck, and an oncoming car had to brake to miss us. Puustjärvi dried his eyes. I probably knew him the least of any of my subordinates. He barely ever talked about his private life or feelings. I knew he played Go in a club, and that had to be a small community. Did he have trusted friends he could confide in there?

When the road turned to four lanes, I sped up to seventy-five miles an hour. We were at Jorvi less than thirty minutes after Puustjärvi had received his call. I left him at the maternity ward door, then headed for the day care, this time without the police light and carefully following the speed limit.

8

"Kervinen's on sick leave and isn't answering his phones," Koivu reported in the Tuesday morning meeting. "Should I send a patrol out to get him?"

"Let's wait until the afternoon. Maybe he's still sleeping. How long is his sick leave?"

"Just this week."

"Got it. Petri will be out on parental leave for a few days. His wife and twin boys are doing well given the circumstances. The babies are in the NICU. Get flower money to me today, five euros per person."

A wave of relief seemed to wash over the room. Puustjärvi had called me the previous evening to say that the emergency C-section had gone well. Even though the babies only weighed three and a half pounds each, they had a good shot at pulling through.

Puustjärvi had asked whether he should tell his wife about Ursula. I'd advised him not to say anything for now. His wife had enough to worry about with the babies. Frankly, I wished I didn't know about the whole mess either. Ursula seemed to be focusing her wiles on Koivu now. Before he met Anu, Koivu had been an easy mark for any woman who took a fancy to him, but I wasn't one to judge him for it. I enjoyed a little flirting myself every now and then.

At the back of my mind there was a flash from the past that I didn't want to think about. Instead I turned to Sasha Smeds's biography. Ursula had read through it and seemed disappointed that it didn't contain anything particularly sensational.

"According to Hackman, Andreas is a terrible drunk and Heli was hopeless as a socialite type of wife, but anyone could see that. Hackman only wrote good things about Sasha, to the point that it seemed like she was probably in love with him. She was a good-looking woman. Maybe she slept with Sasha. Maybe she meant to write about that, and that's why Sasha refused to cooperate with the book anymore."

Ursula swung one of her long legs over the other. Her high-heeled ankle boots were the latest fashion, but I wouldn't have been able to walk in them. Ursula pulled them off like a supermodel, though.

I smirked. "Well, then you can go ahead and ask Smeds to confirm your theory."

"Maria, you don't think a man like Sasha Smeds is content with one woman, do you? Especially since Heli's so bland."

"How should I know? Find out. Not literally, though. I mean ask around," I said and laughed.

"Are you trying to say you've never gotten involved with a suspect? From what I understand, you met Antti as part of a murder investigation."

I would have given anything to have kept myself from blushing. It's true, Antti and I had crossed paths because of an investigation. But I'd known him long before the murder in the Eastern Finland Student Singers, and our relationship hadn't started until after the case was solved. I wasn't blushing because of Antti, though.

"That case was solved before anything happened between Antti and me," I said briskly, even though I knew I didn't need to explain myself to Ursula. "Let's hope this case is closed before the rally world championship. But if it isn't, you can go interview Sasha Smeds again. It's too bad we didn't get anything significant out of Hackman's old coworkers. Let's focus on Kervinen now."

We hadn't found the weapon in the lake, and the bullets fired from it would have deformed into a mess when they hit anything. No identifiable markings would be left on them. So far our informants' inquiries with the local gun fences hadn't yielded any results. I really wanted to know how many times the killer had fired the gun. Knowing how skilled our shooter was might help narrow down the pool of suspects.

The meeting was drawing to a close. "Ursula, you take over the review of the cars, since Petri isn't done yet. Now I have another meeting to go to."

The Police Federation hadn't approved the contract the government had offered us in the fall, so no one had received a raise yet this year. Our department's management team was currently participating in independent negotiations over performance pay, and that meant an endless series of meetings. The best thing about them was seeing Taskinen. Terttu had been sent home for the weekend for a break from testing, but it would still take nearly a week before the pathologist gave his opinion. Jyrki was quiet, but I could have talked less.

During the meeting, I spoke up to say that I didn't like the idea of deciding on my subordinates' personal compensation. The assistant chief of police glared at me.

"People in positions of authority have to be willing to take responsibility for these things," he said. "Your job isn't to please the people who work for you."

I looked at Taskinen and grimaced: the assistant chief of police couldn't be accused of ingratiating himself to his subordinates, but the corporate big shots and city officials were another matter.

"I think this is a group effort. No one solves crimes alone. Performance bonuses should go to a whole unit, not just to one person," I continued. My loathing for meetings grew year by year.

"We have to do something before we end up with a real staffing crisis in the metro area," Taskinen said, trying to calm the waters a bit. "Hardly anyone can live on a police salary here. Performance bonuses are a good start."

"Those of us sitting around this table can't fix the country's housing crisis," the assistant chief of police said angrily. I felt a gentle kick to my shin. It was Jyrki, who followed it up with a grin. I realized then that we were acting as much like teenagers as Ursula and Puupponen had been the previous morning, and I found myself blushing for the second time that day.

Outside it was sleeting again, and the only splashes of color in the landscape were the red cars in the parking lot. Even the bark of the pine trees had lost its bright-brown color and seemed to melt into the asphalt. The Narcotics Unit commander's blue tie looked downright garish among the dark suits.

"Lunch?" I asked Taskinen when the meeting finally ended.

"I'd love to, but not any farther away than downstairs. My next meeting starts in an hour." Jyrki pushed the elevator's call button, and we crammed in with two patrol officers and a junkie. The guy was suffering from such severe withdrawal symptoms that I had to feel sorry for him. I was glad I wasn't in Narcotics, although our cases did often overlap. If alcohol and drugs had never been invented, I would have 90 percent fewer crimes to investigate. I wondered: Was Atro Jääskeläinen in the habit of driving drunk?

We tried to find a quiet corner. Again I thought of Puustjärvi and Ursula, and for a second I wanted to tell Taskinen about their tryst, but all I related was that Puustjärvi's twins had been born.

"Life and death," Taskinen said quietly. "Terttu has been talking about grandchildren for a few years and hoping that Silja wouldn't wait too long." Jyrki cut up his hamburger patty with a look of disgust. I thought it tasted fine, probably because meetings always made me hungry. My phone started playing Bon Jovi's "Always," which meant it was Koivu.

"I got ahold of Kervinen. He sounded pretty incoherent. I think he's on something. Should I send someone to go pick him up?" Koivu said.

"Let's go ourselves. Bring the car out, and I'll hurry and finish my lunch." I grinned apologetically to Taskinen, grabbed my meat with a napkin, and munched on it as I made my way to the parking lot. I knew I was cruel in thinking it, but an addled Kervinen might slip up and confess.

The car windows were steamed up inside, so I wiped them clean. It was still light out, but the sun was low on the horizon and would set by four o'clock. The darkness would last for at least the next three months, which was a gloomy thought. My birthday was the first of March, and I always thought of spring starting then, even though there was still usually enough snow to ski. The year felt like a Ferris wheel that moved slowly from one phase to another: fall was an arduous climb toward a climax, which was somewhere around Christmas and New Year's, January and February were a slow downward descent, and March and April were an easy drop. Sometime soon we'd have to pull out the elf hats and take a picture of the kids for our Christmas card.

Koivu was quiet, probably suffering from lack of sleep again. He wasn't one to complain, though. Kervinen lived in Tapiola high on a hill in what people called the hip flask buildings because of their oblong hexagonal shape and the smaller top floor common area. A two-bedroom apartment in them probably cost a couple hundred thousand euros.

We pressed Kervinen's buzzer three times before a voice asked, "Who's there?"

"Kallio and Koivu."

The door unlocked with a metallic snap. Inside we rode the elevator to the top residential floor, where we found Kervinen's apartment door already open. Newspapers and junk mail lay scattered in the entryway, and the rooms smelled of unwashed clothing and beer. Kervinen leaned in a doorjamb wearing exactly the same clothes he'd had on at our previous meeting. His beard had grown wild, and his hair was matted or protruding at odd angles. His eyes were sunk deep between his cheeks and forehead. He looked as pale and unwell as some of the bodies he'd examined. I'd once lost my temper at Kervinen when he referred to a dead sixteen-year-old girl as a carcass—that's where his nickname had come from. Now the whole department used it. It didn't seem funny anymore, though.

"Have you been to the doctor?" I asked and stepped past Kervinen into the living room. The television was on, and a home shopping network was hawking Christmas lights. I turned it off.

"I am a doctor," Kervinen said.

"When did you last eat?" I asked. "Have you been able to sleep?"

"Don't bullshit me, Kallio. State your business and then get out."

I sat down on the couch, and Koivu sat next to me. Kervinen stood in front of the TV, swaying a little.

"According to your phone records, you spoke with Annukka Hackman the day before her death," Koivu said.

"Yeah, so? For once she agreed to talk to me. Usually she just turned off her phone when she saw it was me."

"What did you talk about?"

"She was my Annukka again. She wanted to meet and suggested Wednesday. Dinner at Tapiontori Restaurant. Just like before. She asked about DNA tests, about how you can tell who's related to who. She said she'd tell me more on Wednesday, at Tapiontori. We were going to drink our favorite chardonnay. I thought she'd changed her mind and didn't want to be with Jääskeläinen anymore. That night and the next morning were like spring instead of November. And then . . ."

Had Annukka really changed her mind?

"Tell me who took Annukka away just when she was going to come back to me!" Kervinen suddenly screamed.

No one had called Kervinen's phone on Tuesday night, but maybe Kervinen was the one who had called Annukka from the Kirkkonummi train station. Maybe he'd learned something before their meeting that had made spring turn back into November, and the disappointment had been too great.

"I can't ever go back to work again. I can't ever open another body bag. Every time it's just Annukka staring back at me," Kervinen said and collapsed into a sitting position next to the TV. "Koivu, could you go buy some more beer? You can get it at the pizza shop down the street. My bank card is on the kitchen table."

Koivu stood up, and I followed him into the kitchen. There were two empty beer crates. The window had a magnificent view all the way to the sea, and on clear days you could probably see all the way to Estonia. I peeked in the refrigerator. The cheese and salami looked desiccated, and the milk was a week old. I didn't want to inspect the vegetables too closely. In the cupboard I found a box of multigrain porridge mix.

"I'll make some hot cereal and try to get Kervinen to eat. What do you think he's on? Look in the bedroom and bathroom for any pill bottles. We can't leave him alone like this."

I'd known Kervinen for seven years, but I didn't know anything about his family or even whether he was originally from the Helsinki area. If I could arrest him and get him into a holding cell, he'd at least be closely monitored, but I didn't have probable cause. Trying to commit him against his will probably wouldn't work either because he wasn't threatening suicide.

"Who's your closest family member?" I yelled while I was mixing the cereal flakes with water. When no answer came, I went into the living room and repeated my question.

"If Koivu could just bring me some beer," he replied, holding his head.

Kervinen's cell phone was on the table, and it was the same model Antti had. I scanned the contacts and found that the first one was Annukka. There was no "Mom" or "Dad," mostly just last names, including "Kallio." One first name appeared in the list, "Esa." I decided to try my luck.

"This is Esa Kervinen's voice mail," the man's voice said. "I'm not available at the moment, but . . ." I hung up and went back into the kitchen to continue stirring the porridge.

"I found Dormicum and ibuprofen with vitamin C," Koivu reported as he walked back in. "There's also a bottle of sleeping pills, with about twenty remaining. He isn't planning suicide or he would have taken all of them. The second bedroom was completely empty with just a couple of cardboard boxes. It looked pretty pathetic."

The porridge was bubbling in the pot, so I added a little salt and set a bowl and spoon on the table.

"Come have some porridge, Kervinen. Butter or sugar?" To my surprise, Kervinen shuffled into the kitchen and sat down at the table.

"Porridge," he said like a child who was learning new words. As the first spoonful reached his lips, his phone started ringing. The display said "Esa." Kervinen let the phone ring, so I decided to answer.

"This is Hannu Kervinen's phone, Maria Kallio speaking."

"Who are you, Hannu's new girlfriend? Where's Hannu? What's happened?"

"I'm a coworker from the Espoo Police. Nothing serious has happened to Hannu, but he's extremely depressed."

"Oh, about Annukka?" Esa Kervinen's voice was exactly like his brother's. "That woman treated him really badly. He should be happy it's finally over."

"Could you come over here? Your brother isn't doing very well on his own."

"I'm teaching all day. School is done at three, so I'll come then. Can I talk to him?"

I handed Kervinen the phone and told him who it was. He answered his brother's questions listlessly and said he was on sick leave. "You don't have to come," he finally said. That was when I took the phone from him. Esa Kervinen promised again to come once school was finished. Just in case I stored his number in my own phone. We waited until Kervinen had finished his bowl of cereal and drunk a couple of glasses of water. He didn't ask Koivu to go buy beer again.

"He's in bad shape," Koivu observed once we were sitting in the car, sheltering from the sleet outside. "Do you think he'd be able to fake innocence in that state?"

"We'll have to ask the police psychologist. I imagine it's possible. Hackman asked about DNA tests. If Kervinen realized that this 'new spring' was just a scam, that Hackman just wanted information from him and not to start a new relationship . . ."

"People are stupidest when they're in love," Koivu said and sighed. I laughed, because Koivu had always acted like a lovesick puppy whenever he was mooning over a girl.

"True. Why did Hackman want information about DNA? She didn't suspect Sasha wasn't Rauha and Viktor Smeds's son, did she? Or Andreas? They were married for nine years before Andreas came. Maybe the boys were adopted and no one ever told them . . ."

I had thought that Sasha resembled their mother and Andreas their father. Regardless, the population registry would tell the truth, and Sasha would have seen his birth information when he applied for his license to marry Heli even if he never had any other interest in his genealogy. So that wasn't much of a theory.

A week had already passed since Annukka Hackman's murder, and the trail was going cold. The footprint analysis from the crime scene hadn't revealed anything, and Hackman's purse only had her and Sini Jääskeläinen's fingerprints on it. I hadn't held a new press conference because there wasn't anything new to announce. When the newspapers asked why Sasha Smeds had been allowed to leave the country, I replied that we didn't have any reason to detain him.

Antti called to say he was picking up the kids, so I went to the grocery store. I hadn't made a shopping list before I left home that morning, and it was hard to remember what we needed. Milk and ground beef, potatoes and tissues. Once back at home I realized I'd forgotten margarine. Antti said he'd grab some from the convenience store. I decided to be a good mother and make mashed potatoes since the kids liked it. Cooking while they watched *Tiny Two* was peaceful.

When the time came to leave our last home, we only had two months to find a new place. We chose the White Cube because it had good access to public transit and was near Iida's music preschool. The convenience store on the ground floor of the neighboring building was also handy, and the kids' day care was within walking distance, although we usually had to carry Taneli halfway. Iida's future school was a half mile away too.

"I put in a grant application to the Cultural Foundation today," Antti said as he handed me the margarine. "I doubt I'll get anything, but I had to try at least. And I've started thinking about Cambridge. That may be my only option."

"We can get by for a few months on my salary, and you'll get some unemployment."

"Yeah, but I just don't want to lie around like that. We need to get out of this miserable apartment. I feel like a man should be able to buy his family a decent house, or at least build one."

I'd been peeling the potatoes I'd boiled for the kids. At that, I suddenly stopped.

"Never in a million years would I have expected to hear those words come out of your mouth."

"Why not? Because our family is a paragon of gender equality, is that it? A woman only makes eighty cents for every euro a man makes in the same job, but luckily in our family it's the other way around! And so you think you can just work whenever you feel like it. Sure, Antti will pick up the slack."

I threw the last peeled potato back in the pot and started mashing them.

"I don't like this apartment either," I said. "Moving here was a mistake, but we can fix it."

"Not on unemployment."

"I appreciate that I was able to be home with Taneli for two years. Now it's nice to be back at work. I would think you'd understand, since work is important to you too."

"But it isn't more important to me than the well-being and happiness of my family!"

Antti started to set the table, and I got out the electric mixer to drown out any angry words I might be tempted to say. Taneli came to see what I was doing. He loved machines and was always happy to help vacuum or fill the washing machine. We were quiet at the dinner table, and after the meal Antti said he was going to the library. Iida asked to go too, but Antti said he was walking.

I filled the dishwasher, then sat down to try to read the Hackman manuscript I'd brought home from work, a copy our unit secretary had printed for me. But Taneli climbed into my lap to complain that Iida wouldn't play with him. So I went in the kids' room with him and we started a car race. Iida then decided that she did want to play with her brother after all, so I was able to slip back into the living room to continue reading.

Auto racing in the Smeds family got its start with Andreas, and he also had greater success initially than his younger brother. The competition between the brothers spurred Sasha to approach his training with more purpose, although both brothers claim their relationship

102

has always been excellent. However, some sources remember tensions in the pit, which at times came to blows. Both Sasha and Andreas deny this.

Andreas's rally career ended with his drunk-driving conviction just as he was on the verge of international success. Afterward the family focused on support-ing Sasha's career, and the results were not long in coming . . .

My reading was interrupted by a toy car, which flew straight into my cheek so hard I felt my teeth rattle. The next car hit my forehead, and I immediately felt a headache coming on.

"What the hell!" I charged to the door of the children's room. Taneli grinned in satisfaction and aimed the next car at me. I raised my hand to stop him, and he flinched in fear. As I lowered my hand, I realized it was shaking.

"Don't throw things anymore. It hurts. Play instead."

Taneli glowered at me, then burst into tears. Gingerly touching my forehead, I felt the beginnings of a lump. I tried to ignore it and lure Taneli into my lap. He didn't want to come.

"Taneli wants Mommy to play, not read," Iida announced.

"Then let's play. How about another car race? I'll play too."

Gradually the game picked up momentum. One of Taneli's cars was a Citroën, and I laughed and said the driver was the future world champion, Sasha Smeds. Iida asked if Sasha was a boy or a girl, then started asking why only men drive rally cars, even though Mom drove our car a lot more than Dad. I was happy Antti didn't hear her.

I didn't get back to the Hackman papers until after the children had fallen asleep. When Antti came home, he didn't bother complaining about me reading for work in bed—apparently walking in the sleet had calmed him down. But we still avoided touching each other.

The title of the fifth chapter of Hackman's book was "The Woman of His Life: Sasha and Heli." Included with the text were several pictures, including a wedding portrait that had printed blurry. Sasha wore a tuxedo, Heli a simple long dress and no veil.

Race-car drivers are swarmed by beautiful women, and Sasha is no exception. But his heart belongs to Heli Haapala, whom he married in 1997. The couple met when Heli, who hails from Kouvola, came to the Smeds farm as a temporary worker in 1996. Heli comes from a middle-class family that includes two younger brothers. Her father is an engineer and her mother works in a library.

When she was young, Heli rode horses and dreamed of becoming a veterinarian, but gradually the environmental movement began to tug at her. Even though she was a city girl, she gained admittance to an agricultural program. Heli was particularly interested in organic farming. She wasn't on the Smeds farm for more than a few months before it became apparent that she could become the lady of the house if she so desired.

"Love at first sight? Well, almost," Heli responds when I ask how their romance began. However, at first Heli didn't like Sasha's rally driving, claiming it was a waste of natural resources.

"But when I saw how hard Sasha trained, my opinion started to change. I respect his perseverance and his will to win. A rally driver has to be in shape practically all the time, and wins are based on overall performance. It's a very demanding sport psychologically and physically."

Unlike some drivers' wives, Heli rarely watches Sasha's races. Her responsibilities on the farm are time consuming. Heli admits that she worries about Sasha on the track, so much so that watching competitions in person is unbearable.

"I think Sasha can concentrate on races better when he doesn't have to worry about me. At home we aren't a star race-car driver and his wife; we're just two equal people."

Heli laughs when asked if she's ever jealous of the women who mob her husband.

"Posing with models and movie stars is part of Sasha's job. I trust him."

Ursula was right—it was hard to find anything sensational in the manuscript. Setting the papers down next to the bed, I closed my eyes. Sleep—and dreams—came quickly. I was in a rally race, and my car was the ancient Fiat Uno Antti and I had sold when the department gave me a vehicle. I didn't know the race course and just tried to avoid the other cars and the crowds along the sides of the road. The children were in the car too, bouncing around in the back without seat belts and screaming warnings. Suddenly the Fiat lost its brakes. I woke up just as we careened off the rocks along the shore of Lake Humaljärvi and plowed into the water.

9

We received the first tire tread analysis results on Wednesday. Because Puustjärvi was still on parental leave, Koivu had to review the report with the technician. Around noon he appeared in my office looking excited.

"I think we got a hit. The Smeds have a bunch of cars, and one of them is a Land Rover, right?"

"Yes."

"About a kilometer from Hackman's car, on Mäyrä Road, we found tracks from where a Land Rover had recently parked. We'll need a warrant to make casts of the tires."

"Good. That lines up with the eyewitness accounts. You have my permission to take the casts, but let's keep this as quiet as we can. The British rally starts tomorrow, and if the media catches wind of this, we'll get slaughtered . . . Do what you can to make everyone think this is strictly routine."

I felt my cheeks burn as if I was doing something illegal. Cases that pointed to influential or famous suspects could be very unpleasant—I'd had ample experience with that. The conviction from the last murder I investigated went all the way to the Supreme Court on appeal, and the process was still underway. If we found a member of the Smeds family guilty of Hackman's murder, someone was bound to point to my husband's environmentalist leanings and accuse me of bias.

Annukka Hackman's death was still in the headlines, and the papers were conducting their own investigations. Although I knew all the big-name crime reporters at least superficially, I didn't know any of them well enough to find out what they were uncovering. In the Hackman case, a source like that would have been helpful.

"I'll give Forensics their marching orders," Koivu said. "Did all the Smedses have alibis?"

"Theoretically, but only the parents' alibi seems solid. Ursula verified that Viktor was having follow-up tests from his heart surgery, and Mrs. Smeds was his driver. Heli's alibi hasn't been confirmed yet, and the brothers are providing each other's alibis. I wouldn't put too much faith in that."

"And Andreas has those DUIs."

"Yes, but that doesn't make him a killer," I said.

"I'm hungry. Keep me company at lunch?"

Lunch with Koivu was always fun, and this time he kept me laughing with anecdotes about surviving alone with his baby, Juuso, while Anu was at the store or aerobics class. I was sure Koivu was exaggerating his ineptitude when it came to changing diapers and bedtime routines, but I let him talk. Little did he know that the infant stage was actually the easiest; parenthood would only become more complicated as the years went by. I didn't say that to Koivu, though. He'd learn soon enough.

After the meal I did some paperwork, although my mind kept wandering back to the Smedses' farm in Degerö. Koivu had said he'd get Forensics out there today. I remembered the rolling fields and the dark pine forests; it was a completely different world than the Turku Highway buzzing outside my window.

A knock came at the door. It was Jyrki.

"Busy?"

"I always have time for you," I answered with a smile. "What's up?" Jyrki sat down on the edge of the desk right next to me, his hands fiddling with a paper clip.

"It's Terttu. Yesterday we had a huge blowup. She's sure she has cancer and that it's because she hasn't had her own life. Supposedly she's always lived according to the dictates of Silja's skating and my work. She believes she's sick because she's been unhappy. According to her, of course, I never even noticed she was miserable."

Jyrki and I had always avoided talking to each other about troubles at home. I guess we didn't want to share the banal "my spouse doesn't understand me" complaints that people who are attracted to each other so often do. Out of respect for Antti, I tried to save my grumbling for conversations with my female friends.

"In a way, Terttu's right. I thought everything was fine, although work does take up a lot of my time. But I like my work, especially now that I'm part of the Interior Ministry's crime prevention task force. I feel like I can really make a difference."

"Yesterday Antti and I had a similar conversation about my work. He was angry that I went to interview Sasha Smeds's manager on Sunday. Apparently earlier in the fall I promised I was going to keep normal working hours from now on."

"You can't always do that, though. That's just how this job is," Jyrki said with a sigh. During my maternity leave his hair had taken on a hint of gray, and a few wrinkles had appeared on his forehead and around his eyes. They animated his otherwise smooth, symmetric features.

"Waiting for the results is the worst thing. Terttu said she's moving out if she survives the cancer."

I took Jyrki's hand and squeezed it. "You've met people in shock before. Don't take her threats too seriously."

Jyrki looked at me for a long time, then wrapped an arm around me. We sat in silence for a while. Another knock came at the door, and

Ursula opened it quickly enough that she saw us touching. We both moved away instantly, but the damage had already been done.

"Maria, I've got the fiber results from Annukka Hackman's clothes. Do you want to look?"

"Yeah, hand them to me. And you did talk with the hospital about Viktor Smeds's follow-up tests, right?"

"Yes," Ursula said, clearly irritated by my double checking. "It checks out."

Taskinen stood up from the edge of the desk to see the report too. He had to walk so close to Ursula that their shoulders touched. The fiber analysis report didn't reveal anything momentous, but it provided a good foundation for further work. Ursula also provided a summary of the interviews with Annukka Hackman's relatives. Most of them had known that Kervinen had threatened her, so they blamed him.

I drove home in the sleet that was still tormenting southern Finland. After the record hot summer, fall had only lasted a few weeks, providing just a handful of clear days before this early winter. Even though I'd tried to spend as much time in the summer sun as possible to store it up for the winter, I already felt like my reserves were depleted.

At home I managed to forget about work for once. I was reading Taneli a picture book on the couch as his bedtime story when my cell phone rang. Antti got to it before I could reach it.

"It's about work. Someone named Andreas Smeds," he said and handed me the phone. "Should I finish the story?"

I stood up and went in the kitchen to talk.

"Kallio."

"What do you think you're doing investigating our car? It was sitting in the garage the whole day when Hackman was killed. What newspaper are you in bed with? There just happened to be a whole pack of photographers lurking in the bushes here when your forensic team showed up. And apparently they didn't have the authority to drive the hyenas away."

It was possible that someone in the building had leaked to the press. I asked Andreas what paper the photographers were from.

"It's all the same pile of shit. I don't try to keep them straight. I called Jouko too. Hopefully Sasha doesn't hear about this before Sunday. Although I guess that's pointless since the British rally is going to be crawling with Finnish media. I hope you feel good about yourself, now that you've ruined my brother's concentration."

Andreas's voice trembled slightly. Maybe he was drunk. Since there was nothing I could do, I cut the call short and went to help Taneli brush his teeth.

The next morning the papers were full of the Rally of Great Britain. "Sasha Smeds Confident Heading into Championship," they proclaimed. I looked at Smeds's boyish smile for a long time. To my relief, Jouko Suuronen hadn't left any messages.

As I drove to work, the sleet was thick, piling up on my windshield wipers. Each winter, the dark days seemed more unbearable than the previous year. The brightly lit advertisements along the roads only made the situation worse. Perhaps simple darkness would have been preferable to the contrast created by the city's lights.

As usual, the conditions for the Rally of Great Britain were expected to be muddy. I felt like I was on my own rally track as I braked to avoid a car that had abruptly cut in front of me.

The rally was also the hot topic at work. The tire tread analysis results were supposed to be ready by the next morning, and the whole unit seemed to be on the edge of their seats about everything having to do with Sasha Smeds. Puupponen was tracking the special stage results on the Internet, and when I returned from a painfully long organizational meeting in the afternoon I saw Koivu and Ursula in the break room watching a news report about the latest rally results.

"What's the score?" I asked as I poured myself a coffee.

"Sasha has fifteen seconds on Sainz. It seems close. Hopefully the Citroën runs well. Earlier this year there was some nonsense with the gearbox," Koivu said.

"Hopefully Sasha can keep his head together," Ursula added. "This is a blood sport, and I worry he might be too soft. He has to risk everything now and push it."

In the evening the difference was only five seconds. The images of cars wallowing and growling in the mud were repeated at the end of every news report. One enthusiastic reporter commentated with his face all aglow:

"The Rally of Great Britain has turned into a true clash of the titans. Facing off we have two Citroën men, veteran driver Carlos Sainz and Finland's latest rally sensation, Sasha Smeds. This is a war with no prisoners."

"Death before dishonor, right?" Antti said, laughing and sitting down next to me. "Even in boxing you aren't allowed to beat each other to death anymore, but in car racing you can go right ahead and kill anyone, even bystanders."

"I don't think they hurt anyone on purpose. Don't they take the biggest risks themselves? It might be interesting to try sometime."

"What, taking risks? Don't you have enough experience already with that?"

"If I die because of my work, it'll be from boredom in the endless meetings," I replied glumly. "We've got our Friday leadership meeting tomorrow morning."

The weather had changed again when I woke up the next morning. The snow had melted and something vaguely resembling the sun peeked shyly through breaks in the clouds. It felt strangely bright, and I had to rummage for my sunglasses in the glove compartment before I drove to work.

Uncharacteristically Taskinen arrived at the meeting a little late, just as I was turning off my phone. I kept it off through the entire hour, so I didn't hear the news until afterward. The tire tracks from the car parked on Mäyrä Road near Lake Humaljärvi and the Smedses' Land Rover had significant similarities.

"The cast is of the back left tire, since the right rear tire print was so unclear it was impossible to draw any conclusions from it," said Hakulinen from Forensics. "The tire is almost brand new, bought and mounted in late October, so it hasn't had time to develop much wear. The tire model isn't very common, but the same tire could be on other cars."

"Would this evidence hold up in court?"

"Only if the defense attorney is a real loser. No one's getting locked up based on this print alone."

That was what I'd been afraid of, but at least the Smeds family would have some explaining to do. I might have made a pretty big mistake letting Sasha leave the country. I called the unit together and arranged to go with Koivu, Ursula, and Puupponen to the Smedses' farm.

"Right now?" Koivu asked. "The rally is on live. They're sure to be watching it."

"Then they'll be home."

"And we'll get in the papers: 'Police Raid World Champion's Family Party,'" Puupponen said.

We went in two cars, my work vehicle and another unmarked car, so it wouldn't be obvious we were police. I remembered how doggedly the paparazzi had lurked around the houses of skiers caught doping. Maybe there would be photographers staking out the Smedses' house too. Puupponen drove my car while I planned our approach. I didn't bother to verify that the family was at home. A surprise would be better.

I figured that it would take less than half an hour to drive from Degerö to the lake where Hackman was killed, and barely ten minutes to walk from the road to the water. The round trip would take about an hour, and maybe either of the brothers, Sasha or Andreas, wouldn't have noticed the other's absence. But how had the killer known about Hackman's swimming outing?

As we drove we met an army of semis coming from the other direction, Russian rigs transporting German luxury cars from the Hanko harbor to the border. They were followed by a long line of passenger vehicles, which made passing difficult.

"Oh, to be a Russian," Puupponen said with a sigh. "On a cop's salary I'll never have enough for an Audi or a Mercedes, but if I were militia in St. Petersburg . . . At Russian prices, I could afford one of those in a couple of months."

"I have a hard time imagining you shaking down tourists," I said.

"Is that a compliment or an insult? Jeez, you women think every guy has to be like Sasha Smeds, rich and daring but still a good family man. You want someone you can look up to and idolize. I'd even be willing to bet you don't really want to earn as much as men." Puupponen brushed a strand of his red hair off his forehead and kept his eyes fixed on the road.

I didn't feel like continuing the conversation. It came too close to what Antti had said recently. When we passed Kirkkonummi, I thought of Puustjärvi. Maybe Puupponen's irritation flowed from the same source as Puustjärvi's guilty conscience: Ursula. Had she turned Puupponen down? At least Koivu and Lehtovuori got along with Ursula. As a young cop my only option had been to be one of the guys, but as a boss I seemed to have taken on a maternal role.

The sun shone on the deep-brown fields, bringing back the ruddiness of the pine bark. Puupponen parked the car next to the much-talked-about Land Rover, and the Smedses' dog rushed to meet us. Its paws left muddy prints on Puupponen's light-colored jeans. We waited for Ursula and Koivu to arrive before going inside.

Andreas was waiting at the front door.

"What is it now?" he asked gruffly, but his face looked pale.

"We need a little more information."

"You can't come bother us now. The race is on, and I'm watching it with Heli and Mom."

"Where's your father?"

No one had talked much about Viktor Smeds yet, and although he had the best alibi of the group, we couldn't overlook him.

"Resting. He can't handle the stress."

Andreas was dressed in all black, and his jeans and sweater made his face look colorless and his eyes oversized. From his breath I caught a whiff of beer. "The worst special stage is on now, and it's pissing rain."

"What's the score?" Puupponen asked, genuinely interested.

"Sasha's thirty seconds ahead of Sainz, and Bosse is up to third. If he gets between Sasha and Sainz, that's just about it."

From somewhere inside the house came a woman's shout, which was quickly stifled, and Andreas went to see what it was. I motioned for Puupponen to follow.

"You and Ursula go watch the rally and try to get something out of Heli and Andreas. I'll talk to Viktor. Koivu, you come with me. The winner won't be decided today."

With a sigh, Koivu followed me. I knocked on the elder Smeds's bedroom door and heard a faint response. Carefully I opened the door.

The room was spacious—it was obviously the master bedroom. In addition to the double bed, there was room for a couple of armchairs with a table between them, a dressing table, and a bookcase. On the left side of the bed lay Viktor Smeds with his eyes closed and face ashen.

"Är det du, Rauha?"

"No, this is Maria Kallio from the Espoo Police and Detective Koivu," I responded in Swedish, ignoring Koivu's stare. Foreign languages had never been his strong suit, and Anu teased him now and then by speaking Vietnamese, which Koivu only knew well enough to say "I love you." At least he didn't grouse about Swedish speakers like some of our colleagues, although he did argue that Russian should be part of the police academy curriculum instead of Swedish. The previous year the department had hired a full-time Russian interpreter, who was kept busy with drug and prostitution cases. In contrast, Swedish Finns mostly broke the speed limit and committed white-collar crimes, and rarely killed each other.

"We didn't get a chance to speak to you on our last visit," I said. "How well did you know Annukka Hackman?"

Viktor Smeds sat up a bit. He was wearing old-man clothes: polyester trousers, a cardigan, and wool socks. His eyes were cloudy and his speech slow.

"I didn't know her. I did meet her a few times, but she wasn't interested in me. Bright girl, but so curious. How's Sasha doing? The doctor won't let me watch. He says it's too much strain on my heart. Rauha wanted Sasha to stop, but here he is on the verge of the championship . . ."

Viktor gave a little smile and rested his head back on the pile of pillows. The veins were raised in his gaunt hands, which also had liver spots.

"How long were you at your follow—"

Just then the door opened with a bang and Rauha Smeds swept in.

"What's the meaning of this?" she hissed in Finnish. "Viktor is resting. He can't be disturbed. Don't you understand he's still recovering?"

I had always imagined the furies from mythology as tall women with dark complexions, piercing eyes, and sharp features. The fury standing before me now, however, bore no resemblance to that. Koivu instinctively recoiled from Rauha Smeds.

"We don't want to disturb your husband, but we have a job to do. We'll try to handle this as calmly as possible," I said.

"Handle this what? You're just like that Annukka Hackman. Questions, questions, questions! How long did I nurse Sasha? Where did Viktor and I meet? Is Heli a good daughter-in-law to me? What business is that of anyone else?"

Rauha walked over to Viktor's bed and took her husband by the hand.

"Min käraste, ska jag vara med dig när polisen avhör dig?"

Viktor nodded. I was amused that Rauha didn't ask my permission to stay in the room. She managed to look majestic in a garment I could only describe as a barn jacket. Her hair was even more unruly than my own, but I hoped mine would gray as beautifully as hers.

"How long did the follow-up visit with your cardiologist last?" I asked Viktor.

"From noon to five . . . They poked and prodded everything," he said, trying to smile. "Rauha, how is Sasha . . ."

"Very well. Try not to think about it. You should be sleeping, but these police!" Rauha looked back at us, exasperated.

"I asked Annukka to leave Viktor alone while the poor man was waiting for his surgery," she said. "He's going to recover, but not without rest." Then she gave me a stern look. "I've always thought of the Finnish police as being very considerate. What's the meaning of your barging in here during the rally finals?"

"These things can't wait."

"Do you really think my husband could have killed Annukka Hackman? Does he look like a murderer? Do you think he'd have the energy to walk all that way through the woods? The papers said Annukka was found in a lake in the middle of the woods."

Maybe Rauha was right. She left her husband's side and gestured for me to follow. She took me to a room upstairs that she called the guest quarters. The window had a view of the fields, and I saw a white-tailed deer running on the edge of the forest.

"Beautiful view," I said.

"The trees have had time to grow back. When my parents returned here, the Russians had burned most of the forest. All the neighboring buildings had been demolished and used for firewood. Only one of our barns was still standing, but the house had survived. I remember my mother saying as we left that she intended to live to be eighty years old so she could come back home. Fortunately she was able to come back in her prime when she was only a little past forty. I don't imagine that's the sort of thing you came to hear about, though. What exactly are you interested in?"

"I'm actually familiar with this area already. My in-laws' summer cabin is at the end of this road. At the moment they're living there year-round."

"Ah. I don't know many of the people in the cabins. But you didn't answer my question. Why are you here now? What do you want?" Rauha crossed her arms and stared at me just like I would when I was interrogating a suspect.

"Could you tell us more about Tuesday of last week? According to the family, you and Viktor were in Helsinki for a heart surgery follow-up exam."

"Yes. We left at ten thirty and got back after six. Luckily we have enough money to take Viktor to a private hospital. On the public side, the line reaches all the way into spring. By that time Viktor probably would have been dead. So that's one good thing about Sasha's hobby."

"Hobby? I thought rally driving at that level was considered a profession."

"It's just boyish foolishness Sasha has dragged out too long. It isn't a profession. I've had a very hard time accepting that he decided to take it so seriously. That's why I wanted the farm to go organic. To give us some sense of balance." It was clear to me that whatever Rauha Smeds wanted to happen happened, regardless of the men in the family. I remembered Antti's bitter pronouncements about gender inequality.

"Of course Hackman wanted to make a fuss in public about a rally star's mother thinking the whole sport was frivolous, but she couldn't claim we didn't support our sons. I'll tell you, honestly, that I didn't like Annukka Hackman. I don't like people who try to profit from other people's lives."

"What car did you take to the appointment?"

"The Škoda. I drove. By some miracle I found a parking spot on South Hesperia Street, so Viktor didn't have to walk far."

During my schooling I'd lived in that area, one of the older parts of Helsinki. I'd jog around Töölö Bay and hang out at the posh cafés like Elite and Kuu Kuu.

I didn't feel like harping on the cardiology visit anymore. Besides, Ursula had already verified the details with the hospital. But I did ask Rauha what the boys and her daughter-in-law had been up to on the day of the murder. Rauha claimed she didn't know.

"A household with five adults like this is pretty unique," I observed. "How do you all get along?"

"Maybe it's unique nowadays, but this used to be the normal way of life. I wouldn't mind a third generation either, but Heli doesn't want children as long as Sasha is racing. I can understand that, of course, since the constant fear almost ruined Viktor's heart. And why wouldn't we get along? Heli and Andreas care for the cattle, and Sasha helps in the fields when he can, just like me. I handle the bookkeeping, and Viktor does light repairs. There's plenty of work and plenty of space for everyone. I like my daughter-in-law and she likes me. Do you have a bad relationship with your mother-in-law? Is that why you ask? Or are you on your second or third mother-in-law?"

I laughed. "First. And I have nothing to complain about." My mother-in-law was in the same situation as Mrs. Smeds, spending most of her time caring for an ailing husband.

"That's good. Hating people is a waste of energy."

A noise came from downstairs, and I realized that Koivu must be watching the race. Had Ursula and Puupponen even bothered to interview Heli and Andreas? I told Rauha she could go back downstairs to watch too.

"Despite it all, I hope Sasha wins, but only if he earns it honestly. The decision the team made last year was infuriating since it was nothing more than money and power dictating who would win. I admire my son's tenacity and how quickly he recovered from that." Rauha stood and headed for the door.

"How quickly did Andreas recover from the end of his career?"

Rauha turned back toward me. Most of her face remained in the shadow of the doorway. "I don't think he's ever recovered," she said.

When we got downstairs, everyone was watching the race. I couldn't make out anything on the screen at first—the camera lens was covered in mud—but the view soon shifted to an aerial shot. Puupponen and Ursula were as enthralled as the people they were supposed to be interrogating. I motioned for Puupponen to join me in the entryway.

"They're sticking to their stories. Heli was on a store run, and the brothers were home. Heli was in Espoo, but she denies going to the lake. And Andreas is backing up his brother. So they could have done it together."

Could Sasha and Andreas have kept something like that a secret in a tightly knit household like this one? Rauha and Viktor were out of the running, so only the younger generation was left. As I watched Sasha on the TV, pushing the limits as he rounded each corner, I thought he must have incredible nerve.

The camera angle changed again, and the commentator exclaimed that Sasha's car was approaching the most demanding section of the seventh special stage. Sasha's lead was already more than thirty seconds, and the commentator shouted with excitement, even though two days remained in the competition. There were only three miles remaining in the stage, so I decided to let my subordinates watch the rest.

Heli sat on the couch looking calm, but her fingers fiddled with the fringe of a throw pillow she held in her lap, braiding and unbraiding the tassels. Andreas was sitting in an armchair, drinking a beer. Rauha stood close by, and reacted physically to every turn of Sasha's car. She relaxed for just a few seconds when the screen showed the cars coming up behind, but the tension returned as soon as the camera shifted back to Sasha's Citroën.

The car raced along a narrow ledge above the seashore, climbing upward. Between the road and the drop was a low rock wall. Mud splashed from the wheels, and the windshield wipers worked overtime to clean it off. Puupponen sighed audibly when Sasha made it through the next curve.

Then, a deer appeared out of nowhere. It jumped right in front of the car, and Sasha had no time to react. He lost control of the vehicle. It careened first into the rock wall, which crumbled, then bounced over the ledge, rolling down the hillside until the cameras lost sight of it.

10

For a moment the only sound was the commentator's stuttering. Then Andreas put his hands over his eyes, Heli stood up, and Ursula started to scream.

"Quiet!" Rauha demanded. "Viktor can't hear about this until he's had his medicine. Andreas, call Jouko. I'm going to check on Viktor."

Rauha rushed out of the room, while Heli stood in the middle of the floor and stared at the television screen. I grabbed ahold of Ursula to get her to stop screaming, and Koivu turned up the TV. Heli looked as if she might faint. Somewhere a phone started to ring. The sound came from Heli's clothing. It took her a few seconds before she pulled the phone out of her shirt pocket.

"Hi, Jouko." Heli's voice was small and high pitched. "I saw on TV. Yes. I'll leave now. Exactly. Call me. Yes." Heli hung up. "Andreas, will you get me the flight schedules? They'll come pick me up in London as soon as I know what airport I'm flying into. Jouko will call as soon as he knows more."

"Those rally cars have the very best safety equipment, roll cages and everything," Koivu said consolingly. "And aren't their suits fireproof too?"

Andreas removed his hands from his face. He got up and walked past Heli without a word. I thought it was strange that he didn't even hug his sister-in-law. It was as if the entire family had fled from around Heli.

"Look, it's burning!" Ursula suddenly exclaimed. The image on TV showed a few flames through the rain. Heli put her right hand over her mouth.

"My bag . . . It's always ready. I have to get my bag," she said. Heli disappeared, and I followed her. She walked upstairs to a room that was apparently her and Sasha's bedroom. She opened a closet and took out a suitcase.

"This is always ready with my passport and clothes for a couple of nights. I knew this day would come. I promised Sasha I would always come immediately if anything happened. I just need my credit cards." As Heli grabbed the suitcase, it was obvious she was used to lifting heavy objects. Still I took the bag from her, and when my hand touched hers, it was ice cold.

"Do you intend to go alone?" I asked.

"That's the plan. I'll be fine." Heli's voice was just as cold as her hand. Andreas appeared in the doorway. There was a strange expression in his eyes, one I couldn't read.

"There's a seat on the four thirty flight to Gatwick. I can't drive you, though. I've had three beers. Should I call you a taxi?"

"I can take her," I heard myself say. Just then Heli's phone rang again.

"Yes? Good. I'm coming on the four thirty flight. It goes into Gatwick. Call me again. I'm not driving myself. Tell Sasha that I love . . ."

Although Heli's voice faltered, there were no tears in her eyes.

"The helicopter has put out the fire and is trying to land near the car now," she said. "They don't know if Sasha and his co-driver, Heikki, survived. Jouko will call again when he knows." She then looked directly at her brother-in-law. "You tell Rauha. Jouko will call you too."

The television downstairs was still showing replays of Sasha's car rolling down the hill. The sports commentator kept repeating how shocking the incident was and that he would tell the viewers more when there was more to tell. The special stage had been suspended.

"I'm taking Heli to the airport," I told my team. "I'll see you at the Christmas party tonight. Make sure they don't need any more help here. Koivu, you check in on the parents."

I knew Koivu could handle whatever would need to be done. As she stared at the TV, Ursula's mascara was a little smudged, making her look vulnerable. I heard Heli in the hall saying something to her in-laws, then she appeared in the living room.

"Shall we go, Detective?" she asked. She wrapped a soft gray wool overcoat around herself. Andreas took the suitcase from me and escorted us to the car. I opened the door for Heli, then went around back to unlock the trunk. As Andreas lifted the suitcase in, he said, "Thank you." Then he quickly returned to Heli's side of the car, where I saw him reach out and lightly stroke her cheek.

"Call when you can," he said.

"I will. I promise," Heli replied.

I placed my police light on top of the car. Once we were underway, I turned it on so the cars ahead of us would move aside. Luckily the Friday rush hour traffic wasn't too bad on the highway. However, Ring III in Vantaa was already gridlocked. Heli sat next to me in silence. I wished I could comfort her, but words weren't going to help now.

"What's your first name, by the way?" Heli suddenly asked.

"Maria."

"Please, Maria. I . . ." Her phone started to ring again. I didn't know the tune it was playing. "Yes? Alive? Ah. In the car. Four thirty. Call the house. The others are there. The police. No, it's fine. They're friendly. Bye."

Heli dropped the phone in her lap, and the tears began to flow. "Sasha's alive but unconscious. They're extracting him from the car right now. He has serious burns. Heikki's injuries are even more serious." She spoke in a choked voice as the tears kept coming. For a second I removed my right hand from the steering wheel and patted her on the shoulder. I wanted to stop the car and give her a hug, but the most important thing was to get her to her plane on time.

"I knew we'd be punished. But why Sasha? Sasha didn't do anything wrong," Heli stammered.

"Punished?"

"Annukka saw us. She spied on us and got what she wanted."

"Saw who?"

"Me and Andreas. Haven't you and your people read Annukka's book? Annukka came snooping around when Viktor had his surgery. That woman had no shame. Once, we even caught her in the house; she'd snuck in and was snooping around Rauha and Viktor's bedroom. The day she caught us, Rauha was at the hospital with Viktor, and Sasha was at trials. We thought we had a couple of days to ourselves. The barn door is never locked. We were just kissing, but that was enough for Annukka . . ."

"Were you and Andreas having an affair?"

"I don't know. I guess."

Heli tried to wipe her tears on the sleeve of her coat, so I told her there were paper towels in the glove box. Puustjärvi had talked about the very same thing—infidelity and punishment—while sitting in the same seat a few days earlier.

"I didn't want to hurt anyone. I just want everyone to be happy. I'm Sasha's wife. I stand by his side at the awards ceremonies and the parties. I smile for the photographers and assure the reporters that I trust Sasha even though he's surrounded by models and movie stars. But I was the one who couldn't be trusted. Annukka said she wouldn't tell Sasha yet.

She'd let him win the world championship first. After that, everyone could read about how his wife cheated on him."

"Who else knows about your relationship?"

"No one. Who else could we tell? The situation is impossible. I can't start a new life with Andreas. That's not possible at the farm. Smedsbo is home for all of us; it's where we have to live."

"How long has this been going on?"

"Since the spring. Andreas says he's always loved me. I feel like I'm in a soap opera. Things like this don't happen in real life. Not to me at least."

Now that would be ironic: Sasha offers his brother an alibi so Andreas can get away with killing the only person who knew about his affair with Sasha's wife. Why hadn't Ursula, who had read the whole Hackman manuscript, said anything about this? As I'd scanned through the book, I hadn't seen anything this juicy.

"Sasha shouldn't have to suffer. Sasha didn't do anything wrong! I see you're wearing a wedding ring. Have you ever fallen in love with anyone besides your husband?"

I dodged the question: "You can't do much about your feelings, and Sasha's accident doesn't have anything to do with you and Andreas."

"Maybe you can't control your feelings, but you can control your actions. And I've ruined everything, and now innocent people are suffering. And do you know what's worse? I should be promising God to leave Andreas if Sasha survives, but I can't. I don't know if I could keep that promise. Police are sworn to secrecy, right? You won't tell what Annukka's book says, will you?"

"I won't personally, no," I said. Had Atro Jääskeläinen swindled us and given the police a cleaned-up version of Annukka's manuscript? If so, where was the complete book?

"It may take hours for them to get Sasha out of the car. Aren't burn injuries horribly painful? Oh, Sasha!" Heli said and burst into tears again.

"I don't think it's a good idea for you to fly alone."

"Well, I'm not so immoral that I'd take Andreas with me on a trip like this!" Suddenly Heli seemed full of rage and self-loathing. It had started to rain, but the streetlights hadn't come on yet. The lights of the oncoming cars scattered in the droplets that collected on my windshield; the wipers couldn't drive them away quickly enough.

"Annukka thought the country had a right to know everything about Sasha's life and about mine. It didn't matter that it would hurt Sasha's parents and my parents and who knows who else! As if this situation was easy somehow. I didn't want this to happen and neither did Andreas. And if Sasha dies now . . ."

I felt helpless in the face of Heli's mess. Even though it was none of my business, I wished I could help. I drove her to the priority-boarding door since her ticket was business class. Half the world already knew about Sasha's accident, and Heli would be taken care of. Still it felt bad leaving her to walk alone into the crowded terminal. She looked so delicate and ready to lose her way.

From the airport, I drove straight to the day care. Seeing the children calmed my mind—both were in good spirits, and Iida proudly showed off the cat she'd made from pipe cleaners and empty paper towel rolls. The day care suffered from a shortage of materials, so we collected empty paper towel rolls at home, and Antti brought paper from work that was blank on one side so the kids could draw. Iida's future school would also be strapped for funds because the technological paradise of Espoo didn't have the money to invest in elementary education.

For a few years Antti had suspected they were just waiting for Nokia and their ilk to found private schools for their employees' children. He'd gone to an elite school in Tapiola himself, which I hadn't grown tired of teasing him about. His education had been somewhat different than what I received in the backwoods of Northern Karelia. Now Antti's old school suffered from serious mold problems, and the classrooms were overcrowded. So much for its reputation.

Back home, I gave the kids mashed potatoes and fish sticks for dinner. I didn't join them, since I'd be eating later at the office Christmas party.

"I assume you're planning on being hungover tomorrow," Antti said as I brushed eyeshadow on my eyelids, sipping a gin and tonic and listening to the Rehtorit sing about Friday making them young again. I knew the feeling, although I didn't have it now. My mind was too full of other people's problems, and the woman looking back at me in the mirror only had a year and a half until her fortieth birthday. I could accept the wrinkles, but the emotional exhaustion felt overpowering. I knew that alcohol wasn't the right medicine, but I couldn't come up with anything else.

Antti joked about how dreary the next morning would be, and reminded me that his own office Christmas party was next week.

"That's a good thing," he said. "Since they're not re-upping my contract, I can tell everyone to their faces what I think of them."

"Are you holding a lot of grudges?" I asked.

"Who me? Never. I'm just a nice guy who wants the best for everyone," Antti replied so bitterly that I was still thinking about it later on the bus. And Antti was nice: even though he hated car racing, he was still genuinely shocked by Sasha Smeds's accident. I just mentioned in passing that I'd taken Heli to the airport, since I couldn't talk about work.

After much consideration we'd chosen the Tapiola Garden Hotel as the venue for our Christmas party in hopes that there might be enough other people in the ballroom to make up for the dearth of female dance partners in our ranks. The party would start with a meeting in a private room, and I would be having my first ham and casseroles of the season. As I waited at the lobby bar for another gin and tonic, Koivu and Puupponen joined me.

"Puustjärvi called to say he isn't coming," Puupponen said. "He's been at the hospital the whole day staring at the twins. His wife is still in bad shape."

Apparently Anu wasn't coming to the party either, even though we all wanted to see her.

"I'm sorry to hear that," I said. "But hopefully we can still have fun without them. How are the Smedses?"

"The old lady drugged her husband into a coma, and Andreas started drinking hard. He even offered us some vodka," Koivu said. "We didn't hang around for long, though. Since Sasha's condition was unclear, we wanted to give them some space. The news will be on soon, so we can see if there's been any new developments before we go down."

Sasha's accident was still the top story. He'd been taken to the hospital in critical condition, and his co-driver was currently undergoing skin grafting, but it was doubtful it would work. Heli would no doubt be with her husband soon. On screen, the familiar Citroën raced along the wet road, then the deer ran in front of it. My muscles clenched again, even though I knew what would happen.

"Did you notice?" asked Koivu. "Sasha didn't even try to brake. He just drove right at the deer. He probably thought he could survive the crash, but he figured wrong."

"No talking about work!" Puupponen said, agitated. "We only have our Christmas party once a year, and I intend to dance with my boss. Come on, Kallio! Let's turn the dial up to eleven and forget about everything else!"

The speakers were blasting Prisoners of the Past's version of "Arctic Wedding," and for some reason the song's theme of unhappy endings was too much for me. I started to cry, but I didn't want to let Puupponen see. He was telling an endless story about some wino he arrested when he was at the police academy. I'd heard the story before, but I still laughed. Puupponen was right. Turn the dial up to eleven and forget the world.

After dancing, we headed for the dining room. Next to the plates were elf hats, which we were supposed to put on our heads. Puupponen led by example, and Kettunen from Narcotics followed.

"Is this seat free?" Taskinen asked, indicating the empty chair next to me.

"Of course," I said, and he quickly sat down. "You probably already heard about Sasha Smeds. Sad situation. The co-driver has three small kids."

"What makes a person intentionally risk his life in a sport like that?"

"Asks the cop."

"A desk cop who's shot his gun once in his whole career, and that was twenty years ago," Taskinen said with a snort.

"Don't you start this 'real men versus pansies' thing too," I said and sampled the red wine that had just been poured in my glass.

It was a light Italian vintage, which paired well with the ham, but for someone like me who preferred strong flavors, it was bland. Still I took another sip. I couldn't disappoint Antti's expectation that I'd be hungover tomorrow.

Ursula's entrance sent a buzz through the crowd, who'd been concentrating on their starter salads. Kettunen had some wine go down the wrong pipe, and the men at almost every table straightened up in their seats. Ursula was wearing a shiny silver minidress, high-heeled silver sandals, and shimmering panty hose. Her outfit was exactly what rapists liked to call "enticing" or "provocative." Most of the cops in the Criminal Division had worked a rape case during their career, and there were some among them who blamed the victims because of their behavior and dress. It would be interesting to know what they were thinking right now.

At about age thirty I accepted the fact that I would never be a tall blond and gave up my inferiority complex, but if someone could revive it, it would be Ursula. Still, I'd sensed some uncertainty underneath her perfect exterior. When I looked at Ursula now, though, sitting between Koivu and Korkeala from Robbery like a newly crowned Miss Universe, I thought I might have been wrong. If she was still in shock over Sasha Smeds's accident, she knew how to conceal it well. Clearly, she intended to have a good time tonight.

Taskinen had decided to let it all hang out too, although he did whisper to me in passing that Terttu's condition was only growing worse. She was filling out her will and the divorce papers at the same time.

"It's almost comical in a way, even though it's cruel to laugh at someone in so much distress," he murmured in my ear. "But let's not talk about that anymore. Do you think I'll have to give a speech at some point?"

Luckily the Criminal Division enjoyed unanimity in the belief that Finnish cops weren't going to play elf games or sing Christmas songs at their office holiday party. Eating, drinking, and dancing were more than enough planned programming. Luukkainen from Narcotics did try to get a song going, but when he got to a line about putting out the candles on Christmas Eve, Puupponen yelled that he should put us out of our misery instead. Taskinen did give a speech, but it was only three sentences long:

"Dear colleagues, we all know the purpose of an office Christmas party is to help us get to know each other and foster a spirit of cooperation between units. But I'm an old-fashioned guy who believes that a spirit of cooperation comes from working together and respecting each other, not from challenge courses and weekend seminars. The purpose of tonight is to have fun, so let's all raise a glass to us!"

Despite my criticism of the vintage, I drank another glass of the red wine. My cell phone was on silent, but I checked it now and then, even though Antti wasn't in the habit of sending me reports about the kids. Koivu had asked Anu to check the TV for any news about Sasha Smeds, so he was checking his phone as well. Ursula was sitting very close to Koivu, and I saw Puupponen staring at them with a crooked smile. I'd thought Puupponen was infatuated with Ursula, but apparently I'd been wrong about that too.

Once we finished our round of gingerbread coffee, the dance band resumed playing in the ballroom. Puupponen came over and asked me to dance again.

"Nobody else has a cool-looking boss like me," he said with a laugh as we moved around the dance floor. "I should take a picture so my mom can see."

I'd dug my old leather skirt out of the closet, and while it didn't quite reach my knees, it was still tame compared to Ursula's outfit. My black shirt had short sleeves because in anything sleeveless I looked like a drag queen. Dancing in heels was no problem for me. Puupponen had a strange, flailing style, though, with long, loping strides that made it hard for me to keep up.

"How is Sasha's wife doing?" he asked between songs. I mumbled something before the band started again, this time with "Besame Mucho."

Puupponen bent so close his lips brushed my left ear. "What if Smeds drove off the road on purpose? What if he's the murderer and thought he didn't deserve to win the world championship?"

I laughed. "You're starting to sound like me," I said. When the quartet's keyboard player launched into a painful solo in the middle of the song, I laughed even harder. The bassist sang, but the guitarist mostly just played accompaniment, and the drummer looked sleepy. Their name was Midnight Fire, but, apart from the keyboardist, they were far from fiery.

After Puupponen, Kettunen from Narcotics asked me to dance, then Autio. Koivu swayed back and forth with Ursula, looking irritated because she had her head on his shoulder. When the band took a break, I went to get a gin and tonic and a bottle of mineral water. The dining room was nearly empty, and I found Taskinen sitting with Lehtovuori in the corner. They were talking about hockey. Taskinen had been a

Battle Axes supporter since his days at the police academy in Tampere, while Lehtovuori was from Lappeenranta and over the moon about the Sputniks' surprise success this year.

"And the Blues have crashed since their name change," I said with a sigh as I sat down with them. "Bring back the Espoo Pucks and their game will improve."

Lehtovuori subscribed to the sports news on his phone and decided to check if there was anything new on Sasha Smeds. Taskinen disappeared to get another drink.

"This says he's in critical condition. Poor guy. Some people get so close to bliss and then fate snatches it away at the last second," Lehtovuori said.

Just then Taskinen returned with a cognac. "I went straight to a double," he announced happily. "We only live once. Maybe it's high time I realized that too. Cheers, Maria."

I'd seen Jyrki drunk precisely once, at a coworker's going-away party. Now he was on track for a repeat, though. When the band returned to the stage, he bowed and led me to the dance floor.

Jyrki was a good dancer, and not nearly as tall as Antti. We did the rumba, with him teaching me the steps as we both giggled.

"Do you remember when we were in this same room for Palo's funeral? Ström was with us too," he said suddenly.

"I remember. Do you still think about them?"

"I do. They both died for no reason. I've been thinking about death a lot lately of course. It's nice that people are having kids at least, like Puustjärvi. Are you planning on any more?"

"Doubtful," I muttered quietly against Jyrki's shoulder. I could smell his aftershave when I got within arm's reach, and I liked it, as well as his closeness. We continued dancing after the requisite two songs; perhaps both of us were trying to stay away from the bar. I noticed that my powder had smudged on the breast of Jyrki's black coat, and I wiped it away with a laugh. I thought of Terttu. I couldn't say I knew her, although we'd met at various family parties and skating performances. I'd always thought the Taskinens were a happy couple.

I raised my gaze from Jyrki's shoulder to see Ursula drag Koivu onto the floor again. Koivu refused the couples dance position and instead started swinging solo to the Beatles' "All My Loving." Ursula looked at him for a second then left the floor, but Koivu continued dancing unperturbed.

"Terttu's always been jealous of you," Taskinen whispered in my ear. "You're so gutsy and decisive. To hear her tell it, I should be married to you instead of her . . ."

"She really said that?" I looked into Jyrki's eyes. They seemed darker blue than normal and a little hazy. The dance floor probably wasn't a good place for such a personal conversation, but I didn't want to stop dancing. Was this how easy it was? You suddenly find yourself aroused by an old friend? Your mind says one thing, but your body says another, with unpredictable consequences? Was that what had happened to Heli and Andreas?

When the song ended, I excused myself and went to the ladies' room, where I looked at myself in the mirror and noticed a twinkle in my eye I hadn't seen in ages. Angrily I slapped my own face, then dabbed on some powder to replace the makeup I'd smeared on Taskinen's coat. When I left, Koivu was coming out of the men's room at the same time.

"Was she in there?" he asked.

"Who?"

"Ursula, damn it. She's been glued to me all night. She's pretty and all, but I'm not interested. I don't want an office Christmas party hookup. Come dance and save me."

I felt far safer dancing with Koivu than I had with Taskinen. Unfortunately, though, the band was now playing the most appalling rendition of Genesis's "I Can't Dance" I'd ever heard. After four songs, I had to get my water, so I left Koivu to try his luck with the civilians.

Back at the table, Jyrki had just finished his cognac and was staring sadly into the round bottom of the glass. Puupponen was holding forth on Sasha Smeds's rally career with some guys from Robbery, one of whom claimed he'd gone to school with Juha Kankkunen, a legendary rally driver. I joined in the chatter and, for a while, managed to convince my colleagues that I was a rally expert, but my glory faded when I couldn't remember what manufacturer Tommi Mäkinen drove for. I did even worse at Formula 1. In vain I tried to change the subject to music. I felt like one more gin and tonic, but I knew that would probably turn tomorrow's mild headache into divine vengeance. For once I surprised myself by being sensible and opting for more water instead. Taskinen offered to get it for me, since he wanted a beer.

After he brought the drinks, he asked me to dance again, and I agreed because the Formula 1 discussion was becoming increasingly heated. The band was back to playing slow, syrupy melodies that caught in the singer's gravelly throat.

"I would never listen to music like this voluntarily," I said to Jyrki at the next break as we were standing at the edge of the floor, holding hands like two teenagers.

"Why not? A wonderful band and wonderful music, the most wonderful night of my life," Jyrki lisped and snatched me by the waist into a tango. Our subordinates stared as we bent and spun to the music, and I was at once bemused and terrified.

The party ended at one thirty, and by that time I'd broken down and had that extra gin and tonic and only danced with Taskinen. Some of our colleagues were headed into Helsinki for more, but I thought it best to head home, because I still wanted to read through Annukka Hackman's Sasha Smeds papers over the weekend. Taskinen thought sharing a taxi was a good idea, although, in reality, my house was significantly out of the way to his. We sat in the back seat hand in hand and side by side, and it felt all too natural. For a moment I imagined how it would feel to be going to the same address.

Jyrki refused to let me pay my part of the fare and insisted on walking me to the stairs. There he kissed me, and I couldn't help responding. I was surprised by how the kiss was so unlike Jyrki, hard and demanding.

At home the house was quiet. I expected to see the cat coming to demand his food, but the kitchen floor was empty. I made a cheese sandwich, drank a liter of water, and thanked my lucky stars I wouldn't have to see Taskinen until Monday.

11

It sleeted the entire weekend, and the kids spent hours in front of the TV. I remembered how I'd disapproved of Moomin videos before I had my own children, but now they felt like lifesavers. Antti read something in Swedish, and I continued with Sasha Smeds's biography, but it didn't say a word about Andreas and Heli. I tried to reach Atro Jääskeläinen to ask whether the police had actually received the final version of the manuscript, but he didn't answer his phone. Sini's cell phone was turned off too. The funeral wouldn't be until next weekend, and by Sunday afternoon I was sick of waiting. I asked a patrol car to visit the Jääskeläinen residence and deliver Atro a request to be at the police station at ten on Monday morning for an interview. Liisa Rasilainen was on duty and called an hour later to tell me no one answered the door but that the patrol had left an official request in the mailbox.

I understood Jääskeläinen wanting to keep his phone off—I'm sure he was as fed up with the constant pressure from reporters as I was. Over the weekend the newspapers had found space for something besides Sasha Smeds's accident: for a change, Carcass Kervinen had both tabloids hounding him. Somehow their reporters had found out that one of the forensic pathologists the police used had dated Annukka Hackman and that we'd interrogated him. Kervinen refused to give any interviews, but Atro Jääskeläinen had told the papers about the relationship, wondering aloud why Kervinen was still walking around free.

Updates on Sasha's condition appeared in every newscast. In addition to second-degree burns, he'd suffered injuries to his lumbar spine. It was probable he'd live, but for the time being it was impossible to say whether he'd get behind the wheel or even walk again. There was a glimpse of Heli in one clip, holding her hands in front of her face and looking small and frightened before the flashing cameras. Two massive security guards stood next to her.

The time of year had arrived when I never had time to get outside when it was light. On Sunday night I went for a run after the kids were asleep, and the streetlights dictated my route. I wasn't usually afraid of jogging in the dark, but now every shadow lurking beyond the light was a threat. The fragility of life felt too present: Annukka Hackman certainly hadn't known she would die when she went out swimming, and Sasha Smeds had been ready to celebrate becoming a world champion. As I ran, I thought of Heli and felt sorry for her. Then I imagined Terttu Taskinen's withdrawn face. There had always been something distant and bitter about her, although based on pictures I'd seen, Terttu had been very beautiful when she was young. Taskinen kept a picture of her from their wedding day on his desk, which Koivu and Puupponen thought was funny for some reason. Why had Taskinen chosen to tell me Terttu was jealous of me?

Just then there was a rustle in the willows, causing me to trip and nearly fall flat on my face. A bushy-haired German shepherd walked out with no owner in sight. The dog jogged along with me for a while, but then turned back. Owning a big dog like that definitely would have made me feel safer, but our apartment was too small. We didn't even have room for a cat.

When I arrived home I realized I was shaking. Antti looked up from the short story collection he was reading and asked why I looked so pale. I told him about the dog, then went into the next room to stretch and remove my sweaty clothes. I felt cold, so I stood under the hot shower for at least fifteen minutes, and even thought about heating up the sauna, but settled for whiskey instead. That didn't help the shaking either. In the end, I put on warm pajamas and thick socks, pulled an extra blanket out of the closet, and climbed into bed under a mound of covers.

In the morning it was well below freezing, and the car didn't want to start despite the engine block heater. Taneli looked like a small animal in his snowsuit and balaclava, which Iida refused to wear because she thought it was too childish.

"I'm the adult and I know that a balaclava is the best choice in weather like this," I said with finality. Some of Iida's friends were already dressing like tiny adults, with crop tops and earrings. There was even perfume made for kids, but I thought preschool was a little early for that too. Sometimes on the weekend I'd let Iida try my makeup, although a little girl with half her face covered in violet eye shadow was an appalling sight. I'd done exactly the same thing as a child before I hit my tomboy stage, at which point I didn't touch makeup for a few years. Then, during my punk phase, I got into heavy eyeliner and black lipstick, which horrified my own mother.

When I pulled into the police department a loud bang came from the left rear tire, and the car's balance shifted. The tire had burst. I managed to get the car into my normal parking spot, where I opened the trunk and found the lug wrench. As I was bending down next to the defective tire, I heard Ursula's voice behind me.

"Are you changing your own tire? Isn't that what subordinates are for—and men?"

I looked up at her. "I guess. But this is my car."

"And we have a meeting starting in five minutes. Makkonen!" Ursula yelled at one of the young guys from Patrol who was walking by. "Handle Detective Kallio's tire and leave the keys at the desk downstairs."

Makkonen obeyed submissively. I didn't know whether I should be irritated or thankful to Ursula, so I wasn't either. In a way she was right, but her interference still bothered me.

"And I assume you don't have a maid?" she asked once we were in the elevator, as I tried without success to rub the mud stains off my gloves.

"Our apartment isn't that big, and Antti usually vacuums."

"Well, I live in a studio and just hired an Estonian girl under the table to come once a week. She irons too. On a police salary I can't afford a legal maid, but I also don't have time for cleaning." Ursula fixed her bangs. That's when I remembered that I'd seen mascara on my cheeks again when I caught my reflection in the car's rearview mirror earlier, so apparently that promise about being waterproof was a scam.

In the meeting I asked Koivu to partner with me for Atro Jääskeläinen's interview. Puupponen thought we also needed to bring Carcass Kervinen in for another talking-to. Today's papers all posited that Annukka Hackman's spurned lover was guilty, and berated the police for going down blind alleys and harassing the innocent.

"Apparently Atro Jääskeläinen is talking to the papers," Koivu said.

"And all this publicity is good for the book he's about to publish. The final version is probably already at the printer, but it looks like he only gave us a draft. I've read and reread the manuscript, but I can't find anything that would cause a splash."

"We didn't find any other version in Hackman's office," I said. "But she could have stored it in a safe deposit box or something. Let's see what Atro Jääskeläinen has to say when he comes in. What's the situation with the murder weapon, Petri?"

Puustjärvi, who'd only returned to work today, sat as far as possible from Ursula. He said there was still no sign of the weapon. But the report had come back on a trail of size forty-one rubber boot prints that had been found during the initial search of the lake area. It continued from Mäyrä Road to close to the place where Annukka Hackman had left her clothes.

"The sole was from a Nokian Kontio Classic, and the boots were relatively new. Should I go check out all of our prime suspects' shoes?" Puustjärvi asked.

"Forty-one is either a man with small feet or a gigantic woman," Puupponen said. "Who would fit that? Atro Jääskeläinen? Or Viktor Smeds? It's strange that the Smeds boys are so tall given how short their parents are." Puupponen glanced at me in alarm, and I grinned back. He enjoyed making fun of my height, and I made a point of commenting on his freckles. Together we'd come to the conclusion that we only ribbed the people we really liked.

Fortunately, the unit's other cases were moving along nicely, but I still left the meeting feeling depressed and cold even though I was wearing my thickest sweater. Koivu and I had arranged to interview Atro Jääskeläinen in one of the downstairs interrogation rooms instead of my office. Being in the same hall as our holding cells put the fear of God in most people, and I wanted that advantage.

"How do you know there's a newer version of the manuscript?" Koivu asked as we exited the elevator in the basement. Someone was pounding on the door of holding cell number three, and an officer was dragging a vomit-covered teenage boy in heroin withdrawal toward the showers.

"I had a conversation with Heli Haapala." For some reason I didn't want to tell Koivu about Heli and Andreas's affair. I didn't think Koivu would run to the papers, but the wall around this secret was becoming increasingly fragile, and Sasha and his parents didn't need anything else to worry about just now. Of course it wasn't my job to protect them, but I felt a strange sisterhood with Heli, although I knew I couldn't let this feeling influence my actions in any serious way.

The patrol brought Atro Jääskeläinen in at seven past ten. He looked bloated and haggard, and his eyelids were like cocktail sausages.

You could see that he'd loosened his belt one notch by the open, worn hole that was now visible.

"Good morning, Mr. Jääskeläinen. Would you like some coffee or juice?" I asked in a friendly tone, but at the same time I turned the Interrogation Room 2 lamp so it left me and Koivu in shadow and shone straight in Jääskeläinen's face. He tried to shift his position in the chair he'd slouched into, but that didn't help.

"So you still haven't caught my wife's murderer? You're protecting Kervinen because he's one of your own. It's disgusting."

"We aren't protecting anyone," I answered. "Has it occurred to you that all these articles blaming Kervinen are protecting the real murderer? Let the police handle the public relations."

"But you aren't telling the press anything!"

"We're saying as much we think is wise. Let's start the interview," I said, then started the recorder. "Present Lieutenant Maria Kallio and Sergeant Koivu, time ten thirteen, November . . ." I hadn't dictated the beginning of an interrogation in ages, and it felt strangely satisfying. I started by asking Jääskeläinen's shoe size, which made him laugh in confusion.

"Forty-one or two."

Jääskeläinen denied owning any rubber boots; he wasn't the walking-in-the-woods type. And he swore he'd turned over every version of Annukka's manuscript.

"How much did your wife tell you about how her work was progressing? Did she tell you everything she'd found out?"

"The book was Annukka's project. I considered putting it off or canceling it when Sasha Smeds refused to cooperate anymore, but Annukka talked me out of it. When will I get the manuscript and background material back? Even though Sasha still didn't win the championship, the accident and his recovery are good stuff for the final chapter. We're just starting to run short on time to hit the Christmas market. That's the best way to honor Annukka's memory, to give her final work to the world."

Koivu and I both asked, in different words, whether we'd been given the final manuscript. We each received the same response: the only version of the book that existed was the one Jääskeläinen had already given to the police. I knew the unit's secretary had made copies of everything, so I decided to let Jääskeläinen have the manuscript disks and other materials back.

"Where is Annukka being buried?" I asked once the official interview was over.

"The service is in Olari Church, then she's being cremated. Annukka said once she didn't want to leave a grave behind, although we hadn't really talked about these things much yet. We only talked about it once after we had two close calls on the freeway back to back. Annukka was only thirty-two, and people her age aren't supposed to die."

After Jääskeläinen left with Koivu, I stayed and sat in the dark interrogation room for a while. I didn't have a clue how we should proceed. It was like I was leading a homicide investigation for the first time. During the last year of my maternity leave, I'd considered pursuing other jobs, like applying for a prosecutor position or Interpol. Perhaps I should have. But of course family stood in the way of the latter. As long as Antti's job situation was uncertain, I didn't dare make any big changes in my own life.

It was possible that Heli had lied about Annukka's discovery of the affair with Andreas, but why would she have done that? A version of the manuscript with the Heli-Andreas revelation probably had existed, and it had probably been destroyed or hidden in the same place as the gun used to kill Annukka. I needed someone to talk to. Maybe Jyrki would be free.

"I just came from a working lunch and thought I'd take a nap on the couch," he admitted when I walked through his door. "I didn't get much sleep last night."

"Terttu keeping you up?" I asked as he sat up.

"At two I made her take a sleeping pill. She hasn't been willing to take sick leave. She says she'll go crazy if she doesn't have something to do. The results are coming at the end of the week. Whatever they say, anything is better than this waiting. And then to top it all off she found a red hair on the collar of my jacket and a smear of makeup on the front."

"You should have said it was Puupponen's," I said, laughing, but my throat felt hot. I didn't want the conversation to go there—I was muddled up enough as it was. "Jyrki, I need some advice. I suspect there's another version of Annukka Hackman's manuscript somewhere. According to Jääskeläinen it isn't in the company safe or anywhere else in the building, but I can't be sure he's telling the truth. I want to execute another search on Annukka's house and the family business, as well as the Smedses' house and Jouko Suuronen's place."

Taskinen's expression tightened.

"That sounds pretty desperate. The press will make it sound like we're fumbling around in the dark," he said. I felt a blush spread across my cheeks; Taskinen was right. And besides, if the new manuscript existed, Suuronen, Sasha, or Heli could have taken it with them when they left Finland and easily destroyed it.

"And we still have a pair of rubber boots to find," I said and started to laugh again, although tears weren't far off. "Maybe we should arrest Kervinen at least for show. Do you remember how big his feet are?"

"Maria, calm down. These cases have always worked out before. Annukka Hackman is no Kyllikki Saari," Jyrki said, referring to the most infamous unsolved murder in Finnish history. He stood up and took my hands, and I let him hold them for a few seconds before I left for lunch.

When I was finishing my salmon pasta, the duty officer at the front desk called to tell me I had a visitor. Since I'd intended to spend the whole afternoon wrestling with a compensation planning questionnaire,

I was perfectly happy with the interruption. When I arrived at the desk to pick up my car keys and meet my guest, there was a surprise in store for me. I'd expected some friend or another, but instead Andreas Smeds was standing in the lobby. This was the first time I'd seen him washed and groomed. He was wearing a trendy black leather jacket, and the rest of his outfit was black as well. The whites of his eyes looked red against his pale face. His cheekbones stood out, and he bit his lip. I decided to take him to my office and call for backup as necessary.

"Heli says hi," Andreas said as we sat down to coffee around the table in my office. I hadn't turned the tape recorder on yet. "She called last night and told me about your conversation. Does the whole police department know yet?"

"No. I—"

"Heli was out of her senses when she told you," Andreas interrupted. "She's always expected a catastrophe, so when Annukka busted us . . ." Andreas gave a crooked smile. "Busted is right—like two kids smoking cigarettes. Anyway, afterward, Heli said we had to tell Sasha. I refused and went to see Annukka to try to talk some sense into her. I got her to promise she'd wait to expose us until after the world championship. It was in her best interest too, since the book would sell more if Sasha won. She wasn't thinking of Sasha's feelings, just the money. No one's feelings mattered to her."

"When did you have this discussion with Ms. Hackman?"

"The day Dad got out of the hospital, sometime in the middle of September. I went to pick up Mom and Dad, but I drove by Annukka's office on the way. No one else was there. Annukka said she was fine sitting on the information. It would give her something to publish that hadn't been in the papers yet."

"Why did you wait until now to tell me this?"

"Because I came to ask you to keep it quiet!" Andreas placed his hands on his knees and leaned toward me, and the alarm in his eyes looked anything but fake. "Sasha's going to recover, but he'll be weak for a long time. Dad is still recovering too, and it's already a miracle he survived Sasha's accident. And Heli is a complete mess. I'm not asking for myself; I'm asking for them."

"Did Annukka blackmail you and Heli?"

"People like her don't like silence; they want publicity."

I wasn't sure what game Andreas was playing or whether he was really a gambler at all. He had at least as strong a motive to kill Hackman as Kervinen did, and his alibi wasn't any great shakes. I knew that I should have called in a witness and had Andreas repeat his story on tape, but I decided to take a risk myself. Maybe the road to solving the crime would be through Heli and Andreas's trust.

"So Annukka promised not to publicize your affair before Sasha's biography appeared?"

Andreas stood and walked to the window. The day was cloudy despite the cold, and the occasional snowflakes looked lost as they fell slowly to the ground.

"Right. We got a couple months of a grace period to arrange things. Of course I should have left and Heli should have asked Sasha to forgive her. That sounds simple, but the reality was a little different. Do you know how it feels to sit ten centimeters from the woman you love and not even be able to touch her? Do you know how it feels to read about your brother's happy, functional marriage and know that it's true and a big fucking lie all at the same time? Do you know how it feels when someone thinks it's their right to reveal your feelings to the whole world as if they belong to everyone, as if anyone should get to comment on them and mock them? 'Look at that goddamn loser,' they'd say. 'When he couldn't keep up with his brother on the track, he tried to take his wife instead.' I'm not arguing that I don't deserve every nasty thing anyone has said and is going to say about me. I'm a good-for-nothing bastard and I know it. But I've never wanted to hurt anyone else."

"I think you already did," I responded quietly.

"Yes, I did."

However cathartic this may have been for Andreas, I needed to get back to what I really wanted to know.

"Did Annukka Hackman tell you where she stored the manuscript to her book?"

Andreas looked at me, startled.

"The newspapers said the police have it!"

"And we do. Do you have a copy of it too?"

"No," Andreas answered, but he turned his face toward the window again so it fell into shadow. "I know this is ridiculous, but can you keep your subordinates from leaking this to the press?"

"I always require my subordinates to respect witnesses' privacy."

"Thank you." Andreas returned to the table and sipped the rest of his coffee. His hands were surprisingly small and his fingers surprisingly slender for such a tall man. Instinctively I looked at his feet as well. His shiny black shoes were at least size forty-four. The Smeds family probably owned any number of rubber boots.

"Heli's coming back to Finland tomorrow. They're keeping Sasha sedated for now to reduce the stress on his body and allow the pressure in his brain to return to normal. At least I can go to the airport to meet her, and there's nothing wrong with hugging your sister-in-law. Oh God, this is so messed up!"

"Be prepared to repeat everything you just told me in an official interview later. And do you know whether Jouko Suuronen is in Finland?"

"He's coming on the same flight as Heli tomorrow. The Citroën team will take care of Sasha. How could he make such a stupid driving mistake? He was the best in the world! If Heikki dies, Sasha will never forgive himself."

Maybe Andreas was afraid that Sasha had found out and caused the accident on purpose. Whatever the case, he didn't seem to have any more information, so I said I had work to do and asked him to leave. I called someone to escort him back downstairs. After the door closed behind them, I remained sitting on the couch. The coffee was giving me heartburn, so I searched for some antacid tablets in my purse. I knew I was probably doing the wrong thing by protecting Heli and Andreas, and it was making me anxious. A strong intuition told me that Heli wasn't capable of murder or of protecting a murderer, but people have done much crazier things for love before.

Since we were running out of options, I decided to issue all the search warrants I'd been considering, knowing I'd end up with half the world breathing down my neck, especially Jouko Suuronen and the media. The compensation planning questionnaire suddenly felt like a pleasant diversion. It was mostly multiple choice, so it didn't require much thought. My colleagues and I had watched with great amusement as the parliamentary election candidates had promised to increase police funding and salaries. People's sense of insecurity was increasing, and the police were seen as the heroes who would drive the drug dealers and motorcycle gangs out of their neighborhoods onto some reservation somewhere. But that required money. No wonder public support for the death penalty had been on the rise. Longer jail sentences would require increased social spending, but executions might save money. Few dared to utter such thoughts out loud, but I knew there were people even in my own profession who'd had enough of constantly catching and interrogating the same people. Lähde and Autio ran a betting pool on our most common suspects, laying down money on how long it would take each convicted knife fighter or rapist to get collared again for the same crime after their release. Usually the one who bet on the shorter time won. Actually homicides had decreased lately, although that was hard to believe if you watched the news.

I almost had the survey filled out when my door buzzer rang. I pressed the green button, curious since most of my colleagues knew my door wasn't locked and always just knocked. Ursula walked in wearing a strangely uncertain expression.

"What's up?" I said as I typed the last few words on the survey form. The typewriter felt clunky and old fashioned, but the form wasn't available in an electronic format yet.

"You probably aren't going to like what you're about to hear, but you're the head of this unit, and I have to file a sexual harassment complaint."

"OK. What's the problem?" I asked calmly, although I couldn't remember ever being so bewildered.

"It's Pekka Koivu. I could have let what happened at the Christmas party go because he was drunk, but today was different." Ursula sat down on the couch and crossed her legs. Her eye makeup and panty hose were both a shiny silver, and her nails had the same silvery polish on them I'd seen Friday night. Ursula had a confident sense of style.

"What did Koivu do?" I had a hard time believing what I was hearing, even though Koivu had tried to get me to spend the night with him when we were at the Helsinki PD. I only had to say no once, though.

"At the Christmas party he tried to grope me under my skirt when I came out of the bathroom. He suggested we get a room together at the hotel. When I said that didn't work for me, he started calling me a whore for giving it up to everyone else in the unit. As if that was any of his business! Today we happened to be in the elevator together, and he pushed me against the wall and stuck his hand down my skirt." Ursula's face burned red, and there were tears in her eyes.

"Were there any witnesses?"

"Of course not! He was careful about where he attacked me. The bathroom hall was empty, and no one else was in the elevator. I demand that he be transferred to another unit."

12

The rest of the day was a mess. Of course I had to call Koivu in for questioning. I caught him at the Jääskeläinen search. He'd promised Anu he'd go straight home from there, but I said he had to come back to the station. Antti would have to pick up our kids. Ursula waited at the station to see if Koivu would confess. Sexual harassment was nothing new in our department, and a couple of times the alleged victim, instead of the accused perpetrator, had been moved into another job. I didn't want that, although I couldn't bear the thought of giving up working with Koivu.

Koivu and I had first met a decade ago when we were both on the force in Helsinki. He then followed a woman to Joensuu in the northeast of the country, but shortly thereafter I ended up filling in as sheriff for the summer in my hometown just up the road. When Koivu's romance ended, he was easy to lure to Espoo. He was a trusted partner and friend, like a brother to me, and I never would have imagined my brother being a sexual predator. When I realized I was already defending Koivu, I started to get irritated with myself. A minidress didn't give anyone the right to grope a woman, nor did her flirting with other men. Nothing did.

It was past four when Koivu finally sat down in my office. Without any introduction or attempt to soften it, I told him about Ursula's accusations. Koivu went pale, took off his glasses, and looked at me like an alien from outer space.

"You don't believe that shit, do you? The truth is exactly the opposite. Ursula was the one who was chasing me around the Christmas party! I even told you so. If anyone was committing sexual harassment it was her, but men aren't supposed to get upset over that; we're supposed to like it! Ursula can tell me I'm hot all she wants, but if I say the same thing it's a crime. Fuck this . . ."

"Did you tell her she was hot?"

"Yes, when she asked if I liked her new party dress. I said it was hot. That's it. And yes, I was in the elevator with her today, but I didn't lay a finger on her. I'm not interested in her."

"So Ursula's lying?"

"Yes. Do you think she's telling the truth?"

I shook my head, but I didn't feel terribly relieved. It was just Koivu's word against Ursula's, and everyone in the building knew what close friends Koivu and I were. I was furious at Ursula for playing with something so serious, and angry at myself that I'd been so enthusiastic to hire her. My instincts had failed me.

"I'll try to talk some sense into Ursula. I don't know if she's mentioned this to anyone besides me yet. Hopefully not."

"Why on earth would she make an accusation like this?" Koivu rubbed his glasses on his shirt sleeve, then put them back on his face.

"Hard to say. I'll talk to her again. You go home, and say hi to Anu."

Koivu shook his head and stood up. Recently, he'd begun to look even more like a teddy bear, with his noticeable belly. Suddenly I felt like patting it, but I didn't. Instead I went to find Ursula, who shared an office with Autio. She was sitting in front of her computer, with a picture of a rally car showing on the screen. Apparently she was tracking Sasha Smeds's condition.

"I had a chat with Koivu," I told her. "He denies harassing you."

Ursula stood up and took a step toward me. The foundation and powder on her face couldn't cover the way she blushed.

"Of course he does. What did you expect? The only question is whether you believe him or me. Don't you understand that it always works this way, Maria? The woman is always labeled as a liar. You always trumpet your feminism, but when the rubber meets the road, you take the men's side. It doesn't feel good. Could you please leave my office?"

I looked Ursula straight in the eyes. They were bright blue, and there wasn't a single clump in her mascara.

"Listen, Ursula, spreading lies about other people isn't part of my feminism."

"Why do you believe Koivu and not me? Did you ask Koivu to prove he hadn't harassed me? Doesn't it say a lot about a man that he chose some Vietnamese girl for a wife? They're so obedient and submissive. No equality required!"

Ursula's description fit Anu Wang so poorly I couldn't contain my laugh. At Koivu's wedding reception, his male colleagues had teased him mercilessly about being henpecked.

"Have you ever met Anu, Koivu's wife?" I asked. "I'm guessing not. Let's just say your little theory doesn't hold much water." I felt like telling Ursula that I knew about the Puustjärvi incident, but fortunately I managed to hold my tongue. That had nothing to do with this.

"So you intend to ignore this?" Ursula asked in a rage. "Well I don't! I'll take it as high as I have to. I'll talk to the ombudsman today and make sure everyone knows my boss isn't taking me seriously. Then we'll see who has to leave!"

"I agree that it's in everyone's best interest that this matter gets cleared up," I replied calmly, even though I could feel my own cheeks burning and wanted to scream at the top of my lungs. Then I left Ursula's office before I could say anything else I might regret.

I had to go sit in my office for a while before I dared to get behind the wheel. The whole time a revolting doubt nagged at me: maybe

Ursula was right. Of course I was relieved that the case would shift from me to the ombudsman and the department's workplace safety officer, but I wouldn't be able to avoid some involvement.

On the way home, the lights from the surrounding cars and buildings seemed to stab at my eyes; all I wanted was complete darkness. Nonetheless, I decided to stop by the Big Apple Mall to see if I could find Antti a fun combination birthday/name day gift, since both were coming up in a couple of weeks. As I wandered the halls of the shopping hell, I felt strangely divorced from reality. Christmas songs played faintly in the background, even though we'd barely made it to mid-November. We'd promised to go to Antti's parents' cabin in Inkoo for Christmas, because the idea of staying in the White Cube was so awful, and Antti's father didn't have many Christmases left. I'd promised to bake the ham, even though Antti's mother didn't approve of such unhealthy fare. The Sarkelas even only drank organic wine nowadays.

I walked up the stairs to the second floor and started when I saw two familiar figures sitting in the café: Rauha and Viktor Smeds. They were holding hands. The Smedses had been together for forty years, and they still obviously felt a great deal of affection for one another. The sight of them made me swallow hard. I tried to slip by them unnoticed but failed. Rauha looked up just as I was walking into the men's clothing store next door.

"Detective Kallio, come over here!" It was a command, not a request, so I obeyed. There were two half-empty café au laits at the Smedses' table, along with a cheese sandwich cut in two. Taking a chair from a neighboring table, I sat down even though I hadn't been invited to.

"Do you know why we're here? We're running away from the police. We left Andreas to handle them. They came at four o'clock and started going through our things. Is that really necessary?"

"You aren't the only ones whose house is being searched," I said.

"What are you looking for? The gun Ms. Hackman was killed with? We don't have any guns other than Sasha's hunting rifle, and it hasn't been used in years. There are always races during hunting season."

"So the rest of you aren't shooters?"

"Viktor used to go out in the forest with the boys. But I don't know how to shoot. My father thought guns were the root of all evil. Luckily he was too old to be sent to the front during the war, because he would have preferred to kill himself than raise a weapon at another person. The boys went to the army of course, although I was against it."

"My husband did civil service. Maybe my son will choose the army to rebel," I offered.

"Maybe. How old is your son?"

"Just two. I'm really sorry about Sasha's accident, but I understand he'll pull through."

Viktor Smeds trembled, and Rauha squeezed his hand tighter.

"We've known from the beginning that something like this could happen," Rauha said. "If you play with death, there's always the danger that the game will go too far."

Rauha's face was hard. I wondered if this attitude toward Sasha's accident was a coping mechanism: her son had chosen his sport and the risks that went with it. Rauha and Viktor didn't fit in the glossy world of the shopping center. People their age didn't appear in any of the advertisements, and if they did, they were what you might call well preserved: slim, barely any wrinkles, always smiling. Viktor was a frail old man who probably couldn't walk from one end of the mall to the other, and Rauha's face bore the years she had lived, but I guessed most of the wrinkles were from laughter rather than tears. Their shopping bag was crocheted out of old panty hose. My mother had made a similar one in the late sixties.

"I think I do know your in-laws, the Sarkelas," Rauha said. "I saw your mother-in-law at the post office yesterday and she expressed her condolences about Sasha's accident. They aren't from Degerö originally, are they?"

"No, they're from Vyborg."

"So they know what it's like to have to leave your home without any hope of returning too. When the police came today and started poking around everywhere, I remembered leaving the farm back in the fall of '44. I was only six at the time, but the memory is still vivid. We only had a few days to pack our things, to dig up the potatoes and the root vegetables and empty the cellars. The cows had to walk for kilometers because all the trucks were busy with the war. Maybe it was a mistake to stay so close, in Innanbäck. Home was only a few kilometers away, but still out of reach. The people from Karelia had to go farther when the Russians took their land. Hopefully it was easier for them."

"My mother-in-law spent her school years in Turku and never adapted to the dialect," I said and motioned the waiter over. I ordered a cappuccino, even though I knew Antti was already waiting at home with dinner.

"It's strange that so many of the people who insist that Russia return Karelia loudly oppose accepting refugees and immigrants to Finland," Rauha continued once the server had left to fetch my coffee. "I would think they'd understand that few people leave their homes of their own free will and that they always want to go back."

My coffee arrived, and I warmed my cold hands on the cup. Rauha Smeds told me they were on their way to the movies.

"Of course I could sic the tabloids on you police, but what good would that do? I didn't choose to have my personal business discussed in public. Annukka Hackman didn't understand that. She thought that everyone wants to reveal all their most intimate details to the whole country. What a strange idea." Then, turning to her husband, she said, "Viktor, the show will be starting soon. And you still have to go—" Rauha cut her remark short and stood up briskly. As she helped Viktor out of his chair, I also jumped up, but Rauha shook her head. They would be fine. After they left, I called Puustjärvi, who was leading the search of Smedsbo Farm, and asked him to leave everything as tidy as possible.

"This guy here's been making a lot of noise. We've been thinking about taking him in." The voice coming across the line now was Akkila's, from Patrol. He'd apparently taken the phone from Puustjärvi. "And he's obviously drunk," he added.

"Andreas Smeds? Don't arrest him if you don't have to," I said. Akkila was known for his hair trigger and excessive use of force.

I sat for a while sipping my cappuccino and watching passersby. The middle-aged women were all in a hurry, each with a family at home waiting for dinner or an aerobics class about to start. The teenagers traveled in packs, the adult men alone. The Somali women usually had two companions and a swarm of children. I didn't feel like I belonged to any group, and that detachment felt good for a second. Then my phone started playing Antti's ringtone.

"I'm coming, I'm coming. I'm just getting a couple of bottles of wine," I answered with unnecessary testiness. There was no escaping reality, and it was pointless imagining that I could. But right now I didn't feel like I had it in me to cope. Antti's present was a bust, but luckily I still had a couple of weeks. Maybe I'd be able to come up with an amazing idea yet.

The world outside the brightly lit mall seemed especially dark. Parking structures had made me uncomfortable ever since I'd been forced to investigate a body found in one. I thought of Rauha Smeds's talk of leaving and going into exile. I hadn't remembered that the Porkkala lease was originally intended to last until 1994. Finland would have been completely different if the Soviets had been that close to the capital for that many decades. Nokia and Neste never would have dared to build their headquarters in Espoo, only six miles from a Soviet naval base, and the whole city probably would have remained a backwater suburb of Helsinki.

I drove home and parked my car next to dozens of others, and breathed in the smell of the neighborhood: gasoline, cold air, and freezer-aisle pizza. During the rest of the evening I did laundry, sewed on missing buttons, and finally went through Iida's clothes. The dresses that were too small would end up at the flea market—I didn't think Taneli would be interested in flowery blouses and frilly bloomers in a few years. The kids were excited about the pile of clothes and demanded to play hedgehog under it. A steady bass thumping came from the unit upstairs: apparently the parents of the teenage boy who lived there weren't home, so he could play his rap full blast for once. I tried to be understanding, since I'd been that age once and had enjoyed blaring my punk records to horrify my family. Still the constant beat irritated me. *At least when I was a kid we had our own house,* I thought. But buying a house in rural Arpikylä on two teachers' salaries wasn't any problem. Unlike in present-day Espoo.

After Taneli fell asleep I opened a bottle of red wine, and after a few drinks realized why I was so agitated: I would have liked to be at the searches, especially at the Smedses' place and Kervinen's apartment. Hanging around at home when all I could think about was work anyway seemed like a waste of time. I wouldn't survive this investigation without Koivu, but how could I suggest that Ursula be transferred somewhere else while the harassment allegations were being investigated? I managed to drink almost the whole bottle of Tollo before I finally forced myself to go to sleep.

The next morning it was sleeting again, and my shoes got soaked in the day care parking lot. Taneli seemed like he was coming down with a cold, but Antti had to be in a project wrap-up meeting, and I couldn't be away from work either. In the morning meeting Ursula sat in the front row and didn't look at anyone, staring instead at the map of Espoo and Kirkkonummi on the east wall of the room, which we used to mark the central locations of all the cases we currently had open. Koivu sat as far as possible from Ursula, as did Puustjärvi. Puupponen was trying to talk about a movie he'd seen the night before, but nobody wanted to listen. Everyone seemed relieved when I moved on to business.

Puustjärvi had been at the Smeds search and reported that Andreas had spent the whole time sitting in the kitchen draining a case of beer and yelling at the cops. The results of the search were slim. The Smeds had a license for the hunting rifle, and it hadn't been shot in years. Our people had managed to go through a few of the disks they found, but none of them had any hint of Annukka Hackman's manuscript.

"We checked all the cars and outbuildings too, but no one bothered digging through the manure heaps or disassembling the milking machines. It's amazing that Smeds's brother could manage alone with the cows, he was so drunk. Maybe the animals don't care about the smell, and the machine does the actual milking anyway," Puustjärvi said.

Our team hadn't gotten into Suuronen's home, though. Suuronen was still abroad and the property wasn't part of any management cooperative that would have a key. I cursed myself for having let so many of my prime suspects leave the country. I'd really made a mess of this investigation.

Lehtovuori had been at Kervinen's place. "We confiscated all of Carcass's diaries," Lehtovuori said. "Very interesting reading. He keeps a list of all the people he opens up, with the cause of death and some really friendly comments. He's a real perv. Do I have to read them all?"

"I assume you looked at what he wrote on the day of Hackman's murder?"

"I did. It's just empty. So is the day after that. And Carcass didn't write anything about Hackman's autopsy."

"Since he didn't do it. How many diaries are there?"

"Ten."

"Read the ones that tell about Hackman and Kervinen's relationship first, and make me a summary. Heli Haapala is coming back to Finland today, as well as Jouko Suuronen apparently. Autio, let's try that search again after the master of the house returns." Knowing that Jouko Suuronen was going to jump on me for searching his house was the least of my concerns.

"And Kervinen had a pair of size forty-one Nokian Kontio Classics," Lehtovuori added. "Small feet for a man. We confiscated them. They're at the lab right now."

I almost whooped with delight. The footprint comparison would take a couple of days, but with any luck they might even find some mud from the lake. A couple of pairs of boots had been brought back from the Smedses' farm too. And the Jääskeläinens had another pair of size forty-one Kontio Classics, apparently Annukka's old mushrooming boots.

"How did Kervinen react to the search?"

"He left. Said he was going to work. His sick leave had run out, and his bosses wouldn't give him any more. But with the way his hands were shaking, I doubt he could hold a scalpel."

"Don't want those Y-incisions turning into Xs," Puupponen said, but no one laughed. It was as if the sleet had invaded our moods. Who had Ursula already told about Koivu's alleged harassment? I wondered as I watched my team trudge out of the room at the end of the meeting. Gone were the normal joking and camaraderie. Had we even had a feeling of unity this fall, or was that just a memory of the past, from the days before my latest maternity leave?

During the meeting the department workplace safety officer had left a message on my phone. Jarmo Alavirta worked in the Traffic Division, and I only knew him from department meetings. Begrudgingly I returned his call.

"Senior Officer Ursula Honkanen has made a report of repeated sexual harassment. She says she also reported the matter to her immediate superior, meaning you, but apparently you didn't believe her or promise to transfer the perpetrator in question to another assignment."

"The perpetrator in question, meaning Sergeant Koivu, flatly denies the accusation."

"And you, as a one-woman judge and jury, decided to leave the matter at that?" Alavirta asked angrily. "A report has already gone to your superior and the chief ombudsman. We will be investigating both Koivu's actions and your own."

"Go right ahead," I snapped and hung up, wishing with all my heart that Puustjärvi had never confided in me. I didn't want to drag him into this mess, but if things got bad enough I'd have to. A few minutes later, the unit's secretary brought me a stack of preliminary investigation reports that needed signing before going to the prosecutor. I read all of them only to give myself something else to think about. Heli and Suuronen's flight would land at eleven, and Autio would be waiting for Suuronen at the airport.

At eleven thirty a knock came at my door. I knew from the style of the knock that it was Taskinen.

"Maria, this is an order from your superior. You're going to have lunch with me at the Rosso in Kauniainen. I'm driving."

"Right now?"

"Well, I'm hungry at least. I woke up at six and ran fifteen kilometers."

"No bragging," I said to lighten the mood, because I knew this wasn't going to be a chitchat sort of lunch. When I stopped in the ladies' room to touch up my lipstick, I was shocked to see how deep the furrows in my brow were. And my hair lacked any luster—it was probably time to visit the salon for a color touch-up.

"Did you have a hangover Saturday?" Taskinen asked in the elevator, where there were others besides us.

"No. Just tired."

"I did. First time in six years. I didn't go running that day." Taskinen tried to grin but failed.

The restaurant was full, so we had to wait for a table. Taskinen told me what was new with Silja and asked if I knew any more specifics about Sasha Smeds's condition. He waited until we were seated at a quiet window table and had ordered our pasta. Then, he got to the point.

"So your subordinate Ursula Honkanen is accusing Koivu of sexual harassment and you for choosing to believe a man over a woman. Ursula just visited my office, and she's prepared to make a lot of noise about this. She threatened to contact the press and the union if she doesn't get justice."

"So what were her demands?"

"Shelving Koivu until the incident has been investigated and then transferring him to another unit or department." Taskinen poked at his salad. "This is going to get ugly. What did Koivu say?"

"That the truth was exactly the opposite, and you saw it yourself at the Christmas party . . ."

"Yes, I did. But you know as well as I do that we're both Koivu's friends, and you know that friends of accused sexual predators almost always say that their friend is a stand-up guy who would never do something like that. Do you believe all of them?"

Our clam pasta arrived, and Taskinen started dumping parmesan on his. I wasn't hungry, but I tried to eat anyway. Low blood sugar could make my hands shake so badly I had trouble pressing the buttons on my phone, let alone applying mascara.

"Maybe it would be best to give Koivu a special assignment directly under me for a while. There's always some office free somewhere in the building," Taskinen suggested cautiously.

"Hell no! We're shorthanded enough with the Hackman case, and we're getting nowhere. You were right about the house searches. We're grasping at straws. Maybe we should just transfer the case to the National Bureau of Investigation."

I tried to use a spoon and a fork to shovel the slick tagliatelle into my mouth, but it escaped back onto the plate. Taskinen's eating was much more elegant. He thought for a few minutes before responding, and I nearly lost patience with his stalling.

"We can define the special assignment any way we want. You and I can design it. You could carve off part of the Hackman case and assign it to Koivu alone."

"But the transfer labels him guilty! Koivu asked me to save him from Ursula on Friday. He said she wouldn't leave him alone. 'She's been glued to me all night' were his exact words. I'm prepared to say that to anyone who wants to hear it, but maybe we should start with Ursula! And you don't even know the rest of the story," I said and groaned, knowing what I had to do. I proceeded to spill Puustjärvi's secret. To my surprise Taskinen started to laugh. I'd never heard him laugh that way before.

"Oh God, what a mess," he finally said. "Should I pity Petri or be jealous of him? The first thing that comes to mind is Palo and his three wives. Or was it four?"

"Just three."

"Some men have their hands full with one. Of course Terttu was waiting up when I came home from the Christmas party, and when she found that hair, you should have heard her. She blew a gasket. I tried to say we just danced, but that didn't help. At least she had a reason to be jealous this time," Taskinen snorted, showing an uncharacteristically cavalier attitude. I was getting the feeling I didn't know my boss at all anymore. Fortunately he moved back to Koivu and Ursula, and together we came up with a plan that would do the least to smear Koivu or interfere with our unit's work.

"Tomorrow and Thursday I'll be in Tampere lecturing at the academy," Taskinen said on the way back to the station. "Terttu's test results are supposed to come on Thursday, and I wanted to be there to support her, but I really can't cancel my lecture. Can I call you Thursday night if I need to talk to someone?"

"Go ahead."

"Thanks." Jyrki's right hand quickly touched my cheek before returning to the steering wheel. "And try to keep yourself together too. We've never had a homicide go unsolved, and you'll figure this one out too. I'm betting before Christmas."

I sighed. "Let's hope so."

I spoke with the heads of Narcotics and Robbery about some joint investigations until three, then was thinking about heading home early when my desk phone rang. The call came from within the building; apparently Lehtovuori was too lazy to walk down the hall. He'd been with the department for twenty years now and had never shown any desire to advance from senior officer to sergeant or to change units. He was a good foot soldier with more of an eye for technical details than human nature. He wasn't at his best in the interrogation room, and I didn't know whether he was the right person to have reading Kervinen's diaries. But now he sounded excited.

"Listen, boss, I was just reading some entries from around the time Hackman and Jääskeläinen got married. Apparently Carcass believed right up to the end that Hackman would choose him instead. It's pretty embarrassing stuff—a grown man shouldn't write things like that. But get this: when the wedding is all said and done, he writes the same entry over and over. 'I'm going to kill her. I'm going to kill Annukka.' Should I pull him in for a grilling?"

13

"Oh, a 'special assignment,' is it?" Koivu said angrily. I'd called him into my office while I waited for Kervinen.

"Right. You'll continue working on our profile of Annukka Hackman, contacting her family and friends and old coworkers. And you'll assist me in interviews as necessary. We'll start with Kervinen as soon as he arrives at the station. Your office will move to the third floor. Jyrki promised some old cleaning closet. It doesn't have a window, but you'll have a desk and a computer."

Koivu shook his head. "This is a nightmare. How can I tell Anu?"

"You haven't told her yet?"

"No. Juuso's been up at night again, and Anu hasn't been able to sleep for a couple of days." Koivu looked a little ragged himself, and no wonder. I wouldn't be able to sleep either if I had a sexual harassment accusation hanging over my head.

"Ursula threatened to go public, so it's best to tell Anu before she reads about it in the papers. Or do you want me to tell her?"

"No, I'm man enough to do it myself," Koivu said in exasperation, then went to move his things.

Man enough. Hopefully I'd never have to ask my own son if he was man enough for anything. The phrase was positive in the sense that a man should be upright and trustworthy, and take responsibility for his actions. But there was plenty of darker baggage tied up in it—and the norms of masculinity—too.

I could imagine how Anu would hit the roof when she heard about the accusations against her husband. I'd blow up too if Antti was mistreated that way. Gender didn't matter—you defended the people you loved regardless.

I looked out my office window to see that the sleet had stopped and the moon shone, looking as delicate as tissue paper. It was almost full and made me long for a walk in the forest. In the city the moon had too much competition. I remembered the fields around our old house, where Antti and I had skied before the children and the beltway came. When was the last time Antti and I had done anything fun together just the two of us? I couldn't remember.

When word came that Kervinen was waiting in Interrogation Room 4, I called Koivu and picked up the diary Lehtovuori had brought me. The death threat was repeated dozens of times, the last one only three days before Annukka Hackman's murder. As usual, Kervinen also reported on the bodies he had examined during this time, but the lines describing his private life were more revealing.

Annukka called and it was like before. She wanted to meet on Wednesday at Tapiontori Restaurant. She must have finally realized that Atro Jääskeläinen is a loser. He couldn't even get Sasha Smeds to work with her on her book, and that book is Annukka's big dream. Annukka asked what I know about DNA. I know everything about DNA if Annukka is the one asking, and what I don't know I'll find out. I've been right to wait.

When I walked in the interrogation room, Kervinen looked almost like his old self: his hair was clean and his clothes pressed, and I could smell his aftershave. But his eyes were as empty as they'd been when Koivu and I visited him at home.

"Hi, Kallio. The boys over in Helsinki aren't going to be happy when they hear you Espoo types ordered me down here in the middle of an autopsy. It was just a junkie, but it still has to be cleared from the queue. Seventeen-year-old boy, chasing the dragon. We've had our fill of them lately."

"Cut the crap, Kervinen. Our team found your diaries. You repeatedly threatened to kill Annukka Hackman."

Kervinen crossed his left leg over his right and glared at me. "People can write whatever they want in their diaries. That's the point of them. I didn't kill Annukka. Jääskeläinen did it when he found out Annukka was leaving him."

"Did Hackman tell you that?" Koivu asked. He was sitting in the shadows next to the tape recorder, sipping a cup of coffee. Maybe I should have left him with Kervinen for a minute. Maybe a man-to-man connection would work best. Most people usually trusted Koivu, whether they were experienced killers or scared old women.

"Annukka hadn't contacted me in a long time. Back in the beginning, after she married Jääskeläinen, she called me a few times and asked me to leave her alone. Then she made her asshole husband do it. In the end they just stopped answering my calls. What else could Annukka's call have meant other than she'd finally chosen me?"

All her family and friends had emphasized Annukka Hackman's persistence and ambition. A coworker from the TV sports desk had said that Annukka would probably sell her grandmother's pet dog to get a story she wanted. Hackman's mother had talked about walking by a movie theater in downtown Helsinki when Annukka was a teenager. A big new Finnish film was having its premiere, and people were lined up to see the celebrities. Annukka said that she intended to become a person other people lined up to see.

Annukka Hackman had asked Kervinen about DNA. Did Sasha Smeds have an illegitimate child somewhere, or had Annukka thought Heli was pregnant?

"In your diary, you said that the Sasha Smeds's book was Annukka's big dream. What did you mean by that?"

Kervinen stared at me as if I was an idiot.

"It was going to be her breakthrough as a journalist. She'd been working on it since before she met Jääskeläinen. Annukka dreamed of an international career, and Jääskeläinen's pathetic little workshop could never offer her anything like that. Annukka spoke perfect English, Swedish, and German. Back when she was still . . . when we were together, we talked about moving abroad."

"Why did she choose Smeds in particular as her topic?"

Suddenly Kervinen blushed. "Annukka was a motorsports reporter and knew Smeds. I don't know whether there was more to it . . . Maybe she was interested in Smeds as a person too, not just as a racer. Annukka always said that an inspiring topic is important in journalism. She never could have settled for working at a local newspaper and writing stories about building permits and military parades. At first she considered a biography of a politician, but they usually want to do those themselves. And Sasha Smeds was a better subject than some tongue-tied ski jumper. Besides, the rest of the world isn't interested in them."

Kervinen now spoke calmly about Hackman as if she was someone he was beginning to leave behind. I was relieved that the worst of his emotional turmoil seemed to be over and that he'd been able to return to work.

We went over his activities on the night of the murder again, and he stuck to his previous story. Still the diary was strong circumstantial evidence. I let him go, but I made it clear that he would be barred from leaving the country at least until his boots had been analyzed.

"Poor Kallio," Kervinen said with pity. "You're on the wrong track again. Go at Atro Jääskeläinen, not me. Jääskeläinen killed Annukka, mark my words."

Kervinen left, but the smell of aftershave lingered in the room. Koivu stared at me, looking irritated.

"I think we should have put him in a cell to think. He's in the defensive stage now, and he's trying to convince himself he didn't do it."

"So you think he's guilty?"

"Everything points that way. But I'll go sit in my own goddamn windowless box to think up some other theories. Want to guess whether I'm going for a beer after work?"

"It does a body good."

"Come with me."

"Sorry. Antti's got something going on tonight, probably a protest rally."

"Who could I protest against?" Koivu said bitterly, then got up and walked out, slamming the door behind him.

I stayed in the sparse interrogation room and listened to Kervinen's answers one more time on the tape recorder. His motive and his death threats in the diary wouldn't be enough to file charges; we needed forensic evidence. Maybe some time in a cell would have broken him.

Ursula was coming down the hall as I dragged myself to my office. My muscles were strangely sore, as if I had a flu coming on.

"So you finally believe me?" Ursula said, smiling happily. "Did Koivu confess? Maybe I don't have to contact the papers after all. Of course they'd be interested to know this kind of thing is happening in precisely the unit that's investigating their colleague's murder."

"Do you really want someone digging through your private life? I'm sure you understand that would mean everything coming out, just like in the Hackman case."

"At least that woman knew what she wanted and was ready to take risks to get it. She was a real pro. You can't get ahead in this world playing softball." Ursula smiled again, then turned into her office.

In the old days, criminal investigation had been a game between the police and the criminals, but now the media had joined the fray. I had tried to maintain a good relationship with the reporters who worked in my area, and usually that had been easy. Now and then we'd had run-ins about them protecting their sources, but I didn't want to endanger anyone's life just to identify some snitch. With this case, the usual informants had been remarkably quiet, so I firmly believed that Annukka Hackman's murder wasn't a professional job. This was a first timer who just knew how to cover his tracks. Who else could that be but Kervinen?

Hackman had dreamed of making a breakthrough. Two decades ago, an ambitious journalist would have longed for her own Watergate, but now exposing the private life of a random celebrity was enough. It didn't demand much journalistic skill. Although I'd always been interested in people, I didn't even try to keep up with all the models, talk show hosts, and tango royalty who rotated monthly on the front pages of newspapers and magazine covers. In a lot of previous investigations it had been helpful to know something beforehand about the victim, but now even that wasn't getting me anywhere.

Once I'd settled at my desk, I set a meeting with Alavirta, the workplace safety officer, for the next morning; he'd left me a message saying he wanted to hear my opinion on what had happened between Ursula and Koivu. I also had several callback requests from Jouko Suuronen, which was no surprise. I'd have the report from the search of his house tomorrow morning, so I decided not to respond just yet.

I was home with the kids by a few minutes past four, and it felt luxurious to have so many hours simply to be. After snacks, we watched *The Moomins* and *Tiny Two* together. Once the kids' shows were done, I left the TV on for the news in case they showed the rally that Antti was going to against George W. Bush and the bombing of Iraq. In the spring the kids and I had gone with him to a march against the fifth nuclear reactor the Finnish government wanted to build, but it didn't help much.

The Iraq protest was only mentioned as a footnote, but I still saw a familiar face before the broadcast ended. Television cameras had been waiting for Heli and Jouko Suuronen at the airport. Suuronen tried to shield Heli, but it didn't work.

"Mr. Suuronen, what's Sasha Smeds's condition right now?"

"He's stable. He needs skin grafts, which is why he stayed in England."

"Will we see Smeds on the rally circuit again?"

"It's too early to say."

Then the same inquisitive journalist attacked Heli.

"Heli Haapala, my condolences. Your husband lost the world championship last year because of a decision by his team and now this year because of a tragic accident. Do you think he'll be up to fighting for the title again next year?"

Looking pale, Heli tried to smile. "There's no way I can answer that. A lot depends on how Sasha's recovery goes." Then suddenly she broke down as her gaze shifted somewhere outside of the camera's field of view. Her eyes filled with tears. The television camera zoomed out, and the still-camera flashes continued firing. It made me sick the way Heli's pain was being turned into public property. Then I saw a tall figure dressed all in black appear from behind the cameras. It was Andreas Smeds. He said something to Suuronen, and together they started guiding Heli past the reporters and photographers.

I was giving Taneli his bedtime snack when Antti came home. Taneli was being a wild man and demanding to feed himself, which meant yogurt all over the kitchen. Iida watched with a look of superiority as her brother made his mess.

"How was the rally?"

"Bloody cold and poorly attended. Your friend Riita Kuurma from the Security Intelligence Service says hi. She was there too. I'm still not sure whether she comes to spy on us or if she really supports the cause."

"She's probably still catching flak over the nuclear plant protest. Should I put some water on? Do you want tea or a red wine toddy? I could use something to warm me up too after I get Taneli down."

I was in our bed reading Taneli a picture book about trains, which he loved, when my phone started ringing. It was in the kitchen, and Iida ran to fetch it for me.

"Iida Sarkela," I heard her say. "Yes, Mommy's home, but she's reading to Taneli. I'll take her the phone."

I handed the book to Taneli while I took the phone from Iida.

"Hi, it's Puupponen."

"Hi."

"Sorry to bug you at home like this, but I thought you needed to hear this right away. I've been through all of the evidence we confiscated from Jouko Suuronen's house, and there's something really interesting, namely a disk with Annukka Hackman's book on it."

Taneli pulled on my arm, wanting me to stop talking and finish the story. "Wait just a second, honey," I whispered to him. "What's the date on the file?"

"There are several versions, but the most recent one is from the end of October. It has a section on Sasha's marriage to Heli."

"Does it—"

"It claims that Sasha's brother is having an affair with his wife. That's quite an accusation."

"And true. Get Suuronen to the station right now, and call me when he gets there. Then we'll let him sweat for a while. I'll get the kids to sleep and then come in."

I'd only managed to sip a third of my red wine toddy, so in a couple of hours I'd be good to drive again. I read the rest of the train book, brushed Taneli's teeth, and sang him a lullaby. Antti read Iida *Pippi Longstocking*. I poured the rest of my toddy into his half-empty glass.

"What now?"

"I have to go in to handle something."

Antti had no reaction.

After I'd put back on my black pantsuit, I redid my makeup. Sasha Smeds winning the world championship would have definitely been in

Jouko Suuronen's interest. Had he told Heli and Andreas that he knew about their secret? Had he trusted that they wouldn't say anything about it before the race series was over and decided to kill Hackman so she wouldn't tell either? Of all my prime suspects, Suuronen was the easiest to imagine as a cold-blooded killer.

I went to sing Iida a lullaby too, and Taneli tossed and turned restlessly in his bed. When Iida started school, the kids would need their own rooms, or we'd have to bring Taneli into our room.

"If I end up on unemployment, then you can work nights too," Antti said as I punched a number into my phone.

"Why do you have to say stupid things like that? We've just spent two weeks on this investigation, and now we finally have the clue we needed at the beginning."

"Will you be all night? I'll make up the couch so you don't wake me."

The light shining from the lamp cast Antti's features in sharp relief. He'd lost weight over the fall. His hair, which was black when we met, had grayed significantly over the past few years. In December he'd turn forty. Impending unemployment and crossing the final threshold into middle age were understandable causes for a crisis, but I didn't always have the energy to be understanding. I thought warmly of Taskinen. He wouldn't have groused at me for wanting to do my job. Then I realized how stupid and dangerous thinking like that was.

Puupponen called at nine.

"We've got Suuronen here now, and he's pretty hot under the collar. It took him a while to answer the door at his place. He was in the sauna and claims he didn't hear the doorbell or the phone. He's had a few beers too, so I'm not sure he's in any shape for an interrogation."

"We'll see. I'll be right over. Get the recording equipment ready. Including video. I want to be able to analyze his body language later. You went to that lie-detecting course in the spring, right?"

Puupponen laughed. "Yeah."

The Police University College had offered a training to teach interrogators how to analyze subject body language. The trainer was an FBI expert from the United States.

In the car I started becoming irritated with myself that I hadn't thought to videotape Kervinen's interrogation. An experienced criminal psychologist might have been able to tell from the video whether Kervinen was telling the truth. The way I kept letting my emotions and empathy for our suspects and witnesses cloud my judgement were hampering this investigation. For a second I considered calling Jyrki, since I really needed a pep talk. Instead I turned on the radio. John Lennon assured me that love was the answer. I grimaced. Love had actually messed up a lot of people's lives instead of making them simpler.

A faint hint of Carcass Kervinen's aftershave still hung in Interrogation Room 4, but the smell of cigar smoke wafting from Suuronen gradually began to overwhelm it. I didn't believe that Suuronen had only drunk a couple of beers during his sauna, since I could also pick up the scent of cognac. Suuronen had been picked up forty-five minutes earlier. He was still on the uphill side of his buzz, but that wouldn't last long. His face and eyes were red, and the knot of his tie hung loose.

"I'm going to file a complaint about you to the Chancellor of Justice," he bellowed as I sat down. "And then I'm going to sic every newspaper in Finland on you. Don't we have laws in this country anymore? What grounds did you have to search my home? Goddamn rubber boots and tire tracks? I already told you I came home on the five o'clock flight from Stockholm on the night of Hackman's murder. Haven't you checked?"

"We have. The plane was a little early, and according to our records, there were no traffic jams that night," I lied. The information about the airplane was correct, but I hadn't remembered to ask anyone to check the traffic reports.

"Goddamn it! If I say there was a traffic jam, then there was a traffic jam. Do I have to buy a goddamn tracker for my car so I can prove to the police where I've been? How about you check my cell phone instead. I was sitting in traffic on Ring I talking to Sasha. You have my permission. I don't have anything to hide!"

Suuronen's hair was damp and a tuft stuck up at his forehead, which he kept trying to smooth back down.

"Nothing to hide, you say? Not even a copy of Annukka Hackman's manuscript at your house?"

I stood up and walked to Suuronen, and to my surprise he flinched. Puupponen's eyebrows went up. As I stood there in front of him, I saw beads of sweat form on his forehead. The interrogation room was hot enough that I felt like taking my jacket off.

"I asked to read the book, of course. I did that back in the spring. That was why Sasha made the decision to pull out of the project."

"In the spring? Be more specific."

"I don't remember exactly! Maybe it was between the Cyprus and Catalonia rallies. Sasha won all the races earlier in the season, then he had a small hiccup in the summer, but . . ."

"Then how do you explain the fact that the disk with the manuscript has files that were updated this fall? Did you start adding to the book yourself?"

Now Suuronen was really sweating. With a groan he took off his suit coat. There were wet splotches under the arms of his blue shirt. He glanced around looking for a drink, but found nothing.

"I want to call my lawyer."

"Go right ahead," I said coldly. Suuronen pulled his phone out of his jacket pocket and pressed a shortcut key. I could hear it ringing, then an answering machine picked up.

"Jalle, damn it, it's Jokke. Call me right now. It's important! I repeat: right now." Cursing to himself, he hung up. "I'm not answering any more questions until I've consulted with my attorney."

"That's fine. You can wait in a cell for him to get here. That'll give you a chance to lie down too. Unfortunately you'll have to leave your phone with the guard, but I'll instruct him to answer it for you."

"What the hell do you think you're doing, girl?" Suuronen tried to stand up but then fell back, clutching his cell phone as if it were some sort of safety handle.

"You're under arrest for concealing evidence and being an accessory to murder," I said, listing off the first charges that came to mind. Puupponen continued raising his red eyebrows, and the freckles on his forehead stretched into ovals. Suuronen sat in silence for nearly a minute, and when he did start talking again, his voice had a forced calm to it.

"Have you read the manuscript you took from my house?"

"Yes."

"So you know what it says about Sasha's wife?"

"Yes."

Without warning, Suuronen pounded his fist so hard on the table that Puupponen and I both jumped, and the desk lamp fell over. "And of course you think I'm just a manager and Sasha Smeds is just a way to make money, right? But that isn't how it is. Sasha's a fucking good guy, and he's my friend! Do you tell your friend that his old lady's cheating on him just as he's about to achieve the biggest dream of his life? Or after he's nearly died? No, you don't, no matter how much it pisses you off when his wife pretends to be sad about his accident. As if that bitch really cared about Sasha! Today, at the airport, I wanted to punch Andreas in the face. That bastard can thank his lucky stars there were so many cameras around. Otherwise, he would have gotten the beating of his life."

Suuronen wiped his brow with his sleeve. His face glowed red, and a vein bulged on his temple.

"I'll ask you one more time," I said. "When and how did you get that manuscript?"

Suuronen had regained his equilibrium. "Arrest me if you want, but I'm not talking until my lawyer is here. Maybe I didn't get it at all. Maybe it was given to me. Maybe someone planted it in my house. Maybe I really did write part of it myself. Just take me to a cell. It won't be the first time."

We left Suuronen with the guard and went to my office for a quick meeting. Puupponen promised to keep his phone on all night in case Suuronen got his lawyer and decided to start talking.

"Um, Maria, what's this whole thing with Koivu?" he asked as I was pulling on my overcoat.

"You haven't heard the rumors? Ursula is accusing him of harassing her."

Puupponen started laughing uncontrollably, and the laughter was so welcome that after a few seconds I joined in too. We giggled until my abs started cramping, and tears washed away my mascara.

"It's lucky for Ursula that Anu's on maternity leave. I wouldn't want to see that fight. Ursula's been annoyed at Koivu since the very beginning. She thinks you show him too much favoritism, and if Koivu wouldn't give in to her attempts at seduction, then of course she'd be pissed. She and I went on a couple of dates, but that's it. There wasn't any chemistry."

I started laughing again and found I was liking Puupponen more all the time. "We're all going to be asked for statements about Koivu and Ursula, which is going to be awkward," I said after I'd calmed down. "You get along with Ursula. Could you try to talk some sense into her?"

Puupponen snorted. "I don't even dare get in the same elevator with her. I don't want the same thing happening to me that happened to Koivu. She's a hot chick, but she's got a screw loose."

"I hate that Ursula's lies are going to harm the credibility of people who've really been harassed."

I remembered my early days on the Helsinki force when I'd had the pleasure of being called a lesbian or a whore when I didn't accept my coworker's date invitations. I felt no sense of triumph at seeing the tables turned on men. Koivu was the one here who was being sexually harassed, and although opposite scenarios were many times more common, that still didn't make it right for anyone to keep quiet about it. Tomorrow I'd have to speak to Ursula directly, even if that meant breaking Puustjärvi's trust.

To my disappointment, Antti was already sleeping when I got home. He'd made me a bed on the couch, even remembering my nightgown and some warm socks. For a bedtime snack I drank a glass of red wine and watched the slowly frosting-over world outside. The moon had set beyond the horizon, and the stars were only a shadow of how they would look in the countryside, away from the light of the city. My abs hurt, and I knew the hysterical laughing fits I'd had that night were evidence of stress. Taneli whimpered in his sleep. I got up to see that his leg had fallen between the slats of his crib. For Christmas we needed to get him a new bed. We just had to find the time to go buy it.

I watched a video until after midnight, then must have fallen asleep. Around four I woke up to a ringing—I'd forgotten to turn off my phone. The call was coming from an unknown number.

"It's Hannu Kervinen, and this is important, Maria. Now I finally know what . . ."

The line went dead. Suddenly I was perfectly awake.

14

I tried to call Kervinen back on his cell phone, but he didn't answer. I tried his landline, but the machine picked up. Antti had also woken up to the sound of the phone ringing and opened the bedroom door.

"I'm sorry, I have to make a few calls. You can just go back to sleep. I might have to go to the police station again, though, so can you get the kids to day care?"

"Has someone died again?" Antti asked with a yawn, then closed the door before I had time to answer that I hoped not. I called the duty officer at the station and asked them to send a patrol to Kervinen's apartment in Tapiola. Then I put some coffee on since I knew I wouldn't be able to sleep until I knew Kervinen was all right. I set my phone to silent and tried Kervinen's number again. He still didn't pick up. I tried to convince myself I didn't have any reason to go to Tapiola. Others would handle it.

I was almost finished drinking my first cup of coffee when the phone started buzzing in the pocket of my robe. It was the duty officer.

"Haikala and Saastamoinen went to the address. They found a man's body lying in the yard, apparently either pushed or a jumper. They haven't made it to Kervinen's door yet, since they have to deal with that."

"The body—is it Kervinen?"

"There's no ID yet. Puupponen is on his way to the scene."

"Thanks. I'm heading that way too."

I didn't want to bother Antti, so I dressed in the previous day's clothes. Downing the rest of my coffee, I grabbed a banana, which I ate in the car on the way to Tapiola. The streets were empty, and all the traffic lights flashed yellow. When I turned in to the apartment complex, I saw Puupponen behind the wheel of a car coming from the other direction.

The parking lot was not quiet, with three patrol cars and an ambulance already there. Senior Officer Mira Saastamoinen was just setting up blue-and-white police caution tape around a shape lying on the ground and covered with a blanket. People stood on balconies and peered out of windows.

"Hi. Get those balconies cleared," I told Haikala. "There may be evidence on one of them." After donning shoe covers and gloves from the car, I ducked under the tape and approached the body. Through the blanket I could see it was contorted in a weird position, arms and legs splayed to either side. I didn't want to lift that blanket, but I had to.

Kervinen's head lolled strangely, and there was surprisingly little blood. His eyes were open, and he had a day's worth of stubble. Farther away on the asphalt I spotted the pieces of a cell phone. When I stood up, I felt like vomiting. I took a few deep breaths and stepped out of the restricted area.

"And now this," Puupponen said in greeting. "Kervinen?"

"Kervinen. I'm going inside to his apartment. Maybe there's an explanation there. With any luck maybe it's the solution to Annukka Hackman's murder. You start organizing interviews with the neighbors and any other potential witnesses. Wake up Lähde and Autio. We need to get to work fast. No one's sleeping in this building anymore tonight anyway. Is the building super on his way?"

"We made the call," Saastamoinen said. "How did you know there'd be a body here?"

Mira Saastamoinen belonged to the department's female soccer team, and we knew each other well. I didn't start explaining the chain of events, though, since too many civilians were within earshot. The wind made my eyes water and whipped my hair in my face. I wished I had a hat. The downstairs door of the building was open, and I went inside to wait for the super. At least there I'd be out of the wind. Someone would have to go tell Kervinen's brother, but that could wait until later in the morning.

The building superintendent appeared after a few minutes. He was a young-looking guy, barely twenty. Along with Hakkarainen from Forensics, we crammed in the elevator.

"Who do I bill for opening this door?" the superintendent asked.

"I'd think that helping the police is everyone's civic duty," I snapped back more peevishly than I'd intended.

"At least I need a signature," the boy said and handed me a paper, which I scribbled on. The elevator stopped on the top floor. When we walked into Kervinen's apartment, we could see the lights of Espoo twinkling through the window, along with a lone ship out on the water. The door to the balcony was open a crack. Patrol had emptied the lower balconies.

The railing was high enough that pushing Kervinen over it would have required some strength even though he wasn't a large man, maybe five foot eight and a hundred and fifty pounds. We'd have to talk to the next-door neighbors first. The balconies faced the forest, but the highest ones were visible from the other apartment buildings around. It wasn't impossible that a neighbor living in one of those had seen Kervinen jump or someone push him off.

On the living room table was a laptop computer. It was turned on, but the screen was dark. With a gloved finger I carefully tapped the space bar, and words appeared on the screen.

"Now I finally know what I have to do. The one who killed Annukka is going to kill me too. But it doesn't matter, because now that Annukka is dead, nothing matters anymore." There was no signature. Taking out my notepad, I wrote down the message word-for-word.

We didn't find any other suicide note in the apartment. The bed was unmade, and based on the smell, the sheets hadn't been changed in ages. Yesterday Kervinen had seemed like his old self, but perhaps he didn't ever clean much. The kitchen was full of empty beer bottles. In a familiar-looking saucepan I found dried porridge, now turning green and fuzzy. I shivered. After the rest of the forensic team rumbled in, my phone rang. Puupponen asked whether I intended to stay at the crime scene much longer.

"There's a really strange letter up here," I told him. "I want your opinion about it. And interview the neighbors from the next balcony over right now. Has someone called crisis support?"

I walked back into the living room. Next to the couch I found Kervinen's Birkenstocks. He'd gone out on the slushy balcony in his socks. That could mean two things: either he'd really decided to jump or he'd gone out quickly because of someone else. But how could a murderer have lured Kervinen out onto the balcony? Kervinen didn't smoke. Jouko Suuronen was the only one of my suspects who seemed to be a smoker.

I glanced into the apartment's spare bedroom. As Koivu had said, there were just a couple of empty cardboard boxes. A layer of dust covered the floor and windowsills. I didn't bother to go in.

I asked some of the forensic team to check out the balcony. "Especially look for signs of a struggle. We can't rule out the possibility of homicide."

Then it occurred to me that I should ask Kervinen to take a close look under the victim's fingernails—and a few seconds passed before I realized some other pathologist would have to inspect this body.

There was a buzzer downstairs to let visitors inside the building. Telephone records would tell us if someone had called Kervinen. On my own phone I checked the time of his call to me, then remembered the pieces of the broken phone on the asphalt. Apparently he'd had his phone with him right until the end.

Puupponen appeared in the entryway. "Things are under control. The boys are on their way over, and Saastamoinen's patrol will start on the interviews with them. What did you want me to see?"

I took him to the computer. The message had been saved at 3:38, four minutes after Kervinen's call. Puupponen bent down to read it.

"'The one who killed Annukka . . .' That's the first ambiguous thing I've ever seen Carcass write. Sorry, his name was Hannu."

"Kervinen didn't necessarily write it himself."

"No, but this doesn't sound like something a murderer would have written to cover his tracks. 'The one who killed Annukka is going to kill me too . . .' Why not just write, 'I can't go on without Annukka'?"

"You're right. Or is he saying that he killed Annukka? First he killed her, then he killed himself. But why did he do it by jumping off the balcony, when he had access to drugs? That's such an easier way to go."

I remembered Kervinen's medicine cabinet in the bathroom. Twenty or so of the Dormicum were left, and a bottle of Cipramil, an antidepressant, had also appeared. That was almost full. Had Kervinen feared he'd be found before the medications could take effect? A blue nylon rope about two yards long lay on the bathroom floor.

I wrote down what Kervinen had said on the phone while I could still remember it clearly. Why had he called me specifically? We'd never gotten along all that well, and I couldn't imagine him choosing me as the last person to talk to in this life. That also pointed to homicide, and another crime I hadn't been able to prevent.

I heard a commotion coming from the hallway and what sounded like an elderly person yelling. A lot of retirees lived in Tapiola. They'd bought their apartments decades ago when the suburb was still spacious and new. When we moved two years ago, Antti had wanted to return to the landscape of his childhood, but it hadn't been possible financially. As for our future prospects, I had a hard time believing a PhD mathematician wouldn't be able to find work, but I'd always considered myself an optimist. At least when I was younger.

I decided to head to the police station to prepare a press release, on the off chance someone who didn't live in these buildings saw something that could help us explain Kervinen's death. There would also be more coffee there, which my body was screaming for. I ordered Puupponen to notify me if anything decisive turned up. Then I remembered Esa Kervinen. Did a teacher's work day start at eight or nine these days? Seven o'clock would probably be a good time to deliver the bad news. I delegated that to Puupponen as well, and told him that Puustjärvi could go along. Maybe it would be good to call on the police chaplain as well.

Kervinen's final diary was still in my office. I flipped through it for answers but with no luck. The last entry was made on the day Hackman called to ask about DNA analysis, the day before her death.

I'm seeing Annukka in two days, then everything will be good again. At Tapiontori, like before. I expect an important surprise. I can finally have her here writing in that empty room, then maybe I'll learn to like this apartment and this life. It's like I'm walking half a meter above the ground, and nothing matters but Annukka.

I remembered what Kervinen had asked Koivu and me in his initial interview: Had we ever been so in love that we thought we'd die if we didn't get the one we wanted? In the same interrogation, Kervinen had seemed to hate Hackman, even though according to the diary just days before he'd thought she was coming back to him and was happy about it. It didn't make sense.

Puupponen called with an update. Kervinen's next-door neighbor had heard voices and steps from his apartment at around two thirty when she got up to go to the bathroom. So far no one had seen anyone going into Kervinen's apartment, and no one had witnessed the fall.

Kervinen and Atro Jääskeläinen had accused each other of killing Hackman. It was definitely time to speak to Jääskeläinen again. I issued the order to have him brought in right away; if no one else had time, I'd question him myself. And Suuronen was still in Holding . . . My head was buzzing, and my thoughts wouldn't seem to come together. At six thirty, my eyes started drooping. I decided to rest for a minute on the couch, but just for a minute. Finding a comfortable position wasn't easy, and I wished I had a blanket. I curled up as tight as I could.

When I woke up, it was to the sound of Antti's ringtone. From the display I discovered that it was seven forty-five. Oh hell.

"Maria. Are you at work or what?"

"Yeah . . ." My mouth was unbearably dry, and my neck was cramped.

"Taneli seems like he has a fever; I don't dare take him to day care. But Iida's demanding to go since apparently they're making Christmas decorations today. Any chance you could take her?"

"My morning meeting is about to start. Take a taxi, and ask it to wait with Taneli while you take Iida in. I'll try to pick her up, and I'll call if I can't."

"So you're assuming that I'm staying home with Taneli without us even discussing it?"

"Yes, I am! We've got another body here, I've been up half the night, and I know I'm about to catch hell from the press, so please stay home. You weren't supposed to have anything special at work today, were you?" I asked, trying to calm down. Antti didn't like being yelled at.

"No, and even if I did, you still probably wouldn't come home," Antti hissed, then hung up the phone without even saying good-bye.

"Shit," I said to myself. We had to get out of the White Cube if all we could do there was fight. Or did it have nothing to do with the place? Was that just an excuse? December would be our seventh anniversary, so maybe this was just a normal marital crisis.

My phone kept ringing, and this time it was Koivu.

"I was just wondering if I can come to the unit meeting while I'm in exile if I promise to sit on the other side of the room from Ursula."

"You haven't heard?"

"What? Did Ursula retract her accusation?"

"No, unfortunately. It's about Kervinen. He's dead." My voice suddenly faltered, and I started to cry.

"Maria, are you OK?" Koivu asked.

"No, not really," I sobbed. "I'll see you at the meeting. I have to calm down now."

Outside it was still dark. The wind had increased to the point that the pine trees outside my window bent like willows. I wiped my face and put on mascara. That, powder, and lipstick salvaged the situation a little but couldn't hide my swollen eyes. But what did it matter how I looked?

Puupponen and Puustjärvi entered the room together.

"How's Kervinen's brother?" I asked.

"He didn't show much emotion. But his wife went hysterical and started screaming about how a person was bound to go crazy if his job was digging around in bodies and then the only woman he ever loved was murdered. Which isn't the worst theory in the world," Puupponen said. He looked exhausted too, and Puustjärvi's face seemed frozen in a permanent expression of misery. The birth of the twins was probably a pretty significant source of stress, along with the fact that he'd cheated on his wife.

The mood in the meeting was oppressive. No one wanted a second homicide investigation on top of the badly stalled one we already had. Ursula glared at Koivu, who was uncommonly quiet, and even Puupponen didn't crack any jokes. Lähde and Autio were going to head back to Kervinen's neighborhood to continue the search for possible eyewitnesses.

"The lady downstairs swears there was an angel in white with Kervinen on the balcony, but I'm leaning away from believing her. She's got a serious case of dementia and spends her days in a care center while the daughter is at work. Apparently she sees a lot of angels," Lähde said.

"I've already written up a press release requesting eyewitness reports. We can eliminate two of the suspects from Annukka Hackman's murder: Jouko Suuronen, because we had him in a holding cell last night, and Sasha Smeds, who's lying in the ICU in a hospital in England. I also think it's extremely unlikely that Sini Jääskeläinen or Viktor Smeds could have pushed Kervinen off that balcony. It also would have been difficult for Heli Haapala or Rauha Smeds. Atro Jääskeläinen, on the other hand, is on his way in for questioning."

"What about Andreas Smeds?" Ursula asked. "And Annukka Hackman's gun is still missing. What if someone used it to threaten Kervinen and make him jump? Then we can't even eliminate the teenage girl."

"Based on the crime statistics lately, I'd almost be more likely to believe the perpetrator was young," Autio offered. He had three teenage children who were reputed to have the strictest curfews in all of Espoo and were required by their father to use a breathalyzer on the weekends. Autio thought that was the only way to keep children on the straight and narrow. Once Koivu had asked whether Autio did drug testing on his kids too, and Autio said it was too expensive on a cop's salary.

"Let's question Jääskeläinen first. Ville, you and Puustjärvi take a crack at Suuronen once his lawyer shows up. Ursula, be ready to come with me to talk to Jääskeläinen. If you're free, come to my office right after this meeting and we'll talk tactics."

I saw a smile flash across Ursula's face. I actually had little intention of talking about Jääskeläinen. This was going to be a conversation about Koivu and not one that I was looking forward to.

Fortunately the smaller cases were moving along nicely, but that was cold comfort. The wind seemed to force its way through the window frames, and I felt simultaneously cold and sweaty in my shabby clothes from yesterday. I wished I could have offered my subordinates solace and encouragement, but all I managed was a minute of silence in Kervinen's memory.

After the meeting, Ursula and I walked together to my office. Our heels clicked out of step in the hallway as my phone kept beeping with incoming messages. The department press officer had distributed the press release and had already received a raft of inquiries and requests for comment.

"Just one call first, if you don't mind waiting," I said to Ursula and motioned to the couch.

"We probably need to hold a briefing, and the chief agrees," the press officer said. "There's already talk of a serial killer."

"Got it. Let's do noon. Call the hyenas together. I'll tell them what I can," I said in resignation. Did Ursula have some instant beauty drops or some other secret weapon I could borrow from her? About all I had in my own bag that might help was concealer. Perhaps intentionally, Ursula was dressed more conservatively than usual in brown corduroy trousers and a matching polo shirt. I wondered again how she had the money for such a large wardrobe.

"So what about Jääskeläinen?" she asked enthusiastically once I'd hung up and sat down behind my desk.

"This isn't about him; it's about you and Koivu. I want to request that you retract your accusation. You know it's baseless. If the department starts a larger investigation into your behavior, there are bystanders who will suffer too, like Puustjärvi and his wife. And there are plenty of people who can testify that you were the one hanging on Koivu at the Christmas party, not the other way around. Do you really want that?"

Ursula sat quietly and looked at her nails, which were also painted brown. Suddenly a tear ran down her cheek, and she muttered, "Of course you're all ganging up on me. That's what always happens. That was why I wanted out of Lahti too. Everyone was all over me there too, and no one ever believed that I didn't . . ." Ursula wiped the tear away. "Of course I know Koivu's your favorite, and that you're under

Taskinen's special protection. But what do you know about me and Puustjärvi?"

"What Petri told me, that you two had sex once."

"Does everyone in this unit have to report to their boss about their private lives too?" Now there was no sign of the tears. Ursula was furious.

"Not at all. I would have preferred never to hear about it, but Petri wanted to clear his conscience to someone. I don't want to spread that around, but I also don't intend to stand by and watch while you try to force Koivu out of our unit with your nonsensical accusations. What do you think you're going to gain from this?"

"I should have known there would be trouble with a woman as a boss! What a queen bee you are, trying to get all the men to dance to your tune!" Ursula screamed. "It's always the same, all you old bitches plotting behind my back. You claim you're a feminist, but you only give me pointless jobs and defend the men no matter what they do."

I let Ursula bluster. Maybe she was right. I hadn't had much time to encourage the newest member of the unit, since I'd had enough on my plate trying to get back up to speed after my maternity leave. Hiring Ursula had been one of my first acts when I got back, and admittedly I'd favored her in the selection process because of her sex. I told her that now.

"But I don't want to get a job just because I'm a woman!" she said. "Is that supposed to be feminism now too?"

"Ursula, calm down. I wanted you in this unit because you seemed competent. What you do in your free time is none of my business, but your work is. Retract your accusations against Koivu before this spirals out of control. We may have a double murder to investigate, and we need everyone's contributions, including yours and Koivu's. You won't have to work together, though, I promise."

"So you're pressuring me?"

"I'm not pressuring you; I'm asking you."

Ursula stood up. "Just wait until the reporters I know hear about this," she hissed, then turned to leave. Once the door had slammed behind her, I put my face in my hands. Kervinen's lifeless eyes appeared before me. We had just talked yesterday, and now his body was in a steel box, waiting to be cut apart.

Thankfully I had a spare shirt, underwear, and panty hose in my office closet. Grabbing them, I headed for the showers, where I found some deodorant and moisturizer someone had left behind. I didn't wash my hair, since it wouldn't have time to dry. I used the concealer under my eyes and tried to tell myself that a homicide detective was allowed to look tired.

The press room was almost full, and I counted a dozen different microphones and tape recorders on the table. The camera flashes made me blink involuntarily. I started by saying that the police needed the public's help in clarifying how Hannu Kervinen had died, then I opened the floor to questions.

"So the police suspect homicide. Does Mr. Kervinen's profession as a forensic pathologist have anything to do with this?" asked the crime reporter for one of the national TV networks, a familiar, sharp fellow.

"That is one of our lines of investigation."

"Mr. Kervinen was also one of the prime suspects in Annukka Hackman's murder, isn't that right?" the reporter continued. "Do the two cases have anything to do with each other?"

"Naturally we're looking into that, but at this point we can't say anything certain."

"How has Ms. Hackman's murder investigation been proceeding? Not much information has been released. Did Kervinen kill Hackman and then take his own life?" asked one of the tabloid reporters.

"That's another line of investigation. Hackman's murder investigation is proceeding, but as you know, DNA analysis takes time."

"Are the police still interested in Sasha Smeds and his family's activities? And has it occurred to you that the police investigation played a role in interfering with Sasha's concentration and possibly caused his tragic accident?"

I didn't know the young man who had raised his voice aggressively and asked that last question. He was dressed in the latest style young people were wearing and a baseball cap with the logo of a Helsinki radio station on it.

"The police have a duty to question all necessary individuals regardless of social status or life situation."

"Including Sasha Smeds's manager? Apparently he's currently in police custody," yelled the same young reporter, causing a stir among the rest of the audience. Who had leaked about Suuronen?

"Mr. Suuronen is assisting us in our investigation," I replied coldly, and in response received a wave of questions that seemed like it would never let up. This balancing act between avoiding the impression of a cover-up and exposing too much took nearly an hour. Afterward I could have eaten a horse. As first aid I downed a couple of salmiakki fish to get my hands to stop shaking, and then I went downstairs to devour a plate of veggie pasta. As I was carrying my dirty tray to the rack, I received a message that Atro Jääskeläinen was waiting in an interrogation room. Immediately I called Ursula. She was busy with an interview for an assault case.

"Tell me when you're done, and we'll go have a chat with Jääskeläinen."

"You still want me there?"

"Hey, this is our job. Tell me when you're free."

On my computer I found an e-mail from Taskinen in Tampere.

He'd heard about Kervinen's death and wanted to tell me to keep my chin up. I teared up again. Jyrki knew the pressure a lead investigator worked under, and he hadn't always been able to stand up to it either. I dialed his number, then I realized he probably wouldn't be able to answer. And talking to Jyrki wouldn't solve anything. On the contrary, I needed to keep my guard up so our warming relationship wouldn't cause any new trouble.

15

It was almost two before Ursula announced she was on her way to Interrogation Room 4. None of the others were free, so Jääskeläinen got our most comfortable room. He still looked bloated and prematurely aged; the bags under my own eyes were mild compared to his. I nodded to Ursula to indicate that she could start the questioning. Atro Jääskeläinen beat her to it, though, asking why the police weren't keeping him better informed about the progress of his wife's murder investigation.

"Things are moving forward all the time," Ursula assured him. "But we need to ask you some follow-up questions. When did you last see Hannu Kervinen?"

Atro Jääskeläinen frowned, then sighed heavily.

"Since Annukka died, I haven't really slept at night. I don't like walking around the house keeping Sini up, so I've been going for drives. It calms me down. Usually I drive on the freeway, but last night I took a different route and ended up in Tapiola. Then the anger hit me again." Jääskeläinen sighed again. "I was driving through town and saw the flask buildings where Annukka had promised to move in with Kervinen. I thought . . . I thought that maybe I could get the bastard to confess since you cops can't seem to. Why do you ask? Did he admit he's guilty?"

Ursula's coffee cup hit the table with a bang. She was speechless. It was my turn to step in.

"Did you visit Kervinen's apartment last night?"

"I tried. The chickenshit wouldn't let me in."

"What time?"

"Two thirty. I rang the bell, and he answered but said he was sleeping. Really he was just afraid of my fist in his face, and that's exactly what would have happened if I'd seen him." Jääskeläinen sat up straighter. Ursula stared at him intently, a challenge gleaming in her eyes.

"Did you know your wife had arranged a meeting with Kervinen the Wednesday before last?" she asked. Jääskeläinen's face closed up like a child on the verge of bursting into tears.

"I heard about it from Sini after Annukka died," he forced himself to say. "The poor girl was beside herself. She thought that I . . . I don't understand why Annukka wanted to meet him unless he knew something that might help her with the Smeds book. And I told him that again last night through the intercom. Annukka never really cared about him. She chose me."

Puupponen was sitting in the next interrogation room with Jouko Suuronen. Maybe Jääskeläinen didn't even know Hackman had made a new version of her book after learning about Heli's affair with Andreas. But how had Suuronen found out?

"Where did you go from Kervinen's apartment?"

Jääskeläinen sighed. "I drove around for a couple of hours and listened to the radio. I was at home a little before four and in bed by five. I slept past noon and didn't even hear Sini leave for school."

Word of Kervinen's death hadn't made it into the morning print editions of any of the papers, but the story had been online since seven. Jääskeläinen was at least good at playing clueless.

"Were there any witnesses to your movements?" Ursula asked.

"A patrol car pulled up behind me on the Turku Highway around the turnoff for Lohja. I was going a little over the limit, but I slowed down when I saw them. They might remember me. I was in my Audi. I can't even touch Annukka's car. I should probably sell it. Sini promised to take Annukka's clothes and things to the flea market. She's a good girl. But why are you asking about what I did last night? That isn't going to help solve Annukka's murder."

Ursula cast me a questioning glance, and I nodded slightly in response. "Hannu Kervinen died last night," Ursula said.

The color drained from Jääskeläinen's face. "Oh my God!" he said, his voice cracking. "I guess I should be happy. Did he leave a confession behind?"

"What did you say to him last night?"

"I asked him to let me in. Then I probably said something about how it was ridiculous for him to think Annukka would have come back to him even if they had met. Look, Annukka and I had an agreement . . ." Jääskeläinen went silent and squeezed his hands into fists so hard his hairy fingers turned red.

"What kind of agreement?" As I waited for him to respond, I considered pausing the interrogation for a while. Some of the witness reports had already come in, and maybe one of them would contradict what he was telling us.

"I take some pretty strong blood pressure medication and it . . . You can probably guess some of the side effects." Now Jääskeläinen was beet red. "And Annukka was so much younger. Of course there are other ways to satisfy a woman, but I still gave her permission . . . Just so long as nothing threatened our marriage. I loved Annukka, and I respected her as a journalist. And of course it stroked my ego that she chose me instead of Kervinen."

"So you gave your wife permission to sleep with other men?" Ursula's voice was triumphant, as if this information meant something important to her. "And you weren't jealous?"

"As far as I know, she never had a chance to take advantage of the arrangement after she broke off her relationship with Kervinen. I gave

Annukka the resources to write the book she wanted to write. Annukka brought life and color into my world. Now that's all gone because of that maniac. I'm glad he's dead!" Jääskeläinen's clenched fists pounded the table.

"I'm going to have to interrupt this interview, but I hope you can stay at the police station for a while," I said. "We'll continue this soon. Ursula, could you please keep Mr. Jääskeläinen company? I have to attend to some other business."

First I went back upstairs to my office and got on our intranet. A whole series of interview reports were waiting—our team had been quick with Kervinen's neighbors. One next-door neighbor had heard Kervinen's buzzer ring in the night but wasn't able to say when. A resident of the adjacent building had seen a male figure at the door to Kervinen's stairwell at about two thirty, but he didn't know whether the man had gone inside. According to the crime lab's report, there were signs on Kervinen's balcony that someone had climbed over the railing, and they had collected numerous fingerprints. However, there were no footprints and no particular evidence of a struggle. We already had a DNA sample from Jääskeläinen taken when Annukka Hackman died, so we could compare it to the evidence collected from Kervinen's body.

I called Antti and asked him to pick up Iida, despite how enticing going home and sleeping in my own bed felt. Antti simply agreed; he'd given up complaining. I didn't want to let Jääskeläinen leave the police station, but I didn't have enough evidence to hold him. And besides, I wanted to know how Jouko Suuronen would explain the disk with the manuscript we'd found in his possession before I decided how to proceed with Jääskeläinen.

I ran back down the stairs because I needed to limber up. I knocked on the door to Interrogation Room 2. Puupponen had remembered to videotape Suuronen's interrogation. When I arrived, he paused the tape.

"A few words, Ville," I said, gesturing for him to come outside. We walked out of the holding area, climbing the stairs half a floor up onto the landing.

"Well?" I asked.

"Suuronen claims Annukka Hackman gave him the disk."

"When?"

"In August. But that's easy for him to claim when Hackman is dead. I'll show you on the video how he scratched his nose and made other gestures that are typical of liars. But that isn't enough evidence to keep detaining him."

"No, it isn't. And actually, the fact that Suuronen didn't destroy the disk is an argument in his favor. He probably assumed the police had the same version. Let him go. Then let's have an interrogation-video watching party when I'm done with Jääskeläinen. Did you sleep at all last night?"

"An hour. I'll still come watch videos with you, though, if I can have popcorn. And by the way, is it true Ursula took back her accusation against Koivu?"

"Where did you hear that?"

"Puustjärvi saw the workplace safety officer. Apparently Ursula sent an e-mail saying it was all a misunderstanding."

I felt like hugging Puupponen for delivering such good news. Of course Ursula had neglected to tell me.

I hoped at least Koivu knew. I walked back to Interrogation Room 4. Ursula had turned the light so it didn't shine on Jääskeläinen, and it seemed like they were having a friendly conversation about Sasha Smeds. Ursula smiled her prettiest smile, and Jääskeläinen didn't seem so glum either.

"Let's continue the interview." I switched the recorder back on, and it whined strangely as if it were breaking.

"How often did Annukka show you the Smeds manuscript?" I turned the light back so it shone on Jääskeläinen's face instead of the seascape picture that hung on the back wall. I hated that painting.

"Annukka didn't like anyone reading her unfinished drafts. I looked over the manuscript in the spring, at the point when Sasha pulled out of the project. After that Annukka said she got all sorts of new, shocking material. She assured me it was all true, and there would be no grounds for a libel suit."

"Did she deliver the manuscript to anyone or have anyone but you read it?"

"No! Annukka was protective of her writing and her sources. Layout was supposed to start a week ago, and she said she asked our graphic designer for a written commitment that he wouldn't breathe a word about the contents of the book. According to Annukka, it had some serious stuff in it that we needed to keep safe. She had a backup copy in her office safe, of course. Sometimes she mailed backups of her work to her parents' house too, but she didn't dare do that this time."

I made a note to ask Koivu to check with the parents, just to be sure they hadn't received a version of the manuscript in the mail.

Then I tried to turn the question around, but I still didn't get the answer I wanted. There was no way to prove that Jääskeläinen knew about the later version of the manuscript. So I had to let him go too.

Jääskeläinen looked relieved, but he lingered in the doorway. "What I said to Kervinen last night . . . was that what made him kill himself?"

"We don't know whether it was a homicide or suicide. I'd encourage you to stay reachable in case we need more information," I said in farewell.

Annukka Hackman's funeral was coming up that weekend, and someone from the unit would need to attend. Perhaps Puupponen would be a good fit. I'd have to ask him later. For now, I desperately needed some fresh air, a long jog in the freezing wind or a few turns on the skating rink. Iida had taken to skating the previous winter, so I'd dug up my ancient skates at my parents' house and tried to see if I could still do it. After a few falls I'd regained my feel for the ice, and we put

Iida in lessons. I'd looked forward to the outdoor rinks freezing, since the indoor facilities had made me anxious ever since I almost lost my life at the Matinkylä Ice Arena while I was expecting Iida.

"Do you want to go out for some fresh air?" I asked Ursula once Jääskeläinen had left.

"I didn't know you smoked," she said.

"No, I meant real fresh air." I headed up the stairs, and Ursula followed me. Outside the frigid wind blew right through my clothes. Exhaustion accentuated the chill, but at least it kept my eyes open and sharpened my senses. Ursula wrapped her arms around herself. It was comforting to see that her nose turned red in the cold too.

"What do you think about Jääskeläinen?"

Ursula snorted. "That man is an idiot. I doubt he knew half of what his wife was doing. Hackman married Jääskeläinen's money and business, not the man. But so what? Idiots are made to be used, and they only have themselves to blame."

"You retracted your sexual harassment complaint." I couldn't help saying it, even though I should have let Ursula tell me herself.

"I did, but don't think that's the end of this. I have my connections."

Ursula turned and went back inside. I yelled after her to check with Traffic for possible sightings of Jääskeläinen, but she didn't answer. It felt ridiculous standing and shouting in the middle of a half-empty parking lot. Instead of Ursula I tried to think about Annukka Hackman. We still didn't know why she'd gone swimming in that lake. Could it have had something to do with Sasha Smeds?

Maybe Hackman really had only married Jääskeläinen because he offered her better job prospects. But could a person really just choose to love someone and stop loving someone else? Maybe their marriage wasn't about love at all. And so what, if they both knew the truth? Marriages of convenience caused fewer messes than marriages built on love. God, I was becoming so cynical.

The cold became unbearable, so I had to head back inside. I fetched my tenth cup of coffee of the day, then went to knock on Puupponen's door.

"Yeah," came the sleepy reply. Puupponen had made an emergency bed out of his desk chair and two others, and he was lying down with his coat over him. "Oh, is it the interrogation video? Do you have popcorn?"

I laughed. "You'll have to settle for salmiakki. Do you want me to grab some?"

Puupponen went for coffee too and lifted a couple of chocolate cookies from Lähde's supply. As I was looking for the right channel for the VCR, I caught a glimpse of a familiar face on the news. Sasha Smeds.

"Rally driver Sasha Smeds is recovering well from the skin-grafting procedure he underwent yesterday," the news reader said. In the corner of the screen they again showed the car rolling down the hill, then the rescue helicopter that rushed Sasha to the hospital. Heli had returned to Finland instead of staying with her husband. Did that mean she'd chosen Andreas?

When Puupponen came back, I moved on to the video. It was apparent looking at Jouko Suuronen that he'd spent the night in jail. His clothing was wrinkled and he hadn't bothered to put his tie back on. His lawyer stayed in the background, but I recognized him from law school. Suuronen claimed he'd met with Annukka Hackman in late summer on the terrace at Tapiontori Restaurant.

"I told Hackman it was in her best interest to let me read the manuscript before it went to press. She didn't want to face libel accusations, so she agreed to have me review the text." Suuronen really did rub his nose as he spoke; he also fiddled with his shirt buttons and shifted nervously.

"I would have expected Hackman to think the more noise, the better," I said to Puupponen. "Politicians' memoirs sell better the more they bad-mouth other people in them."

Suuronen stayed almost calm through the whole interview. It wasn't until Puupponen asked if he'd talked to Annukka Hackman about Heli and Andreas's affair that he became agitated. The irritation overwhelmed his entire bearing, as if Heli had been his own wife.

"Why did that woman want to humiliate Sasha like that?" Suuronen shouted.

"Are you talking about Heli Haapala or Annukka Hackman?" Puupponen asked.

"I don't know!" Suuronen waved a hand impatiently. "To do something like that to such a good man. It's incomprehensible . . ."

Puustjärvi was almost out of the picture. I could only see his left leg, which twitched nervously as Suuronen shouted. Puupponen had handled the talking. Puustjärvi usually preferred to stay in the background if possible. Just then, Puupponen pushed the pause button.

"I don't believe him," he said. "Maybe he stole the disk from Hackman's purse after shooting her."

"But why would he have kept the disk at his house?"

"Because Hackman was dead and no one else could prove she didn't give him the disk!" I could hear the impatience and exhaustion in Puupponen's voice. We both needed to go home and sleep.

I almost felt too tired to drive, but I didn't have a choice: in the morning someone would need to get the kids to day care if Taneli was healthy enough to go. I drove slower than normal, far under the speed limit, and by the time I made it to our parking lot, I was wiped out. I noticed that there was something strange about the landscape: a digging machine had appeared in the middle of our tiny patch of forest, and some of the pine trees had been knocked down. Tears came to my eyes.

For ten minutes I sat in the car bawling about everything: about Kervinen, about this hopeless investigation, about the dead trees. Antti and I had found so much comfort in being able to see that strip of green from the windows of the White Cube. Soon even it would be gone. Maybe Antti would know what was going on in the forest.

When I got upstairs, Antti had just given Taneli half a Panadol for his fever. I picked him up and took him to the couch to sit, where he sobbed and squirmed in my arms. I was ravenously hungry, but I couldn't do anything about that right now. Iida very helpfully brought us a book about tools, which I read to Taneli to try to calm him down.

"Today was really fun at school!" Iida proclaimed. "I learned to crochet. I'm going to make Grandma a pot holder for Christmas, but your present is a secret, Mom. Hopefully I don't get sick too since there's so much work to do at school. And they sent a note home. Parent night is next week. I drew the cats on the note, and Roosa drew the hearts." Iida brought me the lavishly decorated announcement. "Mom, when can we get another cat?" she asked.

"When we move," I replied and tried to continue reading but realized that Taneli had fallen asleep. I carried him to bed. He wouldn't be going to day care for the rest of the week.

With Iida chattering behind me, I dragged myself into the kitchen. "Is there any food?" I asked Antti, who sat at the table reading.

"Iida and I made veggie pasta. There weren't many options. The cupboards were empty and I didn't feel like going to the store with a kid with a fever."

I heated the leftover pasta in the microwave. I felt like a beer, but we were out of those too.

"Do you feel up to making a trip now?" I asked Antti hopefully.

"Gladly. I've been sitting around here all day! I'll take a quick walk at the same time. The chainsaws have been howling all day. All the trees are being leveled, and apparently they're putting in a parking garage."

"That isn't funny," I said with a mouth full of grated cheese.

"Unfortunately it isn't a joke. People want a roof over their cars. Maybe we'll buy a spot in it too." Antti stood up and started opening cupboards. "I'm going to buy everything I can think of. Any requests? And can you be home tomorrow?"

"No, absolutely not! And we aren't buying a covered parking spot. We're moving out of here to somewhere . . . to somewhere with trees and where we can have a cat." I looked outside. From the kitchen window I could see bright lights and a parking lot, behind which there were other buildings. Learning to pick out our window from the parking lot had taken me a full year. That had to say something about how much disgust I felt for this apartment.

"Well, you should probably hold on to your job so we can at least keep paying for this place. Hopefully no one in my job interviews asks what my wife does. I'll have to lie and say we never have any childcare problems," Antti said and disappeared into the entryway. After a few seconds he returned in his coat and boots with a winter hat pulled down to his eyes and started looking for shopping bags in the kitchen cupboard. I always forgot them and had to settle for plastic.

Once Antti was gone, I poured myself a stiff shot of Laphroaig. I knew it was stupid when I had a six-year-old to entertain and a sick two-year-old sleeping, but I didn't have it in me to be sensible. Iida asked what the funny smell was, but I was able to redirect her by suggesting that we read Pippi. That became overwhelming too at the part where Pippi was about to go with her father to the South Seas and leave Tommy and Annika behind in tears.

"Mommy, she doesn't really leave," Iida said consolingly. That made me cry even more. A child wasn't supposed to have to comfort her mother. In my work I'd seen too many children thrust into adult roles, and I didn't want that for my kids. Forcing myself to calm down, I decided to leave the rest of my glass of whiskey until Iida was asleep too.

She was tired like the rest of us and was asking for her bedtime snack by seven thirty and was asleep just after eight. I checked her for a fever too by placing my hand on her forehead, but she wasn't hot. Taneli had kicked his covers off, so I tucked him back in. Then I went back out to the living room and drank the rest of my glass of whiskey, before pouring a little more.

There was no sign of Antti, but the store was open until nine. I tried to think about tomorrow's work. Maybe after the morning meeting I could come home. But that would depend on what sort of lab results were waiting for me. Before seeing those, I couldn't promise Antti anything. I felt helpless in the face of his despondency. Our generation was the first not to exceed their parents' standard of living. Antti had declined any sort of advance on his inheritance, even though his parents' help might have made it possible for us to live somewhere other than a White Cube in the middle of a construction site. When we got married I hadn't even considered things like Antti's career. I only thought I was responsible for my own.

I didn't want to think about our situation right now, though, so I decided to handle one more work task. I called Heli Haapala's cell phone. After a few rings she timidly answered. Of course she didn't recognize my number.

"Hi, it's Maria Kallio from the Espoo Police. I saw on the news that you're back in Finland."

"Onnikki is calving soon, and the organic inspector is coming next week, and I couldn't do anything in England because Sasha's being kept unconscious for now. He doesn't know if I'm there or not. As soon as they let him wake up, I'll fly back," Heli said as if she was under some sort of obligation to explain her decisions to me. I heard her stand up from a chair that creaked, and a television was audible in the background. Then a door opened with a squeak. "I'm sorry for going on like that. I feel like I might explode if I don't talk to someone."

"Don't worry about it. Jouko Suuronen has read Annukka Hackman's manuscript. He knows about you and Andreas."

I didn't know why I wanted to tell Heli this. I heard her walking up some stairs, perhaps on her way to her bedroom.

"Jouko? Has he told Sasha?"

"No, and I don't think he will anytime soon. He's only thinking about Sasha's recovery."

"As we all are, including Rauha, even though she mostly just fusses over Viktor. Sometimes I feel like I'm going to explode with all this acting and pretending. Now at least I have an explainable reason to cry. Of course I realize that Andreas and I had a strong motive for killing Annukka, but we didn't do it."

I tried to imagine what she would see from the windows of the house on a dark November night. The yard was illuminated, and the cows were sleeping in the barn. I hadn't milked a cow since I was a kid, but there was something homey and calming about the smell of a barn, which probably had something to do with my memories from my Uncle Pena's place in the country. Maybe beyond the barnyard lights there was only darkness. I envied that.

"Andreas read online that Annukka's old boyfriend was found dead. Was he guilty?" Heli continued. I said I didn't know yet and ended the call.

I turned off all the lights and tried to use the blinds to shut out the streetlamps blazing outside. Annukka Hackman had been interested in DNA. Was it possible that Viktor wasn't Sasha's father? The couple had been married for years before Andreas was born. Perhaps when it came to Sasha, Rauha had resorted to outside help? Had Annukka discovered that? If so, how? And who had murdered her to keep that knowledge secret?

16

The next morning before our meeting I tested out my theory with Koivu. He'd come to work early to move his things back into his office, and I was glad to help him.

"They always say maternity is a fact but paternity is a matter of opinion. But is that the kind of thing to kill someone over?" Koivu asked, then collapsed contentedly into his chair.

"I guess it depends on who Sasha's father is or whether Viktor knows he isn't."

"Rauha Smeds has an alibi."

"The Smeds brothers don't, and Andreas has been at the top of my list of suspects all along. But why would he have killed Kervinen? What did Hannu know?" I sat down at Koivu's desk and grabbed a piece of the pulla he was munching on. Anu had baked the night before and sent her husband in with treats for the whole unit.

"If Andreas is having an affair with his brother's wife," I continued, "would he kill to protect that same brother? I doubt it. But maybe he would kill to protect his mother, who may have been in his situation in the past, caught up in an illicit affair. Or hey—how do I know Heli told me everything? What if she had an abortion because she didn't know whether the child's father was Sasha or Andreas?"

Koivu began to laugh. "You and your theories! Detective Kallio's crime-solving strategy: if you try every possible option, sometimes you're right! Maybe we should go look at the lab reports. We need some facts, boss."

Taneli had been almost fever-free that morning. I'd taken Iida to day care and promised Antti I'd try to come home early so he could go to work in the evening. Luckily Antti could work from home on the laptop, but only so long as Taneli was asleep. All morning long we were both in low spirits: November 21 had been our cat, Einstein's, birthday, when he traditionally received a mountain of shrimp for dinner. I hadn't bought them at all since his death.

When Koivu and I reached the unit secretary's desk, she was still in the process of collating pages of technical reports and witness statements. I searched through the pile for the fingerprint analysis of Kervinen's computer keyboard. There weren't any foreign fingerprints, and Kervinen's own were smudged. Other fingerprints had been found in the apartment, including mine, as well as a hair that they presumed belonged to me. Kervinen really hadn't cleaned since Hackman's death. The most interesting thing I saw was a report taken from a witness who had seen Jääskeläinen ringing Kervinen's downstairs buzzer but hadn't seen him leave. The morning paper included our request for assistance, and officers were still interviewing neighborhood residents.

Later, at the morning meeting, Ursula made an appeal to interview the Smeds family once more, this time at the station. "We've let them off far too easily, talking to them in their home," she said. "We should drag the whole lot of them down here. At the very least we need to check their alibis for the night before last."

"Maybe Sasha's just pretending to be hurt and caught a private jet back here to kill Kervinen," Puupponen suggested.

We all laughed—which was something we desperately needed. The fall days had grown darker and darker as our investigation had gone nowhere. The night before, I'd dreamed that we found a confession in Kervinen's apartment, but it was only a dream. Puupponen and Puustjärvi began to outline Kervinen's activities from the past few days. He'd been at work since the beginning of the week, so maybe his coworkers and the doctor who prescribed his sick leave would be able to tell us whether he'd said anything about suicide. Ursula was right about the Smeds family. We would have to question them again.

"Ursula and Autio, get Heli Haapala and the Smedses in here for questioning. As far as I know, Rauha and Viktor are unaware of Heli and Andreas's affair. I don't think we have any reason to tell them."

"Well, aren't we being tenderhearted," Lähde said. "If those turds betrayed someone as great as Sasha Smeds, why should the police protect them? God, we've got enough work to do already."

Lähde was eagerly awaiting the end of his days as a cop, with disability pension papers working their way through the system. His back was constantly acting up. It mostly had to do with his sixty-five pounds of excess weight and complete lack of exercise, but Lähde said he'd rather die than eat rabbit food or give up smoking. We hadn't had any serious run-ins for ages, not since he'd finally accepted the fact that he had to answer to a female boss.

I sighed. "You know, Lähde, I just feel like protecting people's right to privacy and their right not to know some things. OK, you all have your orders. Ursula, please let me know what you work out with the Smeds family once you've contacted them."

In my office I remembered what Heli Haapala had said about the organic inspector and calving cows. A couple of times Antti had suggested that he could take up raising organic sheep if he didn't find any other work. My Uncle Pena's farm on the outskirts of my hometown up north had been empty for the past couple of years. Since his death, the estate had tried in vain to sell it, and Antti had threatened to move there.

"That sounds fine. At least your math skills would go to good use. I imagine you already know that nowadays the life of a farmer is mostly filling out paperwork and deciphering EU regulations," I pointed out. Antti had lived his whole life in the city, so it was easy for him to yearn for the romance of a rural idyll. Although a lonely cottage in a north-eastern backwater of Finland did sound more pleasant than the White Cube. The digging machines and chainsaws had already started making noise by the time I'd left to take Iida to day care, and poor Antti would have to listen to them for half the day. If none of the Smedses could come in today, I'd go home to let him work.

I reviewed Hackman's and Kervinen's autopsy reports. Kervinen's cause of death was a broken neck. His body showed various bruises and contusions, the most interesting of which was an abrasion on his neck. "Probably caused as a result of a nylon rope approximately two centimeters in diameter being tightened around the neck," the report stated. The injury had occurred before Kervinen's death. I remembered the light-blue nylon rope lying on the floor of his bathroom. We should have it analyzed for DNA. Had he tried to hang himself first—or had someone strangled him until he went unconscious, then pushed him off the balcony? The samples taken from under Kervinen's fingernails were currently being analyzed. Was his phone call to me cut off when someone wrapped the rope around his neck? A violent headlock could render someone unconscious in under a minute.

Before Kervinen's death, I'd sent copies of his diaries to our criminal psychologist. I now sent an e-mail asking him to look for any hints of suicidal tendencies. Unfortunately Kervinen had stopped writing the day before Hackman's death. Still, perhaps the psychologist would be able to tell us something useful.

The weekend was coming, and it would probably be the busiest time for Christmas parties. That would mean at least a few assaults, and maybe a rape too. It was my turn to be on call, so I was almost guaranteed to have to come in to the station. Antti had his office party on Saturday, and neither of us had remembered to arrange childcare. Damn it.

I ran through the options and landed on the one that Iida and Taneli would enjoy most, Matti and Mikko, their cousins on Antti's side. The boys were sixteen now, and they seemed to enjoy playing with their younger cousins. Antti's sister, Marita, could come in a pinch, but she'd just started a new relationship with a man who lived in Tampere, and they usually met on the weekends. Antti had taken his sister's divorce in stride, but his parents had been shocked even though they knew her husband had abused her repeatedly over several years. In the end I'd intervened when I couldn't stand listening to Marita lie anymore about where her black eyes and broken wrists had come from.

I was sick of knowing too much about other people's lives. I didn't want to read about a tango queen constantly forgiving her husband for beating her or where some professional model had had something trimmed or something added. After the Myyrmanni Mall bombing, Antti was furious when the news showed a picture of the bomber's home.

"Is that what people really want, to go look at the house where a terrorist lived? What are they going to do with that information? I can understand publishing his picture in every newspaper—I guess that can help the police—but this is nothing but voyeurism. The other people in that building still have to live there."

Of course, most of the revelations printed in the papers were carefully constructed messaging. I would have much preferred to read a detailed analysis of the prime minister's child benefit plan than what his kids' favorite bedtime stories were. But a man who read bedtime stories to his children couldn't be a beast whose decisions would swell day care class sizes and reduce elderly people's diaper allowances, could he?

We knew so much more about so many things than our grandparents did, but how much of that information made us wiser than them?

I was just about to call Antti to tell him I was coming home when Ursula appeared at my door.

"I talked to Andreas Smeds. Apparently the parents are on some outing in Turku with the Heart Foundation. Andreas said he can come in for questioning after milking, but Heli's waiting for a calf to be born. What do we do?"

"You interview Andreas today and the others tomorrow. How long will the Turku trip take?"

"Until tomorrow. The cow is supposed to have her baby any second, and there's some inspector there too."

"It would be good if you videotaped the interrogation so Puupponen can analyze it later if necessary. I'm headed home now with these papers. Call if anything important comes up. I'll see you in the morning."

A surprised expression appeared on Ursula's face. "You're going home in the middle of the day when we have a homicide investigation going on?"

"My son is sick."

Ursula shrugged. "It was the same in Lahti. Everyone with small kids was constantly skipping out and making the people without a family do all the work. Then they complain about how hard it is to combine work with family life. But you chose it yourself. No one forced you to make the little brats!" Ursula turned and slammed the door after her. Ten years ago I probably would have agreed. I thought I didn't want a husband or children, that I got along best by myself. The worst thing was that I still had those thoughts sometimes.

When I got home, Taneli only had a slight fever and wanted to play, so I didn't get much paperwork done. Around three he finally went down for his afternoon nap. I read interview records and more lab reports about tire treads, the cars seen around the lake (most of which belonged to local residents), and unidentified fibers found in Annukka Hackman's car. As expected, no meaningful link had been found between the moose hunters and Hackman. We just had to continue our footwork and believe that time wasn't only an enemy.

At four thirty I went to check on Taneli. He was still asleep, and I'd have to wake him to get Iida. His pajamas had blue-and-red cats on them, and his reddish hair curled slightly. He'd inherited that from me, along with his nose, which curved upward like a ski jump at the end and was the same as my father's. Sometimes I thought of couples whose marriages ended in anger. How did they stand to see the person they hated in their children's faces? How did they refrain from directing their anger at their kids?

The whole stairwell echoed with Taneli's protests at being woken up early, and I didn't have the energy to try to calm him down. I wasn't at my best when something woke me up in the middle of a sleep cycle either. I left him in the car to listen to a tape of one of his favorite stories while I went in to get Iida. I locked the car and made sure it couldn't go rolling off anywhere even if Taneli did manage to disengage the parking break. By the time Iida and I came back, he'd nodded off, but in the parking lot at home he started yelling again.

"Make him stop, Mom!" Iida whined. Someone had filled the elevator with cigarette smoke again, so Iida refused to use it, and we took the stairs. When we finally got inside the apartment, I sat the kids down in front of the TV so I could concentrate on making dinner, although canned pea soup didn't demand any great gastronomical skills.

Antti came home around seven. I'd just taken Taneli's temperature, which was normal. I was starting his bedtime story when the phone rang.

"Autio here. I thought you should hear right away. Andreas Smeds confessed."

I felt as if I'd been punched hard in the gut.

"What!" My voice was ridiculously shrill.

"He was screaming his head off and saying 'yes, I fucking shot her.' He was pretty sauced, so we threw him in a cell to sleep it off."

"Wow. Did you videotape the interview?"

"Yes."

I told Autio I'd swing by the station and asked him and Ursula to wait there for me. I read Taneli a short book about a bunny and left Antti to handle the rest.

"A confession," I proclaimed. "Maybe we can get this Hackman case wrapped up. If so, I'm definitely taking a few days off."

Antti laughed. "I've heard that one before," he said, then took over reading to the children.

I was so excited that I couldn't help speeding. The world looked more tolerable now too as fog softened the brightness of the lights and gave the buildings a homier feel. Nothing could make the police station beautiful, though: it was a colossus designed to make a person feel small. I ran up the stairs to our floor and knocked on Ursula and Autio's door. Ursula was in the office alone. Autio was out smoking.

"Congratulations! How did you get the confession out of him?" I said. I couldn't remember Ursula smiling at me that warmly since her job interview.

"Come watch the video. He is drunk, but that shouldn't reduce the value of the confession."

I wasn't so sure of that. The media room was cold. Her hands shaking, Ursula fiddled with the VCR.

Andreas was pale and his eyes were bloodshot. On the video his voice sounded hoarse and unclear. At first he answered Ursula's and Autio's questions with decorum, but as the interrogation proceeded he became increasingly intoxicated, as if he'd downed a bottle of booze fast just before coming in.

"Where was your family's Land Rover on Tuesday the fifth of November?" Ursula asked.

"At home in the yard as far as I remember. It's been more than two weeks since then."

"Did you drive anywhere that day?"

"If I remember right, I was home all day working on the tractor. I've already told you this. You should try taking notes."

Autio had taken the observer's role, while Ursula pressed Andreas. Andreas said he was at home asleep on the night of Kervinen's death.

"I didn't even know the guy. I read in the paper that he was Hackman's old boyfriend. I would have preferred not to know her either."

"So your brother doesn't know about your relationship with his wife. What about your parents? They do live under the same roof after all."

A wicked smile appeared on Andreas's face.

"They couldn't imagine that even I could be that presumptuous. Although I guess I'm going to have to tell them now before Hackman's book comes out, once Sasha recovers a little. I'm leaving. I'm moving . . ." Andreas swayed in his chair and his speech began to slur. "Heli's leaving tomorrow to bring Sasha home. They woke him up, and the doctor gave him permission to travel. I guess Citroën will charter a plane."

"Is Heli traveling tomorrow? That may not work. We'll have to ask Detective Kallio. What was your brother, Sasha, doing on the day of Annukka Hackman's death?"

"Weight training. We have a gym set up in one of the barns. He helped me on the tractor too. And he slept. I'm not my brother's keeper. He didn't leave the house, though. He enjoyed having some time at home. He's a good homebody, our Sasha." Andreas grimaced and leaned one of his hands on his knee. He belched, and Ursula retreated from the smell.

"Did you know Annukka Hackman carried a pistol?"

"Everyone knew. She showed it off to us the second time she visited. Mom was horrified. She's always hated guns. Grandpa was a pacifist, and Mom didn't even want us to go into the army. She started crying the first time she saw me in uniform . . . God." Andreas swallowed. His voice sounded dry. "What do you mean we have to talk to the detective about Heli leaving? Heli didn't do anything! Are you crazy?" Suddenly Andreas stood up, and Ursula reacted by also getting to her feet.

"Take it easy. Or should we put him in a cell to sober up?" she asked Autio, who shook his head.

"Sit down, Smeds." Autio spoke for the first time during the interview. Andreas flopped back into his chair. "Can anyone testify that you were at home asleep in your bed the night before last?"

Andreas blushed. "You'd have to ask the others who were at the farm then."

"So you and Heli weren't sleeping together?" Ursula asked. She tapped her long, golden fingernails on the table. Andreas started laughing.

"No. That isn't a pleasure we enjoy very often. You seem awfully interested in it, though. Cops and reporters. You're all the same. Did you become a pig so you could go rooting around in other people's sex lives?"

Next to me in the media room I heard Ursula draw a breath, then her nails started tapping the chair in front of her.

"Your sex life interests me exactly as much as it relates to the crime we're investigating," she continued on the tape. "You all had a reason to fear and hate Annukka Hackman. How did you know she was at Lake Humaljärvi that night?"

Andreas started chuckling again, although the laugh lacked any joy. I noticed Ursula's muscles tense when she heard the laugh.

"Yes, I fucking shot her. Are you satisfied? I destroyed her life before she could destroy me and my family. And everyone will read about it tomorrow in the papers, right? To hell with the consequences." Andreas tried to look Ursula in the eyes, but his gaze was erratic.

"Where did you throw the gun?"

"In the lake. Is that enough for you? I'm tired." Andreas closed his eyes. Ursula tried to get more out of him, but he didn't answer. After a few minutes he started to snore, and at that point Ursula cut off the interrogation.

"Then we took him to a cell. Should I continue questioning him tomorrow with Autio?"

"Yes, go ahead." I knew Ursula was expecting praise and congratulations, but there was no reason for that. Andreas had obviously realized that if he confessed to Hackman's murder, the police would let Heli out of the country to get Sasha. I asked Ursula whether they'd checked Andreas's blood-alcohol level. They hadn't. Could he have just been pretending to be drunk? And if he had been drunk, would he have been able to put on a farce like that, to ensure that Heli got to travel?

"So there's our solution," said a male voice behind us, making me jump. I hadn't heard Autio come into the room.

"Kervinen's death must have been suicide. Anything for love, I guess."

"We'll see whether Andreas tells us the same story tomorrow," I responded unenthusiastically. "The confession alone won't be good enough."

"I'm the one who got Andreas to confess. Is that why it isn't good enough?" Ursula shouted. "Because it was me?"

"It has nothing to do with that. You did well. Keep doing the same thing tomorrow. I'm going to go have a look at our suspect in his cell, then I'm going back home." I was insanely tired, but I wanted to see with my own eyes what kind of shape Andreas was in.

When the cell door opened, he didn't react; instead, he just lay on the cot. Under his head was a pillow, but he'd tossed the blanket to the floor. I walked up to him and could smell the alcohol on his breath. Maybe Koskenkorva vodka. I shook him by the shoulder, and he mumbled something in response. I picked up the tin cup that was next to the sink. Then I filled it with a little water and dumped it on Andreas's face. He spluttered and opened his eyes.

"What the hell?" His speech was slurred, and he closed his eyes again. He didn't have a belt, the top buttons of his shirt were open, and his shoes had been taken away. The heel of his left sock had been carefully darned with black yarn. Andreas turned onto his other side, and a little spittle dribbled from the corner of his mouth. Questioning him could definitely wait until tomorrow.

In the car I wondered whether I should notify Heli Haapala about Andreas's detention, but then I rejected the idea. I'd let things proceed on their own. Why had Heli fallen in love with Andreas even though he was a reckless drunk who seemed unable to control himself? Was it the typical female misapprehension that only her love could save him? Maybe Sasha was too good for Heli: successful, good looking, pleasant. Maybe Heli felt overshadowed by her famous husband. Maybe it was easier to share the shadow with Andreas.

A terrifying thought crossed my mind: I'd started liking Taskinen more after he turned out to be imperfect like the rest of us, after he'd bowed to pressure to give up on a politically sensitive investigation. After that I wasn't looking up to Jyrki anymore; he was on the same level as me. I'd done my idol worshiping as a teenager; as an adult I wanted someone who could let me be weak or strong depending on my needs. Lately I'd been forced to be the more stable partner, but the situation would balance back out again once Antti figured out his work.

The fog had grown even thicker, and I didn't notice the man in the crosswalk until the last second and had to swerve onto the sidewalk to miss him.

The parking lot at home was quiet, and the neighboring buildings were hidden in the fog. I could feel the humidity curling my hair.

Everything was quiet inside the apartment as well. I checked Taneli's forehead, and his temperature was still normal. Iida seemed to be fine too.

I found Antti sitting on the sofa reading. "Well?" he asked.

"We'll see what he says tomorrow when he's hungover. That's when we usually get the best confessions. There may not be any cause for celebration. One of my colleagues really provoked him." I sat down next to Antti and wrapped my arms around him. We kissed, and it was the restrained kiss of an old married couple, not anything seductive. Still, it was good to just sit together.

Unfortunately, my phone started ringing again. It was Taskinen this time.

"Hi there," I said hesitantly. I knew Jyrki wouldn't have called so late if the news about Terttu was good.

"Hi, Maria. Well, now we know. Terttu's cancer is malignant and she's going in for surgery on Monday, skipping all the lines." Jyrki's voice was quiet, as if he was calling in secret.

"I'm really sorry." I felt the tears coming and tried to blink them away. Jyrki didn't need me crying now. "What are her chances?"

"There's always some hope. I made her take a sleeping pill, and I think she's finally resting. Poor thing. I still have to call Silja. She has a break from practice in an hour."

"Say hi from me. And to Terttu."

"It's probably best that I don't tell Terttu we spoke. I'm taking tomorrow off. We can talk again on Monday."

"Call anytime you need. My phone will be on. I'm on call over the weekend."

I heard a deep sigh on the other side of the line. "Thanks. I already feel better. Good night, Maria."

"Good night."

I didn't realize until I'd hung up that I hadn't remembered to tell him about Andreas Smeds's confession. But perhaps that was best. This call hadn't been from a coworker; it had been from a friend. I started to cry again. Antti didn't ask any questions; he just pulled me into his arms. And that was a good place to be.

17

In the morning my phone was full of messages again. I decided to allow myself some coffee and toast before I answered any of them. But some of that coffee ended up splashed on the morning paper when I saw the headline "Confession in Journalist Murder."

According to unconfirmed information received by this newspaper, a decisive breakthrough has occurred in the investigation of the murder of reporter Annukka Hackman. The murderer has confessed and is now in police custody awaiting arraignment.

Goddamn Ursula. Who else could have leaked that? No wonder I had so many messages. Of course the reporter wouldn't reveal his source. My intention had been to put off holding a press conference until Andreas had been questioned again. Now I'd have to rethink that. Reluctantly, I checked my voice mail. One of the messages was from the department press officer and another was from Heli Haapala.

I called Heli back as I drove from the day care to work, knowing she'd be up early for milking. The hands-free got tangled in my hair and popped out of my ear, though, so I had to hold the phone with one hand and drive with the other. It was one of those mornings again.

The ground was covered in frost and the trees in rime so that sun's rays shining low on the horizon made the branches shimmer with dozens of tiny prisms.

"Andreas didn't come home," Heli said before I'd finished saying my name. "Is he in police custody?"

"Yes."

"The newspaper says he confessed . . . That can't be right!"

"Did one of the papers publish his name? That would be a serious mistake for the leaker and any reputable paper."

"No, but they said someone was arrested, and since I haven't seen Andreas and he won't answer his phone, I assumed it must be him. He hasn't disappeared like this for years. Viktor and Rauha are beside themselves, and I'm supposed to be leaving for England this afternoon. Sasha's surgery went well; he's being transported to Finland the day after tomorrow."

I stopped at a crosswalk for a gaggle of little girls dressed in bright-colored snowsuits. Someone honked behind me—apparently the city's Give us a Brake! Campaign from the beginning of the school year was now a distant memory, as new, more shocking headlines had replaced the news of a young girl's death in a crosswalk.

"I'm glad Sasha's recovering. We need to hear from him as a witness too."

"But Andreas can't be guilty! He swore to me that he didn't . . ." Heli's voice broke with crying, and she hung up. I threw my own phone down on the seat since I needed both hands to shift gears and change lanes. I felt like letting the battery go dead by "accident," but of course I couldn't do that.

At work I dipped into my emergency salmiakki stash for a quick sugar boost, but that didn't help my nerves. The overnight duty officer had delivered reports on familiar themes: domestic violence in a Russian-Finnish family in Suvela and a beating in front of the Big Apple Mall. I decided to start the morning meeting with those to get us moving. First, though, I checked Andreas Smeds's condition in Holding. He'd woken up with an obvious hangover, but he seemed lucid and hadn't asked to call anyone. He'd just asked for a shower.

I glanced at my phone one last time as I walked up to the conference room. A familiar tabloid reporter had sent me a text message. *According to the Internet, Andreas Smeds has been arrested for Hackman's murder. Is that correct?*

Oh hell! Of course the newspapers didn't dare to publish the name of the suspect we were holding without confirmation, but everything was different on the Internet. I was really getting angry. It would be a stupid waste of resources to try to investigate where the Internet rumors had started. And the publicity could work in our favor. Now that we had a named suspect, we'd probably get more eyewitness reports.

"Good morning," I said as I entered the meeting room and took my place up front. "As many of you may have been surprised to read in the paper, we had a breakthrough in the Annukka Hackman case yesterday. Andreas Smeds confessed to shooting her. Congratulations to Honkanen and Autio. However, I'd be interested to know how this information ended up on the Internet. Does anyone have any ideas?"

Sitting by the window, Ursula didn't move. Her red suede skirt was new. Was that the secret to her expensive new clothing? Tip bounties? We had our own tip hotline, of course, as did the papers. Heli and Andreas would become the focus of national criticism, and Sasha would be seen as an even more tragic hero, with no shortage of people wanting to comfort him. Personally I didn't want a role in this soap opera. At least now I didn't have to worry about Heli slipping away, since she'd be under close media scrutiny for the next few days.

"No? No one? I'm afraid this leak might make the investigation more difficult. We'll talk about how to proceed later in the meeting. First, though, a couple of new cases." I tried to calm down as I listened to Lehtovuori discussing an assault investigation that was ready to go to the prosecutor.

"So Honkanen and Autio will continue questioning Andreas Smeds," I said as the meeting circled back to the Hackman case. "I want specific facts: how did Smeds know Hackman would be at Lake Humaljärvi, how far was the shot, how many shots, where did he hide the weapon, and so forth. Just 'Fuck yeah, I shot her' isn't enough. I'll hold a press conference this afternoon, maybe around two. I need facts in hand before then. Puustjärvi, is there anything new from Forensics or the lab?"

"They haven't found Atro Jääskeläinen's fingerprints in Hannu Kervinen's apartment, or fingerprints from anyone else we think might be mixed up in this case. The analysis of the boots came up with bupkis, so we still have no idea who that print belongs to," Puustjärvi said. "Kervinen killed himself and just left that weird message to screw with us. Mark my words."

"But the message on the computer was saved after he called me," I pointed out. "We can't dismiss the possibility that someone else wrote the message."

"But why would this other person, let's say it's Andreas Smeds, leave a message that refers specifically to Annukka Hackman's murderer?" Koivu asked. "Or do you think there could be two different perps here, first Smeds and then someone else?"

"If only I knew. Let's wait for the DNA results from the rope we found in Kervinen's apartment. If someone strangled him, maybe they left something behind. Where in an apartment like that could someone try to hang themselves? Lähde, will you go have a look when you have time?" I tried to remember Kervinen's bathroom. Could he have tried to hang himself on some part of the shower? Forensics hadn't mentioned anything being broken in their report, and few hooks or curtain rods in a normal home would support the full weight of an adult man.

When the meeting was over, Koivu said he wanted to talk privately in my office. I asked him if it could wait, since I first had to organize the press briefing. Two o'clock should give Ursula and Autio plenty of time for questioning, so I went back to my desk and asked the press officer to set it for then. The sun was halfway through its journey to the top of the sky, and seeing it gave me new hope. If only Andreas's confession didn't turn out to be a sham.

"What's up?" I asked Koivu once he was sitting on my couch in his usual position, with his hands behind his head and his legs spread wide.

I was expecting to hear something about trouble at home, but instead he said, "It's this Ursula thing . . ." Then he had a hard time continuing. He closed his eyes, and his glasses trembled with the movement of his face muscles.

"Yeah?"

"It bothers me. I mean, was that it? She makes these baseless accusations against me that half the department hears, then she retracts them. Has half the department heard that too? Shouldn't she have to apologize or something? I can hardly sleep. What if she starts up again? Or accuses someone else?"

Koivu was right. I hadn't really dealt with the situation. On the other hand, forcing a grown person to make an apology felt like the wrong move. That was what you did in a day care or an elementary school. Humiliating Ursula wouldn't bring anyone any kind of satisfaction; it would just be the same sort of power play she'd been making.

"I'm just embarrassed . . . I guess I should ignore it, but some of the guys have been razzing me, asking if I gave Ursula a go because Anu isn't putting out anymore since the baby."

"What guys?"

"Oh, just some shitheads in Patrol. There's no point naming names. And of course a man shouldn't get bent out of shape over stuff like that, but . . ."

"But you are," I said, finishing his thought. Koivu blushed. "I'll try to get both of you around a table after the press conference this afternoon. Then we'll see. Think about what you want to say to Ursula. If the Hackman case really is solved, you should take your comp days. Is Anu planning to extend her maternity leave?"

Koivu shook his head and told me I should ask her myself, which was fair. I wouldn't have liked it either if Antti was telling my coworkers my plans. After Koivu left, I tried to focus on paperwork and sending e-mails, but I was restless. What would Andreas Smeds say today?

I got my answer just after noon as I was coming back from lunch. Autio was on his way in from outside—there weren't many places to smoke in the building.

"He says he already told us everything yesterday, and he doesn't have anything more to say. He won't answer any questions and doesn't want a lawyer."

"Ah. Send him for gunpowder analysis and talk to search and rescue about getting divers back in the lake. We need to find that gun. Smeds can have it his way. We'll put his picture in the paper and ask for eyewitnesses. His name is already online. You don't know anything about that, do you?"

Autio shrugged. "Someone always leaks. Andreas Smeds is a public figure."

He was a few years ago, I thought, *and now he is again.* I tried to psyche myself up to play the triumphant senior detective who only had good news for the media: a breakthrough had happened in the case, one of the suspects had confessed, and the investigation was proceeding apace. Once again it was time to put on my mask, to tie my hair back, touch up my makeup, and straighten my collar. I asked Ursula and Autio to join me since they'd done the dirty work.

During the briefing, the fluttering of camera shutters increased when Ursula commented briefly on the previous night's interrogation, how it had started out routine and ended in a confession. She sounded nervous and overwrought, but she enjoyed the cameras and flashed them the parade smile her colleagues rarely saw. Perhaps she was even irritated when she had to turn the microphone back over to me.

"We have a confession but no motive, and a lot of other details are still unclear."

The public relations officer had brought pictures of Andreas Smeds. I repeated that the police still needed eyewitness reports. One of the tabloid reporters suggested several possible motives, but none of them hit on the real bombshell. The leaker had been smart enough not to reveal Andreas and Heli's affair. If they had, it would have narrowed down my pool of suspects, since only a limited number of people knew about that yet, theoretically just my unit and Jouko Suuronen.

I'd expected to hear from Suuronen, and, sure enough, after the press conference I discovered a message on my phone, full of shouting.

It's Suuronen. I'm at the airport. Tell Andreas to contact my lawyer right now! It's bullshit that I can't talk to him directly! The plane is leaving now. I'm going with Heli to get Sasha. Keep the reporters away from Sasha!

I called Antti to ask him to get the kids from day care, then went to say hi to Andreas in his cell. This time he lay on his back and didn't seem at all hungover.

"Hello, Detective," he said almost cheerfully.

"Hello, Andreas. Jouko Suuronen says hi too. He wants you to contact his lawyer."

Andreas sneered. I sat down on the cement table; besides the cot, there was nowhere else to sit. Everything from genitalia to bible verses had been scratched in the walls.

"We can keep you detained until tomorrow at seven o'clock, then we have to decide whether to arrest you formally. I just held a press conference and identified you as the person who confessed to Annukka Hackman's murder. Is that what you wanted?"

Andreas sneered again. "I may have exaggerated slightly last night when I was drunk," he said.

I sighed. "Do you intend to recant?"

"Well, if it says in the newspaper tomorrow that I'm guilty, then I guess that's the truth. What story do you want to hear, Detective Kallio? I drank half a bottle of booze and then drove to the lake. I shot Annukka and pushed her body in the water. Then I threw the pistol in too."

"What kind of pistol was it?"

"I was so drunk I don't remember. And why do you ask? This conversation can't have any value as evidence."

"No, it doesn't. Is that going to be your answer for everything? 'I was so drunk I don't remember'?"

Andreas sat up. He had Viktor's eyes, which would recede more deeply into their sockets as he aged, just like his father's. At least Andreas was Viktor's son. That much was obvious.

"Do you remember when Sasha was born?" I asked on a momentary whim. Andreas had walked to the sink and was noisily drinking water. His black jeans were grubby, and his plaid shirt stank of sweat.

"I wasn't quite two, so I don't really remember much at all. Dad took me to the hospital to see Mom and the baby and bought me ice cream at the hospital coffee shop. Why do you ask? Are you trying to build a motive for me from some early childhood jealousy? Go right ahead." Andreas tried the cell door, which I'd closed behind me. "Will I have to sit here for long, or will I be transferred somewhere else?"

"You'll sit here exactly as long as I see fit. You seem to have a lot of faith in the Finnish legal system. Just remember that no system is infallible! I'd recommend you either contact Suuronen's lawyer or some other legal counsel. Misleading the police is a crime no matter how drunk you were."

I banged for the guard to come open the door. I still had to deal with Ursula and Koivu's reconciliation before I could get back to the company of sensible people, namely my children. At least the day care hadn't called to report that Taneli's fever had come back.

"Koivu wanted to settle things with you face to face," I told Ursula as we waited in my office for him. She and Autio intended to continue with Andreas later, although I doubted they'd get anything more out of him. Tomorrow I'd have to appeal to the district court to remand Andreas for trial if I thought we had grounds to arrest him. I was so irritated by his antics that I would have been fine with letting him sit in jail for a few days even though it was probably a worse punishment to release him to the mercy of the reporters and paparazzi.

"Why do Koivu and I need you here when we meet?" Ursula asked.

"It's always good to have a witness."

"Yes, and you're known for being so neutral," Ursula snapped back as Koivu walked in. Instead of sitting next to Ursula on the couch, he stood by the window. Neither seemed talkative. I didn't feel like playing day care teacher, so I just waited for them to start the game. Ursula had found a chip in her nail polish and fished for something in her purse. I watched in amusement as she calmly began touching up her gold nails. I tried to catch Koivu's gaze, since he'd been the one who wanted this meeting. Strange how such a talkative person could turn so taciturn when he had to open up about his own feelings instead of interrogating other people.

"I think you owe me an apology," he finally said in a low voice after Ursula had begun her second coat.

"Usually guilty people apologize, not the innocent," Ursula responded coldly.

"You made false accusations against me."

"But they didn't believe me!"

"You're right, because your claims were ridiculous." Koivu was still looking out the window at the darkening afternoon. The moon was already in the sky, shining like a blood orange that someone had sliced in half.

"So I'm supposed to apologize for what you did to *me*?" Ursula stood up and grabbed her purse. "OK. I'm sorry, I'm sorry, I'm sorry.

Are you happy?" And with that she turned on her heels and walked out, slamming the door so hard that the kids' picture on my desk fell over. I set the picture back up. It had been taken at the day care earlier in the fall. Iida's lace collar was a little crooked, and Taneli sneered instead of smiling. That was why I liked the photo so much.

"I think you're going to have to settle for that," I said.

"I imagine so. Maybe I should change units instead of Anu. Why don't you believe Andreas Smeds's confession?"

"Instinct. Which has been wrong before."

"I know. Have you heard anything new?"

"I just visited Andreas."

"No, I mean—" Koivu began, but then his phone started ringing. It was about one of his cases, a convenience store robber caught the morning of Kervinen's death, who'd beaten a clerk after discovering that there was only fifty euros in the bag. Apparently his withdrawal symptoms had become so severe that he wanted to confess. Koivu disappeared, and I decided to head home. When I picked the kids up from day care, Taneli was wearing a bright-yellow shirt that was too big for him, because in honor of Friday he'd managed to dirty not only his actual shirt but also his backup. I knew the laundry hamper at home was already overflowing, but the cupboards were bare.

"Put on Popeda," Iida demanded in the car. The poor kid had been brainwashed with her mom's favorite music and hummed along happily with Pate Mustajärvi as he sang about hitting rock bottom and only having twenty cents in his pocket. A couple of times the ladies at the day care had commented on Iida's song selections after she'd insisted on performing the Ramones' "I Wanna Be Sedated," even though she didn't have a clue what the words meant. I thought my daughter's taste in music was much better than the Shakira and Britney Spears songs her peers preferred.

Even though I was on call all weekend, I didn't have to go in to work other than a quick visit to the court on Saturday afternoon for

Andreas's arraignment. Saturday's papers had already proclaimed him guilty. Atro Jääskeläinen was interviewed in several of the stories. He said he suspected that Andreas had killed Annukka because he couldn't stand the shame of having his drunk-driving convictions brought back to light.

"In her book Annukka really shows the contrast between Sasha and his brother. Sasha is a great man. It's really too bad he missed winning the world championship this year. We're publishing the book as soon as possible, once Annukka's funeral is behind us," Jääskeläinen said in one paper. The story was accompanied by a photograph of him looking forlorn as he sat next to a black-framed picture of Annukka.

The district court session was routine, and I only had to be away from home for an hour. Andreas was there, but he didn't have to say a word. He sat leaning back a bit, eyes closed, looking like none of it had anything to do with him. It wasn't until he heard that he'd be detained in jail for another two weeks that he flinched slightly. For ease of questioning, he would be kept in our building's holding cells. A few reporters and a photographer were waiting outside the court, and I was amused by the way Andreas grinned for the cameras.

On Saturday we also received a couple of tips that a man fitting Andreas's description had been seen behind the wheel of a Land Rover on Gesterby Road south of the lake on the day of Hackman's murder. I wasn't particularly moved by this since publishing a suspect's picture always caused a wave of this sort of thing. There was still nothing to connect Andreas to Kervinen's murder, though. And according to Lähde, there were no probable hanging locations in Kervinen's apartment other than the TV wall mount, but even that was only six feet off the ground.

"It was about as high as I am tall. Maybe he tested it out, then decided it was better to jump," Lähde suggested over the phone.

I'd gone in the kitchen and closed the door to talk because I didn't want the kids hearing a conversation about hanging. So far I'd only told Iida I was a police officer who caught bad guys, but now that she was learning to read it would be harder to protect her from the truth.

On Saturday night Antti went to his work Christmas party, which I hoped would perk him up. He'd spent the day reading unemployment insurance brochures and calculating whether it would make sense to pull Taneli out of day care entirely and only have Iida in half-day pre-school. I'd spent the time cleaning. The White Cube's only good quality compared to our old house was that once I had the kids' toys in some sort of order, the rest of the place cleaned up in an hour.

"Won't Smeds need a farmhand now that Andreas is going to prison?" Antti asked as he slicked his hair back with gel. The hairdo made him look like a mafioso from a 1970s American B movie. Antti rarely commented on the cases I worked, because according to him they affected our lives enough as it was.

"Call and ask. That could be a new career for you. Study to become an itinerant farmworker."

"Actually, there's an interesting project starting in March at Vaasa University, sort of a multidisciplinary dynamic model development thing combining math and economics. I could telecommute, and I'd only have to go to Vaasa maybe every other week. Kirsti Jensen called while you were vacuuming. I'll have to think about it. It's still temp work, but that's better than nothing."

In the end, I didn't need to press the cousins into babysitting; I was able to handle the usual Christmas party assaults and a rape at a local hockey club's party over the phone. The December work schedules hadn't come out yet, but I'd be on during at least one of the holidays. Hopefully it just wasn't Christmas Eve. Christmas violence depressed me the most; it contrasted so much with the joy, peace, and goodwill shown in all the advertisements at that time of year. On the previous Christmas we'd seen a record number of parents lose custody of their children, some as a result of abuse and others because of neglect. There were children who spent Christmas Eve alone, without food or a single present, while their parents were at the bar or passed out on the couch. I assumed I'd be seeing some of them again at work before too long, once they grew up a little.

District Attorney Haimakainen called on Sunday morning. I hadn't seen him at Andreas's arraignment, but now he wanted to be part of the Hackman investigation.

"This is such a significant case that the prosecutor's office should have been alerted immediately when the investigation began," he said.

"I think this is a normal homicide."

"Not with such important people mixed up in it. We need to meet first thing tomorrow morning. Does nine thirty work for you?"

I knew it was best to deal with unpleasant things as quickly as possible, so I agreed. At noon I took a long run around Central Park. When I was halfway around, my phone started ringing. I never carried it on runs unless I was on call. Cursing, I stopped to dig it out of my pocket. I didn't recognize the number.

"Kallio."

"Hi, this is Sasha Smeds. I heard about Andreas. What the hell is he doing?" Sasha's voice was higher pitched and huskier than before; he'd probably been on a ventilator for days.

"What do you mean?" I started walking past a multicolored art installation toward the river.

"I already confirmed his movements in my interview. Or more like how there were none to report. Andreas couldn't have left Smedsbo that night. I can offer you proof of that, on the record, if you'll let me. Talk to Jouko. He can arrange a formal interview when I get back to Finland. Andreas has always had a habit of saying stupid things when he's drunk. He's innocent. You have to let him go."

18

Because of a conflict in the police chief's schedule, the department leadership meeting was moved to Monday morning, so Koivu had to run our unit's usual morning meeting. Outside the sixth-floor windows everything was dark: the streetlights were out. I grimaced and changed the subject when everyone congratulated me for solving the Hackman case. Sasha Smeds's call the previous day certainly hadn't helped the situation. After talking to him, I'd called Suuronen to arrange the interview Sasha had asked for.

"Andreas has always been a basket case, but what the hell is he doing now? Sasha doesn't need anything else to worry about. He's recovering, but his co-driver is still holding on by a thread. They had to amputate his legs, he was burned so bad. Sasha blames himself."

I was starting to believe that Suuronen did care about Sasha and not just the money he made as a result of Sasha's victories. And in the press, Sasha was the incorruptible hero of Finnish rally racing. Annukka Hackman really had needed to look elsewhere—into someone else's life—if she wanted anything juicy in her book.

Taskinen arrived last to the meeting, uncharacteristically late. As the chief of police droned on about the coming year's case closure goals, I looked out the window at the darkness, where shapes were slowly taking form. The sun was still hidden behind the trees, but the color of the sky showed that it would be visible later in the day. Suddenly the meeting didn't feel as exasperating as usual. Strange how the mere promise of light could affect my mood. My allergy to meetings had worsened over the years, and I could only stand them when I got to lead the discussion and set the pace myself. What would the police academy entrance exams say about my ability to work in a team environment now?

Taskinen revealed the cause for his tardiness after the meeting. As the others left, he lingered in the room.

"I took Terttu to the hospital today. I didn't sleep much over the weekend." Taskinen's face looked worn, and for once it was easy to believe he was over fifty. The furrows in his brow were deeper than ever, and the harsh light of the meeting room exposed how much gray was in his hair.

"Is the surgery today?"

"They moved it to tomorrow. Today is still tests. We wrote her will and planned the funeral yesterday. Terttu insisted. Silja's coming next week. She completely broke down when she heard the news. Luckily she has a lot of friends in Canada, and of course her husband. Today you can bet I'm going to run at least ten kilometers as soon as I get away from the hospital. You wouldn't want to come with me, would you?"

"You think I could keep up? You still do a marathon in what, three hours?" I said, trying to lighten the mood. My legs were still feeling yesterday's jog, and I doubted I was up to two long runs in two days. We agreed to chat by phone that evening, since Jyrki was sure to need someone to talk to.

I ran into Koivu when I reached our hallway. "Ciao, boss," he said. "Have you seen the headlines in today's papers? According to the rumors online, Heli Haapala and Andreas are having an affair. And Ursula called in sick. Flu, supposedly."

"Goddamn it!" I yelled as I snatched the paper out of Koivu's hand. Of course anyone could say anything on the Internet. But apparently it was a slow news day, so the print press was willing to report even online rumors to fill space. "Did you talk about this in the meeting?"

"Yep. I said the boss was going to rip whoever leaked this online to shreds. No one looked particularly guilty. Who should we assign to Autio, to continue questioning Andreas?"

"No one for now. We'll just keep him locked up as long as the prosecutor lets us."

I told Koivu about Sasha's phone call. The charter flight carrying his entourage was expected at Helsinki-Vantaa Airport around two o'clock. Sasha would then be transferred to a private room at Helsinki University Hospital for about a week. It was pointless hoping the media would let him rest and recuperate. Now everything related to Annukka Hackman would sell all too well. Once he heard about the affair, would Sasha still be prepared to back up his brother's alibi?

"What did Puupponen report about Annukka Hackman's funeral?" I asked.

"The same things you can read in the paper. People cried and gave speeches about a heroic reporter killed in the line of duty."

Koivu took the paper back from me and opened it to the first spread. The pictures covered half the pages. In one, Annukka Hackman was a beaming bride next to a more pallid Atro Jääskeläinen, and in the another Jääskeläinen placed flowers on his wife's casket in a church.

"That hockey rapist is here too. Nasty case. The victim is only fourteen. So young she believed the player she worshipped really just wanted to show her his trophy case when he took her to his house. I assigned Puustjärvi to interview the victim. Petri's good with kids. I'll handle the dude myself."

"You have my permission to give him the third degree. I'm glad the girl reported it. Are you free around two? If so, let's go to the airport to meet Sasha Smeds. Suuronen promised to reserve a VIP lounge for us for fifteen minutes. This is such a shitty situation that I want to handle it myself."

"Gladly," Koivu said, then laughed. "Read the rest of that paper and you'll know more. The investigative journalists seem to have a leg up on us."

I did as ordered, although reading Internet rumors and the superlatives of funeral reporting made me sick. An article that followed the funeral spread emphasized that Annukka Hackman had been working at the lake, even though there was no hint of that in the evidence. If Andreas was telling the truth, why had he chosen to kill Hackman there? Because it was secluded and a weapon would be easily available?

A call from Antti brought me back to the present day.

"My love. Can you talk?"

"I wouldn't answer otherwise, my love," I said, emphasizing the final word a little sarcastically. We weren't in the habit of using pet names, so they felt artificial.

"I called the University of Vaasa. I'm going for a visit on Wednesday, taking the morning train up and the night train back. They seemed really interested."

"That's fantastic! Can you get the kids today? I think this is going to be another long one. Kisses."

Our life wasn't going to get any easier if Antti had to commute between Espoo and Vaasa five hours to the north. He thought domestic flights were a waste of energy, but now he'd have to fly sometimes. And if he worked from home, he'd need an office. Maybe I'd finally be able to convince him we had to get out of the White Cube. We could go apartment hunting next weekend.

Haimakainen, the district attorney, arrived for our meeting five minutes early.

"This crime is so high profile that we can't keep soft-pedaling the investigation," Haimakainen said in a lather. "Andreas Smeds has a criminal past. And of course he thinks he can give the authorities the runaround because of his brother's position."

Haimakainen was approaching retirement, and he probably thought it would be nice to end his career with a splash. He was thorough in his work and even after three decades as a prosecutor he still had a few shreds of idealism left. Crime could never be completely eliminated, but at least the innocent could be guaranteed some peace while the criminals were suffering their punishments.

"I'm not at all convinced Andreas Smeds is guilty. One drunken confession isn't enough."

"But the newspapers laid out a clear motive for the crime!" Haimakainen said. "Don't make a simple case more complicated than it has to be."

Haimakainen's agitation subsided a bit when I told him about Sasha's phone call. We continued our conversation over lunch, since he wanted to talk about Kervinen too. According to the criminal psychologist's report, changes in Kervinen's handwriting in his final diary entries suggested worsening depression, and the termination of entries on the day of Hackman's death pointed to his inability to process his grief. It was possible he'd committed suicide. And, given his depression, it was unlikely he could have planned Annukka Hackman's murder in advance and in a way that left so little evidence.

When I returned from lunch, I saw Rauha Smeds in the lobby arguing with the duty officer. I tried to slip past her since I still had work to do before going to the airport, but Rauha noticed me.

"Detective Kallio!" she yelled after me.

Rauha was red with rage. Her hair was sticking out every which way and her black coat was covered in dog hair.

"Tell this woman that I want to see my son! I came to bring him fresh clothes because he asked me to. Now I want to hear with my own ears if what those nasty newspapers are saying is true. I nearly fainted when I saw the headlines in the post office today. How can they even publish trash like that? And you aren't taking Andreas's confession seriously, are you? When that boy's drunk he can say anything."

After a moment's consideration, I said, "How about we go to my office for a chat about Andreas and a few other things? The elevator is here on the left." I used my keycard and pressed the button. Rauha smelled like a barn. Apparently she'd been forced to handle the milking while Heli and Andreas were away. She had probably been one of those women who went straight from the maternity ward to the fields, like my own grandmother had been.

When we got upstairs, I asked Rauha if she wanted coffee.

"Tea, please. Preferably herbal."

In the break room I found one suspiciously dry-looking bag of peppermint tea, but Lähde had eaten all the cookies again. As I returned to my office, I found Rauha sitting next to my desk, looking around curiously. She picked up the picture of my children.

"You also have two, and so small still. You never stop worrying about them, though. As a mother yourself, you must know how well we know our own children. I know Andreas isn't a murderer. I'd claim I was one myself to save him, but I can't leave Viktor. His last day could come at any time. All of this has made his condition worse, and I'm afraid to leave him even for a second."

"Unfortunately we can't let anyone see Andreas since the investigation is still ongoing. I wish I could, because maybe you could talk some sense into him and convince him to cooperate. Does Andreas often act violently when he's been drinking?"

Rauha smiled gently. "No. He's like his father that way. First he turns cheerful and then he goes sentimental. Viktor's never been one to drink regularly, though, and neither has Sasha. My father was a strict teetotaler. I never tasted a drop of alcohol before I moved to Sweden."

"What time did you return from the hospital on the day of Annukka Hackman's death?"

Rauha unbuttoned her coat and stirred her tea before she replied.

"It was almost seven. Driving in the dark is difficult, and I would have liked to have left earlier. And we were so worried because Viktor hasn't recovered as he was supposed to."

I wondered how Rauha was bearing the situation: her husband was deathly ill, one of her sons was gravely injured, and the other was imprisoned for murder. It was strange that she didn't ask more about Andreas and Heli. Had she known all along? Could Heli and Andreas's feelings have gone unnoticed?

I remembered how completely oblivious my own parents were to my drinking in high school. I also remembered my sister, Helena's, abortion during her senior year, which my parents still hadn't found out about, and many other examples of how little parents could know about their offspring's lives. It must be even easier for children to keep secrets from their parents once they'd grown up, since there's no reason to keep tabs on adults.

"We're also investigating whether the pathologist Hannu Kervinen's death is connected to Annukka Hackman's murder. Where were you last Tuesday night?"

"Where I usually am—sleeping in bed next to Viktor. Who is this Hannu Kervinen?"

"Annukka Hackman's ex-boyfriend," I replied and poured more milk in my coffee. Apparently Lehtovuori had made it, since he liked it strong.

"Annukka Hackman had plenty of men, and her interest in my son Sasha wasn't just professional either. At first I thought she was just using her book as a pretense to get close to Sasha and break up his marriage." Rauha squeezed more peppermint flavor out of the tea bag into her cup. Her fingers were wrinkled but slender, and her wedding ring appeared a little loose. "And the rest of the family were in their beds too, since Ronja didn't bark. Our dog, I mean. She always makes a terrible racket every time anyone comes in or goes out."

"What about when people move around inside the house?" I asked, thinking of Andreas and Heli.

"Then she's quiet, thank goodness. Old men have to go to the bathroom a lot."

"Are you planning to meet Sasha at the airport?"

"No. Viktor is waiting for me at home. Sasha is being cared for like a king, but Viktor only has me," Rauha said and finished off her tea. "I assume I can at least write to Andreas. I'm sure he's embarrassed by what he said when he was drunk, and now he feels like he can't take it back. He was the same as a child, always acting before he thought. I understand that's why he was such a good race-car driver. He knew how to trust his instincts. But he was always so afraid of success too. I imagine that's why he let himself drive drunk. Some people just can't handle things going right. Thank you for the tea, Detective. Please let my son go free."

Rauha stood up with the dignity of a person who was used to deciding the length of important conversations. I opened the door for her and watched as she walked down the hall with slow but purposeful steps. In pop psychology women were supposed to be divided into two groups: the ones who put their children before their spouses and the ones who put their spouses before anyone else in the world. Rauha Smeds was a good example of the latter type. Was that why her sons started racing? To rebel against their mother? Or to attract her care and attention?

How did the psychologists categorize women like me, who often put work before family and husband, I wondered as I filled out a time sheet. Police and farmers—all stuck in the same swamp of forms that needed filling.

Just then, Koivu stopped by my office. It was time to head to the airport to meet Sasha.

"How did the interrogation of the hockey player go?" I asked once we were on the beltway.

"He confessed. There was no way he could argue against such clear evidence. The neighbors saw the girl coming out of his house hysterical, and the signs of abuse and sperm sample are sufficient corroboration. A goddamn professional player! You'd think they'd have enough women. Everybody fawns over those guys. By the way, have you heard anything from Ursula?"

"No. An employee can be away from work for three days without a note from a doctor. Are they headed to meet Sasha too?" I asked as we passed a van from one of the television channels.

"Of course. The worse Sasha looks, the better. If they can just get someone to cry, the footage will be perfect," Koivu said. "Has the media called you today? The new motive they found for Andreas is seriously juicy."

"No, strangely enough. Maybe it's more effective to ask Heli directly on live TV. The airport may be a real circus."

"Maybe Ursula isn't at home with the flu. Maybe she's doing interviews and making the newspapers bid for the information she has. Want to bet she made copies of both versions of Hackman's manuscript?"

I hadn't thought of that. Of course I'd had colleagues before who couldn't be trusted completely. I hoped Koivu was wrong.

We parked in the VIP lot as close to the door as we could. The airport always gave me a wistful longing to be somewhere else, and on a cold November day like this, even though I hated lounging on the beach, I could imagine myself jetting off somewhere warm and sunny. In fact, I would have preferred that as my reason for being there, as opposed to meeting Heli and Sasha. Even though I had the ability to treat the people I met on cases with professional neutrality, I didn't always succeed. The most important thing now was not to show that to them or my coworkers.

An airport staff member led us to a meeting room. On the way we saw the herd of reporters waiting on the other side of the glass wall.

There were cameras, microphones, and at least one TV crew. One of the reporters recognized me, and ten seconds later my phone started to ring.

"Detective Kallio, you're at the airport too. Have you come to see Sasha or Heli?"

"No comment. And Jouko Suuronen is on the flight too." Something devilish in me made me say that before I hung up the phone, then switched it to silent. The interrogation room was no VIP suite; rather it was a dreary cell whose only decoration was a picture of President Tarja Halonen. She didn't look particularly cheery either. I sat down in a chair full of holes from cigarette burns and stared for a moment through the one-way glass at the travelers walking by.

"Haapala and Suuronen need to be out of the room when we talk to Sasha," I said, more to myself than to Koivu. "The medical staff can stay if it's absolutely necessary. Do you have the recorder ready?"

The first one through the glass doors of the Arrivals area was Sasha Smeds. He lay on a wheeled gurney and was still on an IV drip. Next came the pilot and a doctor. Suuronen followed immediately after, anxiously looking at something on his phone. Heli walked slightly behind the rest of the party, with a wide-brimmed dark-green felt hat pulled down to cover her face.

Koivu opened the door to our room, and we had to shift the furniture to one wall so Sasha's bed could fit in. In my job I was used to looking at people who'd been viciously beaten and killed; still, I cringed when I saw Sasha's face. The right side was still bandaged from the skin grafting, the skin of the left side was tight and lifeless, and his lips were swollen. A bandage was wrapped around his head to cover a wound on his forehead, and matted patches of hair stuck out from it. Sasha's left arm was only bandaged at the elbow, but his right arm and hand were completely covered in gauze.

"No longer than fifteen minutes," the doctor told me in English. "I wouldn't have agreed to this at all if Mr. Smeds hadn't insisted on it."

Sasha's nurse raised the head of the bed. The room was so cramped that Heli was forced to stand right next to me. Up close I could see that her face was swollen as if she'd been crying. The tiny veins on her eyelids were blue, and her nose was red. She gave me a faint nod. Suuronen carelessly barged into the room, bumping Sasha's bed in the process, then apologizing profusely.

"Sasha, do you want any of these people to leave?" I asked.

"Heli and Jouko can stay." Sasha's voice was still strangely high like a prepubescent boy. "And Dr. James doesn't understand Finnish."

While the others left, Koivu started the voice recorder and recited the name of the interviewee and the others present. I closed the door, perhaps subconsciously expecting all the reporters and photographers to run in at any moment.

"You said you had something to tell us about your brother, Andreas Smeds's, movements the evening of Annukka Hackman's death."

"Right. Or rather I don't have anything at all to say about them. When my parents left for the hospital, my brother, my wife, and I stayed home. Then Heli left for the store a little after three. I was worried about her going so late, because she doesn't like driving in the dark and the road conditions weren't great. I worked out in our gym and helped Andreas fix the tractor. Even though we weren't in the same room the whole time, I'm absolutely certain I would have heard it if Andreas had left. I hear engines, Detective. It's part of my job. Andreas couldn't have killed Annukka Hackman."

Sasha stopped talking and, with his healthy hand, reached for a cup in a holder connected to the side of the gurney and lifted it to his lips. His movements were slow, and as he drank, he made the same glugging sound as a child who's just learned to drink on his own but still can't control the angle of the cup or the amount of liquid coming out of it.

Suuronen lost his cool. "Damn it, Sasha, do you have to act so noble? Andreas deserves a punch in the teeth, not you defending him."

Sasha lowered the cup and responded quietly. "It isn't his fault my wife stopped loving me."

"I've never stopped loving you!" Heli exclaimed.

Dr. James turned his head from person to person, looking concerned.

"Mr. Suuronen and Ms. Haapala, could you please leave?" I said as I stepped to the door and opened it. Suuronen walked so close to me that I could smell the cognac on his breath. Heli had tears running down her cheeks.

"Sasha, if Andreas doesn't retract his confession, we're going to need you to testify in court. Is it possible that Andreas left the farm by foot or bicycle, then changed over to a car later? Were all of your vehicles in the yard or garage, or could he have used . . ." I tried to think desperately what other machines they might have besides the tractor, but all I could think of was a combine harvester.

"We store one tractor in a barn on the other side of the pasture, but I would have heard that too. And Andreas doesn't ride a bike. He was in a hurry to get the John Deere in shape before the snow started sticking. Andreas handles the plowing for our road maintenance association, and the plow only fits that tractor. I'm ready to swear on anything that Andreas could not have left Smedsbo Farm without me noticing."

"Did you notice him leaving?" Koivu suddenly asked.

Sasha flinched. "What?" he asked, his voice cracking.

"You said he couldn't have left without you noticing. Did you notice him leaving?"

"No, I didn't!"

"And did you leave the farm that night?"

"No." There were beads of sweat on the bare side of Sasha's face now, and the doctor glanced at us in concern.

"That's enough," he said. "The flight was taxing, and my patient needs to rest now. Has a police escort been arranged for our ambulance during the transfer?"

That I didn't know, since it was the airport staff's responsibility. I stepped outside to ask the airport's assistant security manager, who was standing guard outside the door. Soon, two sets of patrol officers from Vantaa appeared.

"Do we have to go through the crowd, or can we take a back way to the ambulance?" Suuronen asked the security manager.

"You and Ms. Haapala have to go through customs, but Mr. Smeds and his medical attendants can go straight to the ambulance." I doubted they would have been so flexible with a no-name passenger who broke his leg on a package vacation. Suuronen grimaced.

"Could one patrol come with us?"

The Vantaa cops nodded. The nurse and Dr. James set off guiding Sasha in the other direction with a pair of police officers marching after them.

"I don't give a shit about you," Suuronen said to Heli. "But for Sasha's sake I'm ordering you to keep your trap shut with the media out there. You could have at least tried to gussy up the truth and shift the blame to Andreas. Then at least you'd still have a chance. Stupid bitch!"

Heli didn't answer; she just slowed down so she didn't have to walk next to Suuronen. I matched Heli's pace, and Koivu automatically moved to her other side. There was no line at passport control. The party's luggage had come, and Suuronen loaded his own and Sasha's on two carts, one of which he pushed at one of the Vantaa cops. Heli only had the same roller bag she'd had packed in her closet the night of Sasha's accident.

Customs didn't stop us, but outside the glass doors the concourse erupted in a hell of blinding flashes, and a wall of humanity instantly surrounded us.

"Heli, is it true you're having an affair with Sasha's brother?"

"How have these rumors affected Sasha's recovery?"

"What is Sasha's condition? Didn't he come back on the same flight?"

Suuronen muttered "no comment" at every microphone pointed at him, and Heli didn't even say that. I took her bag and started to blaze a path through the scrum, even though I didn't know where we were going. Koivu shoved the overly enthusiastic ones away. We all followed Suuronen, who walked directly to the VIP parking lot. The Citroën I'd seen in his driveway was waiting there. I remembered the cognac on his breath and wondered if he was OK to drive.

Just then, he turned and yelled at Heli. "What are you doing here? Take a taxi, you whore!" Heli cringed as if she'd been struck, and I'd had enough.

"I assume you guys have a breathalyzer," I said to the Vantaa officers. "Mr. Suuronen isn't going anywhere until he's been tested. If you tip the scale, you're taking a taxi too, Suuronen."

"Goddamn it," Suuronen yelled, but he didn't have a choice.

The result was 0.04.

"Listen Ms. Detective, I know my limits. Now go rake Andreas over the coals. Tell him he's better off behind bars because if he gets out he's going to answer to me," Suuronen said. "And, Heli, you should have seen all the women Sasha had to choose from. God, they were beautiful. Any other man would have cheated, but not Sasha. Think about that, you fucking floozy!"

Suuronen slammed the door of the Citroën and sped off. Heli looked at the ground, her face empty.

"Heli, you can start out in our car. We'll take you to Kaunianen where you can get a taxi. There won't be any reporters there," I said.

Our car was only a few spaces away from Suuronen's. I nodded to Koivu to take the driver's seat and got in the back with Heli. She'd pulled the brim of her hat down again and clutched a grubby white handkerchief.

"I didn't want this publicity," she said and sniffed. "Things are already messed up enough, then to have all of those reporters coming at us too. They turn Sasha into this idol I don't even recognize anymore.

I know it's pointless trying to blame anyone else. I'm responsible for my own feelings. I didn't want this, though. I just wanted a normal life. Tending the house and taking care of the cows. But why am I trusting you! How do I know there aren't microphones hidden in this car? Tomorrow I'll be reading in the tabloids all about what 'anonymous sources' say about Heli's motives."

"The car isn't bugged," I said firmly. Koivu shook his head. As Heli wept quietly, I wrapped my arm around her. It felt right. Heli had done some stupid things, but who was I to judge? I knew from experience how painful it was to feel too much for the wrong person.

"Can Andreas be convicted for something he didn't do?" Heli asked after calming down a bit. Christmas lights shone in the shopping centers along Ring III as people drove through the slush to make their holiday purchases. They were all living their small, normal lives, the lives so many others thought were so useless. People thought you had to be in the newspapers or on TV for your life to have meaning. But how many of those people lugging their shopping bags through the sleet really would have traded places with Heli and Sasha if they'd known the truth?

"What would you like me to say to Andreas?"

"I can't even think right now. Maybe I shouldn't even go back to the farm, but I don't know where else I'd go . . . Rauha can't handle the animals herself for long."

The lights of downtown Espoo loomed hazy on the horizon as we turned toward Kauniainen. I looked at the back of Koivu's neck. His hair had grown over his collar, and before long he'd be able to pull it back in a ponytail. His dark-blue corduroy jacket, which he'd been wearing for a few years now, was tight around the shoulders. Thank God at least Koivu was satisfied with his life. That was a comforting thought.

We dropped Heli off at the Kauniainen taxi station. I gave her my card and told her she could send a message to Andreas just by e-mailing me. Tomorrow I'd have to talk to the public defender assigned to Andreas.

"What do you think?" I asked Koivu as we drove to his house to drop him off.

"I don't think anything. My elbow is bruised from hitting a camera and I need a drink."

"I know the feeling. Say hi to Anu," I said as we pulled up to his place. "Or wait—I'll come up and say hi myself. I haven't seen my godson in weeks."

Anu was clearly glad to have company. She made tea as she quizzed me about my experience with nursing. We arranged for them to come over in a couple of weeks for a little Christmas get-together, and I told Anu that as a mathematician Antti could calculate exactly how much mulled wine a breastfeeding mother could safely drink. We all laughed at that, and the darkness didn't seem quite so impenetrable as I walked down the stairs to the car. Just as I was opening the door, Antti called.

"It's me. Something really strange just happened. Iida got a big package in the mail, and the package slip says the sender is Jani Väinölä. Wasn't that the same guy who blew up our mailbox a few years ago? What's he trying to do now?"

19

It took me a few seconds to understand the significance of Antti's words. A package for Iida. Sent by Jani Väinölä, who a few years earlier had blown up our mailbox. Väinölä knew I had a daughter named Iida. Antti told me that the package was waiting at the Olari post office. A package that was unlikely to be an innocent gift.

First I called Dispatch. I ordered them to send the nearest patrol car to Olari and also call out the bomb squad. Better an overreaction than risking civilian lives. When had Väinölä been released? I didn't remember anymore the length of his sentence for his mishmash of crimes. I plugged in my hands-free and started driving toward Olari as I asked Dispatch to look into Väinölä's status. When they called back, I learned he was in prison in Helsinki again after he'd failed to return from a furlough. While he was out, he'd done some drug dealing, which had increased his sentence further.

That knowledge calmed my nerves a bit. The chances that Väinölä had managed to send a bomb from prison were slim. Still my hands shook so hard I couldn't dial the number of the Helsinki prison, which wasn't in my contacts. Simply driving was hard enough.

The Olari post office was located on the second floor of a red brick building. A patrol car was already on scene, and the evacuation was underway. A teary-eyed young woman rushed out the door with a baby stroller, and I nearly ran into her. The patrol hadn't told everyone there was a bomb threat, had they? Ever since the Myyrmanni Mall bombing, people had been hysterical, constantly fearing that death could come at any moment. Personally I'd known for years that no one was ever safe anywhere. Now I felt responsible for the distress of these people fleeing the post office. Maybe that's why I went inside.

"I have to get my coat. It's cold out there!" one of the postal workers yelled at Officer Akkila.

"Just get out. We have blankets." Akkila's expression was tense; he was scared too. The worker was wearing a thin sweater and a short skirt, and she trembled with fear and cold. Akkila grabbed her by the arm.

"Stay out of here," he hissed at me. "We're going to shut the doors and hope the bomb squad gets here before anything happens. What the hell's going on?"

"We'll see." I tried to call the Helsinki prison again, and managed to reach one of the assistant wardens.

"Jani Väinölä is in his cell. And of course we check all outgoing packages. There shouldn't be anything to worry about." The warden promised to check their log to see who Väinölä had sent mail to. He'd call me back once he had that information.

The bomb squad arrived in two vehicles with lights flashing. I wondered when the first reporters would show up. What if this turned into a bigger story than Myyrmanni? That would be the thought on their minds. Give us this day our daily catastrophe, that we may sell more newspapers. Praise be to Jani Väinölä, who provided us something to put in our headlines.

"So we have a possible mail bomb," the squad leader, a Sergeant Aspholm, said calmly after I'd explained the situation. "Finding the package will be easiest if we know the tracking number. What's your storage system like?" Aspholm asked the postal worker in the miniskirt, for whom Akkila had gone to get a blanket.

I called Antti and asked him to look at the tracking number on the package slip.

"Is there a bomb in the package?" Antti asked. I heard Iida humming something in the background.

"Don't know yet. Maybe Väinölä thought about us when he read about the Hackman investigation and figured it was time to get revenge. We'll see. The bomb squad is headed into the post office now."

Gawkers had gathered in the square next to the post office and on a nearby elevated walkway, and a couple more patrol cars showed up to keep order. The bomb squad donned their safety gear, then sent a dog in first.

I couldn't see the package storage room through the post office's windows, so I moved away from the building. If there was an explosion, I didn't want to be standing anywhere near the glass. I tried to hop in place to stay warm even though it felt stupid. As if I were dancing with death.

An airplane flew over surprisingly low, as if it were off course. Its rumble made the people gathered in the square shift restlessly. People had appeared in the windows and on the balconies of the nearby buildings, but I still felt alone.

The fear that my job would hurt my family only grew worse with time. For the two years I'd been out of the policing world, I'd felt safe. And after the bombing of our mailbox, an apartment building had felt like a safe place to live. That was an illusion, of course. Annukka Hackman had carried a pistol, and that pistol had led to her own death.

A snowflake fell on my nose, followed by another. I walked down to the parking lot and lifted the windshield wipers of my car so they wouldn't freeze to the glass. I felt like getting in and sitting down, but then I wouldn't be able to see as well when the bomb squad came out. When the phone rang, I jumped. It was my mother. I didn't answer, because hiding the truth from her would have taken too much energy. Time stood still as I waited for some sign from the windows of the post office: an alarm, an explosion, an all-clear signal. It felt as if I'd been standing in that square for hours when I finally saw the post office door open, and the bomb dog and Sergeant Aspholm walked out. Aspholm took off his helmet. As I ran over to him, he noticed me and smiled.

"That's quite a feat of dollhouse construction, with built-in cabinets and all. There's a letter too, although the sender isn't much of a word-smith. No sign of explosives, though. I think you're safe to take your daughter her new toy."

Aspholm patted the dog, who gave a happy yelp. The patrol offi-cers came over, along with the remaining postal workers. The crowd of onlookers seemed to grumble, as if they were disappointed nothing exciting had happened after all. I walked into the post office, past the front desk, and into the package storage room. Brown wrapping paper and bubble wrap littered the floor. I felt like it was my responsibility to clean up the mess I'd caused.

The dollhouse was wonderful: two stories, six rooms, and even a little sauna upstairs. The outside was painted red with a black roof, and the window trim was white. The kitchen and bathroom had fixtures just like a real house. I could still faintly smell the paint from the final touch-ups.

The letter was on the roof of the dollhouse, in a normal brown envelope, unsealed. I opened it and found a sheet of graph paper with a note written in all caps.

HI. I MADE ONE OF THESE FOR A FRIEND'S KID AND THOUGHT YOUR LITTLE GIRL MIGHT DIG ONE TOO. GREETINGS FROM THE BIG HOUSE. J. VÄINÖLÄ.

There had to be something more to this. Was the paint poisonous or was there something dangerous besides a bomb hidden in the cabi-nets? I sniffed the house like a dog, stroking the surfaces and inspecting every single part. The postal worker watched me, puzzled.

"We need to have the package slip for that," she said in irritation. "Since it's been opened and everything. Is it yours?"

"I don't have the package slip," I said and giggled with pure relief at someone talking about something so mundane. "Of course I can come back and pick it up tomorrow," I said and started winding the bubble wrap back around the dollhouse. Iida would love it, even though we'd have to cram it into the children's already-cramped room. I grabbed some string from the counter to tie the bubble wrap, then I collected the brown wrapping paper and threw it away. The postal worker watched the whole time as if she was afraid I might steal something.

"You can just bring the slip tomorrow," she finally said. As I carried the package out to the car, I decided to make one more call. I reached the assistant warden of the prison again. He was on the treadmill in the gym. In the background I could hear pop music playing and people grunting.

"So what's up with Jani Väinölä?" I asked.

"Not much. He's got a couple more months to go."

"Did he get religion?"

The warden laughed. "Not that I know of. He's the same as he's always been."

"Skinhead and everything?"

"Well, he has a little hair now, but the ideology seems the same. He hangs out in the wood shop, but there's not much work in that industry these days."

"Does he have a girlfriend?"

"Nobody visits him but other guys who just happen to be free at the moment. Why do you ask?"

It was embarrassing, but I went ahead and related the story.

"Maybe he regrets the bombing," the assistant warden said. "Damn, I think I just pulled something. I gotta get off."

Väinölä sorry? I didn't know what to think. I'd always tried to believe there was a little good in everyone. That faith was constantly tried, though.

I drove the few blocks home. The snow had intensified, a coarse, cold precipitation that blew at my windshield from the passing cars and wormed its way under my collar when I got out. An old woman who lived in our building was fighting with the door; a drift had piled up in front of the threshold and she couldn't pull the door past it. I set down the dollhouse and opened the door for her. The old woman, the dollhouse, and I didn't fit in the same elevator, so I walked up the stairs to our floor. Soon it would be Taneli's bedtime.

Antti came to the door and breathed a sigh of relief when he saw the package.

"So it really was a false alarm?"

I shook the snow from my hair, leaving a small pile on the entryway floor, which quickly turned into a puddle.

"Apparently. Strangest thing. Iida, come look. There's a package for you!"

Iida rushed into the living room and started ripping off the wet plastic, with Taneli enthusiastically helping. Iida squealed with joy when she saw what was inside.

"Did Santa bring it?" she asked.

"No, just a nice man named Jani. You can write him a thank-you note and send him some gingerbread cookies."

"Won't anyone else make him gingerbread cookies?" Iida asked as she tried to fit her Barbie in the dollhouse living room.

"I don't think so. I do have a feeling Santa Claus might bring some furniture for that house, though."

Antti had saved me some fish soup from dinner, but I wasn't hungry. I told him about my conversation with the prison warden while Iida whipped up some temporary furniture made from Legos, with Taneli helping and hindering her in turns. Soon the living room floor was full of toys and packing material, but I didn't care. No one had tried to blow up Iida. All was well in the White Cube.

In the morning I cursed when I stepped on a tiny Lego. At first I felt like my ankle was sprained, but it gradually got better. Getting the kids moving was hard; they'd both been up late playing with the new dollhouse. Outside, I saw four inches of snow on the windowsill. The world was as soft as a fluff ball. I packed the kids' sleds, because the day care's yard had a small hill. It was negative four degrees Fahrenheit, so the snow wasn't going away anytime soon. The children shivered in the car while Antti and I dug it out. The previous night I'd been so befuddled by the episode with the dollhouse that I'd forgotten to put the cover on the car. Luckily, I'd had the presence of mind to plug in the engine block heater, though.

When I got to the station, Koivu had brought the morning papers to the meeting room. "Sasha Returns Home Brokenhearted," said one. On the cover of another was a picture of Heli and half of my face. "Sasha and Heli—Divorce!" it proclaimed. I didn't want to read the articles, but I had to skim them at least.

"Rally racing star Sasha Smeds is facing his greatest challenge. For the second time the world championship slipped through his fingers, this time due to an unfortunate accident. Seriously injured, Smeds also learned recently that his wife is having an affair with his brother, Andreas, who was forced to end his own career on the rally circuit several years ago due to a drunk-driving incident. Fortunately Sasha has the unshakeable support of the Finnish people behind him," said one article. Another wrote:

> Sasha is a modern-day explorer, a rally vagabond who risks his life so viewers can enjoy the thrill of competition. The role of the good wife keeping the home fires burning isn't enough for all modern women, and temptations can become overpowering. It's tragic that Sasha's disappointment in his wife came just as he needed her support the most.

A cough behind me interrupted my reading. I looked up to see Ursula's face, pale with red splotches.

"Morning. Feeling better?"

"No. I just came in to submit my sick leave paperwork. I'm staying out until after Christmas for psychological reasons." Ursula handed me the paper. "The department doctor thinks my depression is being caused by the cover-up of the sexual harassment incident. I need time to recover." Ursula crossed her arms. She really did look stressed, and her hair had none of its previous shine.

"Can we speak privately after the meeting? I have something else I'd like to talk about." I'd have to press Ursula about the leaks.

"I'm not obligated to stay for the meeting. I'm on sick leave," Ursula said coldly.

The rest of the unit started gathering around us, as it was time to start.

"And I don't need to meet with you privately," Ursula continued. "I'd rather speak my mind in front of everyone. I think you're a shitty boss and you don't want any other women around threatening your position. You keep too much work for yourself because you don't trust the rest of us. The Koivu thing was the last straw. Make him investigate all the rapes now! I used to wonder if you were sleeping with him or with Taskinen, but now I think it's both! Don't count on me ever coming back here," Ursula said and turned to leave.

I knew I was beet red, and I felt like vomiting. Still I had to turn and face the rest of my unit; there was work to do. Puupponen glowered after Ursula, Lähde stared at the tips of his shoes, and Koivu gazed out the window. He was also blushing.

"OK, Koivu. What do you have to tell us about our hockey star?"

Koivu turned to look at me. "He says the girl lied and told him she was eighteen. Which is reasonable, since she was in a bar. He denies forcing her to have sex, but the girl's bruises say otherwise."

The meeting went as it did every morning. Once again I left the Hackman case for last.

I asked Autio and Lähde to continue questioning Andreas. "We should consider whether the evidence supports continuing to hold him, given Sasha's testimony," I said. Of course I would have liked to interrogate Andreas myself, but after what Ursula had said, that felt difficult. And I did trust my subordinates—all of them except Ursula, that is. Getting someone to stand in for her while she was out on sick leave would be impossible, and to make matters worse, Puustjärvi came to see me after the meeting to announce that he wanted to take the next week off as parental leave. The twins had come home, and his wife needed him there. What was I supposed to say to that?

Fortunately the snow illuminated the world even without the sun. Suddenly I realized there was less than a month to go until Christmas, and we still hadn't taken that Christmas card picture. Maybe we could shelve that and have Iida draw something instead.

I was reviewing a final report with Puupponen on a fistfight that had happened in Olari when the phone rang. I didn't recognize the number, so I answered. The voice seemed strange at first, and the caller didn't bother to introduce himself.

"What the hell is this about that slimeball Suuronen having a version of Annukka's book that I haven't even seen? Annukka never would have given that loser anything! Did he rob our office? I already have the book at the printers. Am I supposed to pull it back now?"

"All along we've assumed we received the correct—and only—manuscript version from you, Mr. Jääskeläinen. Apparently there's another version in existence."

"Apparently! And now I'm reading about it in the paper even though we're talking about my wife's life work here. This is outrageous. Where's the manuscript now?"

"In our evidence locker. We'll be sure to return it once the investigation is over."

"Well, at least you've found the killer. It's just too bad we don't have the death penalty. That man deserves it. And I'm going to tell him so if I get to see him in court. Who do I have to contact about getting my manuscript? I'm at least going to go talk to Suuronen."

"Go right ahead. For now the disk with the manuscript will remain with us."

"Well, shit!" At that point, the telephone started beeping. Perhaps Jääskeläinen would succeed in getting Suuronen to reveal how he got the manuscript. I certainly wanted to know that too.

"Wake up, boss," Puupponen said. "Dreaming about Christmas vacation?"

"No, summer break on a beach full of ripped hunks bringing me beer," I shot back.

"Oh. What would Antti think about that?"

"A girl can dream, can't she? OK, where did we leave off?"

Once we'd handled the paperwork, to my surprise Puupponen lingered in my office chatting about this and that. I knew he dreamed of becoming an author, and I assumed he wanted to talk about that. I let him beat around the bush for a while in the stereotypical way for people from Savo.

"I guess she has some sort of mother complex," Puupponen finally said.

"Who?"

"Ursula. Once, right after she joined the unit, we were having coffee, and she talked about her childhood. Her parents divorced when she was a year old, and her dad didn't really keep in touch. Her mom is an economist, which is why Ursula studied economics at first too. There were plenty of stepfathers, and her mother blamed Ursula whenever one of those marriages failed. I guess Ursula felt like she could never be good enough for her mother. But that's just my opinion, based on Finnish cop sauna psychology," Puupponen said with a snort, then went on his way.

Over the course of the day the cold eased up a bit, but the trees were still blanketed in snow, and the exhaust fumes from the Turku Highway hadn't managed to foul the drifts in the yard of the police station. I hoped Iida and Taneli were wearing enough, because if Iida had to dress herself, she usually forgot her sweater and wool socks. Just as I was planning to head to lunch, Autio stopped by my office. He had a habit of wearing the same dark-gray double-breasted suit, and once someone had suggested that he must have bought two or three at the same time. In the summer his tie was light blue, in the winter dark red. Sometimes I envied men, because a suit was such a versatile piece of clothing. Once I'd worn a tie with a pantsuit, but I caught so much flak for it that I never tried again. And besides, the tie looked idiotic over my breasts.

"We've run into some detours with the charges against Smeds. He's retracted his confession, and, as you know, his brother's providing him with an alibi. There isn't any circumstantial evidence, so I don't see any reason to hold him anymore." Autio fiddled with his tiepin, which was an image of a jaguar.

"What about a charge of intentionally misleading the authorities?"

"And what would be the point of that?"

"Has Smeds said why he confessed in the first place?"

"He just claims he was so drunk he didn't understand the questions. The interrogation is on video. You can look yourself."

"It doesn't matter. Just question him as a witness now. I'll handle releasing him."

My stomach growled angrily, as if it were protesting releasing Andreas. After handling his release paperwork, I drafted a press release about the current state of the investigation, then went downstairs for a yogurt; low blood sugar was making me angry.

I decided to stop in and see Andreas before he was released from his cell. In the past few days, he'd grown a short black beard and mustache, which looked strange on a man with blond hair and blue eyes. He lay on his cot looking indifferent, as if it was all the same whether he was in jail or at home.

"How you doin', Christer Pettersson?" I said. Andreas started.

"What do you mean?"

"It's the same scenario as Olof Palme's supposed murderer: you confess and then take it back depending on the circumstances. I'm sure it's been nice hiding from the media in jail, but be ready to have a hundred of them piling on as soon as you're out. The press release about your discharge is going out any second."

Apparently the yogurt wasn't enough lunch, because I was still irritated. "Also be prepared for a charge of misleading the authorities. Whether you were drunk or not when you confessed, we've wasted a crap load of time because of your nonsense, while the real murderer is still free."

Andreas turned his face to the wall.

"Now get up. We need this bed!" I felt like grabbing him by the shoulder, but I kept myself under control. Andreas slowly sat up.

"Now the whole world knows what a good man Sasha really is," Andreas said bitterly. "So good he'll even give his brother an alibi after he's slept with his wife."

"And even while that same brother is acting like a three-year-old brat. Heli's a mess, by the way."

Andreas turned to face me. "What do you mean?"

"Read the papers on your way home."

"Are they writing bad things about Heli? Shit." Andreas jumped up. "They have no right. I'm leaving the farm. Sasha has the money to hire a dozen farmhands to fill my job. Worse things have happened to people than not getting to be with the person they love." Andreas tried to sound cynical, but his eyes betrayed his true feelings.

"Yes, you can leave. That's easy. But what about Heli? Do you intend to ask her what she wants?"

"Heli won't leave Sasha," Andreas said and leaned his head against the wall.

"Be sure you let us know where you end up. We'll still need to question you." I opened the door and yelled to the guard that Smeds was ready to go. Then I went upstairs to get my workout clothes from my closet and headed down to the gym to take out my frustrations on the punching bag. A right for Ursula, a left for Andreas, and another right for myself. Why the hell had I let Andreas's confession upset my investigation since I'd known the whole time he was lying? Why was I letting what happened to the Smeds family bother me so much? And then there was the continuing problem of Ursula to deal with. God. I'd had enough of this.

After an hour in the gym, I was so wiped out I couldn't feel angry about anything anymore. I ate a meat pie, which left a sinfully greasy taste in my mouth. After washing that down with a glass of buttermilk, I felt like a new woman. I answered a few reporters' calls, trying to make them think we still had a suspect even though Andreas Smeds had gone free. I didn't do very well. Three weeks had passed since Annukka Hackman's death. That was at least two-and-a-half weeks too long.

And of course the coffee was out in our break room, so I went up a floor to find some. When I caught a glimpse of Taskinen at the end of the hall, I ran after him. Terttu's surgery was scheduled for today, and Jyrki had said he'd call me so we could talk more yesterday, but he never did. When he saw me, his face quivered, and it took a second before he regained his composure.

"Jyrki, how's Terttu?"

"Hard to say yet." Jyrki took me by the arm, but the gesture didn't quite constitute a hug.

"You didn't call yesterday."

"I can't dump all of this on you. You have your own life to live!"

The door to the next office opened, and Assistant Chief of Police Kaartamo appeared in the hallway. Quickly I pulled my arm from

Taskinen's hands. Kaartamo and I tolerated each other out of necessity, but we interacted as little as possible.

"So I hear you've released your prime suspect," Kaartamo said. "That investigation seems to be dragging. Is it still as wide open as before?"

"We're getting more lab results all the time," I replied.

"The PR side of things could use some work. Can you trust all of your subordinates, Kallio? You need to get tough down there." Kaartamo gave a wry smile. "At least you have a good relationship with your own superior. That's a good thing."

"Don't worry, I'll find out who's been leaking information," I said, then hastily headed back to my office. Kaartamo had an annoying habit of prying into not only our investigations but also the private lives of everyone who worked in the department. Taskinen didn't need any more worries. And neither did I. Still, Kaartamo was right about one thing: I had to put Ursula over a barrel, even if it meant visiting her at home.

I was just opening my office door when my phone started ringing. When I tried to get it out of its belt holster, half my coffee splashed on the floor and my pants. Damn. By the time I got the phone out, the caller had hung up. I wiped up the worst of the mess on the floor, then went to the restroom to try to get some of the stain out of my pants. They were a light gray wool, so I was probably looking at a trip to the dry cleaners.

After I'd dealt with the coffee spill, I dialed the number of the call I'd just missed.

"This is Sini," said a young voice.

"This is Maria Kallio from the Espoo Police. Did you just try to call?"

Sini sighed. "Yeah, but I don't know if it's anything. I was home because we don't have classes this week, and I heard Dad yelling at you over the phone about that book Annukka was writing. I remembered something. When I heard Annukka talking to Kervinen that time, she said she was going to 'give it to him' at Tapiontori. Of course I thought she meant sex. But what if she gave Kervinen the manuscript and my dad found out about it?"

"What do you mean, Sini?"

"Well, Dad's been storming around all day shouting about how he didn't really know Annukka and she was such a bitch for not telling him important things. He's been really messed up ever since she died. It's like I don't even know him anymore. He gets drunk and cries and yells a lot. But he's all I've got."

Atro Jääskeläinen. The spouse was usually the perpetrator. And Jääskeläinen had admitted to going to Kervinen's building the night he died. Maybe he killed Annukka out of jealousy. After all, who besides Atro Jääskeläinen would have known about Annukka's swimming excursion at the lake?

"Where is your dad now?"

"He just left somewhere," Sini said, sniffing. "He said something about some manager that he wanted to go punch in the mouth."

Despite it all, I nearly started laughing. Suuronen wanted to beat up Andreas, and Jääskeläinen wanted to beat up Suuronen. Such manly men! I tried to calm Sini down and thanked her for calling. For her sake I hoped Atro Jääskeläinen wasn't guilty.

For our sakes, I hoped he was.

20

That evening I could barely stay awake long enough to give Iida her good-night hug. Apparently that session with the punching bag had really drained me. Antti tried to come on to me after Iida fell asleep. Hearing about the job in Vaasa had put him in a better mood, and I didn't want to ruin that for him. So I went along with it, even though I knew my responses to his caresses were purely mechanical. Some things are easier for women than for men.

"If I get that job, we can say good-bye to this apartment," Antti murmured against my neck as we lay quietly side by side after making love. "Housing costs can't go up any more than they already have. And I'm up to taking on some renovations, so we'll find something."

"Of course," I replied from the border between sleep and wakefulness. I fell asleep in Antti's arms. At three o'clock I woke up shivering without my nightgown. I went to the kitchen for a drink of water, then crawled back in next to Antti, but by then I was wide awake. Antti turned over, but his steady breathing told me he was still asleep. I tried to relax using the techniques I'd learned in my prenatal classes, but my thoughts started wandering to other people. Was Heli sleeping? And where? In a double bed with an empty space for Sasha or in one of the smaller rooms at the farm? Was Taskinen awake? I heard Taneli laugh in his sleep. That relaxed me a bit, and eventually I slipped back into unconsciousness.

In the morning I learned that Atro Jääskeläinen really had visited Suuronen and kicked up a fuss outside his house, resulting in Suuronen calling the police. Jääskeläinen didn't get arrested, though.

"Bring him in for questioning," I told my team during that day's meeting. "Suuronen too. Let's see if he's still claiming he got that disk from Hackman. That seems like the only way forward. We haven't ever failed to solve a homicide before, right?"

I knew my smile was fake, and Koivu's grin seemed forced too. I had to speed through the agenda before my next meeting started. Somehow I'd been roped into helping to plan the next Women's Police Day, which was being held in Espoo. I didn't quite know what I thought about it—no one ever organized a Men's Police Day. And did male nurses or midwives ever get together? I'd told Antti I was never joining the Association of Professors' Wives.

The meeting was held outside of town at the hotel that would host the event. The world shimmered in the light of the rising sun. Antti would have a beautiful day traveling up to Vaasa.

Fortunately the woman in charge of the meeting had some verve, and none of the other women seemed to have any need to repeat things that had already been said just to hear themselves talk. If we'd wanted that, we would have invited some men. I promised to deliver a presentation on the increase in female violent crime, even though I knew I'd regret it when it came time to prepare. Fortunately that wouldn't be for months. The meeting ended an hour earlier than I'd expected, so on a whim I decided to visit Lake Humaljärvi. The scene of the crime hadn't received enough attention. Maybe it hadn't been the site of Annukka Hackman's death simply because it was an easy place to steal her gun. Maybe the lake itself had some significance.

I left my car at the same turnout where Hackman's vehicle had been found. Trading my high-heeled ankle boots for proper galoshes, I set out trudging through the snow. In the forest it was only about four inches deep, so walking was relatively easy. I could see animal tracks everywhere: A moose had gone here, a fox over there, and what creature left those tiny double tracks—a weasel? The sun warmed the back of my coat, and great blue tits twittered as they flitted from tree to tree. For a moment I could imagine it was spring. Finding the trail under the snow was a challenge, and a few times I took wrong turns and ended up too far to the west, near the old Soviet trenches. During the lease of the naval base to the Soviets, known as the Porkkala Parenthesis, the border had gone through Lake Humaljärvi. That's what Puustjärvi had said. Part of the Soviet Union had been inside Finland, within artillery range of the capital. Trains moving between Helsinki and Turku shuttered their windows when traveling through the Parenthesis area, and any fisherman who accidentally crossed the border was subjected to intense interrogation at the Soviet base and then again on the Finnish side of the border. Smedsbo Farm had also been in the Parenthesis area. Could that have something to do with Hackman's death? She'd been poking around the farm. Had she found something there related to the Soviet period that the Smeds family didn't want revealed?

I walked to the shore near the place where Hackman's things had been found. This was where she'd undressed and donned her wet suit and dive boots. Did Hackman see her murderer or did the shot come as a surprise? And how many shots were fired? Maybe Hackman had tried to swim away from her attacker, diving for as long as she could without coming up for air, then . . .

I tried to imagine how this peaceful landscape had looked during the Soviet period before the bunkers were demolished and the guard towers were torn down. I stared at the ice, which rippled a little as the wind pushed water under it. It probably wouldn't support a person yet. I threw a rock onto it and heard a deep, clanging sound. The rock skittered across the surface, then disappeared under a small snowdrift in the middle of the ice.

On the other side of the lake I could see fields and farmhouses. We'd repeatedly interviewed the residents, with little result. Did those houses exist during the Parenthesis? I tried to ask the landscape, but the only reply I received was the melancholy song of the ice. So I gave up and returned to my car.

Back at the office, I found a note on my desk telling me that Koivu and Autio had been downstairs going at Atro Jääskeläinen for half an hour already. Jääskeläinen had come to the station voluntarily. I headed down to take the temperature of the interrogation. Jääskeläinen was still being questioned as a witness, but I hoped my boys could also start poking some holes in his story.

"Detective Lieutenant Kallio joined the interview at thirteen thirty-two," Autio dictated to the tape. It was easy to understand what Sini had meant when she talked about the change in her father's personality. It was apparent just looking at him. In the space of three weeks, Jääskeläinen had put on considerable weight. His clothes didn't fit anymore, he'd developed a third chin, and he was now wearing his wedding ring on his little finger. He'd shaved carelessly, leaving long hairs sprouting here and there on his cheeks.

"Finally, Detective Kallio! Your damn minions here keep reading me the riot act while robbers and murderers are running around free. Why did you let Smeds go?"

"There wasn't enough evidence against him. Did you see Jouko Suuronen last night?" I asked, knowing that my subordinates had probably already asked the same thing.

"How many reports of that do you need? At first he opened the door, but when he saw who it was, he closed it again. I could charge him with assault. My arm got caught in the door. Do you want to see the bruise? How dare he claim Annukka gave him that disk? Annukka never would have done that!"

"At any point have you suspected that your home or office was broken into?"

"No! And we have an alarm system. A few CDs were stolen from Annukka's car in August, but they didn't take the stereo, so I didn't bother calling the police. Annukka didn't want to. But . . ."

"How did they break into the car?"

"Annukka thought she left the window open when she ran down to the corner store to pick up the newspapers. She would have told me if her manuscript was stolen!"

"She didn't even tell you what was in it," Autio pointed out.

At this, Jääskeläinen became irate. Jumping up, he started to scream profanities at anyone and everyone. At the police, at Annukka, at Kervinen. His face burned so red I worried he was going to have a heart attack.

"Mr. Jääskeläinen. Atro! We want to find out how that manuscript ended up in Jouko Suuronen's possession—just like you do. And you can help us best by answering our questions instead of throwing a fit. Tell us about the car break-in—" I began, then my phone rang. More work for the Violent Crime Unit. The duty officer told me that a Russian woman had been found unconscious in the basement of her apartment building. She'd been rushed to the hospital, and the officers suspected she'd been sexually assaulted.

"I have to go," I said. "Koivu and Autio, you continue. Let's talk later about next steps."

"Prostitute?" I asked when I arrived on the scene.

"Probably. There're two or three apartments in that building with an indeterminate number of Russian and Estonian women staying in them. We've raided it a few times, and you can guess how many of them had proper visas."

"Aha. So I can get background from Patrol. I'll see who I can spare. And we can't question the woman right now, right? But she's going to live?"

"The doctors are still looking her over."

Back at my office, I assigned Lehtovuori and Lähde, along with a Russian interpreter, to interview the woman once she was able to talk to us. Everyone knew that Russian prostitution was happening, but it was ridiculously hard to get a handle on. Women came and went, no one dared talk to the police, and they changed apartments and phones constantly because there was big money behind the operation. And the criminals were the women, not their clients. That's because so many of the people who made the laws were also customers. For years a tenacious rumor had been going around the station that Assistant Chief of Police Kaartamo enjoyed variety in his sex life and didn't mind paying for companionship. Of course people always gossiped about bosses, but the idea didn't feel impossible.

I was glad that we were going to get to make contact with at least one of the prostitutes, since it might give us an opportunity to free a few people from human trafficking. I called Lehtovuori again and ordered him to arrange a guard for the woman at the hospital.

Then my thoughts returned to Annukka Hackman. Why didn't she tell her husband the full contents of her book? He had a right to know—after all, he was her publisher. I went to our conference room, which we also used as a case room, and found the pictures of Annukka Hackman's body. Things rarely went well for lone rangers in real life. A couple of times I'd had to take stupid risks in my own work, but I wasn't going to do that anymore. A case I'd investigated just before my maternity leave, the murder of a politician named Petri Ilveskivi, had shown me how productive working as a group can be. That was sure to be the case now too. Koivu and Autio would get Jääskeläinen to talk, and someone else would succeed with Suuronen.

At four it was time to go pick up the kids. When I arrived in the yard of the day care, Iida rushed up to me.

"Mommy! My shoe broke! Look, I have the school's extra shoes. They're way too big."

Minna, one of the day care workers, also came over.

"Hi," she said. "I noticed when we came in from our morning play that Iida's foot was soaking wet. The toe of her shoe separated from the sole."

That's all I need, I thought. There was no point fixing cheapo winter boots from the megamart, and Iida needed shoes fast. Then I caught myself: a broken winter boot was a pretty small problem compared to the previous day, when I thought someone had sent Iida a mail bomb. Be thankful for a small, boring life.

I decided to drive to Tapiola—maybe I could feed the kids fast food while I was there. Antti hated hamburgers and the disposable ideology of the restaurants that served them, so I felt like I was doing something on the sly when I walked into McDonald's with the kids. The line was long and the smell of the grease made me ill. Iida began demanding a toy with her kid's meal, and Taneli joined in the chorus. For girls they were offering ponies with pink tails and monsters for boys, the cashier informed me. I didn't want either, but I didn't feel like fighting, and of course Iida wanted the girl toy, and Taneli wanted the monster. Gender roles were learned quickly in day care. But it wasn't like the world would be a better place if my son played with plastic ponies and my daughter tried to frighten him with a monster.

I ordered just a salad, because I knew I'd end up eating half of Taneli's meal. Of course he wanted the same thing as Iida. There was no space downstairs, and maneuvering upstairs with a two-year-old and a full tray was a chore. Iida careened headlong through the people toward a free window table.

Christmas had already arrived in the Tapiola shopping district, and all the windows were full of Christmas advertisements and lights, Santa Claus flying in his sleigh, and cheery songs. I pitied the salespeople who had to listen to the same Christmas tracks for a month on end, since I had a hard time simply surviving a shoe purchase with the music playing. Taneli was angry because we didn't buy him anything, so I went to the children's clothing department to get him some new gloves. The excitement of riding on the escalator cheered him up, and I barely managed to tear him away from it. A violet sequined dress with spaghetti straps caught Iida's eye, but the cut was far more appropriate for an adult, with an open neckline and back, accentuated waist, and short hem with strings of sequins dangling from it. Something like that would have looked fantastic on Ursula but not on a six-year-old.

"Mommy, can I have this? It's so cute!"

"I don't think you need a new dress."

"Our preschool Christmas party is soon."

Suddenly I realized that Taneli had disappeared as we were fighting. Hopefully he hadn't gone back to the escalator! I could just see my child tumbling over and being strangled by his hood on the belt. Ignoring Iida's protests, I grabbed her hand and started dragging her toward the down escalator. I reached Taneli just as he was stepping onto it. The whole place was teeming with adults, but no one had tried to stop him.

"Mom, I want that dress!"

"Be quiet!" I picked up Taneli, and he squealed and squirmed, wanting to walk on his own. Iida started crying, and I felt as if the entire shopping center was staring at us disapprovingly. One more career woman who can't handle her kids. Oh hell.

In order to make peace, I suggested that we go to the library. I checked out a couple of books for myself too, hoping to escape from reality in bygone England or a world of fantasy. I had a hard time convincing Taneli that the Moomin book he wanted was already on our bookshelf at home. On our way back we walked through Tapiontori Square. The fountain was silent, and stars twinkled over the central office tower. The Tapiontori Restaurant was only half-full since it wasn't quite dinnertime.

"She said she was going to give it to him at Tapiontori." That was what Sini had said Annukka Hackman had promised Kervinen. And what if the thing Kervinen was supposed to get was waiting for him here? Atro Jääskeläinen had said Annukka sometimes mailed copies of

articles and manuscripts to people for safekeeping. Could Annukka have mailed something to the restaurant, to be retrieved either by herself or by Kervinen?

I'd have to check.

"Let's go to one more place," I told the kids and led them into the restaurant. Luckily there wasn't any Christmas music playing.

"Hello, I'm Maria Kallio from the Espoo Police," I said to the bartender as I flashed my badge. "You had a regular customer, a reporter named Annukka Hackman. I'm leading her murder investigation. Has your restaurant received any mail addressed to her?"

The bartender gave me a suspicious look. Police detectives didn't usually conduct criminal investigations with two children hanging on their coattails and an armful of picture books.

"To Annukka Hackman . . . No, nothing comes to mind. I know the case, though. We hardly ever receive mail addressed to customers, but wait a minute and I'll ask the manager."

The bartender disappeared into a back room. Iida had sat down in an armchair near the bar and was looking like an expert as she flipped through a business magazine, and Taneli was flirting with a woman sitting at a nearby table by hiding behind my back, then peeking out and smiling. Why didn't I ever come here for lunch with Taskinen? *I mean for dinner with Antti?* I thought, correcting myself.

The bartender came back. He was carrying two envelopes, a large A4-size one and a smaller padded mailer.

"There wasn't anything for Hackman, but these have been sitting on the manager's desk for weeks. This bigger one is addressed to an Ulla Aalto, and I think it came in the summer, and this other one . . . I think it says Kervinen."

I felt like snatching the envelope from the bartender, but instead I extended my hand with feigned calm. I'd seen Annukka Hackman's large, clear handwriting on enough documents that I easily recognized it.

Tapiontori Restaurant, H. Kervinen, for pickup, the envelope said. I looked at the postmark date. November 4. That was the day before Hackman's body was found, two days before her intended meeting with Kervinen at this restaurant. Cautiously I felt the envelope. There was something thin and rectangular inside, presumably a floppy disk. There was no sender listed on the outside.

This was exactly what I'd been looking for. "I'll give you a receipt for this," I told the bartender and started fishing for my notepad.

"But shouldn't it go to this Kervinen?"

"It should, but he's dead too. I'm taking it now."

I could barely write legibly. What version of the manuscript had Annukka sent Kervinen?

I put the envelope in my bag in a zippered pocket. The excitement made me impatient, and I was agitated as I drove home, with no patience for Iida's questions about what an exchange rate was, even though my only real principle of parenting was that children's questions deserved answers. I felt like driving to the police station and assigning someone to read the manuscript immediately. Should I call someone to pick it up? No—I only had two hours until Iida's bedtime, and I wanted to read it myself. But had Antti taken our laptop with him on his trip to Vaasa?

Fortunately the computer was at home. I would have liked to start reading immediately, but the children wouldn't stand for it. I read them their library books at a record pace and glanced at my purse every fifteen minutes. Of course Taneli had no interest in going to sleep, and Iida kept asking when Daddy was coming home and spent ten whole minutes brushing her teeth. What had I been thinking earlier in the day about lone rangers and working as a team? Someone else could have already read the disk. Ursula was right. I was a selfish bitch who didn't know how to delegate.

When the breathing in the children's room had quieted to slow, sleepy sniffles, I finally opened the envelope. The disk was a standard black Canon floppy. I carefully slid it into the computer, then copied it to the hard drive and then to another disk. Every noise from the stairwell made me jump as if someone could just come through the locked door downstairs. I checked the chain on the door and lowered the blinds, then laughed at myself in derision.

When I'd finally opened the file directory, I clicked on the Table of Contents. First came the Introduction, which I'd read. Then Chapter One, Rauha and Viktor's Story. That hadn't been in the versions I'd seen so far. Sasha's parents' background had only been covered briefly in a chapter about his childhood. Now his childhood years were in another file, as Chapter Two. No other chapters had been added.

What was Rauha and Viktor's story about? My head buzzed as I opened the file.

21

Rauha and Viktor's Story

Translated from Viktor Smeds's original Swedish manuscript by Annukka Hackman

Dear Andreas and Alexander. By the time you read this, I'll already be gone, so I can tell you with peace of mind who your father really was. I was not the man you thought I was.

I was born in Leningrad in 1935, not in 1938 like all the documents say. My given name was Viktor, that's true, but my last name was Rylov. My father died in the Winter War at the Battle of Raate Road, blown up by a tank. My younger sister, Natalia, starved to death during the Siege of Leningrad, and my mother never recovered from that. Mother died in 1952, on the opening day of the Helsinki Olympics.

I don't remember much about my father, because he was away from home so much serving in the army. Natalia and I were both conceived while Father was on leave. Mother worked in a makhorka factory rolling cigarettes. I still remember the way she smelled. We lived in a room that was smaller than the woodshed at Smedsbo. The toilet was at the back of the yard, and we heated wash water on the stove once a week. We weren't any poorer than anyone else I knew, though. Everyone was poor. My mother was a communist, because she didn't dare to be anything else. Babushka, my father's mother, hated the Finns because they killed her son. I remember being afraid of many things: the rats people said bit little children's fingers and toes, the Militsiya, Uncle Vladimir who lived next door and beat my mother and me when he was drunk.

I wasn't particularly good in school, and that was probably partially because I began my studies during the war and partially because of malnutrition. I didn't have many dreams other than getting to eat as much butter as I wanted. Before the war I'd been able to taste butter. But during the war, we lived on cabbage and rutabagas, or, when times were particularly bad, wallpaper paste and grass. I dreamed of eating butter with a spoon straight from the dish. That time didn't happen until I was here in Finland, though.

My memories of my childhood are disjointed and fragile. Your mother says I don't want to remember and I'm shutting it out. My Leningrad wasn't the city of bridges and empire architecture I've seen in pictures. It was a limited area of backstreets, our house, the school, and the cemetery where I went to remember my father. Natalia was buried on the Field of Mars in a mass grave my mother didn't even remember the precise location of. After the war my mother's health declined steadily, but we were never able to get her to a doctor. When the lung cancer was discovered, it was so far along nothing could be done. By then I'd quit school and spent my days working in a shoe factory and my nights caring for Mother. I didn't think I was lucky or unlucky. Life was just like that. During her final weeks, Mother prayed often, and I feared the neighbors would hear. The only god allowed was Stalin.

After Mother passed away, I was called into the army. I was sent far from home, to Baku in Azerbaijan, but I enjoyed it there. I was an infantryman in the 114th Rifle Division. The warmth was intoxicating after the terrible winters of Leningrad. I was used to bullying and violence from my childhood, so the army felt like home. And besides, soldiers had a better life than civilians. We had food, clothing, and a dry place to sleep. I didn't have to make any decisions myself. Everything was decided for me. Routine created a feeling of security: there would be food tomorrow, and no one else would be lying in my bed in the evening. I didn't have any other plans for the future, so I decided to stay in the army if they would let me. This decision was strengthened by learning that I might be able to go abroad, perhaps to Poland. I didn't want to go back to Leningrad and the shoe factory. I was a good shot. That was the first thing I'd ever been better at than anyone else. Eventually I was invited to join the Communist Party. You didn't refuse that.

In the end, the army sent me to Finland. I was disappointed when I heard. Finland would be even colder than Leningrad. I didn't know much about the country, other than it had been beaten in two successive wars by the Soviet Union and was now such a faithful ally that it had agreed to lease us the Porkkala area for fifty years. And that was the area I was going to now, to defend my nation from the capitalists' attempts to destroy communism.

I arrived in Finland late one night in early May 1952. When we crossed the border at Vainikkala, I didn't know that I would never return to the land of my birth. I sensed a shift, but I thought it was just the change of environment. I had no idea I would change myself. At first I was disappointed that the landscape bathed in the moonlight wasn't any different from the parts of Karelia we'd already traveled through. We rode past Helsinki and through Espoo, and the morning gradually dawned. The journey from Baku had lasted for days, and I'd only slept a little. When our transport finally stopped at the border of Espoo and Kirkkonummi to check our papers, I thought I was dreaming. I didn't know the sea could look like that.

Of course I'd caught glimpses of water before in Leningrad, but only lakes and rivers. I didn't learn to swim until I was in the army. The sea smelled different, though, and I could make it out even through the stench of truck fuel and dirty men's sweat. The sea. I hoped I could get close to it. I wished I could dive into it. Soon my dream was realized when I was stationed close to the shore, at a farm named Smedsbo on the Degerö Peninsula. I was assigned to guard the border. Sometimes

I was on the northern border at Lake Humaljärvi, sometimes on the western border at Ström. I was given a bicycle, and during my free moments I often rode to the beaches at Kopparnäs and Degerö to swim.

Life at the Porkkala base was much more luxurious than in the Soviet Union. The base had its own school, a movie theater in a former church in Kirkkonummi, and all sorts of goods and foods that I'd never heard of before in the store. Mandarins in tissue paper, good strong coffee, tobacco that tasted different from what my mother had taught me to smoke as a child. That summer was magical: white nights, warmth, and even an occasional feeling of camaraderie with the other residents of the base.

One late summer evening I was on my way to my shift at guard post number three in Ström. That was when I saw the girl for the first time. She stood behind the barbwire fence on the other side of the border zone and looked at me curiously. She wore a blue dress and had thick, light-brown curls. I shouted to her not to come any closer, in Russian of course. To my surprise and wonder, she responded in Russian. I heard her voice clearly, even though the distance between us was dozens of meters. There were barbwire fences on either side of the border, with a patch of sand about ten meters wide running down the middle between them. The sand was raked once every guard shift, so smooth that it even betrayed the tracks of mice.

The girl's name was Rauha, she told me, which meant "Peace." She missed her old home. Did the squirrels still collect nuts under the back eaves? Did the swans still come to Degerö Bay?

What's the name of the house? I asked.

Smedsbo, Rauha said, and based on the description I could tell it was the same house I lived in.

Of course I shouldn't have talked to the Finnish girl. But her voice was so bright and happy even though she spoke of sad things. Later I got so close to her that I could see how blue her eyes were, like the sea on a summer day. Of course there were women on the base too, the officers' wives, the teachers, and the cooks. None of them lived at Smedsbo, though, and besides, I was a shy boy. When I told the other men stories about my exploits, they were only stories. The officers had prostitutes, and some of my barracks mates had spent time with girls in Baku, but I'd never dared. I immediately became infatuated with this girl, though: she wasn't afraid and she didn't treat me like an enemy, even though I was one of the people who had driven her from her home. When she smiled, I didn't need any other sun. I fell in love without knowing what the word even meant.

Later I learned that Rauha and her parents had often come to the border, especially in the early days of the lease. The guard at that time, Artur, had been a nice old man, Rauha said, easily paid off with cigarettes and chocolate.

Paid off to do what? I asked.

To let us over the border to the hills at Malm where we could see our house, she said. *Have they cut down any more of the forest?*

I didn't know, since I didn't have any point of comparison. I told her how the trees looked, even though Rauha didn't understand the more complicated expressions I used. Her father had taught her Russian so she could read Tolstoy in the original language. *Father is a wise man,* Rauha said. *He doesn't hate anyone.*

Do you want to come across the border again sometime? I asked, even though I feared someone would see us. The guard posts were only a few hundred meters apart, and the border zone had been razed. On our side of the barbwire there were openings spaced one kilometer apart so we could get in to rake the sand strip. I didn't know about the Finnish side, though.

Yes, the girl said. *Whenever is best for you. Will you always be the one on this guard shift?*

I don't know, I replied.

Of course I was afraid. I'd seen how rule breakers were punished. Maybe I'd be shot along with the girl's family. In the early days of the base the Finns and the Soviets had had more contact. The children had played together and swum in the Siuntio River. Later the army had built a swimming barrier across the river.

When I came on shift the next day, I waited for the girl, but she never came. Three days passed before she returned. Now she was wearing a blue-and-white striped dress with a slender waist and flared skirt. I'd never seen anything more beautiful.

What do you want in return? she asked.

I don't want anything, I said, although I would have liked to touch her, her soft cheeks, her smiling lips, the hair that the summer breeze blew into her face.

When will it be possible? she asked.

I don't know yet. Maybe when Sasha is on shift with me. Sasha is a good man. I'll speak to him. But only to the hills. Anything else is too dangerous. Tell your parents that.

I thought it was strange that anyone could long for a place the way Rauha and her parents did. The family had lived on the farm for more than two hundred years, but the new main house was only two decades old. Although I'd lived seventeen years in the same room in Leningrad, I didn't want to go back there or to Baku. I didn't know whether Babushka or Uncle Vladimir were still alive. It was irrelevant to me.

Sasha said he'd turn a blind eye when I helped the girl cross onto the base but he wanted money in return.

What will you do with Finnish money? I asked, since we only used rubles on the base.

You're so naive. Don't worry, I'll find a use for it. Two hundred marks and I'll turn my head.

At that time, I didn't know if that was a lot or a little, but I learned from Rauha's expression when I told her. I was standing on the sand strip, raking it, and she was standing right near me on the other side of the barbwire.

And the same amount for you? she asked.

No, for me just a smile, I said and reached across to stroke her cheek, ignoring the barb that caught ahold of my sleeve. The girl didn't push my hand away.

You're nice, she said. She pronounced her words in Russian unlike anyone else. It was like birdsong to me.

I knew how dangerous this all was, but ignoring the danger made me feel like a man. So what if I was executed because of this girl? There were crazier things to die for, like communism and the fatherland. Those were just ideas, but Rauha was real.

Tell Sasha that he'll get the two hundred marks. I'll give them to you to take to him. When Rauha left, she blew me a kiss. There was no way to kiss through the barbwire.

They came two nights later with the money and waited on the other side of the line while I took it to Sasha. Of course we were forbidden from leaving our guard posts, and of course we ignored that rule. Sasha looked away as the Smeds family walked over the sand strip and through one of the openings in the wire we used when we raked. I was so afraid I nearly fainted. In the dusk they walked the kilometer to one of the hills and saw their home. I watched the three figures: the girl's tall, slender father, Albert; her mother, Alma, who was as small as her daughter; and the girl herself, Rauha. I was seeing what homesickness meant.

When they came back, Albert asked why I'd helped them. I didn't know how to answer.

I think you've taken a fancy to my daughter, he said. I blushed.

After that, I was transferred to the Lake Humaljärvi day shift, even though I didn't want to go. I longed for Rauha, but I couldn't think of any way to see her. I couldn't just go poking around other guard posts during my free time. Fortunately there was Sasha.

That girl came looking for you, he said one night. *I told her where you are now. She told me to say hello. How does she know Russian?*

I didn't want to talk about Rauha with anyone, even Sasha. She was something that belonged to me alone. Still I suggested to him that he could pretend to be sick and I could promise to cover his shift. Our commander had a taste for vodka and was easy to fool.

After working double shifts for three days with no success, I finally saw Rauha.

I've missed you, she said.

Me too, I said. I kissed my fingers and pressed them to her cheek, and she let it happen. I decided I had to get somewhere with her where we could be alone. The danger of being seen together in the open border area was too great.

In the fall we began to hear rumors that Porkkala would be returned to the Finns, perhaps as soon as the following year. The base was restless. No one wanted to go back to the Soviet Union, me least of all. Finally, on the eleventh anniversary of the Moscow Armistice, on the nineteenth of September, 1955, we learned that the Porkkala Naval Base would be returned to Finland in January.

After hearing this, I went to the border to wait for Rauha. She came, her face glowing.

I get to go home, she said.

I have to return to the place they claim is my home, I replied. *Away from you. I don't know where I'll be taken. No one does. But wherever it is, it will be the wrong place because I won't be with you.*

Come over the border, she said. *Come and stay with me.*

That isn't possible, I said. *If I try to cross the border, my comrades will have to shoot me. I don't want to force them to do that. And the Finnish authorities have returned deserters before. But maybe I could swim. Maybe I could swim over on Lake Humaljärvi. I could hide in the rocks, pretending that I'd drowned, until it's dark enough to come out.*

When? I'll get a boat. I can row to Storholmen Island to wait for you. Then we can row together to shore. That isn't too far to swim. I'll arrange it all.

I believe you.

Rauha was just a girl, but she knew what she wanted. You know your mother. When she decides something, that decision sticks.

The autumn nights were cold and I wasn't a good swimmer. In addition, I had to stage my drowning during my guard shift, which meant leaving my uniform on shore, so I wouldn't be recognized as a soldier on the other side. I decided to at least keep my underwear on, but everything else, including my footwraps and boots, had to stay. The guard shift ended at three. I staged my drowning at two. I left my clothes on the shore and threw my gun in the water. On the previous evening I'd talked about how much I liked swimming, even though I had trouble with cramps sometimes and was afraid of slipping on the rocks around the lake.

For several hours I hid, shivering, in a damp, mossy crevice where I could barely turn around. I didn't dare to climb out until it was dark enough. As I climbed, I tore a long scratch in my shin, which stung in the water. I didn't know whether my clothing had been found. The rocks were cold, and my body was stiff with fear and the chill. The water felt frigid. I tried to slip into it with as little sound as possible, but I lost my footing and caused a splash. I tried to stay underwater, but I couldn't hold my breath for long. When I rose to the surface, I heard Petrov's familiar voice issuing commands in Russian: *"Tšto eto?"* I knew that the searchlight would find me soon, then would come the shots.

I swam for my life. That's the only way to describe it. I swam, fearing with every stroke that I would lose my strength, that the water would swallow me. It's hard to swim quickly and silently at the same time. The searchlight flashed on the shore, but no shots came. Maybe Petrov trusted that the Finnish authorities would handle me.

When I got near the east side of Storholmen, I saw a boat. It began gliding toward me like a dream. I was so cold I didn't think I could make it. When I finally grasped the side of the boat, I was so exhausted I couldn't climb in, and when Rauha tried to pull me up over the side, the boat took on water. Finally she ordered me to grab the rope on the stern and she would drag me to the island. My arms were so cold and tired I could barely hold on. I'll remember the number on the side of that boat, seventeen, until the day I die. Some of the fishermen in the area had permission to work in the border waters, but only during daylight hours, and the boats they used were numbered.

On Storholmen, I crawled ashore like an animal. Rauha wrapped a blanket around me and rubbed and shook me until my blood started to flow again. She gave me clothing and a thermos of hot coffee. I hadn't eaten since morning, and I was trembling with fear and hunger. I was embarrassed that I'd made Rauha row us to land by herself, but I couldn't have done it.

I'm fine, she said. *We have a bicycle we can ride to where my family is staying in Innanbäck. Father will take us to Karjaa tomorrow, and we can go by train to Turku. They'll start looking for you, so it isn't safe to stay here. You can't speak Russian. You have to learn a few words of Swedish tonight. And later you'll have to learn all of it. You'll become my second cousin from Kokkola, Viktor Smeds. The parson of the Swedish parish in Kokkola is my father's cousin. He'll add you to the parish register. They did that after the Civil War when members of the Red Guard fled to Sweden, which is another thing we can do. We have family near Stockholm. I'll teach you the language.*

I listened as Rauha spoke, and through the darkness I could only make out her silhouette, not her face. Perhaps I fainted, perhaps I fell asleep, but when I woke up we were already on the shore of the mainland. I told Rauha that I should ride the bicycle and she could sit on back. She refused. In the end we took turns riding along the potholed roads in the trembling light of a flashlight. A couple of kilometers before Innanbäck, the batteries ran out.

Don't worry, Rauha said. *I know the road. I'll get you there.*

Inside the family's dwelling in Innanbäck there was hot soup waiting. I'd never eaten anything better. After I'd finished, I had some learning to do. *Thank you. Good day. Good-bye.* Swedish was a strange language. The bed they put me in that night was soft.

Albert's cousin from Kokkola came to visit. He rode here with some acquaintances, which was why he didn't arrive until the middle of the night. That was what Alma told the neighbors.

I managed to sleep for a few hours, wishing Rauha was next to me. The morning train from Karjaa left at eight o'clock, and Albert drove us there in a Ford, which he had borrowed from a neighbor.

From Turku you'll go to Kokkola, where my cousin, the parson, will then take you to Sweden in his motorboat, he said. Sometimes it's good for priests to know smugglers.

Rauha took care of everything. She bought the train tickets; she set out our food. We couldn't speak Russian on the train, but Rauha pointed things out through the window. House. Car. A man. I nodded and repeated. I'd never studied a foreign language, but to my surprise it wasn't hard. Later I learned German and some Finnish too.

The parson was waiting at the Kokkola station. He looked like Albert. We didn't share a common language, and we could only speak Russian in the sacristy, behind closed doors. *Look, this is the parish register,* he said. *This will give you a new life. There's space on this year, at the end of November in thirty-eight. What day do you want?*

The twentieth, I said to Rauha, since it was my real birthday, although in April of '35. It would be easy to remember. I became three years younger than I was.

You were born in a sauna, mother Johanna Smeds, father unknown, the parson said. Apparently Johanna had gone to Sweden and died there several years earlier. As long as I didn't return to Kokkola, no one would ever doubt my identity. Since I was now only seventeen, I needed a guardian. Albert would do.

These certificates attest to your identity, the parson said as he handed me some papers. *When you turn twenty-one you'll have to apply for a government identity card. Conscription is in two years. Take care that you learn Swedish by then. Rauha will teach you.*

That night, Rauha and I were housed in neighboring rooms. The parsonage was cold, and I couldn't sleep. What if the authorities found me anyway? There was no way this would work. I knew nothing about Finland. I didn't know Swedish or Finnish, and I didn't know anyone but Rauha. I didn't have a penny of Finnish money, and I didn't even own the clothes on my back. My only hope was Rauha. Rauha who knocked on my door and came to me, who comforted me and stroked me and kissed me. *How do we get married in Finland?* I asked her. I belonged to the church now; I'd been baptized and gone to confirmation school. Did I have to start believing in God? What I wanted to do with Rauha was forbidden before marriage.

For three days we hid in the parsonage, where we sat in Rauha's room and talked. *My name is Viktor. I'm from Kokkola, but I live with my mother in Uumaja. I want to move to be with my relatives in Inkoo. My girlfriend's name is Rauha.*

In the fifties the world was different. Few had a television, and of course the newspapers said nothing about a soldier who had escaped from the Porkkala base or drowned in a lake. They did look for me, and even went as far as Innanbäck. I asked who Rauha borrowed the boat from, and she said she hadn't borrowed it. She'd stolen it. No one knew.

On the fourth day we traveled to Vaasa and then by boat to Uumaja and from there by train to a farm near Stockholm that was owned by Sten Jansson, a member of Rauha's family. He'd give us work and let us stay for a while. There I learned the language that would become my mother tongue. I loved this language, because Rauha spoke it. Rauha, my new life.

It wasn't an easy winter, and I wouldn't have survived without Rauha. I was ill and couldn't work, and I had nightmares. I was so afraid. Jansson was an old bachelor with a taste for drink, who worked us too hard for starvation wages. All throughout the winter we followed the progress of Porkkala's return to Finland. First we heard that only reporters and soldiers could go there. Later, in the spring, permits would be issued to civilians.

We're going home! Rauha exclaimed, but I didn't have any home but Rauha.

When word came in a letter from Albert that the family could move back to Smedsbo in the spring of 1956, we quit our jobs. Old Man Jansson didn't like it and leveled all manner of threats at me. I waited in terror for him to expose us to the authorities. All through those first years I was afraid, and the only place my fear faded was in Rauha's arms.

Albert and Alma were at Smedsbo on the very first day possible. I wondered what had happened to my few possessions, whether my comrades had taken them or thrown them away. I never knew. We arrived at Smedsbo in April, nearly a year after I first set foot in Finland. I already spoke Swedish quite fluently, but I was afraid of speaking with strangers.

I'll just say you're shy, Rauha promised. Still, I feared being found out, but no one asked anything. Sten Jansson drank himself to death six months after we left. The animals had gone untended, and we mourned the cows who'd starved to death and the dog who'd been choked by his own collar more than we mourned the man.

I survived the move, and I even survived my military service almost two years later. Albert tried to convince me to apply for a deferral as a farmworker, but I wanted to get past it as soon as possible since it was what I feared the most. I was assigned to the shore batteries at Upinniemi. We did a lot of cleaning up after the Russians, exploring bunkers and mapping out the island defenses. A few times my fellow soldiers wondered how I was so good at guessing how some military detail was organized in the Soviet army. Of course I didn't guess, I knew. That made me smile inside. In the army I suffered pneumonia and had to spend two weeks in the hospital. Rauha came to see me when she could, and that was where I proposed.

When you got home from the army I was planning to ask you, if you hadn't done it yet, she said. *Of course I'll marry you.*

So we became man and wife on Midsummer in 1960. Everything was perfect. I liked my new in-laws, and I'd gotten to know the villagers. Someone at the wedding remarked on how small my family was; the only person there from my side was the parson. I said that I was born out of wedlock and that none of my mother's siblings had survived. Occasionally someone asked about my childhood in Uumaja, but usually they left me alone. *That new son-in-law the Smedses have is quiet, but he's a good worker,* they'd say. *His Swedish is strange, but he speaks the truth. Do you want to join the hunting club? I have a good dog you could buy.*

Over the years my fears faded. Leningrad and a young man named Rylov were just a story from long ago. I had a place in the world as a husband. In the early sixties, Albert's back started to bother him, so more and more of the work on the farm fell to me. I felt useful to the people I loved.

We weren't immediately blessed with children. Rauha had several miscarriages in the early years. After a while the doctors said we should let her body rest. We wanted each other, so abstinence was difficult. Using birth control felt wrong, but we had no choice. We waited a year or so. Andreas, when you were born, you were a true miracle. We named you after my father, Andrei. Sasha was born two years later, and he was named after my fellow guard, Sasha, whose full name was Alexander Nikolayevich Tikhonov. Sometimes I wonder what happened to him. Did he ever get back to his home in Pervouralsk or did he just wander the Soviet Union, which doesn't exist anymore? Leningrad has been replaced with St. Petersburg. And I have a new homeland, Finland.

I'm sorry that I couldn't tell you about my childhood or my family. You asked sometimes why you didn't have any cousins on my side. I lied and said that I'd been an only child. *Why don't we ever visit Kokkola?* you asked. *What would we do there?* I said. *Our home is here.*

Albert died in 1973, Alma ten years later, and the parson who'd helped us in 1989. The only ones who know the truth anymore are me and Rauha. When your mother is gone too, you can tell our story. Then there won't be any danger of us being charged with a crime for what we did. Yes, it was fraud; yes, it was against the immigration laws, but it didn't hurt anyone, and it gave us decades of joy and two wonderful children. I'm proud of your rally career, Sasha, even though the publicity for the rest of the family has sometimes brought back my fear of being discovered. And I'm just as happy, Andreas, that you are continuing the traditions of your mother's family on this land. Viktor Rylov became Viktor Smeds. I don't know where I'll end up after I die, but I can't imagine that I won't be able to be with Rauha then too. My heart will never stop being with her.

22

I read the account again. Was this really Viktor's story? Was it true? And how had Hackman gotten her hands on it? What had Heli said? *"Once, we even caught her in the house; she'd snuck in and was snooping around Rauha and Viktor's bedroom."*

Viktor's story explained why Annukka Hackman died at Lake Humaljärvi and why she'd been asking about DNA—a test would have shown that Rauha and Viktor weren't second cousins after all. Protecting their father would have been a motive for Sasha and Andreas to collude in the crime and support each other's alibis. Viktor's immigration violations and fraud had stretched over decades, compounding the seriousness of his crimes. No wonder Annukka had been so secretive about her manuscript.

I felt like sending a patrol to Smedsbo Farm right then. Instead I made a few more calls, first to the hospital where Sasha was receiving treatment. His condition was stable, and he was sleeping. He was unlikely to walk for several more weeks.

Then I called the private hospital where Viktor had had his surgery.

"I'd like information about Tuesday, the fifth of November, when Viktor and Rauha Smeds came in for Viktor's follow-up examination after his heart surgery. Were they there the whole day?"

"Wait just a moment . . . I'll have to check." I heard typing and papers shuffling, and in the background I could even make out the sound of an ambulance.

"Viktor arrived around noon with his wife and left at six. The doctor wasn't completely satisfied with his recovery, so they administered an EKG and . . ." The receptionist rattled off a series of medical terms that went in one ear and out the other.

"Was Mrs. Smeds present throughout the entire exam?"

"The notes only indicate that she brought him in and picked him up. No taxi or ambulance was necessary. You could ask the doctor who carried out the tests, but he won't be in until the morning shift."

"Yes, please have him call me as soon as he can. It doesn't matter how early."

Goddamn fucking Ursula, I thought. Had she actually confirmed the elderly Smedses' movements with the hospital? Or had she simply verified the appointment and their arrival, but forgotten to ask whether Rauha had stayed and waited for Viktor the entire time?

I tried to remember the cars that had been spotted at the lake three weeks earlier. Did they include a green Škoda or anything similar? I couldn't leave the kids alone and go to the police station to rifle through my files and find out. And none of my subordinates were likely to be working overtime. It was already ten thirty, but I still called everyone's cell. Only Lehtovuori picked up, but he couldn't remember either.

Was it Andreas, Sasha, Heli, or Rauha? I wondered. I had to talk to someone. Koivu would have been the natural choice, but at this time of night he was usually trying to get the baby to sleep. Taskinen was home alone, and I doubted he would be asleep yet. I was just dialing his number when the front door opened. I was so startled I dropped my phone on the table, but then I heard Antti's familiar steps.

"Hi. You're back early. I didn't think your train was coming until twelve."

"I made the early one. And I got the job. I can start right after Christmas, and the funding is good for at least five years. The pay is two grades higher than what I'm getting now, and the trains are really fast." Scooping me up in his arms, he kissed me more passionately than he had in ages.

"That's great," I muttered distractedly against his dark-red sweater.

"Hey, I just caught the early train home specifically so I could tell you the good news before you fell asleep. And then all you have to say is 'that's great'? I even bought champagne, so let's light some candles and celebrate, if that's OK with you."

I broke away from Antti's embrace. My mood was too unsettled for champagne and candles, and in truth I would have preferred to use Antti's early homecoming to let me go back to work. This was how it had been before, and this was how it was always going to be: there was just no way I could fill all the roles I had to play.

"Yes, let's celebrate, but can I keep it to one glass? I need to be sharp tomorrow. We just had a surprise turn in the Hackman case, which is probably going to solve the whole thing. I want to be with you, but I need to make one more call."

When I reached Dispatch, I asked the duty officer to send a car to stake out Smedsbo Farm and let me know what the situation was at the house. Who would end up leaving, Heli or Andreas? I wondered what I'd do in Sasha's place, but I didn't have a clue. Hopefully I'd never be faced with that decision.

Antti poured the drinks and lit the candles. He talked happily about his research plans and suggested that we start looking for a new apartment that weekend.

"Interest rates are so low right now, and maybe we could accept a little help from my parents. Mom's right. She can't take the money with her when she goes, and that inheritance advance might be just what we need."

I only heard half of what Antti said since part of my brain was still reviewing the Hackman case. The uniformed patrol called to report that everything seemed peaceful at the Smedses' place. A single light burned in the yard and another in one window of the house. Based on the description, it was in Heli and Sasha's room. Antti was tired after traveling so far, so after a single glass of champagne, we went to bed. He fell asleep quickly, but I stayed awake. I watched the rays of light that swam through the blinds onto the walls and sheets, and wondered whether anyone was sleeping at Smedsbo tonight. At some point sleep won out, and I found myself sitting on a train to Vaasa with Viktor Smeds, who was speaking in Russian. I only understood a few words, *umer* and *da svidania*, "death" and "good-bye."

In the morning the same old assaults and domestic violence incidents were waiting for me at the office. One family, the Salminens, had the father, mother, and seventeen-year-old son all sitting in cells, and the three younger children had been taken into state custody. During the morning meeting, I assigned Lähde, Lehtovuori, and Autio to handle the most acute cases, since Autio had recently taken a special course on recognizing and preventing domestic violence.

"And then we still have the Annukka Hackman case, but things have changed. We now have strong evidence that points at the Smeds family again. We already have one patrol car posted close by. Puupponen, Puustjärvi, and Koivu, you'll come with me to the farm. We'll leave at ten after handling a couple of other things. It's probably best to take two cars. The secretary will bring you a new version of the Hackman manuscript, and you can read it for yourselves. Take a look at Chapter One; it's different from the first chapter in the version we recovered from Hackman's safe. Puustjärvi, I need you to check the witness reports again from the lake area on the day Annukka Hackman went swimming. We're looking for any sighting of a green Škoda. Puupponen, will you please check Ursula's report on Viktor and Rauha Smeds's alibis? Then call her and check the alibis again."

Just then my phone vibrated. The number displayed was from the private hospital where Viktor had had his surgery. Hopefully, it was the cardiologist and I'd still be able to reach him after the meeting.

I was.

"Of course I remember Mr. and Mrs. Smeds. Viktor's coronary arteries were so congested that his operation came down to a matter of weeks, and his recovery hasn't gone as we hoped. Mrs. Smeds did bring Viktor to the appointment, but she wasn't here the whole time. Some people wait in the waiting room, but others run errands in the city. She was here in plenty of time to pick him up, though."

"Did you notice anything strange, in Rauha Smeds, I mean?"

"Of course she was nervous. Viktor's health has been touch and go. We arranged for them to come back in a month, which is coming up next week. You don't see couples like them very often. After forty years of marriage they're still like newlyweds. I was surprised to see Mrs. Smeds leave her husband's side even for those few hours."

"Thank you. Unfortunately we'll probably have to bother you again."

When a knock came at my door, I assumed it would be Puupponen, but instead I looked up to see Taskinen.

"Maria, do you have a moment?" If Jyrki hadn't looked so miserable, I would have said no.

"Yes, but only a moment. We've just about got the Hackman case solved. Come on in."

Taskinen remained standing in the doorway. There was a wrinkle in his collar, which shocked me. It was like seeing any other man showing up unshaven and smelling of booze.

"Don't worry about it. We'll talk later. I just wanted to say that . . . that getting through all of this is a lot easier knowing you're around." Taskinen's gaze locked on mine for a few seconds. I tried not to look away. Fortunately Puupponen jogged up.

"Maria, according to Ursula, the hospital told her Mrs. Smeds was there the whole time."

"So she claimed she asked?"

"Well, yeah. How would I know if she hadn't?"

Puustjärvi pushed into the doorway next to Puupponen, jostling Taskinen aside. Koivu stood behind Puustjärvi, in the hall. "The eyewitness reports don't include a green Škoda, but there was a dark-gray car of about the same description. It could be a match. The license plate was KC something just like the Smedses' car. The person behind the wheel was short and drove unusually slowly down Gesterby Road back to Kirkkonummi a little before five on the fifth of November."

"OK, let's get going. Koivu, you come with me. Petri and Ville, tell the patrol car standing guard that we're on our way. And let's play it cool."

The day was cloudy, with a dark, ruddy color in the west that promised more snow. I drove, and there was something strangely calming about it.

"Koivu, things like this shouldn't happen. Failing to thoroughly check an alibi is such a basic mistake." I braked to avoid a tractor-trailer that rounded a corner and blew through a yield sign right in front of me. "Put the light on top and give that guy a scare."

Koivu grabbed the light and reached out the window to place it on top of the car.

"Maria, we don't know that Ursula screwed up here. Maybe whoever she spoke to at the hospital made a mistake. Maybe they just assumed that Rauha stayed during her husband's appointment. I'm still having a hard time believing Rauha Smeds is a cold-blooded murderer, though. Couldn't it still be the boys? What the hell is going on with this road! Does the city not have any snowplows anymore?"

After the bridge over the bay on the west side of town, the road had been plowed, and I accelerated. At first the snow came slowly, but by the time we reached Kirkkonummi it was driving hard enough that I had to switch the windshield wipers on full speed. On one straightaway there were two cars off in the ditch, and traffic was down to one lane with police directing the flow. When they saw our flasher, they motioned us past the line.

"Apparently no one's hurt," Koivu observed calmly. "You only have to see the remains of a six-month-old after she went through the windshield to remember to always use a car seat."

"When was that?"

"When I was just starting out in Helsinki. What were you thinking of doing when we get to the farm?"

"We'll put them all in different rooms, then question two at a time. Hopefully my Swedish is good enough for Viktor. Why don't any of us know Russian?"

The snowstorm obscured the top of the Degerby church tower and almost made me drive past the intersection leading to Degerö, because the road sign was also covered in snow. The rolling hills and fields were covered in a blanket of snow perfect for skiing. A couple of miles to the west was the hill where Rauha's parents had gone to look at the home they longed for. The patrol car was tucked away in the forest three hundred yards from the Smedses' farm where it was out of sight of the house.

"Car twenty-three, this is Lieutenant Kallio. Who's inside?"

"Four individuals, two men, two women. Car twenty-three over."

I asked the patrol car to follow Puustjärvi's vehicle down the lane.

When I parked in the farmyard, Ronja the dog rushed out to greet us. Heli was sweeping the main steps, which seemed insane given the way the snow was coming down.

"Oh God," she said when she saw how many of us there were. "Did you come to badger Andreas again?"

"No. Are the others home?"

"Rauha is in the living room resting, and Viktor's probably reading. Andreas is upstairs packing. He's going somewhere today and won't tell us where." Heli swallowed and wiped a snowflake from the corner of her eye.

"And you're staying?"

"I don't know. Sasha doesn't want to talk about it yet. He says he needs some time."

"What do you want?"

Heli snorted. "It doesn't matter. There are no good options for me." She opened the door, and I kicked the snow from my shoes before entering. The scent of fresh-baked bread filled the entryway. The door to Rauha and Viktor's room was closed, but someone was bustling about in the kitchen.

"Puustjärvi, you go find Andreas. Puupponen, you take Heli upstairs and keep her company. You two stay on guard here," I said to officers Airaksinen and Saastamoinen. Koivu followed me into the living room, where we found Rauha Smeds working next to the traditional baking oven. She was wearing a well-worn flowery apron. Her hair was covered with a scarf in the same fabric, but it couldn't completely tame her gray locks, which fell over her forehead and ears. Rauha's right hand was in a bowl of dough, and her left wiped flour from her cheek.

"Hello, Detective."

"We need a word, Rauha. Are you at a good stopping point?"

"The last loaves are just about to go in the oven. Life must go on even if the younger generation has done themselves such a disservice."

Rauha looked straight at me, and for a moment I was sure that everything I'd read in Annukka Hackman's book was completely made up. There had never been any Viktor Rylov, just two second-cousins who met by chance in Kokkola. After our morning meeting I'd asked a colleague in that city to track down the church registries from the late thirties. It would be possible to determine whether something had been added after the fact, since the composition of the ink and the handwriting varied from decade to decade.

"Is your husband sleeping?"

"He had another bad night. He's been having nightmares. Sasha's accident has been too much for Viktor, and we couldn't hide this business with Andreas and Heli." Rauha turned out a lump of dough onto the floured table and began to roll it into long snakes. Her movements were quick and sure, and the braiding was done in an instant. Then a second and a third loaf took shape, and each was placed on a baking sheet under a cloth near the oven to rise.

"Would you like some fresh Inkoo-style bread?" she asked and wiped her hands on her apron. Then she started brushing the dough off the table and into the bowl.

"Thank you, but no. What does the name Rylov mean to you? Viktor Rylov."

"Who's he?" Rauha continued her tasks without any change in expression.

"A Soviet soldier who disappeared from the Porkkala Naval Base in September 1955. He was a border guard from Leningrad. We found the latest version of Annukka Hackman's manuscript. How did she get her hands on Viktor's autobiography?"

Rauha turned toward the kitchen with her bowl, and Koivu and I followed her. After dumping the flour from the bowl into the compost bin, she washed her hands. I let her finish before saying, "Let's sit down around the table in the living room." As I took Rauha's arm, I felt tall next to her. Rauha calmly removed her arm from my grasp.

"You don't need to lead me around. I'm not going to run away." She closed the kitchen door behind her, then took a seat at one end of the table. Koivu and I crawled onto one of the benches that ran along the sides. The snow had drifted halfway up the windows, and the fields were barely visible. The wind had reached a crescendo, howling plaintively and rocking the electric lines. Koivu fished the tape recorder out of his bag and was just turning it on when the living room door opened.

Viktor Smeds was wearing a brown striped undershirt and thick woolen trousers with drooping suspenders. He wore two pairs of wool socks, so his feet looked abnormally large compared to his slender legs. His wispy hair stood up as if he'd just gotten out of bed, but his eyes were sharp. His hands were steady too. They held a hunting rifle, pointed straight at me.

"Leave my wife alone," he said in soft, singsong Finnish. "Back up. Leave this house."

Rauha had turned to look at Viktor. "Dear, what are you . . ."

"You've always said you know what to do. Now it's my turn to decide. Lock the kitchen door."

The door between the living room and kitchen had an old-fashioned lock with a long metal key. Rauha locked the door and put the key in a pocket in her apron. Viktor still aimed at me. I heard Koivu breathing heavily, and I could smell my own fear in my sweat. The last time anyone had threatened me with a gun was before my children were born. If Viktor shot me now, I'd never see Iida and Taneli again.

"How many policemen are there in the house?" Viktor continued.

"Six."

"Bring them down here, along with my son and daughter-in-law. The man can go get them. The lady policeman stays here. If you try anything, she dies."

I felt Koivu hesitate. The barrel of the hunting rifle was only a few feet from my heart, and I'd seen the damage a weapon like that could do at that distance.

"Go," I snapped. "Tell Airaksinen and Saastamoinen to remove their weapons. Come back in with your hands up."

I knew Viktor wouldn't gain anything by shooting me, but was he able to grasp that too?

"How long have you known?" I asked Viktor in Finnish, since I was so scared I couldn't speak any language but my own.

"I only know that you've come to get me," Viktor managed to say before the door opened again. I turned my head as much as I dared and saw Heli and Andreas walk in with Koivu behind them.

"Come closer, Heli and Andreas." Now Viktor had switched to Swedish. "And you, Detective, get up off the bench and back up to my son."

I did as Viktor ordered, even though my legs were weak and standing up seemed to take an eternity. Slowly I backed up to where I imagined the living room door was. I caught the scent of Heli's hair near me.

"Stay there. Rauha, come over here."

Rauha stood up and obeyed. That would have been the right moment to attack, but we didn't have time. Viktor wrapped his left arm around his wife and awkwardly held the rifle with his right. The barrel of the rifle touched Rauha's chin. Andreas was breathing hard behind me.

"Come in everyone, just don't come too close," Rauha said to the two patrol officers who were now apparently standing behind me at the living room door. "Andreas, do your parents one last service and make sure the police don't have any guns. I've never been able to tolerate guns. All they are is trouble."

I wondered whether Koivu had called for backup while he was out of the room. Viktor Smeds didn't seem to have any sense for modern police technology. Mira Saastamoinen took off her gun belt and threw it in the entryway, and Airaksinen wasn't wearing one.

"Mom, they don't have any guns," Andreas said after giving us all a cursory pat down. "What's going on here? Neither of you could have had any reason to kill Annukka Hackman. And you were in the hospital when it happened."

"Your father was, but I wasn't." Rauha's voice was steady, and she had a smudge of baking flour on her right eyebrow. She had wrapped one of her arms around Viktor and helped him support the rifle toward her own jaw.

"But why? You couldn't have done that for us . . ." Andreas's voice faltered as he gestured toward Heli.

"For your father. Your father wanted you and Sasha to know after he died. He wrote his story before his heart surgery and left it in a drawer with the family history. On the envelope he wrote, 'To Alexander and Andreas, to open after my death.' And of course that thieving woman found it! Oh, Viktor," Rauha said, smiling gently. "If only you could have been a little more careful. I would have told the boys everything."

Puustjärvi shifted behind me, and the dog scratched at the door. Someone's phone rang, but no one answered. The windowpanes tinkled as the wind threw snow against them. The rest of the world was out there beyond the snow, but here, in this world, there were only ten people.

"Mom, what did Annukka find?" Andreas's voice was as tremulous as a small boy suddenly confronted by some incomprehensible and upsetting claim by people older than himself.

"Your father's biography, which reveals that he isn't my second cousin from Kokkola but rather Viktor Rylov, a Russian deserter, who's been living in Finland with false papers for nearly fifty years. Annukka said we'd committed a lot of crimes—falsifying documents, lying under oath, illegal immigration, and desertion in time of war. What a great story, she said. 'Rally hero's father expelled from country.' These kinds of revelations didn't come along every day."

"Did she tell you she'd found the papers?" I ventured to talk for the first time, and my voice sounded strangely hoarse and hard.

"She came here one day in September and handed me Viktor's envelope. We didn't even know it was missing." Rauha's nostrils flared like a cat smelling something suspicious. Hackman had returned Viktor's autobiography like any book borrowed from the library and thanked them for the interesting material, which she had copied and was currently translating into Finnish.

"I promised her everything, the moon and the stars, a million euros, but she only laughed and said that the truth was more important than money and that our crimes had to be exposed. I said that it was also illegal to invade a person's home and take their property without permission, but she just said that money and the right lawyer could solve that, unlike what we had done. According to Annukka, Viktor didn't belong in Finland. As if he had anything to do with Russia anymore!"

Rauha moved and the barrel of the gun brushed her jaw, but she seemed to ignore it. Viktor stroked her cheek with his left hand. Heli had wrapped her arms around herself as if for comfort. I felt the warmth of Koivu's body behind me.

"When do we rush them?" he whispered, but Viktor heard him.

"No tricks! Andreas has to hear how it all happened, and Heli can tell Sasha. After that it will be time for silence."

Rauha continued her story.

"I told Annukka that Viktor was in poor health, that he was living on borrowed time, that the surgery had failed. She had no mercy. I couldn't stand the thought of being separated from Viktor, of not being able to sleep next to him. For forty years we've only slept apart on the nights I was in the hospital giving birth to the boys. When Viktor had his surgery, I slept next to his bed. We don't have much time left. I didn't want to sacrifice a second of that."

Heli sniffed.

Viktor coughed, which made the rifle give a loud click, and we all jumped.

"Don't come any closer," he said, and the words sounded like a prayer. Rauha lifted her left hand and wiped the sweat from her face.

"Of course I didn't want to kill her, but there was no other way," she continued. "She enjoyed making me beg. I intended to go to her house in Espoo and ask her one more time to keep quiet. I tried to call her from the hospital, but she didn't answer. I called her again from the public phone at the Kirkkonummi station. She only laughed and said that she was on Gesterby Road going to Lake Humaljärvi to see what it was like to swim for her life in the frigid water. It was just a game to her. I decided to go after her and drove like a madwoman. I don't know where I left the car. When I arrived at the shore, she was already in the water. I saw her purse and knew that there was a pistol inside. I only fired once, and that was enough."

Andreas groaned. I saw him place his hands on Heli's shoulders, but she didn't even try to take them.

"Where did you throw the gun?" I asked.

"I drove to the Vårnäs Bridge and threw the gun, Annukka's phone, and her keys into the water. I didn't think it would occur to anyone to look in the reeds there. Now you've heard everything there is to hear. You can leave now. We want to die together, just the two of us."

No one budged.

"And what about Hannu Kervinen?" I asked.

"Who?" Rauha's expression was genuinely confused. "Oh, the pathologist? I didn't have anything to do with him."

"Didn't you?" I asked, then thought of the message Kervinen had left behind. *"The one who killed Annukka is going to kill me too."* A violent death led to others. Some people preferred to die than to live without each other.

"I never even met the man," Rauha said grimly.

"He died because he couldn't live without Annukka," I said. "He was the same as you. He wouldn't give up the person he loved for any price. He thought Annukka Hackman was worth a love that great."

Out of the corner of my eye, I saw Heli jerk Andreas's hands off her shoulders and shake her head. Andreas looked back at her like a person bereft of hope.

"Father," he said. "Put down the gun. I don't want to lose you too."

"There's no way they're going to send you back to Russia any time soon," I added. "And they probably never will."

How thin my voice sounded, and how little impact it had. I remembered the last time I'd tried to talk a gun out of a shooter's hand. I'd failed.

I wondered if it would help if one of us tried to rush outside. We could shoot through the window and wound Viktor, but he would be likely to kill Rauha, making him a murderer too. We had to try to talk our way out of this. I tried to catch Andreas's gaze. Perhaps he'd know what to say. I saw Puupponen fiddling with his phone behind Koivu's broad back. The dog whimpered outside the door.

"Andreas. I love you and Sasha so much. We both do. Try to clean up your mess," Rauha said quietly. "I love you, Viktor. Now."

Viktor pulled the trigger. It clicked. By the time he pulled it again, Koivu, Andreas, and I had already jumped on the couple. Andreas made it to the gun first, and I grabbed Rauha's hands.

"Nje zarjožena, nje zarjožena," Viktor said.

I heard Heli laughing hysterically and saying, "Sweet Jesus, I took the bullets out of the magazine the night before last! I was afraid Andreas would do something to himself and took the bullets out!" She was on the floor kneeling, and Mira Saastamoinen bent over her.

It wasn't until we had Viktor and Rauha in handcuffs that I started shaking. The Smedses still held each other's hands, and I was secretly happy I wouldn't be the one who had to separate them from each other when they reached Holding. Viktor had to be detained as well, since it was unclear when he'd learned about the murder. The list of charges against each of them would be long and complicated.

The snow had nearly buried the police cars. Someone had let Ronja inside and she walked from person to person whimpering strangely. She kept smelling the handcuffs and trying to lick them off Rauha's wrists. I asked Rauha if she wanted to take off her apron and thought of the misshapen bread that had now risen too much and that someone would have to throw in the compost.

"Let's get moving," Puustjärvi said to Viktor, and Mira Saastamoinen took Rauha by the arm.

"May I at least stop at the door to the barn?" Rauha asked, and I nodded. Viktor followed behind her, and for a moment they stood in silence at the barn door.

"Let them ride in the same car, Mira," I said to Saastamoinen. I swallowed when Rauha turned to say good-bye for the second time in her life to the home she thought she would never see again.

23

"Can I ask you for a ride somewhere again?" Heli asked once the patrol car had disappeared beyond the hill. She'd wept aloud as she hugged her mother- and father-in-law good-bye, and her face was still wet. Ronja had tried in vain to force her way into the cruiser with the old couple.

"Yeah, there's room in my car." I wasn't in any hurry to leave, since I was still shaking. I'd gone in the kitchen to drink some juice and made Heli and Andreas drink something too.

"It's better for Andreas to stay here. He can manage alone with the animals for a few days. And this is his home, not mine. I'm going to the hospital to tell Sasha before the media finds out, then I'll go somewhere. It doesn't matter where. I'll just get my suitcase."

I didn't see Heli and Andreas's good-bye, but the fresh tears on Heli's face told the story. I sent the others off in the second car because I thought Heli might need someone to talk to. For the first part of the drive she was quiet, and I retreated into my routines, planning our after-action review and the press conference. We'd have to send Forensics to Vårnäs Bridge first thing in the morning. I'd also have to talk to Ursula, regardless of her sick leave. Her failure when it came to Rauha's alibi was inexcusable. And all the leaks—which I was certain she'd been the source of—had caused an inordinate amount of trouble for the investigation.

"It's strange," Heli said at the Degerby intersection. "This is the first time I've realized it. At first I always thought it was nice when Sasha came home or we met up abroad, but then it started to feel forgettable. Last spring I was driving back from the airport and felt so happy and light like I was floating half a meter off the ground. It was so nice to get home, to get away from the rally world. But I was right here when I realized that the real reason I wanted to get home was because Andreas was waiting there for me. Last spring was like a drug. I couldn't keep away from Andreas, and he couldn't keep his hands off me. But now it's November and there's no escape from this emptiness."

"Thanks to you, at least one person's life was saved."

"No, it had nothing to do with me. It was just random luck. I took the bullets because I was afraid for Andreas."

"Does it really matter who you saved by doing it?"

"Just before Viktor pulled the trigger, I was planning to try to grab the rifle from him. I was afraid that Andreas would attack him, and I wanted to get there first. But in the end I didn't dare. I didn't want to die after all."

I left Heli shivering in the snow at a taxi stand in downtown Espoo. I asked her to give her contact information to the police, and after a moment's hesitation I encouraged her to call if the darkness started to feel overwhelming. Because Heli wasn't a suspect anymore, I went ahead and hugged her good-bye.

Dodging snowplows, I drove to the police station. Bryan Ferry's "A Fool for Love" was playing on the radio, and listening to it finally brought the tears. I sat in my office for a few minutes before going to the after-action review. I'd have to talk to a therapist. It was pointless thinking I could get over being threatened with a gun by myself. I didn't feel any triumph or relief now that we'd solved the crime. All I felt was sorrow.

Maybe love made people crazy or maybe it made them see everything in a new way. Sometimes it made things brighter, sometimes it distorted the world. People did insane things for love. They broke laws and hurt the people closest to them. They killed each other. They killed themselves. But would it be better not to love or was even the most hopeless love better than no love at all? Wasn't the ability to love what made us human?

I didn't know.

ABOUT THE AUTHOR

Photo © 2011 Tomas Whitehouse

Leena Lehtolainen was born in Vesanto, Finland, to parents who taught language and literature. A keen reader, she made up stories in her head before she could even write. At the age of ten, she began her first book—a young adult novel—and published it two years later. She released her second book at the age of seventeen. She has received numerous awards for her writing, including the 1997 Vuoden Johtolanka (Clue) Award (for the best Finnish crime novel) for *Luminainen* (*The Snow Woman*) and the Great Finnish Book Club prize in 2000. Her work has been published in twenty-nine languages.

Besides writing, Leena enjoys classical singing, her beloved cats, and—her greatest passion—figure skating. Her nonfiction book about the sport, *Taitoluistelun lumo* (*The Enchantment of Figure Skating*), was chosen as the Sport Book of the Year 2011 in Finland. Leena lives in Finland with her husband and two sons.

ABOUT THE TRANSLATOR

Photo © 2015 Aaron Turley

Owen F. Witesman is a professional literary translator with a master's in Finnish and Estonian-area studies and a PhD in public affairs from Indiana University. He has translated more than thirty Finnish books into English, including novels, children's books, poetry, plays, graphic novels, and nonfiction. His recent translations include the first seven novels in the Maria Kallio series, the locked-room mystery *Cruel is the Night* by Karo Hämäläinen, and the dark family drama *Norma* by Sofi Oksanen. He currently resides in Springville, Utah, with his wife, three daughters, one son, two dogs, a cat, six chickens, and twenty-nine fruit trees.